Praise for the novels of Susan Mallery

"Sweet and fun… This two-in-one romance starts a new series that Mallery's many fans will devour like a Christmas cookie."   —*Booklist* on *The Christmas Wedding Guest*

"Mallery packs in the Christmas spirit, with friends and family coming together to celebrate. The result is alluring, well plotted, and sure to please."
                    —*Publishers Weekly* on *The Christmas Wedding Guest*

"Mallery's authentic characters and their refreshing summer escapades are sure to resonate. The emphasis on the power of friendship and the joy of new romance make[s] this sparkling novel a sure hit with women's fiction fans."
                    —*Publishers Weekly* on *The Friendship List*

"Susan Mallery never disappoints and with *Daughters of the Bride*, she is at her storytelling best."
   —Debbie Macomber, #1 *New York Times* bestselling author

"Mallery brings her signature humor and style to this moving story of strong women who help each other deal with realistic challenges, a tale as appealing as the fiction of Debbie Macomber and Anne Tyler."
                    —*Booklist* on *California Girls*

"Mallery combines heat and sweet in a delicious tale destined for beach blankets."
                    —*Publishers Weekly* on *The Summer of Sunshine & Margot*

SUSAN MALLERY

the
CHRISTMAS
WEDDING
GUEST

HQN

HQN®

ISBN-13: 978-1-335-45855-1

Recycling programs for this product may not exist in your area.

The Christmas Wedding Guest

First published in 2021. This edition published in 2022.

Copyright © 2021 by Susan Mallery, Inc.

For questions and comments about the quality of this book, please contact us at CustomerService@Harlequin.com.

HQN
22 Adelaide St. West, 41st Floor
Toronto, Ontario M5H 4E3, Canada
www.Harlequin.com

Printed in U.S.A.

To Kim, Belle's mom—
thank you for sharing your adorable baby with me.
Writing about her was such a highlight.

And to the wonderful readers
in the Susan Mallery All Access group on Facebook
who helped come up with many of the fun Wishing Tree
Christmas traditions and names of the local businesses—
you'll see your last names sprinkled throughout the book.

Join the fun: Facebook.com/groups/susanmalleryallaccess.

Also by Susan Mallery

…and the beloved Fool's Gold romances.

For a complete list of titles available from Susan Mallery,
please visit www.susanmallery.com.

the
CHRISTMAS
WEDDING
GUEST

One

_____

"IT'S A VACUUM," Reggie Somerville said, trying to sound less doubtful than she felt. "You reinvented the vacuum?"

Gizmo stared at her, his hurt obvious, even behind his thick glasses. "It's a *smart* vacuum."

"Don't we already have those round ones that zip across a room?"

"They're not smart. They're average. Mine is smart."

Reggie was less sure about the vacuum's intelligence than her client's. Gizmo had a brain that existed on a different plane than those of average humans. His ideas were extraordinary. His execution, however, wasn't always successful. A basic knowledge of coding shouldn't be required to work any household appliance—a fact she'd tried to explain to him about fifty-seven thousand times.

She eyed the triangular-shaped head of the vacuum.

The bright purple casing was appealing, and she liked that it could roam on its own or be a regular stick vacuum if that was what she wanted. The printed instructions—about eighteen pages long—were a little daunting, but she would get through them.

If the trial went well, she and Gizmo would discuss the next steps, including her design suggestions. Once those were incorporated, they would start beta testing his latest invention. In the meantime, she would be doing a lot of vacuuming.

"I'll get you my report in a couple of weeks," she said.

Gizmo, a slight, pale twenty-year-old who lived with his extended family just north of Seattle, offered her a small smile. "You can have until the first of the year. I'm going to be busy with Christmas decorations for the house. We started putting them up just after Halloween, and it's about to get really intense. I've worked out some of the kinks from last year, so the animatronics look more real. It's taking a lot of time. My grandma's really into it."

"Sounds like fun."

"We're launching the Friday after Thanksgiving, but we'll be upgrading everything through December. Come by close to Christmas. You'll be blown away."

"I can't wait," she said with a laugh.

She and Gizmo talked for a few more minutes before she walked him out of her home office. When the door closed behind her client, Belle, her one-hundred-twenty-pound Great Dane, poked her large head out from behind the desk.

"You didn't come say goodbye to Gizmo," Reggie said. "I thought you liked him."

Belle shifted her gaze to the purple vacuum sitting in the middle of the area rug, obviously pointing out that potential death still lurked.

"It's not going to hurt you," Reggie told her. "It's not even turned on."

Belle's brows drew together, as if she wasn't willing to accept the validity of that claim. Reggie tried to keep from smiling. Belle made a low sound in her throat, as though reminding Reggie of Gizmo's last invention.

"Yes, I do remember what happened with the dog walker robot," Reggie admitted.

The sturdy, odd-looking robot had started out well enough—walking a very concerned Belle around their small yard. Unfortunately, about ten minutes in, something had gone wrong with the programming, and the robot had started chasing her instead. Belle, not the bravest of creatures, had broken through the screen door in her effort to escape the attack, hiding behind Reggie's desk for the rest of the day.

Gizmo had been crushed by the failure and had needed nearly as much reassurance as the dog. Sometimes, Reggie thought with a sigh, her job was the weirdest one ever.

"I'm going to leave this right here," Reggie told Belle. "It's turned off, so you can poke at it with your nose and get used to it."

Belle took two steps back toward the desk, her body language clearly saying she would never get used to it, and why couldn't Reggie have a regular job that didn't threaten the life of her only pet?

"Or you could sit on it," Reggie pointed out. "The robot weighs about ten pounds. You're more than ten times that size. You could probably crush it like a bug."

The dog's brown eyes widened slightly, filled with affront.

Reggie held in another smile. "I'm not commenting on your weight. You're very beautiful and way skinnier than me."

She settled on the sofa and patted the space next to her. Belle loped all of three strides before jumping up and leaning heavily against Reggie. The soft rose-colored sweater Belle wore to protect herself from the damp cold of mid-November looked good on her dark gray fur. Reggie put an arm around her dog and pulled her phone out of her pocket. A quick glance at the screen told her she'd missed a call. From her mother.

She tried to ignore her sudden sense of dread. Not that she didn't love her parents—she did. Very much. They were good people who cared about her. But they were going to insist she come home for Thanksgiving and Christmas, and she couldn't think of a single reason to refuse.

Last year had been different. Last year, she'd stayed in Seattle, with only Belle for company, enduring the holidays rather than enjoying them. She'd given herself through New Year's to mourn the breakup and subsequent humiliation that went with the man of her dreams proposing at the Lighting of the Trees on the Friday after Thanksgiving, arranging an impromptu celebration party on Saturday and then dumping her on Sunday.

After sharing her happiness with nearly everyone she knew, having her friends coo over her gorgeous ring and ask about wedding plans, she'd had to explain Jake had changed his mind. She assumed. His actual words, "I can't do this. It's over. I'm sorry," hadn't given her much to work with.

Hurt and ashamed, she'd buried herself in work and her life in Seattle. She hadn't returned home to Wishing Tree even once since it had happened, preferring to lick her wounds in private. She'd told herself she was healing, but Reggie knew the truth was less flattering. She was hiding, and it was time to suck it up and get over herself. She'd worked hard to put Jake behind her and move on with her life. Thanksgiving was next week, and she was going home, like she did every year. Besides, it wasn't as if she was still mourning her ex-fiancé. She'd gotten over him, and now it was time to demonstrate that to her hometown…and possibly herself.

"At least, that's the plan," Reggie told her dog and pushed the button to phone her mother.

"Hey, Mom," she said when the call was answered.

"Reggie! It's you. You'll never guess. It's so wonderful. Your dad and I are getting married."

Reggie blinked a couple of times. "You're already married. Your thirty-fifth wedding anniversary is coming up next month. I thought we'd have a party or something." She and her sister had talked about the possibility a couple of weeks ago.

Her mother laughed. "You're right. Technically, we're married. We eloped and I have to tell you, I've always regretted not having a big wedding. Your father pointed out I've been upset about that for the last thirty-five years, so maybe it was time to do something about it. We've decided we're renewing our vows with a big wedding and a reception afterwards. It'll be the Wednesday before Christmas."

"You're having a wedding?"

"Yes. Up at the resort. We're inviting everyone. It's been so much fun, but the planning is getting out of hand. I was hoping you could help me."

"With your wedding?"

"Yes, dear. Are you feeling all right?"

"My head's spinning a little."

"I know it's a surprise, but I'm so happy. You're coming home for Thanksgiving, aren't you?"

"I am."

"Good. So I was thinking you could just stay through Christmas. There's plenty of room down in the basement for you to work. You could handle your business in the morning and help me in the afternoon. It's only five weeks, Reggie. You have a job that lets you work from anywhere."

While that was technically true, Reggie wasn't thrilled at the thought of packing up her life and moving in with her folks for over a month.

"What about Belle?" she asked, hoping bringing up that subject would help shift things.

"You know we love her."

"She's afraid of Burt."

"Oh, they're fine together. It's all a big game."

Reggie thought about how Belle quivered with fear every time she saw her father's small dachshund in the room. Burt was normally good-natured, but he'd never taken to Belle and spent most of his time running after her and biting her ankles. Belle, for her part, tried to keep out of his way, frequently traversing a room by going from tabletop to sofa to chair, often with disastrous results.

"I want her to be a flower girl," her mother added.

"We'll get her an adorable dress and she can have a basket of rose petals hanging around her neck."

Reggie rubbed her dog's back. "She'd look good as a flower girl."

"See? Say you'll come home and help with me with my wedding, Reggie. I need you. Dena's busy with school, and she's developed terrible morning sickness. I have no idea where she got it from—I was fine with both my pregnancies, but she's wiped out. You've been gone too long. It's time to come home."

Almost the exact words Reggie had told herself, minus the wedding guilt.

"Mom," she began, then held in a sigh. Why fight the inevitable? Once she was home, she would be happy she'd done the right thing. Plus, it was Wishing Tree at Christmas—nowhere else in the world came close to that little slice of magic.

"Sure. I'll be there. Belle and I will drive over the day after tomorrow."

"I'm so happy," her mother squealed. "Thank you. We're going to have fun, you'll see. We haven't had the first snowfall yet. Maybe you'll be home for that, and you can go to the big town party. All right, now that I know you'll be home for the holidays, I have yet another favor to ask you."

Reggie wasn't sure if she should laugh or moan. "What did you do?"

"Nothing, really."

"It has to be something or we wouldn't be talking about it."

"Yes. Good point. Dena's class is going to do a knitting project for their holiday charity. Normally I'd be happy to manage it for her, but this year with the wedding and all, I just don't have time. I was hoping you could do it for me."

Reggie closed her eyes. "Mom," she began, then stopped, knowing she was going to say yes in the end, so why fight it?

Every year students at the local elementary school came up with several charity projects to do in December. Since Dena, Reggie's older sister, had started teaching there, the family had also gotten involved. For the past couple of years, Reggie's mom had been in charge of that project, organizing supplies and students, paving the way for their good deed.

"This is why I've avoided coming home," Reggie said weakly.

"No, it's not. You avoided coming home because Jake Crane was too stupid to realize what he had with you. I hope he spends the rest of his life regretting his decision and fighting a very painful rash."

"Go, Mom."

Her mother laughed. "I can be supportive."

"You always are." Reggie smiled. "Fine, I'll be the knitting queen."

"Wonderful. I'll email you the information you'll need to get up to speed. You're going to have a great time with the kids. In the meantime, be thinking about wedding favors. Something we'll make ourselves, so it will be really special. I was playing with the idea of painted coasters, or we could make soap. I've always wanted to learn how to do that. We could go botanical or floral."

They were going to make soap? "You know you can buy really cute little soaps, Mom. They sell them online."

"I'm not buying the favors. I want this to be a project for us to do together. Anyway, I'll see you soon. Let me know when you leave Seattle so I can start worrying when you're not here on time."

"How about if I just show up unexpectedly so you don't have to worry at all?"

"Where's the fun in that? I can't wait to see you. I'll give Dad your love."

"Thanks, Mom. And congratulations on the wedding."

DENA SOMERVILLE HAD known being single and pregnant would offer challenges, but she'd never thought she would be sick every second of every day. *Her* mother had always talked about how easy her pregnancies had been and the fact that the women in their family popped out babies with barely a pause in their days.

Sitting on the floor in her bathroom, leaning against the wall, while wondering if she was done throwing up for this hour, Dena decided either her mother had been lying or Dena had been adopted.

It wasn't supposed to be like this, she thought, turning over the damp washcloth on the back of her neck and wishing she could magically transport herself eight weeks into the future, when her doctor had promised the nausea and subsequent vomiting would finally end. Alas, she had yet to figure out how to move through time at will, so she was stuck with the unpleasant reality of knowing that in an hour or two, the waves would return, and three times out of five, she would oh, so elegantly puke with little or no warning.

What really got her was the fact that she'd had a plan. A good plan, a sensible plan. A plan that could almost be called superior. She'd always been the girl with a plan, and she'd always done the work to make it happen. She didn't believe in luck or fate—she put in the time and effort required, even when it was hard.

She'd fulfilled her childhood dream of being a teacher and she loved her job even more than she'd thought she would. When her Grandmother Regina had passed away, dividing her estate between her two granddaughters, leaving stocks and bonds to her namesake, Reggie, and the Wishing Tree B and B to Dena, she'd moved into the spacious apartment above the old carriage house and had spent her summers updating the place.

Although Dena had been less than successful in the romance department, she'd kept putting herself out there. She'd signed up for a dating service and had traveled to Seattle every other weekend for five months in an effort to meet *the one*. She'd used three different dating apps, had told anyone who would listen she was in the market. She'd gone on group dates, blind dates and double dates.

After two years of honest effort, she'd accepted that she wasn't likely to find Mr. Right, or even Mr. Good Enough. At that point, she'd had to start asking herself the hard question—did giving up on love also mean giving up on having a family? The answer had come quickly enough, and it had been a big fat no. She loved kids, and she wanted kids of her own.

Being a logical, fact-driven person, she'd taken an entire year to research IUI—aka intrauterine insemination, or what her sister referred to as the turkey baster method of getting pregnant—and another six months to make the decision to have the procedure. She'd scheduled it such that her due date would align with the end of the school year, thereby giving her the whole summer to spend with her baby.

She'd picked out colors for the nursery, she'd investigated the best day care options, and she'd typed up notes for when she sat down with her family and told them what she wanted to do. She had a wonderful support system, including her parents, her sister Reggie, and the staff at the B and B, all of whom had become like family to her. She'd even managed to get pregnant right out of the gate.

She'd tried to think of everything, but she'd never considered the possibility she would be laid low by morning sickness.

The combination of the cool, damp washcloth and the cold tiles beneath her butt seemed to ease the nausea enough for her to risk standing. When she was on her feet, she paused to see if her stomach would punish her, but all seemed calm. With a little luck, she would get through the next couple of hours without the need to barf.

Tightening the belt on her robe, she walked to her balcony and stepped out into the freezing, dark morning. As always, the sharp, cold air shocked her lungs and made her shiver, but the last whispers of nausea faded in the chill.

It was barely six in the morning, and much of the world was still asleep. This far north and only a month from the shortest day of the year, daybreak was nearly two hours away. She looked up at the bright stars twinkling overhead. Although it was cold enough to snow, the weather had been remarkably clear. The mythical first snowfall had yet to occur.

Soon, she thought with a smile. Soon there would be snow and the celebration that went with it, because Wishing Tree was that kind of town.

She glanced toward the main building of the B and B and saw the kitchen lights were on. Ursula, their gifted but snarky chef, had already gotten to work on breakfast. Once that meal was done, she would put together box lunches for any guests who had ordered one. That endeavor was followed by batches of cookies, brownies and scones that they sold in the lobby every afternoon. Ursula's last task before heading home was to create appetizers for their evening wine-and-snacks event.

Sometimes she made little quiches or put together a really great cheese plate. Her stuffed mushrooms were popular, as were the crab puffs. And the wine. All beautiful Washington wines from the great wineries: L'Ecole, Painted Moon, Northstar, Lake Chelan, Doubleback and Figgins.

"Ah, wine. How much I once loved you," Dena murmured, then laughed. At least she could still eat the food—or most of it, when her stomach would cooperate. Soft cheeses were a no-no, and these days olives made her gag, but otherwise, she was all in.

A light clicked on, illuminating the back patio of the unit below. The ground floor of the carriage house had been split into a storage room for the B and B and a stand-alone suite for guests who preferred something more upscale and private. The space came at a premium, but they rarely had trouble filling it—especially during the holiday season.

The current resident, a ridiculously good-looking man who had arrived two days ago, was booked through the day after New Year's. Dena was nearly as excited about the thought of all those weekly charges filling up her bank account as she was by the eye candy. Most of her guests were couples and families. Attractive single men didn't often find their way to her B and B.

Not that his marital status mattered to her. She had accepted that love wasn't in her destiny—and she was pregnant, so getting involved with a guy made no sense. Oh, and there was the added fact that based solely on looks, he was miles out of her league. Still, an expectant mother could gaze and admire, she thought with a smile.

So far he was a quiet neighbor who didn't slam doors or turn up his TV too loud. Last night she'd heard guitar music coming from his place—a song played several times in a row. The soft rendition had lulled her to sleep, so she wasn't about to complain.

The cold seeped through her bathrobe and made her shiver. Dena sucked in one more breath before heading inside to start her morning. She brushed her teeth, then dressed quickly. Once in the kitchen, she ate the only breakfast she was able to keep down these days. An avocado and egg salad sandwich on rye bread. Possibly gross in most circumstances, but her doctor had given it a thumbs-up.

She glanced longingly at her coffee maker, thinking how incredibly close the two of them had been, back before her life had been defined by something the size of a lima bean. Not that she had regrets—giving up coffee was so worth it for her baby's sake, but at least she'd known that deprivation was coming. It was the morning-slash-afternoon-slash-early-evening sickness that was going to do her in.

But for now her tummy was quiet, so she filled her

water bottle, retrieved her lunch from the refrigerator and headed downstairs to her car. If she could get a little cooperation from her body, she was going to have a good day—mostly because every day she was teaching was a good day. Plus there were so many things to look forward to. On Friday she would be announcing the charity project chosen for the third-grade class. Then, next Monday, they would have their monthly career day presentation. If she remembered correctly, they were hosting a plumber, a veterinarian and a Christmas tree farmer. So many possibilities, she thought as she walked to her car. She was, in every way possible, the luckiest person on the planet, and she had the life to prove it.

Two

REGGIE BENT AT the knees and hoisted the fifty-pound bag of dog food over her shoulder. One of the reasons she'd decided to get a dog a couple of years ago had been to make herself get out of the house to go on walks. Working at home made it easy to get too sedentary. But she hadn't counted on having to incorporate an upper body strengthening routine into her life, simply to handle the bags of dry food she bought for her roommate. On the bright side, now she could easily lift fifty pounds and toss it into the back of her SUV, next to the box of presents she'd packed.

Belle stood on the porch, watching anxiously. In addition to being, um, well, less than brave, Belle had a touch of separation anxiety. She forever seemed worried that Reggie would simply take off and leave the dog on her own.

"You know that's never going to happen," Reggie

pointed out. "You're coming with me. You saw I'd already started packing your suitcase."

Belle whined low in her throat, apparently not reassured by the reminder.

Reggie stacked a second bag of dog food on top of the first, then added three cases of canned food. She returned to the house to double-check everything was locked up and the furnace turned down to sixty.

One suitcase was already by the door. She went through the second one on the sofa, double-checking that there were plenty of sweaters, coats and flannel onesies for Belle. She added a few of her dog's favorite toys and several bags of Greenies treats. Belle licked her lips when she saw the familiar bags.

"Yeah, not until we get to Wishing Tree," Reggie said. "Okay, I think that's everything."

She closed the suitcase before pulling Belle's pink collar out of her jeans back pocket. "All right, pretty girl. Let's get this on you."

Belle sat patiently while Reggie fastened it into place. Once that was done, Reggie carried out the suitcases before returning for her coat, her handbag and her dog. She got Belle settled in the back, confirmed the car reindeer antlers were secured, then got in behind the wheel and started the engine.

"We'll stop for burgers on the way," she told Belle. "At that place you like."

Belle wagged her tail as she looked out the window. Belle was very much a girl who enjoyed a burger.

Reggie drove north out of Seattle. She would take Highway 2 most of the way, before turning off for the smaller highway to Wishing Tree. The town was about twenty miles south of the Canadian border, and about a hundred fifty miles east of Seattle. She'd already checked the state's department of transportation website and knew she would have a relatively easy drive with bare and dry roads the whole way.

Thinking about the lack of snow was a nice distraction, but eventually she found herself admitting that she was both happy to be going home and a little apprehensive.

Maybe a year was enough time for everyone to forget what had happened to her, she thought. At least Jake wasn't living in Wishing Tree anymore. Paisley, her best friend and source for all the local news, had let her know that Jake had been promoted to manager of one of his family's properties in Colorado after his stint as assistant manager of the resort just outside of Wishing Tree. The promotion had happened right after the first of the year. Although Paisley was often the go-to person for any interesting gossip, in this case, she had insider knowledge. Not only was she firmly on Team Reggie when it came to the breakup, she was also the events manager at the resort.

"I'll be fine," Reggie told herself out loud, before turning on the radio. She knew she was over Jake, but she had to admit she was glad she wouldn't be running into him. The conversation would be awkward, and she also didn't want anyone thinking she was still missing him.

An hour later, she was willing to admit that anticipation at the thought of going home was outweighing trepidation. She'd been silly to stay gone for so long, she thought. She was too strong to let a man come between her and returning to Wishing Tree.

Her cell phone rang. Reggie pushed a button on her steering wheel to activate the hands-free function.

"Hello?"

"Hey, you. How's the drive?"

Reggie smiled as she recognized her sister's voice. "It's easy. Belle saw a deer and tried to jump out the window, but I convinced her to stay inside."

"Your windows are open?" Dena asked, sounding surprised. "It's like twenty-eight degrees here."

"No, the window's closed. Belle doesn't worry about things like windows and walls getting in her way. You know that."

"That's my favorite dog niece. Is her suitcase bigger than yours?"

"Kind of, but that's because she's more fabulous than me. How are you feeling? Still barfing everywhere?"

Dena sucked in a sharp breath. "I try to not barf *everywhere*, as you put it. But yes, I'm still sick."

"Mom said her pregnancies were easy. I'm sorry yours isn't the same."

"Me, too. But hopefully in a few weeks the all-day morning sickness will start to ease. I'm also tired a lot. I nearly fell asleep in class yesterday. That's supposed to pass, too."

"There's a lot of passing in pregnancy," Reggie teased. "I didn't know that."

"Me, either, but hey, we're learning together."

"I'm excited about the knitting project." Reggie watched a truck come up close behind and then zoom around her. As she was going exactly four miles over the speed limit, she waved at the guy and wondered if she would see him getting a ticket a few miles up the highway.

"Are you sure you want to take it on?" Dena asked, sounding concerned. "It's a lot of work. I could—"

"No, you couldn't," Reggie said, interrupting her sister. "Dena, you teach full-time, you manage the B and B and you're pregnant. Don't you think that's enough? I've read over the material Mom sent, and I'm happy to step in while she's busy with planning her wedding. Besides, it'll be fun and my good deed for the holidays. I've been practicing with the circular loom I bought. The kids are going to have a great time."

"Thanks for helping my class."

"Not a problem."

"Some of the parents will be joining the sessions," Dena said, her voice slightly tense. "We'll talk about that when you get here."

"The more people who help, the more hats and scarves we'll get done. I think the parents joining in is a good thing."

"We'll talk later," Dena repeated.

"Sure. Just don't tell Mom I already left. I don't want her worrying about me on the drive."

"What? Our mother, worry?" Dena laughed. "When has that ever happened? By the way, she can't decide if she wants us to be bridesmaids."

Reggie winced. "It's her wedding and she gets to say what happens, but I'm a big, fat no on the topic."

"Me, too. I'd be worried about the whole throwing up thing."

Reggie grinned. "That would change the mood of the happy event."

"Yes, and none of us want that to happen. Are you really okay about coming home?"

The change in topic was unexpected enough that it took her a beat to catch up. "It's past time. I love being home for the holidays. I'm not going to let what happened a year ago keep me from spending time with my family."

"That's a good attitude. How much of it is fake?"

"About forty percent."

"That's still pretty good." Her sister's voice turned teasing. "Want me to ask around, see if I can find some nice guy looking for love? Dean's still single, and he's yummy-looking."

"Thanks, but no. Dating my ex's best friend would be weird."

"Oh, right. Sorry. Not a good suggestion."

Reggie laughed. "It's okay. Even if I ignored the BFFs with Jake thing, I've dated nice guys nearly all my life. I want to try someone a little bad. In part for variety and in part because when he breaks my heart, it won't be such a surprise."

"Maybe it would work out and you'd live happily ever after."

"Uh-huh. Because *that* happens every day."

Reggie saw flashing lights up ahead and moved to the far lane as she passed the speeding truck, now pulled over by the highway patrol.

Karma, she thought with a smile. How could anyone not believe?

"I'll see you soon," Reggie said.

"Yes, you will. I love you, Belle."

Belle woofed at the sound of her name.

"Make your mom stop for burgers," Dena added.

Reggie smiled. "It's already the plan. Love you, sis."

"Love you, too."

TOBY NEWKIRK CONSIDERED himself a fairly together guy. He had a successful business that employed over two thousand people across the western United States. He had an eight-year-old son who was happy and smart and had plenty of friends. He had a nice home, and he took care of his grandmother. He paid his bills on time, had a college fund for his son and could bench press his own weight without breaking a sweat. Okay—he broke a sweat, but he could still do it. So why did the thought of a private meeting with his son's third-grade teacher make him feel both guilty and apprehensive? Harrison was fine. He was reading above grade level and had the beginnings of what Toby thought might be a heck of a fastball.

He shook off his sense of dread, then signed in at the main office, after which he was told to report to Ms. Somerville's classroom.

The hallways of Wishing Tree Elementary were quiet—all the kids were in their monthly musical assembly. Harrison had mentioned it over breakfast, saying the high school choir would be performing.

Toby found Dena Somerville at her desk. Harrison's teacher was a year older than him, and he'd known her much of his life. She was of average height, with medium brown hair and brown eyes. Boringly ordinary, her younger sister, Reggie, had always complained about Dena and herself, back when he and Reggie had been in high school, and more significantly, an item.

A lot of years ago and even more miles, he thought, knocking on the open door. There had been nothing ordinary about Reggie Somerville.

Dena looked up and gave him a wan smile. "Toby, hi. Thanks for stopping by. This won't take long."

She waved to the chair by her desk—an adult-sized

chair, for which he was grateful. There was no way he could squeeze into one of those kid chairs.

As he sat, he noticed Dena seemed a little pale—as if she wasn't feeling well.

"Everything all right?" he asked, not sure if he really wanted to hear the answer. Sometimes when a guy asked a woman what was wrong, he got back way too much information. The more they shared, the easier it was to respond wrong, and then it all went to crap.

"Harrison's doing great," she said, looking away and swallowing. "Give me a second, please."

She seemed to be breathing more deeply than normal, and her hands shook a little as she reached for the mug on her desk. He would swear that for a second she started to turn green, but then she exhaled sharply and relaxed.

"I'm good."

He had no idea what had just happened. All he knew for sure was he wanted to be far, far away—the instinctive male need to bolt when something female-based and uncomfortable happened.

Instead of running—a response that was both wrong and cowardly—he stayed where he was and waited.

Dena gave him a relaxed smile. "I wanted to let you know that Harrison's idea was chosen for our holiday project. I'll tell the students on Friday. All the third graders will be using circular looms to knit scarves and hats for children in need. We'll start work the Monday after Thanksgiving, and we have three weeks to get them done and delivered."

"That's not a lot of time."

"I know. A problem we face every year. We've talked

about starting the projects in early November, but that never seems to happen." She smiled. "We'll need to work hard to ensure we can get a lot of hats and scarves made between now and then."

"I was planning to volunteer to help on whatever project was picked."

"I was hoping you'd say that." Her gaze settled on his face. "But there might be a complication."

"Which is?"

She looked away, then back at him. "I'm sorry. This is going to fall under the category of too much information, but I felt you had the right to know because, well, because of Reggie."

He frowned. "Your sister?"

She smiled. "How many other Reggies do you know in your life?"

"She's the only one, but I haven't seen her in years." At least ten. No, twelve, he thought. Not since he'd taken off near the end of his high school senior year. "I heard she lives in Seattle."

"She does, but she's coming back for the holidays." Dena waved her hand. "My mom normally shepherds the holiday charity project through to completion, but my parents are renewing their vows with a big wedding and reception, so she doesn't have the time this year." Dena offered him a cautious smile. "Reggie's going to be taking charge instead."

Toby didn't know how to react to that nugget of information, but was saved from having to figure it out when Dena turned green again. She grabbed her desk and audibly panted.

"Are you all right?" he asked.

She shook her head and continued to breathe heavily. Just as suddenly as her color had changed, it returned to normal and she sagged back in her chair.

"That was a bad one," she murmured. "I thought I was going to throw up for sure." She looked at him. "Sorry. I shouldn't have said that."

"You're sick."

"Not exactly." She paused. "I'm pregnant."

"You're..."

Dena chuckled. "Wow, the look on your face. Yes. I had artificial insemination a couple of months ago."

She'd done that? He knew the procedure existed, but he'd never known anyone who had done it. Or used it. Or however he was supposed to think of it. "And now you're sick?"

"According to my doctor, the nausea will pass in a few weeks. Until then, I'm scaring a lot of people."

"Me included."

"Sorry." She smiled at him. "Back to the charity project. Given your past relationship with my sister, I wasn't sure if you'd be uncomfortable working with her. That's why I wanted to let you know what was happening."

He'd only been back in town about a year himself, and in all that time, he'd barely thought about Reggie. He heard a few things—like where she lived and the fact that just when he and Harrison had moved here, she and Jake Crane had gotten engaged and broken up, all in the space of a weekend.

"Dena, that was a long time ago. I doubt Reggie even remembers who I am."

"Oh, I'm pretty sure she remembers. You were her first real boyfriend. Girls don't forget that."

Information he would think about later, he told himself. "I'd have no problem working with her on the charity project, and I'm going to assume she'll say the same about me."

Dena grinned. "I'll have to let you know. I haven't talked to her about you yet. I wanted to check with you first. You're an involved father, which I respect. I know Harrison is always your priority. That's nice to see."

"Thanks. So we're good?"

"We are. If you could act surprised when Harrison tells you about his idea winning, that would be nice."

"I'll be appropriately blown away." He started to stand, then hesitated. "Am I correct in assuming the pregnancy is also something not a lot of people know?"

"You are. I would appreciate your discretion."

"You have it. And, ah, congratulations."

"Thanks. I'm due right after the end of the school year, so I'll be able to finish up with my class."

They talked for a couple more minutes, and then he made his escape. As he drove back to the center of town and his office upstairs over the retail store, he tried to figure out which surprised him most—Reggie returning to Wishing Tree or his son's single teacher getting pregnant through artificial insemination.

He didn't have any moral judgments on the latter. While he didn't know Dena beyond her capacity as Harrison's teacher and Reggie's sister, he considered her an intelligent, thoughtful person who wouldn't make the decision of becoming a single parent lightly. It wasn't an easy task—and he would know. He'd found out about Harrison when the boy had been three months old. One second he'd been a regular single guy with zero responsibilities, and the next he'd been holding a baby who was his son. The amount he'd known about kids in general and babies in particular could fit on a matchbook cover and leave room for advertising. But he'd figured it out.

As for Reggie, he'd spoken the truth when he'd pointed out to Dena that their relationship had happened a couple of lifetimes ago. Sure, he'd been crazy about her, and back then, he'd fantasized about them spending the rest of their lives together, but so what? They'd been young and in love and now they were neither. Working with her on the charity project would be no big deal. It might even be fun to get to know each other again.

As for risking his heart, he knew that wasn't going to happen. Not counting Reggie, he had incredibly bad taste when it came to women. If he only had to worry about himself, he might take a chance, but there was more on the line. And in his world, Harrison was the only thing that mattered.

Three

WHILE THE REST of the planet barreled forward, wanting to know what the future would bring, Wishing Tree, Washington, was more content to meander. There was plenty of high-speed internet to be had and a burgeoning high-tech area on the outskirts of town. The new outlet mall was a big hit, and there was talk that several of the state's larger wineries were thinking of putting in a tasting room, but at its heart, Wishing Tree was only ever what it had always been. Homey, family-friendly, and completely and totally Christmas-centric.

The north-south streets celebrated all things holiday. There were names like Jolly Drive and Reindeer Avenue. The east-west streets were all named after trees. Noble and Spruce, even Mountain Hemlock Highway. Instead of a traditional town square, there was The Wreath—a circular area where all important events took place. Parades (and there were several) began and ended there. The tree lighting took place in The Wreath. The town's Advent calendar had a place there. Stores circled The Wreath, and if a retail space became available, there was always a sizeable waiting list of businesses wanting the prime location.

As Reggie drove slowly along the familiar streets, she felt an easing of a tension she hadn't noticed until now. Being back was right, she told herself. Seattle was great and she loved her life there, but coming home to Wishing Tree, especially for Christmas, was pretty wonderful, too.

Her parents lived in one of the older neighborhoods. The brick houses sat on oversized lots. Wide porches offered lots of space for holiday decorations. Right now there were plenty of scarecrows and turkeys in front lawns. The Friday after Thanksgiving, all that would change as the town appeared to flip a switch and begin what was, for them, the best season of all, with the Lighting of the Trees.

From the back seat, Belle began to whine, as if she recognized where they were and couldn't wait to see her grandparents. Reggie noticed the absence of snowmen in the decorating. Town rules—no snowmen until the first snowfall. And the definition of *snowfall* was very specific, at least in Wishing Tree. It had to snow steadily for at least fifteen minutes, at the end of which the ground had to be lightly dusted. If that happened, the first snowfall was declared. Horns sounded and everyone headed for The Wreath to celebrate.

The first snow was incredibly late this year, Reggie thought, taking in brown, bare lawns. With a little luck, she would still be around when it happened. After all, Wishing Tree had had a white Christmas every year of its existence. There was no reason to think this year would be any different.

She pulled up in front of the familiar two-story brick house. There were big windows and a wide porch. She and Dena had grown up in this house. She knew which stairs creaked when she was trying to sneak out and exactly how long she could shower before the hot water ran out. She knew the sound of rain on the roof in her upstairs bedroom and which part of the basement was comfortable to work in and which part creeped her out.

The front door opened and her parents rushed out. Belle nearly went through the window in her eagerness to get outside and greet them. Reggie hurried around and let out her dog. Belle burst forth with all the joy her giant body could contain, rushing toward two of her favorite people in the world.

"Who's a beautiful girl?" Reggie's mom said, holding her arms open wide. Reggie's father got between them, taking the brunt of Belle's body blow as she slammed into them before circling, barking and whining, wiggling with happiness and drenching them with kisses.

Reggie watched her parents, trying to see if anything had changed since they'd visited her in Seattle a few months before. Her dad had a few more gray hairs around his temple. Leigh, her mom, would never let that happen to her own hair. She visited her stylist regularly for a cut and a little root touch-up. Her medium brown hair was the same color it had always been— the same color Reggie had inherited, along with her mother's brown eyes.

Reggie joined her parents, moving more sedately.

Her dad held her tight. "How was the drive?" he asked, before passing her off to her mother for another hug.

"Good. Easy. We stopped for burgers."

Leigh cupped Belle's huge head in her hands. "Did your mom get you a burger because you're a good girl?"

Belle's long tail whipped back and forth, stopping suddenly when a sharp bark filled the air. Reggie saw Burt, her dad's twenty-two-pound dachshund, run out of the house toward them. Belle immediately slipped behind Reggie, her tail tucked between her legs.

"You really need to learn to handle him," Reggie said before bending over and greeting Burt. "Hey, big guy."

Burt wiggled with happiness as she patted him, before glaring at Belle and giving a low growl. Belle retreated further.

Leigh put her arm around Belle. "Just stand up to him. He's not as brave as he seems. Show him who's boss, pretty girl. That's all it's going to take."

Good advice, Reggie thought. Sadly, Belle had not yet mastered more than a few words of the English language and couldn't understand much beyond the tone of the message. The finer details, and the advice, were lost on her.

Her mom shepherded the dogs inside while Reggie and her dad took care of the luggage. The suitcases went upstairs into Reggie's old room, and the dog food was stored in the kitchen pantry. Last, Reggie carried her laptop and Gizmo's vacuum downstairs into the basement rec-room-slash-craft-room-slash-spare-office.

She set them on the long worktable, noting there were sample wedding invitations spread out, along with a printed guest list. It seemed her parents really were serious about renewing their vows and having a big party to celebrate.

She went back to the main level, noting there were a few changes from her last visit. The hardwood floors had been refinished and the walls painted. There was a new stove in the kitchen—a nice six-burner model replacing the one that had been older than her.

The living room furniture—used for guests—was as pristine as always. It was pretty much the only place pets weren't allowed. In the family room, however, the big sectional and two recliners were worn from use but still comfortable. She thought maybe the TV was a little bigger than the last time she'd visited, but otherwise, all was as she remembered. Including Burt nipping at Belle's ankles and the Great Dane yelping before jumping on the sofa, where she stood trembling, her expression one of outrage and fear.

"Oh, Belle," Reggie said, settling next to her dog. "You have got to grow a spine. Seriously, your daily poop weighs as much as he does."

"There's a thought," her father said, leaning over the back of the sofa and kissing the top of her head. "It's good to have you back, kid."

"It's good to be back."

"I need to get to the shop."

Leigh walked out of the kitchen. "Dinner's at six thirty, Vince. Not six forty or six forty-five."

He grinned. "Tell me again. Why am I marrying you?"

Reggie's mother smiled. "Because you'd be lost without me."

"That I would."

They kissed. Then Vince waved and went to the garage. Burt stared after him, sighed when the garage door closed, and curled up in his bed by the recliner on the left. Belle eyed him suspiciously before collapsing on the sofa, resting her head on Reggie's lap.

"So, where are we with the wedding?" Reggie asked as her mother took her seat in her recliner.

"Sometimes I think I'm organized, and other times, I'm not sure. Dena and I were discussing the bridesmaid issue yesterday."

"She mentioned that. Mom, it's totally up to you. If you want us to be bridesmaids, then we're in. If you don't, we're fine with that."

"Thank you. I'm leaning toward no. It's not as if this is a real wedding."

Reggie nodded, trying not to show her glee. "But you still want Belle to be your flower girl."

"Of course. You'll need to make her a dress. Something pretty with lots of lace and maybe a train."

"A train might scare her, Mom. She could think she was being chased."

"All right. Then just a pretty dress in either red or green."

Reggie stroked Belle's face. "We'll put you in red because that looks good on you, doesn't it?"

Belle slapped her tail against the sofa.

"Do you want to have a wedding shower?" Reggie asked.

"No. I'm too old. And no gifts."

"People might want to bring something."

Leigh waved her hands. "Have them donate to the town benevolent fund in our name. It's not like your father and I need anything. We're fine with what we have. We just want a big party."

"And a wedding."

Her mother smiled. "Yes, and a wedding."

Reggie went upstairs to unpack. Belle followed, glancing around anxiously, as if expecting Burt to burst out from around a corner and attack her.

"You're fine. He's zonked out by the recliner," Reggie pointed out.

Belle's worried expression didn't relax.

Reggie led the way to her old bedroom. It had been updated the summer she'd come back from her first year of college. The pale blue walls were restful, and she'd packed up her high school memorabilia, leaving the shelves and surfaces mostly empty.

Belle walked over to the huge bolstered dog bed in the corner and sniffed.

"He hasn't been on there," Reggie told her. "Mom keeps the door closed."

Belle didn't look convinced and sniffed every inch before finally settling down. Reggie unpacked Belle's things first. She stacked her dog's coats, booties and scarves on the landing by the stairs and put her pajamas in a drawer in the larger dresser. She'd just put her own suitcase on the bed when she heard footsteps on the stairs and a familiar voice calling, "You made it."

Belle leaped to her feet and hurried out to greet Dena. Her tail whacked Reggie in the thigh, causing her to jump and cry out.

"That's going to leave a bruise," she muttered, following her dog to greet her sister.

They hugged. Reggie looked at Dena's pale face. "How are you feeling?"

"Less barfy this second, which is always nice."

"You don't look pregnant."

"Not yet," Dena said, heading into Reggie's room and collapsing in the chair by the small desk. "I was going to keep the whole thing a secret until I was three or four months along, but with me throwing up, I've had to tell people I'm pregnant, not sick. I hate it when my plans get messed up."

"You can't plan for a baby."

Dena grinned. "You can if you try hard enough. So, you're back. How does it feel?"

"It's too soon to tell, but mostly good. I've decided I was being ridiculous thinking people would care about my personal life. It's been a year and Jake's gone and no one's going to say anything."

Dena glanced away, then back at her.

"What?" Reggie demanded as she opened her suitcase and picked up a stack of bikini panties.

"You're right about Jake. No one's going to care. But the thing is, I'm not sure they won't still be chit-chatting about you."

Reggie slid the underwear into the drawer. "What are you talking about?"

"I didn't want to mention this before—when you were dealing with the breakup. But Toby moved back to town about the time you and Jake ended things."

Reggie's first thought was they hadn't "ended things." Jake had dumped her with zero explanation. But as her sister's words sank in, she realized that wasn't exactly the point.

"Toby as in Toby?" she asked, sitting on the bed. "The Toby I dated in high school?"

"That would be him, yes."

Toby—she hadn't thought of him in forever. He'd been her first love, her first boyfriend, her first everything. They'd had a fight, she'd ended things and two days later, he'd taken off, never to return. Or so she'd thought.

"How is he? Have you seen him? He's been back a year and no one told me?" She tried to remember what, if anything, she'd heard about him. "His grandmother still lives in town, right? And his dad died a couple of years ago."

"Yes to all that," Dena told her, looking concerned. "He opened a Judy's Hand Pies in The Wreath and moved the corporate headquarters to Seattle."

"What?"

Reggie's voice was enough of a yelp to cause Belle to raise her head and check for danger. Not finding any obvious threats, she put her head back down.

"He's in Seattle?"

Dena shook her head. "Mostly he's here. I think he goes over there every few weeks, but he lives here, with his grandmother, up by String of Lights Park."

The more well-to-do part of town, Reggie thought absently. "Hey, how do you know so much about him?"

Her sister drew in a breath. "His eight-year-old son, Harrison, is in my class."

"What?"

Reggie came off the bed and put her hands on her hips. "Toby has a son in your class and you never thought to mention it to me?"

Dena shifted uncomfortably. "I know. It's bad, huh? I just didn't know what to say, and when I thought about telling you, it kind of felt like I shouldn't."

Too much was coming at her too fast. "So he's married."

"No. There's no wife. Harrison doesn't say anything about his mom and I haven't asked. Toby comes to all the parent-teacher stuff. He's a good dad. He really loves his kid."

Toby was back and he had a son?

"Wow," she said, returning to the bed. "I don't know what to think or say about that."

"At least it's not Jake."

Reggie laughed. "True."

"He's a really great guy," Dena began.

Reggie held up both hands. "Stop, you. No. Just no. Don't even think about setting me up with someone I used to date in high school."

She was going to say more, but Dena went pale and seemed to sway a little in her chair.

"What?" she asked, suddenly anxious. "Are you all right?"

Dena shook her head and deliberately slowed her breathing. "Give me a sec. It's the nausea. Hopefully it'll pass."

"There's a trash can right there," Reggie said helpfully.

Dena managed a slight smile. "Thank you. So thoughtful."

"I try."

She continued breathing deeply for a few seconds, then relaxed. "Okay, I'm better."

Reggie studied her, not sure she was telling the truth.

"Are you doing all right with the pregnancy and all?"

Dena's mouth twisted. "If you're asking if I'm having

second thoughts, then no. But I will admit being pregnant is harder than I anticipated. I thought I'd come up with the perfect plan."

"You know what they say about God and having plans. They make Him laugh."

"I've always thought God would be happy about my planning. It means less work for Him."

Reggie laughed. "Okay, good point. How can I help?"

"There's nothing much to do while I gestate. Oh, but I do appreciate you taking over the charity knitting project for Mom. If you hadn't agreed, I would have had to—"

"Holy crap!" Reggie sprang to her feet. "Harrison's in your class. I'm going to be working with Toby's son."

Dena cleared her throat. "Yes, well, more than that. Toby's one of the parents who is, you know, helping out."

No, Reggie thought firmly. "Not happening."

"Why not? According to you, he's just some guy you used to go out with."

"Don't use my own words against me, please."

Dena grinned. "Where's the fun in that?" Her smile faded, and her tone grew cajoling. "Come on, you'll be making hats, and they're for homeless children, by the way. Children who don't get enough to eat and are cold."

"Don't try guilting me into not wanting to throw a little hissy fit here."

Reggie took several sweaters out of the suitcase and crossed to the closet, where she put them on a shelf. When she turned back to her sister, she said, "I'll work with Toby. I'm sure it will be fine. What's the big deal?

We're both grown-ups. I barely remember what he looks like."

Dena gave a slightly wicked laugh. "Oh, you'll recognize him. And for the record? He looks good."

"IT'S CHRISTMAS TREES," Micah Ruiz said, staring out at the rolling hills covered with trees. Hundreds of trees. No, he corrected. Thousands. Tens of thousands.

"Yup," his friend Steve Burdick said with a grin. "That's what they call 'em. We have grand firs, blue spruce and Fraser firs."

"You know the difference?"

Steve's grin widened. "I do now."

Micah chuckled. "How long did that take you to learn which was which?"

"A couple of months."

"You really own a Christmas tree farm."

"I do."

"In a town called Wishing Tree."

Steve looked at him. "You seem a little slow on the uptake. Should I worry about you?"

"Just trying to take it all in. Hearing you say you bought one and seeing it are two different things. So, what's the plan?"

"The Christmas tree lot in town opens the Saturday after Thanksgiving. The one out here opens the same day. People can drive out and pick a cut tree, or they can go choose their own and chop it down themselves."

Micah shook his head. "You're trusting people with axes?"

"They sign a waiver."

"That's the holiday spirit."

Micah glanced around at the endless rows of trees,

the mountains beyond and the bright blue sky over-head. He'd always thought of himself as a city guy, but the past few months had taught him the value of solitude in a beautiful place.

He and Steve walked back to the truck, then drove the short distance to the country store just off Mountain Hemlock Highway, where the owner —a woman who had to be in her eighties—made a surprisingly excellent cup of coffee.

Mrs. Bevins, small and bent, with glasses and curly white hair, smiled when she saw them.

"Back again, boys?"

"We can't resist you or your coffee," Steve said easily. "And I wanted to show Micah where the cut tree lot would be."

"Just out back," Mrs. Bevins said. "Steve and his guys will set them up Saturday morning. I process the payments here." She winked at Micah. "You could keep me company, if you wanted. You're a fine-looking man."

Steve snorted. "Yeah, he's always had the face."

Mrs. Bevins poured them each a mug of coffee. "I might have other interests, but his face is nice, too."

Micah thanked her while keeping his distance. Years of practice made dodging eager fans—or bold old ladies—second nature to him. He had a sixth sense about wandering hands and knew just when to get out of the way.

When he'd first been starting out with the band, he'd welcomed the attention and had taken advantage of the offers. He'd had a failed marriage early on—one that had happened and ended so quickly, neither of them had been affected by its demise. After a few years, he'd learned to be a bit more discerning about who he took to his bed. Then he'd met Adriana, and from that moment on, there hadn't been any other women.

He'd always been a big believer in love. His ballads were incredibly successful, and he earned nearly as much from other artists covering his hits as he earned from recording them himself. But believing in and writing about love hadn't prepared him for what it was like to actually feel it for himself. Adriana had rocked his world (no pun intended) and opened his heart in ways he hadn't imagined.

Sometimes at night, while she was sleeping, he would sit up and watch her, grateful beyond words that she was in his life. When he thought about how unlikely it was to find the one person who made everything right and fall in love and have her love you back, well, it made his head spin. She had been the greatest of highs, and losing her and their unborn child had nearly destroyed him.

He returned his attention to the present and walked outside with Steve. There was a big fenced-in space in the rear, with gates in the front and back.

"We've already marked the trees we're going to cut down for sales here and in town," Steve told him. "We'll start cutting Monday so they're ready in time."

"I remember when the closest you came to farming was knowing the best pot dealer in every state."

"Hey," Steve said, glancing around as if to make sure no one was within hearing distance. "That was a long time ago. Pot's legal in Washington State now, and I don't do that anymore."

Micah laughed. "You're a little sensitive."

"I'm not your partying drummer. I'm a family man

with a kid, and I'm a respected member of the community."

"Fair enough. You've come a long way."

Everyone in the band had, Micah thought. They'd been teenagers when they'd started out. Now, nearly twenty years later, they'd moved on. They were married—most had kids. He'd been the last to settle down, but once he'd found Adriana, he'd been all in.

"How's the B and B?" Steve asked, leaning against the fence.

"Comfortable. I have a quiet room in the old carriage house."

"Getting recognized everywhere you go?"

Micah grimaced. Being spotted was an occupational hazard. "Some. Most people just do a double take, then keep moving. I can handle it."

"Finding your way around town okay?"

"Mostly keeping to myself."

Steve studied him. "You need to get out. Mingle with people. Soak up the atmosphere. It's why you're here."

His friend was right. Micah had come to Wishing Tree hoping to find a little holiday spirit. He'd managed to heal his body from the accident that had injured him and taken Adriana, and mostly recover from the loss of his wife, but he'd yet to find his way back to writing. In the past year, he hadn't so much as come up with a refrain, let alone an entire song. He'd tried writing alone and with a writing partner, but neither had produced anything. He'd always done well with holiday-themed music and hoped hanging out in a place known for celebrating the season would help him jump-start his creativity.

It had to work, he thought fiercely. He was done performing. He was nearly forty and more than ready to let the kids have all the fun on stage. But writing, composing, that was different. That fed his soul, and his inability to create left him feeling frustrated and worthless.

"In the meantime, I need a favor," Steve said.

Micah looked at him. "Sure. Name it."

"Monday is career day in Noah's class, and I'm supposed to be there. There's no way I can get the tree lots up and running and show up for that. I talked to Noah and he's fine with having you instead."

Noah was Steve's eight-year-old son. While Micah would gladly rush into a burning building to save the kid, he was less sure about speaking at career day.

"What am I supposed to say to them?" Micah asked, sounding doubtful. "Nothing about being a rock star is wholesome."

"Talk about songwriting. How you came up with 'Moonlight for Christmas.' Play a couple of your greatest hits. The presentation is maybe fifteen minutes. You can wing it."

Micah wanted to say no. He hadn't been in front of a crowd for nearly four years, not since he'd married Adriana. The closest he'd come to sharing was at the grief group he'd joined after he'd lost her last year. But Steve and the rest of the band had been there for him in the almost six months it had taken him to recover physically from the accident. Since leaving the physical rehab facility, he'd been hanging out with one or the other of them, avoiding his home back in Malibu, restlessly searching for a way to return to songwriting and figure out how to be happy again—assuming that was possible.

His heart told him to say no, that it would be too

hard, but his head said he had to keep moving forward. Whatever he was looking for wasn't behind him. Besides, he'd always been willing to fight for what he wanted, whether it was a better deal with his record company or winning over Adriana.

"I'll be there," he said, before he could talk himself out of it.

"Thanks," Steve said. "I'm grateful. I'll text you the when and where. The elementary school is pretty close to the B and B."

Micah laughed. "It's Wishing Tree, bro. It's not like anything is far."

"Makes it easier not to get lost."

Micah hoped that was true. He could use a little not getting lost in his life. Not to mention some musical inspiration. And maybe a little Christmas spirit to fill up the empty places inside. A big ask for the small town, but hey, wasn't this the time of year to expect a miracle?

Four

DENA PARKED ON the side of the carriage house. When she'd first inherited the Victorian B and B, she'd assumed she could start walking to work, what with the B and B so close to the elementary school. But being a teacher meant carting files, folders and overflowing plastic totes back and forth, meaning she had to either drive or get some kind of urban burro to help her carry everything. She'd elected to use her car.

She left her car unloading for later and walked across the paved driveway to the front of the large, three-story Victorian. Mid-November should mean plenty of snow on the ground, but not this year. Despite the brown grass, the yard still looked pretty with the brightly colored metal turkeys, gourds and Pilgrims nestled among the plants. Pumpkins sat on each of the steps leading up to the front door. Harvest wreaths hung on the front door and in front of each of the first-floor windows.

The Friday after Thanksgiving, the decor shifted from Thanksgiving to Christmas. Dena took care of the interior decorating—it was one of her traditions—while she hired professionals to do the outside of the B and B. No way she was comfortable getting up on a twenty-foot ladder!

She went inside and did a quick scan of the living room with its comfy sofas, ornate end tables and the massive fireplace along one wall. She checked for out-of-place books or guest items left behind, but found all was well. Past that was the reception area. The reception desk was actually an old bar from a brothel that had existed a hundred fifty years ago, when gold and lumber had first put Wishing Tree, then known as Trading Post, on the map.

Winona, her fortysomething general manager and right-hand woman, looked up and smiled.

"How did it go today? Feeling any better?"

"I only threw up once, and I made it to the bathroom in time."

"Yay. A victory."

"A really small one. Everything good here?"

"Yes. The Pinkertons called again, looking for space over Christmas." Winona sighed. "I wish we could accommodate them. They're such a wonderful couple."

Dena agreed. The Pinkertons had been coming to the B and B for Christmas since before Dena had inherited the place. They were older—charming and warm—with a love of crafts of all kinds. Every year they showed up with unexpected gifts for the guests and staff. One year Mrs. Pinkerton had made little stuffed Christmas mice ornaments for every tree in the B and B and for each guest to take home. They'd said this year they were going to be visiting family rather than coming to Wishing Tree, so Dena hadn't held a room for them, but a change in plans had them requesting a reservation.

"You'll let them know if anything opens up?" Dena asked, already knowing the answer.

"Yes. I'm confirming the December reservations this week. If anyone cancels, I'm calling them right away."

Winona ran through the guest list with Dena and handed her the December menus to review.

"Have you met your roommate?" Winona asked with a grin. "He's very swoon-worthy."

"He's not my roommate. He lives downstairs."

"Giving you even more access. You share the court-yard. Maybe he'll see you and invite you in for a night-cap."

"Unlikely. Besides, I can't drink."

"Oh, yeah, I forgot. So a bite to eat or a quickie up against the wall."

Dena wrinkled her nose. "That's romantic."

Winona's smile turned knowing. "You're judging because you've never been taken up against a wall. It can be very exciting."

"I'm not sure how the logistics would work or if my thigh muscles would be up to the task." She leaned against the bar. "And before you get too lost in your fantasies, have you made sure there isn't a Mrs. Swoon-worthy around?"

"He seems very single. I'm thinking of calling dibs."

Dena laughed. "You go ahead. I doubt he's my type anyway."

"Oh, honey, he's everyone's type."

"I'm taking that as my cue to leave. I'll see you later."

"Yes, you will."

Dena walked back toward the carriage house. She let herself into the small walled courtyard that led to the entrance to the upper and lower apartments. The bottom one took up half the ground floor. Her upstairs apartment covered the downstairs unit and the storage area, giving her two spacious bedrooms, two bathrooms and a small study. The corner kitchen had lots of light, and there was even a small fireplace in her living room.

She'd just fished her key out of her handbag when she heard a low male voice say, "Hello. I think we're neighbors."

Dena turned and saw the mystery guest standing just inside his open front door. He was, as she and Winona had discussed, completely and totally swoonworthy. About six-two or -three, with dark hair and piercing blue eyes. His jaw was square, his shoulders broad. He was lean and strong at the same time, and his smile was whatever was better than perfect.

"Um, hi," she said, wondering how, exactly, one did it up against a wall. It sounded uncomfortable to her, but if the man in front of her was doing the asking, she was willing to risk the—

Ack! She had to get a grip.

She pulled her mind back to the present moment and walked toward him, hand outstretched.

"I'm Dena Somerville. Welcome to the Wishing Tree B and B."

"Micah Ruiz."

They shook hands. As she felt the heat of his skin against hers, she was fairly sure she experienced a jolt all the way up to her elbow. A kind of tingly, zippy buzz that made her want to step a little closer to find out if he smelled as good as he looked.

Horrified by her wayward thoughts, she deliberately pulled her hand free and took a half step back.

"Is your room all right?" she asked, striving for what she hoped was a welcoming yet professional tone. "Do you need extra towels or anything?"

His dark eyebrows drew together just enough to make him look delightfully quizzical, yet thoughtful and incredibly handsome.

"Why would you ask that?"

"What? Oh." She laughed. "Sorry. I'm the owner."

"So you have access to the good stuff."

She glanced over her shoulder and lowered her voice. "I can, in fact, get you an extra bar of goat's milk soap anytime you need one."

"That's a lot of power."

"I try to use it wisely. As someone who gets to see the menus in advance of them being posted, I'll tell you that tonight, the Snacks and Wine hour is not to be missed. We're having fried mac and cheese bites, with a veggie plate because balance is important."

"I don't think I've ever had a fried mac and cheese bite."

"Then you have to try one. Or twenty. They're a little addictive. Of course, all the food we serve is amazing. I say that because Ursula is the best chef in the valley."

One corner of his mouth turned up. "Ursula? Named after the *Little Mermaid* Ursula?"

"No, and please don't mention that particular movie around her. She's not happy being portrayed as a villain." She paused. "Villainess. Anyway, come over to the main house between five and seven and you'll be dazzled."

"I thought it was snack and wine *hour*," he said, his low voice teasing.

"Yes, there is that. You should come." *With me, as my date. We could get to know each other better and—*

Dena shook off the thoughts. Later she would read one of her pregnancy books and find out if there was a mental component to the gestating process.

She gave Micah a quick wave before retreating. Once she was safely upstairs and in her apartment, she set down her handbag on the entry table and wondered why Micah hadn't been one of the guys to show up on her dating app—back when she'd been doing the dating thing. She would have said yes to him in a heartbeat.

Of course, she was merely ordinary, and had he seen her picture as a possibility, he would have no doubt passed her by. Alas.

She lightly pressed her hand to her belly. "Not to worry," she told her lima bean. "No dating for me. You're all I need in my life. And I say that with love, rather than to pressure you."

TOBY CAREFULLY USED the hook to bring the yarn up and around on the circular loom he'd bought at a local craft store. The charity project was starting in a little over a week, and he wanted to be proficient enough to help teach the kids what to do. One of the advantages to being the CEO of his own company, he thought humorously, was that he could work on crafts in the middle of the afternoon if he wanted to.

Satisfied with the three rows he'd completed, he

stored the loom in a desk drawer. He would take it home with him tonight to work on over the weekend. Harrison had said he wanted to practice as well, and even get a start on making a hat or two. His son wanted this to be the best charity project the third-grade class had ever done.

His son had a big heart, Toby thought, moving his mouse to wake his computer. He was a sweet, caring boy with an easygoing nature. Given the family genetics, Toby knew he'd gotten lucky in that respect. Things could have been a lot different.

He looked at the spreadsheet in front of him, but instead of reviewing the numbers, he found himself thinking about the past. Probably because of what Dena had said about Reggie coming back. He hadn't thought about her much in years, but in the past couple of days she'd been on his mind, along with a lot of things he'd done his best to forget.

Toby's father had been a mean drunk and not much more pleasant when he was sober. Toby had been a troubled teenager, only relaxed and comfortable on the football field. Academics had never interested him, and he'd rarely found a rule he was willing to follow. If he'd grown up in a town big enough to have a tough crowd, he would have run with them. But in Wishing Tree, there hadn't been any really bad kids. Still, he'd had a reputation.

One that Reggie Somerville had ignored, he thought, remembering how she'd shocked the hell out of him the spring day she'd walked up to him as he stood by his locker. She'd had on her cheerleader uniform, with its short skirt and tight sweater. Back then, she'd worn her brown hair in a high ponytail that had bounced with every step. A sophomore to his junior, she'd looked him right in the eye before saying, "You should ask me out sometime."

That was it. A single sentence that had rocked his world and muddled his brain. He'd been unable to speak. Or move. He'd just stared at her until she'd given him a smile and turned and walked away, her skirt swinging and ponytail bouncing.

Later that afternoon, he'd finished PE about the time she'd finished her cheerleader workout. As if pulled by gravity, they'd met by the waist-high chain-link fence that divided the field. He'd tried to act cool and was sure he'd failed. Still, he'd managed to ask her out for Saturday night.

"I'd like that," she'd told him.

"Your parents going to approve?"

She'd cocked her head, as if considering her answer. "Probably not, but they won't say I can't date you. They'll tell me to be careful." She started to turn away, only to face him again. "You're going to come to the door to pick me up, and then you'll come inside and meet my dad." The smile returned. "He sounds a lot meaner than he is. Just be respectful. Tell him you won't drink or speed, and that you'll have me back five minutes before my curfew."

"That's a lot of rules. I'm not a guy who plays by the rules."

The smile had never wavered. "You're not as tough as you think, Toby Newkirk. You pretend not to do what's expected because you're bad, but the truth is, you're waiting to find someone who cares enough to make you do the right thing. That would be me."

She'd walked away then, just like she had earlier

that day. He'd shown up when she'd said he would, had suffered through a fifteen-minute interrogation from her father, and had brought her safely home *ten* minutes before curfew.

And that had been it. For the next year, he and Reggie had been a couple. Attraction had grown into genuine love and through most of his senior year, she'd been the one he turned to when things got so bad at home he had to worry about hiding the bruises.

It had all come to an end the week after their senior prom, he thought now, knowing time had blunted the pain of the last time they'd spoken, but not his regret for his part in it. He'd hurt her, and in her mind, he'd betrayed her. That it hadn't been on purpose hadn't mattered. Not to her. He supposed now it was just old news to her.

But not back then. He remembered her tears as she told him it was over. Two days later, his father had surprised him in his sleep, coming at him with a baseball bat. Toby had managed to get in a couple of blows, enough to disorient the old man and allow Toby to escape. Faced with the reality that if he stuck around much longer, his father would kill him, he'd taken off with the idea that he would never come back. He'd been angry, hurt physically and emotionally, and brave in the stupid way of eighteen-year-olds who think they know everything.

Nearly twelve years later, here he was. Back where he'd started. Older, wiser and a whole lot clearer on what was important.

He glanced at the clock, then stood and stretched. Harrison was due to stop by the store on his way home, and Toby would take a few minutes to greet him, as he always did.

The corporate offices of Judy's Hand Pies, Inc., were located just outside of Seattle. Toby drove over every three or four weeks to meet with his senior staff. The rest of the time, he worked remotely from Wishing Tree. His second-floor office was plenty big, and he liked being in the middle of town.

Downstairs was the Wishing Tree branch of Judy's Hand Pies, complete with a small test kitchen and, in the summer, an outdoor eating area. He made his way to the main floor and entered through the kitchen. Shaye Harper was busy helping a customer.

"Hello, Mrs. LaBella," Toby said when he caught sight of his former chemistry teacher. "How are you feeling today?"

"Excellent, as always, Toby. My daughter is bringing her family over for the weekend, and I want plenty of hand pies for them to snack on."

Mrs. LaBella had never been a fan of his in high school. She'd rightly assumed he could do well in her class, if only he applied himself. He'd resisted anything that resembled studying and had only passed because Reggie had been disappointed by his string of D grades. Just to make her happy, he'd worked enough to get Cs in all his classes, except for advanced algebra, where he'd accidentally gotten a B.

One of the disadvantages of small-town living was knowing practically everyone by name. When he'd first returned, Mrs. LaBella had offered little beyond a stern greeting and a sniff, but over time, he'd won her over. Well, he hadn't. Harrison had.

His former chemistry teacher took her box of pies

and left. Shaye waited until the door closed behind her before saying, "I don't get it. The seasonal turkey hand pies do really well. But it's turkey, stuffing and vegetables, which is exactly what we'll all be eating next week. Why are people buying them when they'll have the same meal in a few days?"

He reached for one of the pies himself. "Anticipation. It helps set the mood for the holiday. We'll sell them through Sunday, then pull them from the menu until two weeks before Christmas."

"Retail is weird."

"Retail is about managing inventory and fulfilling wants."

Shaye, his newest hire and a recent resident of the town, grinned. "Are they going to be covering that in my marketing class next semester?"

"They are, but they'll call it something different."

He split the pie and handed her half. As she took it, her engagement ring caught the light. Shaye hadn't just moved to town—she'd also found love with Lawson Easley, a returning soldier.

Shaye nibbled on the hand pie. "It's really good, but I still don't get why people want to eat turkey and stuffing a week before Thanksgiving."

"And yet they do."

"Based on your anticipation logic, then why not a hot dog hand pie right before Memorial Day?"

He chuckled. "We've tried, but we can't get the flavors right."

"You're probably using the wrong relish."

"Maybe."

The door to the store opened and Harrison burst in,

his great-grandmother at his heels. Harrison rushed over, dropped his backpack and hugged Toby.

"Hi, Dad. School was great. I got an A on my math test and Ms. Somerville said the parent sign-up sheet for our charity project was already full. She's getting lots of calls from people in town who want to come help."

Toby smiled at his son, then smoothed his floppy blond bangs out of his face. "You need a haircut."

Harrison groaned. "Not a haircut. It's too soon."

He released his father and greeted Shaye before circling around behind the counter. "May I have a hand pie, please?"

"Sure," Toby told him. "Let Shaye get it."

"He's so polite," Grandma Judy said with a laugh. "You were never that polite."

"I was too busy getting into trouble."

He spoke easily, even as he studied his grandmother. He'd never planned to return to Wishing Tree, but after his father's death, Judy had aged seemingly overnight. He'd worried about her living alone and knew asking her to leave her hometown would be too hard on her, so he'd joined her here. It had taken six months to relocate the corporate headquarters from Austin to Seattle.

He'd bought a big house out by String of Lights Park, choosing one on a quiet cul-de-sac. Harrison had a yard and knew a couple of the kids in the neighborhood. The center of town was a short ten-minute drive, and Harrison's school was five minutes south of that.

Harrison picked the seasonal turkey pie, causing Shaye to sigh and shake her head. His son settled at one of the tables to eat it while Toby got him a carton of milk to go with it. Judy sat with him until he was done, then ushered him out the door.

"We'll see you at home," she said.

"I'll be there by five."

He watched them get into Judy's compact SUV, then caught sight of a woman walking a dog on the other side of The Wreath. At first the dog held his attention. The massive, dark gray Great Dane wore a colorful blue-and-green knit sweater. Both the dog and the outfit were unusual enough to be noteworthy, but when his gaze slipped to the woman holding the leash, he felt a firm kick in the gut.

He knew that walk—the one with the little bounce. Long brown hair had been cut to jaw length, and the cheerleader uniform had been replaced with jeans and jacket, but he recognized her all the same. She was the grown-up version of the teenager he'd given his heart to all those years ago. She'd been his first time, his first love, his first everything. And as Dena had warned him, Reggie was back.

Five

MICAH HAD BEEN hoping for a little more Christmas from the town of Wishing Tree. On his Saturday morning walk, all he'd seen was Thanksgiving and harvest decorations. There were plenty of turkeys and gourds and pilgrims but not a single elf or snowman to be seen.

Steve had told him Christmas arrived the Friday after Thanksgiving and that he would be overwhelmed by holiday cheer and seasonal decorations. Micah hoped that was true—he could use a little inspiration. So far his attempts to write a holiday love song had been a dismal failure. He'd yet to string together more than three chords, and the closest he'd come to even a single phrase was, "I love you at Christmas," which was hardly going to win him a Grammy.

He stood in the middle of what he thought might be the town square, although it was round, and someone at the B and B had told him it was called The Wreath.

The big open area could easily host a pop-up fair or a giant Christmas tree. There were businesses circling it, including a couple of restaurants, a pet boutique, some store called Wrap Around the Clock and, most important to him, a coffee place.

He walked into Jingle Coffee and stood in line. The store was crowded and warm, with all kinds of mugs for sale and several kids clustered around what looked like a hot chocolate station.

He ordered a large drip coffee to go, then headed out, only to pause at the front wall, where a bulletin board had a big calendar showing town events through New Year's, along with different notices. Someone was selling a "gently used" Barbie DreamHouse. Someone else had found a large great white shark's tooth on a chain by the bookstore.

There was a reminder about the first snowfall, explaining it really did have to snow for fifteen full minutes and cover the ground to be the actual first snowfall. When that occurred, horns and sirens would sound, and all those interested should meet in The Wreath for the celebration.

"These people need to get a life," Micah murmured to himself.

He saw that on the first of December, the city Advent calendar would begin. Residents were reminded that participation was encouraged, especially when the daily activity involved helping out a neighbor.

He went outside and told himself that small towns were different from his life in LA. Not that he had a life in LA anymore—he hadn't lived in his house in over a year. Not since he'd lost Adriana and the baby. First he'd been in the hospital for a couple of weeks, then he'd had nearly five months in rehab, relearning how to do things like walk and dress himself. He'd spent a month in Australia, thinking the change in scene would help him recover, but it hadn't. Since then he'd been moving from place to place, looking for something he couldn't define. Which made finding it nearly impossible.

He walked along the storefronts, gazing in windows. He had to circle around a couple of women pushing strollers—a painful reminder that if the drunk driver had swerved left instead of right, he and Adriana would have had an eight-month-old now and it would be his first Christmas. Instead, Micah was alone with a battered psyche and enough memories to sink a ship...or a man.

Micah finished his coffee and tossed the paper cup into a recycling bin. The day was clear and sunny, but bitterly cold, and his thin jacket wasn't doing enough to keep him warm. He told himself when he got back to his room at the B and B, he would go online and order something warmer to be shipped overnight. Maybe he'd get a couple of plaid flannel shirts while he was at it.

He was still chuckling at the thought of owning a flannel shirt when his phone rang. He answered without checking to see who had called, then wished he hadn't when he heard a familiar female voice say, "What's so funny?"

"Hello, Electra."

"You're not going to tell me?"

"It would take too long to explain."

He heard her sigh. "I see you're still being difficult. Micah, I've told you the solution. Come back to LA where you belong. I know the house in Malibu has too many memories, so I'll help you sell it. You can buy something else in Venice or Hermosa Beach. If you don't want to be by the water, you can find something amazing up in the Hollywood Hills."

"Did you call me to talk about real estate?"

"No. I called to talk about the variety show. I want to make sure you're not backing out. You've been in a mood lately, and you're unpredictable."

A mood? He'd lost his family. That wasn't a mood. But he knew better than to state the obvious. Electra would turn it around to be about her, and he would end up apologizing for something he hadn't done because she was simply better at manipulating people.

"I'll be there," he told her. "I'm doing the show."

"And you're singing 'Moonlight for Christmas'?"

"Yes."

"People love that song so much. I've been talking to Billy about releasing a new version of it. Maybe we can get into the studio in the next few days and make that happen."

"I'm not coming back until the show."

"Why not? After we recorded the new version, we could go somewhere and write together. I know you're not writing on your own, Micah. You need me."

He needed a lot of things these days—he needed to start living again and he needed to sleep. He needed to find his inner voice, the one that whispered lyrics and suggested melodies, but he didn't need to spend even five minutes with his ex-wife.

"No, thanks," he said, trying to keep his voice friendly rather than curt. "I'll get there on my own."

"You're so stubborn. Fine. I'll see you in a few weeks."

"You will."

She hung up without saying goodbye, because that was Electra's way. He put his phone back in his pocket and started for the B and B, his good mood squashed by their conversation. Electra had a gift for sucking the joy out of any moment. Funny how twenty years ago, she'd been the most exciting creature he'd ever met. Of course, he'd been a kid and hadn't known better.

He took Grand Avenue to Jolly Drive and turned right. The B and B stood in a row with other Victorian houses, although the B and B was by far the biggest. At the last second, he went into the main building, thinking he might get another cup of coffee and see if there were any scones left from breakfast.

As he stepped inside the common living room, he was hit by welcome heat, the scent of a wood-burning fireplace and the sound of Dolly Parton singing "With Bells On." His upstairs neighbor, Dena, he thought she'd said, was on a stepladder, reaching up to dust the big mirror above the fireplace.

She wore her long brown hair in a braid that came halfway down her back. She had a Washington State Cougars sweatshirt on over jeans. When she saw him in the mirror, she moved down the two steps before hurrying to the wall and pushing a couple of buttons. Dolly instantly went silent.

"Sorry," she said with a grin. "I checked to make sure all the guests were gone before cranking up the sound system. Not everyone appreciates my taste in music."

"Dolly Parton is iconic."

"She is, but you'd be surprised the number of people who don't like country music. Especially the old stuff. They think it's too twangy."

"But you like it?"

"I do, a fact that humiliated my baby sister, so there's an advantage. Did you walk around town?"

"Yes. It's a bustling place."

She had freckles, he thought in surprise. And large eyes. She wasn't wearing any makeup or jewelry and obviously hadn't dressed to impress.

"I'm not sure *bustling* could ever be used to describe Wishing Tree, but people do enjoy getting out on a Saturday morning." She paused. "You look cold. Can I get you some coffee? We have scones, as well."

"That's what I came looking for."

"Oh, good." The smile returned. "Maybe I'll take a break from my chores. The scones were awfully good this morning."

He followed her into the large dining room. About a dozen tables were scattered around—some seating two, others seating six or eight. The room had big windows, several sideboards and hutches, and wainscoting painted creamy white.

Dena stepped into the kitchen and washed her hands, then returned with a plate of scones. She set them on one of the larger tables before walking over to a carafe and pouring him a mug of coffee.

"How do you take it?" she asked.

"Black is fine."

She put that down, filled a second mug with hot water and added a tea bag, then took one of the chairs. Micah did the same, sitting at an angle to her.

She seemed far more intent on his cup of coffee than him, he noted. Confusing, but okay. He had the thought that she had no idea who he was, something that happened occasionally.

"Ursula makes a superior cup of coffee," she said, sounding wistful.

"You don't drink coffee?"

"I'm cutting back." She offered a smile. "But I can have scones, so all is not lost. Plus, I must have burned off at least one scone's worth of calories with all my dusting." She broke the blueberry scone in half on her plate. "The cleaning staff comes through the public areas every day, but I try to do a deep dusting every weekend to help out. It gives me time to think, and if no one is around, I get to listen to music."

"Like Dolly Parton and anything with twang."

She laughed. "That's right. It's very restful after my day job."

He took a bite of the scone. "Wait, you said you own this place. You have another job, as well?"

"Uh-huh. I'm a teacher. I inherited the B and B from my grandmother Regina a few years ago. Winona, my general manager, handles the day-to-day running of things. I pitch in when I can and get a few perks like knowing the menus in advance."

"You're busy."

"I couldn't just sit around and do nothing with my day."

As he picked up his coffee, he realized that "sitting around and doing nothing" pretty much described his life these days. He wasn't writing, he wasn't performing and he didn't have a weekend job, "just to help out." Being around Dena was leaving him feeling a little useless.

"So you know what the snack is tonight," he said, his voice teasing.

"I do. It's mini pizzas, which don't sound amazing,

but they are. Ursula makes a killer pizza dough, and the sauce is homemade. There will be a selection of different flavors. Plain, pepperoni, mushroom." She swallowed, then laughed. "Just thinking about them is making my mouth water. You have to come tonight and taste them."

"How do you know I'm not here every night?"

"Because I usually am and I haven't seen you. Plus I get a report of who shows up and who doesn't."

"You keep track of your guests."

"I want to make sure they're having a good time. We send every guest a survey, asking what they enjoyed and what they didn't. If the Snacks and Wine hour isn't their thing, that's fine, but if they don't like the food, the atmosphere or the music selection, then I need to know that so we can make some changes."

She sounded earnest as she spoke, as if she meant what she was saying. Most people did, he reminded himself. They wanted to do a good job and make other people happy. He knew he liked hearing that one of his songs had touched someone deeply or been played at their wedding. He liked that his music was significant in people's lives.

"You're a good innkeeper," he said lightly.

"I hope so. I'm still learning. Winona has been here nearly a decade, so I depend on her a lot. So, yes on Snacks and Wine tonight? We're serving a saucy cabernet from Painted Moon Winery. All the wines we serve are from Washington State."

"Buy local," he said lightly. "All right, I will see you at five."

She shook her head. "I won't be here. I wish I was going to be able to make it, but my sister Reggie is back for the holidays, and I'm going out with her and some friends. A girls' night kind of thing at Holiday Spirits. It's in The Wreath."

"Is having your sister home a good thing or a bad thing?"

Her smile nearly blinded him. "It's very good. We're super close, and she's been avoiding town for about a year now. She had a bad breakup last Thanksgiving. The guy she'd been dating proposed on Friday, they had a party to celebrate on Saturday and then he dumped her on Sunday. If I was big and burly, I would have beat him up."

"You don't seem vengeful."

"I'm usually not, but this was a special circumstance."

"I'm sure the judge and jury would have viewed it that way, too."

She laughed. "I know it's wrong to hurt someone, but he made me so mad. Who does that? If you ask me—" She stopped talking midsentence and looked at him.

"Sorry. I've been going on and on, and you've been very polite to listen to me. I'm going to leave you now to enjoy your morning while I get back to my dusting."

"And Dolly," he teased.

"Yes. And Dolly."

Dena rose and collected their empty plates, along with her mug, and took them to the kitchen. Micah stayed where he was for a few more minutes, smiling when the music resumed. When the song ended, he went out a side door and walked over to the carriage house and his one-bedroom suite. Once inside, he got out his guitar and a pad of paper, then sat on the sofa and waited for inspiration.

Two hours later, he'd crossed out as many lines as he'd written and couldn't come up with even the beginning of a melody. He'd hoped Wishing Tree would help with his creativity, but so far there wasn't any magic to be found. If it wasn't here, he wondered if it was anywhere. And if it wasn't, the problem wasn't the magic—it was him.

REGGIE SHIVERED IN the cold night air. This time of year sunset was barely after four, so by seven, the temperature had seriously dropped. She wore a scarf, gloves and a hat, but she was still freezing by the time she and her sister arrived at The Wreath.

"How can it be this cold and not snow?" Dena asked with a laugh as she tugged open the door of Holiday Spirits. "It's just plain wrong."

"Maybe, but the stars kind of make up for it. The sky is amazing."

The building was long and narrow, with a jukebox at one end. Booths lined one wall, and the twenty-foot bar lined the other. The décor was wood-centric and the drink menu eclectic. They'd serve beer or a glass of wine, but not graciously. Holiday Spirits was all about the hard liquor.

The specials were listed on blackboards. Every imaginable kind of liquor was represented on the mirrored shelves. Most of the time the snacks were minimal at best, but every few months there was a cocktail tasting menu with five courses and a different drink for each course. Reservations and a designated driver were both required.

Reggie smiled. She'd always loved this place—with its attitude and fancy drinks. As a teenager, she'd dreamed about being old enough to come here. She'd had her first, um, well, *legal* drink here, the day she'd turned twenty-one. She'd been on plenty of dates that had ended here, but mostly Holiday Spirits was where she hung out with her friends.

She spotted Paisley by one of the booths, waving frantically.

"There," Reggie said.

Paisley met them halfway and hugged Dena, then Reggie.

"You're back! How's Belle?"

"Pouting. She was upset I was leaving, so Mom's letting her have the recliner while I'm gone."

With a blanket covering her, Reggie thought, grinning at the memory of her dog getting comfy for the evening.

"I'm so happy to see you. Stop leaving. It makes me sad."

Reggie laughed. "I live in Seattle."

"Yes, well, I've never approved of that, have I?" Paisley, a beautiful, leggy blonde with plenty of smarts and enough sarcasm to be interesting, turned to Dena. "How are you feeling? I think we should seat you on the outside, in case you have to run off and, you know."

"Barf?" Reggie asked cheerfully.

Paisley winced. "Please don't say that word. I have a very sensitive gag reflex."

Reggie hung her and her sister's coats on the hooks outside the booth, then realized another woman was already seated there, a petite redhead with a tentative smile.

"Hi," Reggie said, holding out her hand. "I don't think we've met. I'm Reggie."

"Shaye."

Paisley, Reggie and Dena slid into the booth.

"I've told you about Shaye," Paisley said. "She moved here over the summer and got engaged to Lawson Easley."

Shaye held up her left hand. "It appears to be legal."

"Congratulations," Reggie said. "Both Paisley and my sister have said nice things about you."

"Thanks for letting me hang out with you," Shaye told her.

"You're always welcome," Dena said, then wrinkled her nose. "I tried to get Camryn to join us, but she didn't want to leave the twins."

Howard Troll, the owner, walked over to their table. "What'll it be, ladies?"

"A coquito for me," Paisley said.

Reggie grimaced. "Too much coconut. Howard, I've been dreaming about a Santa's Sleigh for weeks."

"What's that?" Shaye asked. "The drinks here are all so exotic."

Dena sighed. "A Santa's Sleigh is brandy, amaretto, eggnog and ice cream."

"Practically a meal," Reggie said with a laugh. "Try one, Shaye. If you don't like it, I'll drink yours."

Shaye smiled. "Sounds delicious."

Howard looked at Dena, who shrugged apologetically. "A virgin strawberry daiquiri, please."

"Virgin?" Howard sounded outraged.

"I'm pregnant."

Howard, closer to sixty than fifty, stared at her. "You're not married."

"Yes, I know."

He clicked his tongue. "You kids today. Virgin it is." He turned away, then back. "You want a nice turkey sandwich on whole wheat with a side salad?"

Paisley's blue eyes widened. "But Howard, you hate to cook."

"We gotta take care of her."

"So you went from disapproving to nurturing in eight seconds?"

He grinned. "I know how to move with the times."

"I'm fine, Howard," Dena told him. "But thank you."

When he left, Paisley stretched out her hands toward Reggie. "How are you? Is it okay being back? Are you nervous or having flashbacks?"

Reggie thought about her day. "Except for walking Belle, I haven't left the house until tonight. I'm good. Not nervous and no flashbacks."

Paisley gave Shaye a quick recap of Reggie's engagement and subsequent dumping last year. As her friend spoke, Reggie mentally poked at her heart for sadness. The biggest emotion she could find was regret for time wasted mourning a relationship that obviously hadn't been meant to be.

"I feel horrible," Paisley admitted. "I hosted the engagement party."

"No guilt allowed," Reggie told her. "You were being a good friend. No one knew Jake was going to be such a jerk. We're done, I really am over him, and I've found my way home. I vote we drop the topic forever."

"We should," Dena said firmly. "So, what's new?"

"I'm busy up at the resort," Paisley said. "Lots of

holiday parties." She smiled. "Your parents' wedding. I'm looking forward to that."

"We'll try to keep things easy," Reggie told her.

Paisley looked at Dena. "Does she know?"

Reggie immediately went on alert, not sure how many more "surprises" she could deal with.

"I told her yesterday," Dena said, then smiled at Shaye. "This is just such an info dump for you, but there's this guy."

"There's always a guy," Shaye said with a laugh.

"Reggie dated him in high school."

Howard returned with the drinks and a small cheese and fruit plate.

"Only hard cheese," he told Dena. "It's safe for you and the baby. Healthy."

"Thank you," Dena said, her voice sincere. "You're very sweet."

"Yeah, don't let that get around."

Paisley stared at him as he left. "This is a side of Howard I've never seen before. It's kind of freaking me out."

"Me, too," Reggie said, picking up her drink. "To good friends."

They toasted. Then Shaye said, "So about the guy?"

"I'll tell it." Reggie took another sip of the delicious cocktail. "We were madly in love in high school, and then we broke up. He took off and I haven't seen him since."

"Then he ended up starting Judy's Hand Pies," Dena added. "Named after his grandmother."

Shaye's eyes widened. "My Toby?"

Reggie was pleased Paisley and Dena looked as startled as she felt at that particular statement.

"I mean, I work for him," Shaye said.

"Oh, *that* 'my Toby,'" Dena said.

"Is he single?" Paisley sipped her drink. "Asking for a friend."

"As far as I know," Shaye told her.

Reggie bumped Paisley. "Your quote unquote *friend* isn't interested."

"Maybe I was asking for Dena."

"You weren't."

Paisley's smile was unapologetic. "I wasn't. You should so get back together with him. Everyone adores a first-loves-reunited story. Plus, it's Christmas."

"Bite me."

"So that's a maybe?"

"Yes, Paisley. Toby and I are getting back together. I've spent the past decade pining for him. I can't wait for us to fall madly in love. It's going to be epic."

Paisley grinned. "Sarcasm becomes you."

Reggie raised her glass. "It's a classic look that flatters all of us."

The women laughed. Reggie looked at her sister. "Please change the subject."

"Well, I have news," Paisley said, looking excited. "There's a rumor the town is going to start having a Snow King and Snow Queen again."

Reggie and Dena exchanged a happy look.

"Really?" Dena asked. "I miss having a royal couple for the holidays."

"What's a Snow King and Queen?" Shaye asked.

"People are randomly, or not so randomly, chosen to be the honorary hosts of the holiday season here in town," Paisley said. She sipped her drink. "They judge cookie contests, participate in Advent events. They used to be a married couple. Then it was whoever put their name in the hat. Oh, if there's a Snow King and Queen, maybe they'll start having the Holiday Ball again. That would be fun. Everything will be set up over the next few months so we're ready to go with them next year."

Reggie listened to her friends and her sister discuss the possibilities. Despite the fun of having a Snow King and Queen, she found her mind drifting back to Toby and the fact that he'd moved back to Wishing Tree. She was willing to admit she was a bit intrigued at the thought of seeing him again. Just out of curiosity, she mentally added. Yes, they'd been an item, and yes, he'd broken her heart, but so what? She'd moved on and gotten over him. She had absolutely zero interest in the man romantically. Zip. Nada. None.

Mostly she wanted to see how he'd changed from the teenager she'd been so desperately in love with. She'd been crazy about him for months back then. She'd thought he'd been interested in her, but he'd never bothered to ask her out. Finally, she'd decided the best way to get his attention was to challenge him. She'd been shocked and thrilled when the tactic had worked.

She'd figured out fairly quickly that Toby wasn't the kind of guy who played games with other people's emotions. He'd always been straightforward with her, saying what he meant, doing what he promised. Which made what he'd done after she'd given him her virginity so unforgiveable.

She returned her attention to the present. He was old news, she told herself. A curiosity—nothing more.

Six

DENA LEFT HOLIDAY Spirits a little after nine. She loved
her sister and her friends, but hanging out with them
while everyone but her was drinking wasn't the thrill
she had hoped it would be. She was tired and hungry.
The cheese plate Howard had brought her had become
a communal affair and had been devoured quickly. She
wanted to go home and see if there were any mini pizzas left, then go to bed. Not exactly the Saturday night
of her dreams, but she was okay with that.

She stepped outside and shivered in the cold. Thank
goodness home was close. She hurried the short distance to the B and B, used her key to let herself in the
back door, then flipped on the lights.

After tossing her jacket, gloves, hat and scarf over a
chair, she studied the contents of the refrigerator, smiling when she saw the container of mini pizzas. There
were plenty to make a meal. There was also a lovely,

fresh salad with a note that said, For Dena, because Ursula was looking out for her.

Dena turned on the smaller of the two ovens. Yes, it would take longer for the pizzas to heat that way, but dough was never the same when warmed in the microwave.

She'd just started sorting through the mini pizzas, trying to decide how many she wanted versus how many she could reasonably eat and not be too stuffed to sleep, when a loud knock on the kitchen door made her jump.

She spun and saw the shape of a man standing outside. A second look told her the person in question was Micah. She crossed to the door and let him in.

"Hi," he said, shivering in the cold, one hand clutching his coat closed, the other holding a guitar. "I saw the light go on and wondered if I could beg a few mini pizzas?"

"Of course," she said automatically, stepping back to let him in, all the while trying not to notice how incredibly handsome he was. His dark hair gleamed in the overhead light, and his deep blue eyes were large and expressive. Or maybe it was his mouth—full and tempting, but still masculine.

"Dena?" he asked, his voice slightly concerned.

"Huh?"

Oh, crap! She'd been staring.

Humiliation rushed through her, making her turn away and struggle for control. What was wrong with her? Why was she acting like an idiot? All good questions she would try to answer later.

"Sorry," she murmured. "I was lost in thought. Mini pizzas. There are bunches. Come pick the ones you want and I'll heat them in the oven. I also have salad, and we have beer and wine."

She was going to say more, or possibly ask about the guitar, when a wave of nausea hit her out of nowhere. It was swift and powerful and there was no resisting it. She barely had time to make it to the kitchen sink where she threw up the glass of water she'd had an hour ago.

As soon as she'd vomited, her stomach returned to normal. The cold, clammy sensation receded, and except for the lingering embarrassment and the fact that she was standing at the sink, she could almost pretend nothing had happened. Almost.

She carefully rinsed out her mouth, washed her hands, then sucked in a breath as she wondered what on earth she was supposed to say to her guest.

Whatever small hope she had that he'd left faded when she turned and saw him standing in the same spot. The coat was gone, and the guitar was lying across a chair. His expression was quizzical, the drawn-together brows making him even better-looking.

"You all right?" he asked cautiously.

"I'm great."

"Stomach flu?"

"Pregnancy."

"You're pregnant?"

"Yes. Nine weeks." She sagged against the counter. "I'd planned on keeping it a secret, but that's not happening. About a week ago, the morning sickness hit, and it hit hard. Worse, it's not just in the morning. It's all day and without warning. Once it passes, I feel fine. Sometimes I can control it, but obviously not tonight. Sorry about that."

His gaze was intense, and she had no idea what he was thinking. She doubted he was admiring how beautiful she looked as she puked out her guts. Or was it puked up?

"Where's the father?"

Ah, that. She raised one shoulder. "There isn't one."

"You're carrying the Baby Jesus?"

She laughed, instantly feeling better about their conversation. "Not that I know of. I had IUI. Intrauterine insemination." At his blank look, she added, "A sperm donor and a turkey baster."

"It wasn't really a turkey baster, though, right?"

"It was more medical than that, but the concept is the same. I'm thirty-two, and I can't seem to find someone to fall in love with. I really want to have kids, so I decided to stop waiting and make it happen. I have a good job, a supportive family and a network of friends."

She told herself to stop talking—that she didn't need to justify her decision to him.

He smiled, and the simple act stole her breath.

"You're impressive," he told her.

"Thank you."

"I'm disappointed about the Baby Jesus."

"I'm pretty sure God would pick someone else if he wanted to do that again."

"It would have made a great story. You still up for mini pizzas?"

One cue, her stomach growled. "I am. I hope that doesn't gross you out."

"I'm tougher than I look."

She was more interested in knowing if he was as *good* as he looked, but there was no polite way to ask that question. Plus, saying it would imply she wanted something from him, and to be honest, all her musings were more fantasy than anything else.

They picked out their snacks and she put them on a cookie sheet, then slid it into the oven and started the timer. She showed him the collection of beer and handed him the opener. After getting water for herself (yum), she tossed the salad with a little dressing and put it on the table. They sat across from each other at the small table.

"You didn't go to Snacks and Wine tonight, did you?"

"I didn't."

"You have to be more social, Micah. It's good for you. Plus, we always have such lovely guests. I think you'd really enjoy talking to them."

He drew his brows together again. Man, did that work for her.

"Sometimes situations like that are awkward," he told her.

"Why? No offense, but you don't have any trouble talking to me. Is it groups of people that bother you?"

She wasn't sure what kind of response she'd expected, but him bursting into laughter wasn't it. She couldn't tell if he was laughing *with* her or *at* her. Except she wasn't laughing at all and couldn't figure out what was so funny.

"Sorry," he said, clearing his throat. "You don't know who I am, which makes me wonder why I assumed everyone else would."

He wasn't making much sense, although she realized the bigger problem was that he obviously was someone important and she had no idea who. She searched her memory for a flicker of recognition, but there wasn't any. So he probably wasn't an actor. Then who? Royalty? A porn star? Male model?

"I'm a singer/songwriter," he told her. "Until a few years ago, I was lead singer for Darryl John James. It's a rock band."

"I know who they are," she said. She did. Sort of. She'd heard of them. Kind of.

"You're lying," he said with a grin. "You couldn't name one of our songs, which is okay. There's not enough twang for you."

"I do like country music," she admitted. "Sorry."

"Don't apologize. Everyone has different tastes."

"Yes, well, so the guitar isn't to help you pick up women?"

The laughter returned. "No. I'm working on something, but it's not going well."

He was writing a song? How did anyone do that? She couldn't imagine.

"I'm going to feel ridiculous when I google you later, aren't I?"

"A little, but don't take it personally. I like being a regular person, and that doesn't happen very often. Although it's been nice in town. People have recognized me, but most of them just leave me alone."

The timer dinged. She busied herself plating the pizzas and carried them over to the table.

"I don't even know what to ask," she told him, picking up a veggie pizza. "Tell me about the band."

"We started when we were in high school. There were three of us originally. The band name is our middle names."

She winced. "Darryl?"

He chuckled. "James."

"Thank goodness. Darryl would be tough. So, how did you get from high school band to famous?"

"We were discovered playing at a party. That got us a record deal. We started touring and we took off. I'd been writing songs since I was maybe ten or eleven. Once we had a label, I worked with some brilliant guys and got a lot better at it. I've had a few writing partners, but lately I'm writing on my own."

He paused to finish his mini pizza, then reached for a napkin. "'Moonlight for Christmas.'"

"I know that one!"

"I wrote it with my ex-wife."

"It's a great song."

"Thanks."

Everything about this was surreal. It was one thing to think of Micah as the hot guy in the carriage house, but to discover he was famous kind of knocked her sideways.

"I don't think any of the guests would be a problem for you," she told him, "if you wanted to risk Snacks and Wine."

"Thank you."

"I won't say anything to anyone."

His dark blue gaze locked with hers. "I never thought you would."

They stared at each other. She felt tingles all the way down to her toes—ridiculous, yet true. How he would laugh if he knew.

"So, um, what are you doing in Wishing Tree?"

"Looking for inspiration. I haven't been able to write for a while, and in the past I've had good luck with holiday songs. A former bandmate and close friend moved here a few years ago. He's been telling me to spend Christmas in Wishing Tree, so here I am." He picked up another pizza. "Steve bought a Christmas tree farm a few years back."

Her eyes widened. "Steve Burdick?"

"That's him. You know him?"

"His son, Noah, is in my class." She smiled. "I'm his third-grade teacher."

"Then I'll see you Monday. I'm filling in for Steve for career day."

She told herself cheering would be tacky. "The kids will enjoy meeting you. You'll be their very first rock star guest."

His mouth twisted. "To be honest, I have no idea what to talk about. Eight-year-olds aren't my target audience."

"Probably best not to discuss life on the road."

The humor returned to his eyes. "You're assuming a lot."

"Am I wrong?"

"No."

She grinned. "Then maybe talk about what it takes to write a song. Or show them a few chords on the guitar. Or what it's like to record a song. Everything's digital these days. Do you still go into a studio with the band? Stuff like that."

He leaned back in his chair. "Thanks. Those are all good suggestions. I feel better."

"Anytime. Now eat your salad. It's good for you."

One eyebrow rose. "So, you're a bossy teacher."

"When I have to be."

"Good to know."

REGGIE KNEW THE third Santa's Sleigh had probably been a mistake, but she and her friends had been having such a good time. Back in Seattle she went out some, but not like this. Still, making up for lost time in a single night was going to lead to a very tough morning. She would have to remember to hydrate and take something for the inevitable headache.

"You're a bad influence," she told Paisley as they approached Reggie's house.

"Only sometimes," Paisley said, hugging her. "I'm so glad you're back. I've missed you. Calls and texts aren't the same."

"I agree. I'll talk to you tomorrow. Oh, and text me when you get home so I know you're okay."

Paisley laughed. "What on earth would happen to me?"

"But you will text?"

"I will. Love you."

"Love you, too." Reggie started for the front door.

"Oh, and I'm really glad you and Toby are back together," Paisley yelled from the corner.

Reggie waved her off and walked into the house. She was going to take a lot of Toby grief from her friend. She could already feel it. She would have to—

"How was your evening?"

The voice came from the shadows of the living room. Reggie jumped, managing to hold in her strangled scream.

"Mom! You scared me. It's nearly ten thirty. You didn't have to wait up."

Belle came skittering out of the living room. Reggie braced herself for the impact of her dog rushing into her, wanting to be greeted.

"Your father went to bed, but I wasn't tired. Did you have fun?"

"We did. I met Shaye, who's new to town, and she seems nice. Dena cut out early. I think her morning sickness is really getting to her." Reggie took off her coat, scarf and gloves.

"I couldn't help hearing what Paisley said. About Toby."

Oh, no. That was how rumors got started.

"It was a joke, Mom. We talked about the fact that Toby's back in town and that we used to date. She was teasing. It wasn't anything more."

Her mother studied her. "Are you sure?"

Reggie made an X over her chest. "Yes. I haven't seen him since high school. Paisley was just being funny, and later I plan to kill her."

Her mother smiled. "That seems a little extreme. All right, darling. Have a good night."

"Thanks, Mom."

Reggie walked through the house to let Belle out for a late-night potty break. The Great Dane shot Reggie a look of incredulity, then reluctantly headed for the chilly backyard. She was back in seconds, shivering and acting offended.

"The temperature is not my fault," Reggie pointed out.

Belle turned her back to show her displeasure.

"Maybe you'd like to sleep downstairs tonight, not with me," Reggie grumbled, not really meaning the threat.

Belle ignored her and headed for the stairs. Reggie followed, petting her dog as she went.

"There was a really nice Chihuahua at the shelter. Maybe I should have taken him home instead. They eat a lot less, and you can probably pick up their poop with a tissue."

Belle shot her the "I can't hear you" look before walking into the bedroom and going to her big, fluffy bed.

Reggie followed her and knelt on the floor. "You're right. I'm sorry. I won't speak of it again. You're my favorite, and I love you very much."

Belle nuzzled her cheek.

Sad but true, Reggie thought. Belle was her most successful relationship. At least her doggy companion never hogged the remote.

AFTER SPENDING MOST of the day translating Gizmo's technical instructions into something the average person could understand, Reggie was ready for a break. She got out a thick coat for Belle and a matching scarf for each of them and took her dog and herself out for a walk.

Funny how quickly she was settling into a routine with her parents, she thought, walking toward the center of town. While she didn't want to make the living arrangements permanent, she was glad she'd agreed to return for the holidays.

She greeted people they passed. Most steered clear of the giant dog, which was fine with Belle. She was afraid of strangers. And squirrels, vacuums, aerosols, firetrucks and, of course, Burt.

So far there was an uneasy canine truce. Burt had only gone after Belle twice, and she was almost relaxed as she walked through the house. Reggie suspected the little dachshund was lying in wait, ready to attack when least expected.

She inhaled the cold, crisp air. The skies were still gloriously blue—not a cloud to be seen. The Thanksgiving decorations stood proudly at nearly every house—not a snowman or a hint of Christmas anywhere.

"This is a weird little town," Reggie murmured. Belle seemed to nod in agreement.

They reached The Wreath and began to walk the outside circle, a path in front of all the stores. Snowdrops Florist had beautiful harvest arrangements in the window. The Nothing-To-Do-With-Christmas store had a lovely display of beach-themed gift items. They passed Joy's Diner, Jingle Coffee, Poorman Bank and Yule Read Books, her steps slowing with every store until Belle finally turned and looked at her.

"I know," Reggie whispered. "I can't help it. I'm scared."

An emotion Belle could get behind. Still, the Great Dane tugged on the leash as if saying she had to get over it.

"Like you do that."

But standing in The Wreath with her dog staring at her wasn't a good look. She sucked in a breath for courage, then started walking again, right up to Judy's Hand Pies.

She paused in front of the store. There were dozens of pies on display in the window, some sweet, some savory. The smell of freshly baked pies had her mouth watering and Belle nudging at the door.

"We can't," Reggie told her. "No dogs allowed."

Belle's head dropped.

Reggie studied the store, with its bright awning and inviting window display. She knew a little about the company—she'd read a couple of articles once she'd learned Toby was the owner. He'd started selling hand pies out of the back of his truck and had graduated to food trucks and then stores.

She remembered when his grandmother would sell the pies in town. Having them for dinner had always been a treat at Reggie's house.

The front door pushed open, and Shaye waved at her. "Hi. Good to see you again."

"Hi, Shaye. It's my first time by the store. If the visual doesn't draw you in, the smells will."

Shaye laughed. "That's what we're counting on." She shivered. "It's freezing. Come on inside."

Reggie motioned to Belle. "Thanks, but I can't leave her out here."

"Bring her in. I'll pretend not to notice." Shaye approached Belle. "Hi, beautiful girl. What's your name?"

"This is Belle."

Belle sniffed the offered hand, then looked at Reggie for confirmation. "It's okay. We like Shaye."

Belle inched forward and allowed herself to be petted, and then they went inside.

The scents were even more delicious in the store. Reggie liked the high ceiling and the seating area off to the side. There were pies, sodas, milk and water, along with to-go boxes in all sizes.

"Saturday was fun," Shaye said as she washed her hands at a small sink. "Thanks for including me."

"I'm glad we got to meet. You've been here since the summer, right? So this is your first Christmas?"

"It is. I'm looking forward to experiencing all the traditions." She dried her hands. "Now, what can I get you?"

Reggie eyed the selection. "A mushroom pie for me and a seasonal turkey for Belle."

"It has cranberries in it. Is that all right?"

Reggie smiled. "Dogs can eat cranberries, and Belle is a big fan."

Shaye got them each a pie. Belle gulped hers in a single bite, then licked her lips as if asking for more.

"You'll spoil your dinner," Reggie told her, holding on to her own pie. She took a bite, then tried to catch a piece of crust as it crumbled. Belle darted forward and snatched it before it hit the ground.

Shaye laughed. "They're messy but delicious."

"Yes to both," Reggie said, grabbing a couple of napkins just as the front door opened and a boy rushed in.

Reggie would guess he was eight or nine, with pale blond hair and brown eyes. Neither were remarkable, nor was the boy, but there was something familiar about him. Something that made her body tense and her fight-or-flight response kick in. Even as adrenaline poured through her and she thought about bolting, a man stepped into the store.

No, not just "a man." Toby Newkirk.

They stared at each other. Reggie had no idea what he was thinking, but she battled a rush of emotions. Guilt, curiosity, concern, anticipation. They swirled together and sat uneasily with the pie. Even as she realized she couldn't speak, she knew she had to explain her presence, and hey, maybe why there was a giant dog splitting her attention between the last of Reggie's pie and Toby's son.

"Hello, Reggie," Toby said, his voice casual, as if he wasn't the least bit surprised by her presence.

"Toby." She did her best to smile. Not sure if she

succeeded, she turned to his son. "Hi, I'm Reggie, and this is Belle."

"I'm Harrison. I've never heard of a girl named Reggie."

"I'm named after my grandmother Regina." She wrinkled her nose. "Reggie seemed like a better choice. Belle, can you say hello?"

Belle looked from Harrison to Toby and back. She took a tentative step toward the boy and sniffed twice before resting her massive head on his shoulder and sighing heavily.

Harrison laughed as he wrapped both arms around her and hugged her tight.

"She doesn't usually warm up to people she doesn't know," Reggie said with a grin. "She likes you."

"What kind of dog is she?"

"A Great Dane. She weighs a hundred twenty pounds."

Harrison's eyes widened. "That's a lot."

"It is." Reggie glanced at Toby. "We were on a walk and Shaye invited us in. The store is nice."

"Thank you."

Okay, this was incredibly awkward, she thought, not sure what she was supposed to say or not say. The last time she'd seen Toby, she'd been seventeen and heartbroken. She'd accused him of betraying her and violating everything they were supposed to mean to each other. His impassioned "it wasn't what you think" hadn't moved her at all, and she'd broken up with him, turning her back on him and walking away.

She'd cried for three days, waiting for him to show up and try to convince her she was wrong, but he never had. A little later, she'd learned he'd simply up and left town, never to be seen again. Until, apparently, last

year, when he'd returned with his son and his hand
pie fortune.

"Can I walk her?" Harrison asked his father.

"That's up to Reggie."

"Sure. She's really good on the leash."

She waved to Shaye, then stepped outside with
Belle. Harrison and Toby followed. Reggie handed
over the leash. Normally Belle would have shot her a
look of incredulity, but instead she simply moved close
to Harrison, prepared to go where he went.

Harrison started down the walkway, Belle at his
side.

"A Great Dane?" Toby asked. "What were you thinking?"

"I know. I wanted a midsized dog, but there she was,
looking so scared and sad, trembling in the corner of
her kennel. She'd been brought in by a family who
couldn't handle her. They said a neighbor had abused
her, but I think it was more than just a single incident.
Once I saw her, I couldn't leave her there. So I took her
home. She's actually really sweet, although not what
anyone would call brave."

Harrison tried to walk across the middle of The
Wreath, but Belle came to a stop and wouldn't budge
until he returned to the path.

"She's a rule follower," Reggie added.

"She is." He angled toward her. "It's good to see
you, Reggie. It's been a long time."

Good to see her? What did that mean? The moment
was beyond surreal. She had no idea what she was feeling. Or supposed to feel. "It has been."

"I've been back a year, and this is the first time I've

run into you. I take it you don't spend much time in town these days?"

There was so much to deal with in those two sentences. She couldn't decide which to address, then decided to ignore it all.

"I'm back for the holidays. My parents are renewing their vows with a big wedding." She smiled. "They eloped the first time around, and my mom has always had regrets. I'm helping with the planning."

Harrison and Belle turned and started back toward them. Reggie watched them rather than risk looking at Toby. So much was the same, but so much was different. He seemed taller and broader than he had before. A man now, rather than a teenager. She wondered what else was different—not that she would ask.

"I understand we're dating again," he said conversationally. "How's that going?"

Her mouth dropped open. She consciously closed it, feeling heat flare on her cheeks.

"You didn't just say that."

He flashed her a smile that made her knees get a little wiggly. "I heard it from two sources. One of them was my grandmother. Rumors are flying all over."

She covered her face with both hands. "No. This isn't happening." She forced herself to look at him. "Paisley was joking, okay? It was meant to be funny. I'm sorry someone overheard us. We're not dating. I mean, obviously you know that."

Where was that ground-splitting earthquake when she needed one?

"Stupid small towns," she muttered, walking toward Harrison. "So, we have to go now. It was nice to meet you."

"Can I walk Belle again sometime?" the boy asked.

"Sure. She would like that."

Belle inched toward Harrison. Reggie pulled her back. "Come on, Belle. We have to get home."

Belle sighed heavily before walking with her. She turned twice to look at Harrison.

"You'll see him later," Reggie told her. "I was just humiliated. Could you have a little compassion for me?"

Belle shook her head, implying she could not.

"I'm going to let Burt loose to go after you."

Belle's knowing look implied she didn't believe that for a second.

"You're right. I wouldn't do that. But jeez, why did Toby have to say that? Who else is talking about us, and what do I do now?"

Belle bumped her gently, offering support but no real advice.

"I'm going to ignore the whole thing," Reggie told her. "Maybe then it will just go away."

Seven

MICAH ARRIVED AT Wishing Tree Elementary School fifteen minutes before he was expected. He signed in at the front desk and was given directions to "Ms. Somerville's" classroom. Once he arrived, he waited in the hall as he'd been told to, telling himself there was no reason to be nervous. He was going to talk about music and songs—he could handle a room full of eight-year-olds. Besides, he knew Noah had his back.

A few minutes later, he was joined by a woman his age and a man a few years younger. They introduced themselves.

"I'm a veterinarian," Sally said, shaking hands with him. She had a couple of small covered kennels with her.

"I'm a plumber," Tim added.

Micah hadn't thought this part through, so instead of saying something sensible, blurted out, "Former rock star."

They both stared at him. Tim blinked first.

"Micah Ruiz. From Darryl John James? Holy sh—" He looked around and lowered his voice. "I'm mean, wow, that's incredible. What are you doing here?"

"Visiting friends. My former drummer, Steve, owns the Christmas tree farm outside of town."

Tim nodded at Sally. "That's Micah Ruiz."

"I got that," she said with a sigh. "You'll go last, Micah. No one wants to follow you."

Before he could figure out how to respond to that, the door to the classroom opened, and Dena stepped out.

His first thought was that she looked good. He liked how she wore her hair back in a braid and had little gold hoop earrings. Despite the lightly applied makeup, he could see the freckles on her nose and cheeks.

She wore a long-sleeved T-shirt with a colorful turkey embroidered on the front, and a long brown skirt. Teacher clothes, but still appealing.

"Hi, everyone," she said with a smile. "Thanks so much for coming to our monthly career day. You've introduced yourselves?"

"Oh, we know who he is," Sally muttered.

"Micah Ruiz," Tim said, his tone reverent.

"A fan, I see." Dena smiled. "Okay, so who wants to go first?"

"I will," Sally said, walking into the classroom.

"Then Tim, then me," Micah told Dena.

Dena glanced toward Sally. "Do I sense tension?"

"I think she wanted to be the star of the day."

"And she's upset because you're famous?"

"Only in her mind. The average eight-year-old has no clue."

Dena grinned at him. "Humility? Unexpected."

As she spoke, she lightly put her hand on his upper arm, as if guiding him inside the room. In his business, he was touched all the time. Tugged at and pulled, sometimes by security and often by fans. Most of the time he ignored the contacts—they meant nothing. But Dena's gentle touch caught him off guard and sent a faint whisper of awareness through him. It was gone nearly before he registered it, but it had existed. A reminder that he was still alive. That life went on and so did he.

And if he was healing enough to notice when a beautiful woman touched him, maybe other parts of him were coming back to life, as well. Maybe the creative part of his brain would awaken and start to make itself known.

He walked into the room and spotted Noah. The kid grinned at him, then nudged the guy sitting next to him and pointed.

Sally talked about being a veterinarian. She'd brought along some kind of snake, along with a tarantula. Both had about half the students squealing and trying to get out of the way while the other half crowded close.

When her surprise guests were back in their carriers, she shot Micah a look as if to say "top that" before retreating to the back of the room.

Tim talked about being a plumber and how important it was not to pour grease down a drain or put anything foreign in a toilet. Then it was Micah's turn.

He got out his acoustic guitar and walked to the front of the classroom. Dena had pulled out a stool for him and gave him an encouraging smile that did little to quiet the nerves in his gut.

He sat down and introduced himself. "Noah's dad couldn't join us today because he's a Christmas tree farmer and this is his busy season, so I offered to come instead."

"Do you cut down Christmas trees?" a girl asked.

"No, I'm a songwriter."

Nearly all the students stared blankly.

"What does that mean?" one of the boys asked.

"I write songs. Someone has to."

There were more blank looks.

"All the music you hear in movies or commercials or on TV or in church, all those songs were written by someone."

He played the opening notes for "Let It Go" from the Disney hit *Frozen*.

"My mom hates that song," one girl volunteered.

Micah grinned. "It was written by Kristen Anderson-Lopez and her husband, Robert Lopez. How about this one?"

He played the opening to "Moonlight for Christmas." A few of the kids looked confused but several nodded.

"'Moonlight for Christmas,'" one boy said. "My mom says it makes her cry but in a happy way. My dad gags when he hears it."

Micah laughed. "I wrote that song. It was my first hit. I wrote it with my ex-wife a long time ago. Who knows the song?"

Several hands shot up.

"Why don't you sing it with me?"

He started to play the song. When he started singing, a few of the students joined in. Sally glared, but Tim was an enthusiastic participant. When he'd finished, Micah showed them all a few basic chords and how putting them together in a different way created different songs they knew, and then his time was up.

Dena asked everyone to clap for their guests. Sally left quickly, but Tim hung around for a few minutes before heading out. Micah answered some questions while packing up his guitar. He was about to duck out when a bell rang and all the students jumped to their feet.

Dena looked fondly at them as she opened the door. "Stay in line. I'll see you in a bit."

In a matter of seconds, the room was empty.

"Recess," she said by way of explanation. "Their chance to burn off energy in the middle of the afternoon." She smiled. "Thanks for coming. You did great, and the kids really loved—"

She went completely white and pressed her lips together even as she started frantically looking around the room. Micah had a feeling her morning sickness had just made an afternoon appearance. He rushed toward her, grabbed her arm, then applied pressure on her wrist.

"Take a breath and hold it for a count of four, then exhale slowly," he told her.

Her eyes widened slightly, but she did as he requested, repeating the breathing cycle. About a minute later, he felt her relax and he released her wrist.

She stared at him. "What did you do?"

"Applied pressure to your pressure point. I'm not sure what it does—maybe triggers some nerves that calm your stomach. It can be effective."

Question filled her brown eyes. "You saved me. I was about to throw up, and given what I had for lunch, that would not have been pretty."

"You should be fine for the next few hours."

"Pressure points, huh? I'll have to check them out."

"I can show you the most likely spots, if you want."

An offer he meant in the spirit of one human helping another, he thought, noting how she took what he would guess was an involuntary step back.

"Thank you. I would appreciate any help with my morning sickness."

The words and the body language didn't line up, so which was one telling the truth? He told himself it didn't matter—that Dena was simply his landlord for the month he was in town. Still, he found himself wanting to help her feel better. He liked being around her—there was something calming about her normally high-energy state. Inexplicable, but still true.

"You know where to find me," he said, picking up his guitar.

She walked him to the door and thanked him for helping with her students. He nodded and left, his mind suddenly captured by the hint of a melody and the faint whisper of *I thought I'd be by myself again*. Words that made no sense, but might, someday, become a part of something.

TOBY STUDIED THE data his sales manager had sent him. Nate Martz was determined to expand Judy's Hand Pies into grocery stores around the country—a huge step that required a drastic change in their business model. The pies would have to be shipped frozen and then cooked by the consumer.

Toby had resisted the idea for nearly two years, but Nate had started to wear him down. To that end, he sent monthly reports with sales projections. The numbers were impressive, but Toby wasn't convinced. Not only was the grocery store frozen market tough to break into, but he also wasn't willing to compromise on quality.

Currently the pies were made in several processing plants across the western half of the US. They were shipped to local stores and baked on-site. The food trucks also baked their pies in specially designed ovens, which meant the inventory was always fresh and hot. Ceding control to a consumer who might or might not bake the pie correctly didn't sit well with him, although he'd agreed to an experiment. Currently there were several hundred pies sitting in a freezer in Seattle. Every few weeks, a couple of dozen were baked and eaten by volunteers to determine if they still tasted as fresh.

His cell phone buzzed. He glanced at the screen and saw he had a message from Shaye.

Mrs. Somerville is here and would like to speak with you.

Toby grinned. Mrs. Somerville? Shaye was mistaken. The only one of the Somerville women who would stop by to see him was Reggie.

He'd enjoyed running into her yesterday, even if they hadn't had much of a chance to catch up. Her bolting had been his fault—he couldn't help but tease her about the rumors he'd heard of them dating.

He didn't know how the talk had started, but Wishing Tree was the kind of place where people loved to share gossip. No doubt much like every other small town. Sunday, while he was in the park playing catch with Harrison, two older women had asked him about his relationship with Reggie. They'd explained that they'd judged him too harshly when he'd been a teenager and were happy to give him a second chance now. The taller of the two had winked at him and said Reggie looked like the kind of girl who would have pretty babies.

Earlier that morning, Shaye had asked about when he'd been in high school and dating Reggie, leading him to believe that the rumor mills were working overtime. Now Reggie was here.

He picked up his phone. Be right down.

As he stood and started for the stairs outside his office, he wondered what she wanted. Dena had mentioned she would be in charge of the charity project. She could be stopping by to talk about that. Or she could be using it as a pretext for them to hang out.

He hadn't thought of Reggie in years, but in the past few days, she'd been on his mind. Memories, most of the excellent variety, had haunted him. When he'd left Wishing Tree, she'd been the person he'd missed the most—even more than his grandmother. While his plans had been vague, he'd always assumed he and Reggie would stay together forever, eventually getting married and starting a family. But she'd broken up with him, and he'd left town, and he'd never intended to see her again.

Funny how that had suddenly changed.

He walked in the back entrance to the pie shop, prepared to give Reggie a bit of a hard time before accepting whatever plan she'd come up with, but she wasn't the one waiting for him. Mrs. Somerville, Reggie's mother, stood by the pie case and smiled when she saw him.

"Hello, Toby."

"Mrs. Somerville."

She waved her hand. "Leigh, please. Thanks for taking a minute to speak with me. I'm sure you're busy running your empire. I know what Vince is like when he has to deal with the business side of things instead of working with the guys on the cars. It's consuming."

She nudged several grocery bags sitting on the floor next to her. Chips and a pineapple stuck out of one of them.

"I was doing my Thanksgiving dinner shopping when it occurred to me that it would be nice to have friends around the table. Usually it's just Vince and me and our girls, but I was wondering if this year, you'd like to join us. With Harrison and your grandmother, of course."

Toby felt like a cartoon character. He wanted to hit the side of his head to see if anything was lodged in his ears. Reggie's mom was inviting him and his family over for Thanksgiving? Sure, he knew them well enough to say hello, and she and her husband had been pleasant enough when he'd been dating Reggie—after the initial grilling. She was a regular customer in the store, and they lived in same town, but Thanksgiving dinner was a whole different level.

Unless the invitation hadn't come from her. Was this Reggie's way of spending time with him without making a big deal of things? Had she sent her mother rather than come herself?

That had to be it, and to be honest, he was more than a little interested in spending some time with Reggie.

He didn't know much about her life now. He knew she lived in Seattle and had some kind of design business, but nothing other than that.

"I'll need to check with my grandmother," he said. "If she's up to attending, then we'd be happy to join you. Thank you for asking."

"My pleasure," Leigh said with a smile. She handed over a piece of paper. "That's my cell and also Reggie's. Just let me know what you decide. We eat about three." She laughed. "A ridiculous time, according to my husband, but it's tradition. I hope we'll see you Thursday."

With that, she picked up her bags of groceries and headed out. Toby held the door for her, then closed it. Shaye stared at him quizzically.

"Was that as weird as I think it was?" she asked.

"Yup."

"You don't really know her or her family. I mean, you used to date Reggie, but that was in high school. Or am I missing something?"

"You're not."

"But you're going?"

"That's up to my grandmother."

"Okay then. Lawson was right—this is the oddest little town ever. You going back to work?"

Toby glanced at the clock. "I think I'll take a break and swing by the house."

Shaye grinned. "To ask your grandmother if she wants to join you with your ex-girlfriend for Thanksgiving?"

"Something like that."

WHEN TOBY AND Harrison had first moved to Wishing Tree, they'd lived in the house where Toby had grown up. Getting the business started had taken all his time, so he hadn't bothered to look for something bigger until the store was open, but once that happened, moving had become a priority.

Judy had protested that she would be fine on her own, but Toby had insisted she move with them. She was getting older, and he wanted her to be around people. Plus, she was family.

He'd found a great house just north of the central part of town. There was a huge en suite bedroom downstairs, perfect for Judy. She had access to the family room and kitchen without having to navigate the stairs. He and Harrison had taken over the second floor, using the bonus space as a media room. Their bedrooms weren't above Judy's, so her space was quiet. An intercom allowed her to call them downstairs whenever she needed them.

He drove home and walked inside. His grandmother was in her favorite chair in the family room, reading a book. While she used the tablet he bought her for things like Facebook and email, she preferred to read the old-fashioned way.

She looked up when he entered. "You're home early."

"I'm going back to the office. I just wanted to talk to you first."

He sat on the sofa. Nearly all the furniture in the house was new. Judy had kept a few antiques she'd had since she was a young woman, but otherwise, they'd started over. The big sectional was deep and wide, with overstuffed cushions and plenty of pillows.

"Leigh Somerville came to see me today," he began.

"Reggie's mother? I know who she is, of course, but

we've never traveled in the same circles." Judy smiled. "It's a generational thing."

"She's inviting us to Thanksgiving."

Judy's smile broadened. "Is she?"

"Yes."

"With Reggie."

"I'm guessing she'll be there."

She put down her book. "I always liked Reggie. She was a sensible girl who knew what she wanted. I wish you hadn't blown it with her."

He winced. "Hey, you don't know what happened."

"I know it was your fault. You told me yourself, when you were packing to go. You said you'd ruined everything and there was no reason to stay."

A time he didn't want to recall. "You know I didn't leave because of her."

His grandmother seemed to shrink a little, as if the memories of that time were too painful to be remembered. "Yes, I know."

He involuntarily rubbed his left arm—the burns there, compliments of his father's cigarettes, had mostly faded. He had scars from beatings with a belt and what he would guess were interesting X-rays showing multiple broken arms.

"What about Thanksgiving?" he asked. "Would you like to go there? I know it's very last minute, so if you'd rather have dinner here, just the three of us, that's okay, too."

"Dinner with Reggie and her family would be nice."

He narrowed his gaze. "This is just a night with friends. No matchmaking."

"Why not? You need to be married."

"Harrison and I are fine."

"I don't worry about him. He's going to be a happy, healthy man. But you've been alone too long. Let someone in, Toby. You need a little love in your life."

"I'm doing fine without it."

He got up before she could ask about sex—because she would, and it wasn't a topic he wanted to discuss with his grandmother. He walked over and kissed the top of her head.

"I'll see you tonight."

"Yes, you will."

He drove back to the office. As he waited at one of the five lights in town, he found himself wondering why he was suddenly so interested in Reggie. From the second he'd seen her walking her dog, he hadn't been able to get her out of his mind.

Maybe it had something to do with how much he'd loved her once. Or how he'd lost her. The latter had shattered him, leaving a greater impact than any one of his father's blows. It had been the Tuesday after prom, the Tuesday after the night she'd finally given herself to him. They'd made love, going all the way, the first time for both of them.

After a year of dating, they'd done everything else many times, but the act of making love had been even more incredible than he'd imagined. The feel of her body, the way her gaze had been so trusting, her hands so sure, had thrilled him. He'd spent the next two days feeling like he could fly.

Monday afternoon, in the locker room, he'd admitted that to his best friend. Someone must have overheard them because by the next morning, word had spread all over school that Reggie Somerville was the best sex of his life.

Given his reputation for trouble, no one would ever think she'd been the only sex of his life. Instead, she'd been humiliated and had wrongly assumed he'd been the one to betray her by broadcasting something that should have stayed between the two of them, and making it seem cheap instead of beautiful. She'd ended their relationship, and days after that, he'd left town.

He parked in his spot and made his way upstairs.

If only, he thought, entering his office. If only he hadn't said anything. If only she'd listened when he'd tried to explain. If only his father hadn't been a mean SOB who wanted nothing more than to take out his anger at his sorry life on his only son.

But it had all happened, and there was no going back. He picked up the paper with Reggie's number on it and smiled.

Maybe the past couldn't be undone, but there was always the present and the future. It seemed to him that Reggie had gone out of her way to make both a little more interesting.

Eight

DENA TOLD HERSELF she was just being neighborly. A half hour into Snacks and Wine, she realized Micah wasn't going to show up, which meant he was missing out on all the yummy bruschetta goodness. As the owner and therefore hostess of the event, it made sense to ensure *all* her guests were happy. To that end, she went into the kitchen, put several bruschettas on a plate, grabbed a beer from the beverage refrigerator and hurried across to the walled courtyard by the carriage house. She knocked once and took a step back, more for his safety than because she was being polite. She had a bad feeling that there was a fifty-fifty chance she would want to throw herself at him the second he opened the door.

Not only was the man fifteen kinds of gorgeous, but she was still reliving the tingles from when he'd touched her. The fact that she'd felt tingles while fighting nausea was a testament to how powerful his—

The door opened. Micah grinned when he saw her, sending heat and more tingles all through her body.

"Dena, hi." He glanced at the plate she held. "If I won't go to the appetizers, you'll bring them to me? I'm not sure that's the lesson you want me to learn, but I'm not going to turn them down."

He stepped back, an obvious invitation. She told herself to act normal and not simper or preen—good advice considering she was bad at both.

She walked into the downstairs suite, heading directly for the small table and chairs in the corner. When she'd set down the plate, she pulled the bottle of beer out of her jacket's front pocket.

The smile returned. "I thought the event was Snacks and *Wine*," he teased.

"It is, but you wanted a beer before, so I assumed that was your preference. I can go get you a glass of wine if you'd rather."

"A beer is great. Thanks. Want to join me?"

Oh, could she? Dena reminded herself of the pledge to pretend normalcy and shrugged out of her coat. "Thank you. That's very nice of you."

He crossed to the kitchenette and pulled out a mug. "The owner of this establishment thoughtfully provided me with a tea selection. Want something herbal?"

"Yes, please."

While he heated water in the microwave and opened his beer, she took a seat at the table. A quick glance at the living area showed her that Micah was relatively tidy and that he'd brought more than one guitar with him. She could see at least three cases propped up against the wall.

He carried over her mug, along with a small plate

for the tea bag. When he was seated, she said, "Thanks again for helping out in class. The kids loved your presentation. They're going to be talking about it for days."

"I was happy to help. It was fun for me, too."

"I wish we still taught music, other than the monthly assembly. It's such an important part of learning. But we just don't have the budget. How did you learn to play?"

"I taught myself. I was always interested in learning, and I picked it up fairly easily. Once I decided I wanted to get serious about starting a band, I did odd jobs to pay for lessons."

"You were determined."

"I was."

She looked at him and found him studying her. The sensation of having his full attention was unnerving.

They were sitting relatively close together. She could easily stretch out her hands, and then they would be touching. Of course, then he would recoil in horror and she would be humiliated, but right up to that point, the fantasy was pretty fun.

"How did you learn about pressure points as a remedy for morning sickness?" she asked, more to distract herself than because she wanted the information.

Micah frowned. "Why would you ask that?"

"Wasn't I supposed to?"

"But you know about…" He leaned toward her. "You didn't google me?"

"No. Should I have? I've been busy with school and the B and B."

Dena did her best not to feel foolish. She wasn't a "google someone" kind of person. Did he really expect that she would—

"I'm sorry," Micah said, his tone sheepish. "I just assumed. Most people do."

They stared at each other, as if unsure who should say what. She moved the plate of bruschettas toward him. "They're really good."

He laughed then, breaking the tension. "You're a food pusher."

"I am. I inherited the trait from my mother. I can't help it."

He took a piece and bit into it. "Delicious."

She grabbed one for herself. While she couldn't eat the blue cheese and fig toppings, there was also a fresh tomato and basil mixture and one with sharp cheddar and pear.

When he'd finished his, Micah wiped his fingers on a napkin and picked up his beer.

"I was married," he said, his voice quiet, his eyes filled with what she could only describe as sadness. "Adriana was five months pregnant when we were T-boned by a drunk driver. She and the baby were killed instantly. I was badly injured. In her first trimester, she had bad morning sickness. I learned about pressure points to help her."

Dena tried to take in what he told her. The stark words painted an uncomfortable visual, filling her with emotions she couldn't name beyond sadness and grief at the unbelievable loss.

"I'm sorry. How long ago did this happen?"

"Just over a year. I spent last Christmas getting transferred from the hospital to a rehab facility, which made what I was going through worse."

She felt her eyes begin to burn—a sure sign that tears were not far behind. She did her best to blink them back.

"Ignore my emotions," she said, clearing her throat. "The hormones make it hard for me to have any kind of self-control." She sniffed. "So in a way, this is your first Christmas alone."

"Yes."

"I'm glad you're in Wishing Tree. It's a good place to get lost in the spirit of the season."

"That's what I'm hoping for."

A single tear escaped. She brushed it away. "We really have to change the subject."

He gave her a faint smile. "You pick."

"Did Noah tell you about the school charity project?"

"No. What is it?"

"We're making hats and scarves for kids in need. Students were asked to submit ideas for our project, and this is the one that was picked. Harrison, a friend of Noah's, suggested it. We're using circular looms to knit the hats and scarves."

She reached for another piece of bruschetta. "My mom usually takes charge of things like that, but she's busy right now, so my sister, Reggie, is going to be running the work sessions. Reggie's back in town through New Year's. My parents are renewing their vows and she's helping with that, too."

"Reggie is going to be busy."

"Yes, she is."

He seemed more relaxed, she thought, watching him eat and sip his beer. He was just so handsome, but not in an off-putting way. There was an ease about him— she supposed he was a man comfortable in his own skin. It was hard for her to imagine he was famous.

"You really wrote 'Moonlight for Christmas'?"

"I did."

"With your ex-wife? Wasn't that awkward?"

He chuckled. "We were married at the time. Electra and I—"

"Electra? Seriously?" Dena couldn't help grinning.

"Not her real name."

"Astonishing."

"It is. We met when she auditioned to be a backup singer for our first tour. Darryl John James was still a new band, not sure if we were going to make it. She and I discovered we both liked to write songs."

"If she's your ex-wife, you discovered other things, as well."

His eyebrows rose. "Ms. Somerville, you shock me."

"I doubt that. Was that your first hit?"

"It was. Things just took off from there."

"While I won't be googling you, I think I have to download some songs and listen to them."

"Yeah, don't do that."

"Why not?"

"You're not going to like them. There isn't any twang."

She laughed. "I like other kinds of music. Besides, I know you now. The songs will be special because of—"

She set down her mug and tried to suck in air as nausea hit her hard. Control seemed impossible, so she was going to have to make it to the bathroom. No way she was throwing up in the sink again. It was too humiliating to consider.

Before she could try to remember where the restroom was, Micah was out of his chair and crouching next to her. He took her forearm in his hands and pressed in several places, his dark blue gaze locked with hers.

"Breathe," he murmured, "Hold it for a count of—"

"Four," she said, already feeling better. "I remember."

She concentrated on her breathing and the way she immediately relaxed. His fingers were warm, his body close. It was only when heat and desire replaced the need to throw up that she realized he was still crouched next to her and they were still staring at each other. Which meant he probably knew she was far less interested in any medicinal touching and way more into anything else he wanted to do.

Humiliation crashed through her. She pulled back and tried to smile.

"All better," she said brightly, aware she probably sounded like an idiot. "You have the touch." She paused, hoping he didn't misunderstand. "I meant, well, just you're very good at what you do."

Ack! Worse!

He moved back to his chair. "Are you all right?"

"Fine. Great. Thank you for your help. I'm going to have to study up on how you do that so I can take care of myself." She held in a moan. Really? Had she just said that? "With the nausea."

One corner of his mouth turned up. "Yes, I got that."

"Great. Fine. Excellent. I'll be going. You enjoy those bruschettas."

She stood, grabbed her coat and made her escape. Once she was safely in her own apartment, she curled up on the sofa and vowed that she would do better the next time she saw Micah. Or maybe she would simply avoid him altogether. That seemed the much safer alternative.

REGGIE CLEARED THE craft table in the basement. She collected one of the plastic bins in the corner and tossed all the mismatched odds and ends into it so she could have some work space. She put tubes of watercolor paints into one of the drawers in the big storage unit on the wall, and stacked craft paper on the shelf.

Once she had empty desk space, she laid out the wedding invitation designs her mother had picked out. While the invitations would be sent via email, Reggie found making decisions easier if she could see the designs in print rather than on a screen.

She'd narrowed her favorites down to three when she heard a crash from upstairs. Seconds later, Belle came tearing down the stairs, Burt right behind her, barking and nipping at her heels. Belle jumped onto the sofa, looking scared and frantic.

"Burt!" Reggie scolded. "Leave her alone."

Burt was unimpressed with her admonition and continued to growl. Belle whimpered.

"I wish you'd stand up to him," Reggie said with a sigh. "It's the only way to make it stop."

Belle's hurt look made it clear the Great Dane thought Reggie should do a much better job of protecting her delicate self.

She returned her attention back to the invitations— all Christmas-themed. Not a surprise, given the season. She narrowed her selection down to one, then went in search of her mother. At the top of the stairs, she called for Belle, who made a frantic dash for the stairs, taking them two at a time, leaving Burt yapping in the basement.

She found her mother in the family room, sorting through a large plastic bin of Christmas decorations. Reggie feigned shock and disapproval.

"Mom! We haven't had Thanksgiving yet. What are you doing?"

Her mother smiled. "Yes, this is me, violating the Wishing Tree code. Technically, I'm not decorating. I'm sorting." She held up a Santa troll. "He's looking shabby. Is it time to move him on to his reward?"

"Never. Mom, we have to have a Santa troll."

Her mother frowned. "He really does need a bit of a spruce. I'll take him downstairs and see what I can do. Did you pick an invitation?"

"I've sorted them in the order I like them, but these are your invitations. You have the final say."

Reggie sat next to her mom on the sofa. Belle jumped up next to her, leaning heavily against Reggie and eyeing the stairs, as if waiting for Burt to appear. Reggie spread out the invitations, then tapped the one she liked best.

"It's beautiful, it's easy to read and it's very much your style."

Her mother picked up the sheet of paper, reading the text before studying the design. "I like it, too," she said. "Let's do this one."

"That was easy." Too easy, Reggie thought. Usually her mother liked to change her mind at least twice before coming to a decision.

"I like it, and we have to get them emailed to everyone. I sent a save-the-date card last month, but the invitations need to go out."

"All right. This one it is."

Her mother had already given her the email address file of all the guests, so sending out the invitations wouldn't take long. A good thing, because at some point she had to get working on her project for Gizmo, not to mention the other work she'd brought with her.

"I've decided on the wedding favor."

Reggie wrapped her arm around Belle and braced herself for the announcement.

"The soap?" she asked cautiously, thinking that would be a long process, considering none of them actually knew how to make soap.

"No, I want to give away Christmas cactus. I've ordered little custom pots that are just so sweet, along with several flats of Christmas cactus. You can transplant them for me."

Reggie stared at her mother. "Is everyone getting a plant or is it one per couple?"

"One per couple. So only sixty or seventy." Her mother patted her arm. "It won't take you but a minute to get it all done."

Reggie thought about pointing out she also needed time to work, but knew then her mother would get that hurt look that made Reggie feel small and mean.

"Did you order potting soil?" she asked instead.

"Yes, a special kind for the cactus. Maybe we could tie little ribbons on the pots. Red and green, for the holiday."

"Sure. Let's do ribbons."

Her mother smiled. "I'm glad you approve."

"It's your wedding, Mom. You get to pick whatever you want."

Leigh rubbed Belle's ears. "I want my beautiful grand-dog to be my flower girl. Your mommy's going to make you a lovely dress and you'll be the prettiest girl ever."

Belle's tail wagged.

The flower girl dress! She'd forgotten. Reggie held in a groan, thinking she was going to have to make a list to keep track of all her wedding duties. There was also running the third-grade charity project, but she didn't want to think about that, mostly because she knew Toby would be one of the parents helping and that meant spending time with him. As their last encounter had been fifteen kinds of awkward, best not to go there.

"I need to clear my head," she said out loud. "Want to go for a walk, Belle?"

Her dog shifted away, sliding down on the sofa until she was curled up on a cushion, her back to Reggie, her eyes closed.

Reggie's mother laughed. "I think that's a no."

"I have to agree with you. Lazy dog."

THE AFTERNOON BEFORE Thanksgiving, Micah was ready to throw a chair through the window. He'd spent most of the day trying to write, and no matter what he did, he ended up with crap.

He'd made lists of words to get things started. He'd googled holiday phrases and traditions. He'd taken three walks, had attempted to take a nap and had even tried going for the ridiculous with a song about a Christmas aardvark. A little after five he had absolutely nothing to show for his day. Not a note, not a word.

He'd planned on writing a Christmas song for Adriana, but at this point, he would be thrilled to get out a stanza or a refrain about a damned aardvark, but he couldn't do that, either. Whatever combination of talent and work he'd once had to create music was gone, or at least in deep hiding. What he didn't know was if it would ever come out.

He paced the length of his suite three times, after which he again thought about tossing the chair through the window. Only he'd never been destructive—not in that way—and saw no reason to start now. Besides, this was Dena's place, and he didn't want to hurt her. Or disappoint her. Ridiculous, but true.

He tried some slow breathing and quickly lost interest, so he stood up, swore under his breath and then grabbed his jacket. He had to get out of his room, and right now the only place he could think of to go was the uninspiringly named Snacks and Wine.

He circled around to the front of the house. The temperature had to be well below freezing. The jacket he'd ordered from REI kept his body warm, but his hands were freezing. Gloves, he thought as he ducked inside. When he got back to his room, he was ordering gloves.

He hung his coat on the rack by the front door and glanced around. There were about ten or twelve people in the large living room, a few more in the dining room. Several were holding small plates and glasses of wine. A couple of guys had beers instead. A few people glanced at him and nodded. No one did a double take or came over to speak with him. Very much in keeping with how things went in Wishing Tree.

He walked past the reception area, glancing around, looking for Dena. Winona, the manager, greeted him.

"Food and drinks are in the dining room." The implication being he should help himself.

"Thanks. Is Dena here?"

Winona pointed. He turned and saw her chatting with an older couple. She was laughing at something they said, her body relaxed. She had on a dark green sweater over jeans. Her long hair was loose.

As he watched her, he wondered why she'd felt she had to have a baby on her own. No, that was the wrong question. The right one was, why was his gender so stupid sometimes? Dena was attractive, smart, kind, funny and easy to be with. There was no reason she shouldn't have found a hundred guys who wanted to fall in love with her and get married. But she hadn't, so she'd made the decision to have a child on her own. He mentally added the word *brave* to her list of attributes.

He made his way to the dining room, where he found a selection of "Italian-style" Washington wines, along with meatballs, melon and prosciutto. He filled a small plate, took a glass of wine, then went to find a place to sit. He'd just settled on a chair in a small alcove when Dena joined him.

"You made it," she said, sitting next to him, an end table between them.

"I did. Snacks and Wine. It needs a better name."

She laughed. "I know. Something catchy. I keep telling myself I need to do some brainstorming, but somehow it never happens."

"How are you feeling?" he asked.

She sighed. "Tired. And apparently I look that way, too. Three people have asked me if I'm getting enough rest."

"Just a few more weeks and you'll get through the first trimester."

"That's what I tell myself. I can't wait for bursts of energy and a positive outlook on life."

"You're pretty positive most of the time."

She laughed. "I am, but between the nausea and the exhaustion, I'm less perky than usual." She leaned back against the chair. "So, what are your plans for Thanksgiving?"

He sipped his wine. "Checking up on me?"

"You know it. I want to make sure you have somewhere to go. Otherwise I'll be dragging you to my parents' house, where you will be forced to watch football with my dad while he complains about having dinner at three in the afternoon. At the same time, Belle, my sister's Great Dane, will cower from Burt, my dad's twenty-pound dachshund. Poor Belle just can't seem to learn that she's the bigger dog."

"Thank you for worrying, but I'm having Thanksgiving with Steve and his family."

She eyed him with a faint air of disbelief.

"You're sure?" she asked.

"Cross my heart. You can ask Steve."

"Okay. I just wanted to make sure you weren't going to be alone."

"I'm not."

"It's just as well you have somewhere to go. We'll be dealing with a lot of wedding talk."

"That's right. Your parents are getting married. That should be fun."

"I'm happy for them. It's a little odd, but hey, so are most parents. Reggie and I are thrilled that we won't be bridesmaids, but Belle, the Great Dane, is going to be a flower girl."

"I want to see a picture of that."

Dena laughed. "I promise you several. Reggie's making her a dress, and then I think the plan is to hang a basket of flowers around her neck. It should be charming. How are the meatballs?"

"Delicious. Did you want some?"

"I'll get them." Dena glanced toward the dining room. "And melon. I can't have the prosciutto."

"No processed meats."

"No soft cheese, no alcohol." She sighed. "No coffee."

"You miss coffee?"

"Yes. Decaf just isn't the same. Coffee and I were good together. It was a long-term thing and we were happy."

"You'll be together again soon." He rose. "I'm going to get you some food."

"Oh, you don't have to. You're my guest."

She started to stand, but he waved her into her seat. "I'll be right back."

He went into the dining room and put meatballs and melon on a plate, then poured her a glass of juice. But when he returned to the alcove, Dena's eyes were closed, and her head was leaning against back of the chair. Her slow, even breathing told him she'd fallen asleep. Unexpected tenderness swept through him, followed by a fierce sense of protectiveness.

Adriana had done the same thing, he thought, quietly sitting next to Dena, prepared to watch over her. Adriana had been embarrassed, but he'd found it charming. He still did.

He supposed it made sense that he was thinking of his late wife more these days. Being around a pregnant woman was bound to bring back memories. As he sipped his wine, he thought about how the images from the past were less sharp than they had been. They no longer cut like glass. Instead, they were a comfort. Recollections of a happier time that made him hopeful about the future.

Without thinking, he stretched out his arm and took

one of Dena's hands in his. She didn't waken, instead shifting toward him and lacing her fingers with his. In the background he listened as the playlist moved on to another song. At first he didn't recognize the opening bars, but then he smiled as George Strait began singing "Ocean Front Property." The man had a great voice, he thought with a grin, and just enough twang to keep Dena happy.

Nine

"YOU SHOULD JOIN US," Reggie said, stretched out on the bed, Belle by her side. She shifted her phone to the other ear.

"If I skipped Thanksgiving, my mother would hunt me down and kill me," Paisley said cheerfully. "As it is, I'm only staying for the day, and you know that makes her crazy."

"She does like time with her favorite daughter."

"I wish. I'm her only daughter. Okay, have a happy Thanksgiving. Let's plan something for the weekend. I have a couple of daytime events at the resort, but we can party into the night."

Reggie laughed. "Last time I was home by ten thirty."

"We're older now, and therefore more responsible."

"Is that what we're calling it? Talk to you when you're back."

She hung up and smiled at Belle. "Paisley is the youngest and she has four older brothers, all of whom are married. They're going to spend the whole day giving her dating advice."

Belle frowned slightly.

"I know. They should leave her alone, but do they listen?"

Reggie sat up, then took a shower. Thirty minutes later, she was dressed and made up, with her hair blown out. Downstairs, she found Dena seated at the kitchen island, Belle at her feet.

"How are you feeling?" Reggie asked her sister. "Still getting sick?"

"Yes. And I'm tired all the time." A little color stained her cheeks. "Last night I fell asleep at Snacks and Wine."

"While talking to a guest?"

Dena avoided her gaze. "Not exactly, but still. It was embarrassing."

From the family room, their father yelled at a flag thrown in a football game, and their mother chided him for yelling.

Dena shook her head. "Some things never change."

"I know. It's just a matter of time until he starts complaining that we're eating at three." Reggie pulled a bottle of sparkling cider from the fridge. "So you'll feel special at dinner."

"Very sweet."

"The turkey is giant. It's just the four of us. Mom must be in the mood for leftovers."

"I'll take some home with me." Dena smiled. "Did you already do your stuffing-is-gross rant?"

"Yes, both out loud and in my head."

Reggie had spent the early part of the morning helping her mother, chopping vegetables and cooking sausage for the stuffing. For those who didn't like their bread product basted in turkey blood, there was dressing, cooked in a casserole dish.

"You hungry?" she asked Dena.

"A little."

"Go watch the game. I'll make you a salad." When she hesitated, Reggie gave her a little push toward the living room. "Go!"

Dena joined their parents. Reggie pulled ingredients out of the refrigerator, turned and nearly ran into Belle.

"You're being stealthy," she complained with a laugh.

Belle eyed the cheese and cooked chicken breast.

"Not for you."

Reggie expected a protest, but before Belle could make one, Burt careened into the kitchen. His little feet slipped on the hardwood floor, sending him plowing into Belle, who shrieked and then took off down the hall. Burt went after her, obviously loving the game.

"If you'd stand up to him, he would leave you alone," Reggie called after them.

She confirmed that neither of her parents wanted a salad, then went to work. While she admired Dena, Reggie couldn't imagine being that brave. Deliberately choosing to get pregnant was life-changing. There were weeks Belle was all the responsibility Reggie could handle.

She called Dena back to the kitchen.

"Here you go," she said. "Healthy goodness. I even used kale."

Dena wrinkled her nose. "I don't like kale."

"It's good for you. It's dark and leafy, so it has to be healthy."

"It tastes yucky."

"That's mature."

Dena laughed and joined her at the island. Belle returned to her bed in the kitchen, but kept her eye out for anything that fell.

"I'm excited to start the charity project on Monday," Reggie said. "I've been practicing and I'm getting pretty good."

Her sister eyed her humorously. "How much of your enthusiasm is about Toby?"

Reggie had done her best to forget about him. "None."

Dena raised her eyebrows. "Really?" She drew the word out to several syllables.

"Yes, really. Why would I be interested in him? I don't know anything about him. I knew him when he was, what? Seventeen? Eighteen? He's a totally different person now."

"He's kind of sexy."

"Then you date him."

"He's *your* boyfriend."

"He's not! What part of 'it's been years' is unclear to you?"

"So you have no interest in him?"

Reggie thought about her brief yet embarrassing encounter with Toby. They hadn't exchanged more than a handful of words, and most of those had been her babbling.

"He's probably dating someone."

"Not that I've heard," Dena told her. "Regardless,

I'll change the subject because I'm just that great a person."

"Thank you."

"You're welcome. How's it going with the wedding?"

Reggie told her about the invitations and the replanting of the Christmas cactus.

Dena winced. "I can help. I can work on some when I get home from school."

"Between lesson planning, running the B and B, barfing and being exhausted? I don't think so. You focus on yourself and the baby."

"Winona runs the B and B. I'm just backup. The barfing is a little better. I've been using some pressure techniques, and they seem to help."

"How'd you learn about those? I've never heard of them."

Dena looked at her salad. "One of the guests at the B and B."

Reggie studied her sister. There was something in her posture. Something that made Reggie ask, "What aren't you telling me?"

Dena's eyes widened. "Nothing. Why?"

"You're hiding something."

"You're imagining things. You just listed everything going on in my life. When would I have time to hide anything?"

Reggie wanted to keep pushing, but their mother walked into the kitchen, and the moment was lost.

"When you're done with your salads, could you start setting the table?" Leigh said. "I want to use the good china and the nice glasses. Oh, and add three place settings."

Reggie looked at Dena, who shrugged.

"We're having company?" Reggie asked.

"Just a couple friends. Nothing special."

"Who?" Dena asked.

Their mother smiled. "You'll see."

Knowing pursuing the topic wouldn't help, Reggie carried their empty plates over to the sink, then followed Dena into the dining room. They made quick work of picking out linens and putting an old-fashioned candelabra on the buffet.

Dena touched the tall white tapered candles. "We probably shouldn't light these. If Burt goes after Belle, she could easily bump into the buffet and poof, there goes our happy Thanksgiving."

"A house fire isn't what any of us longs for."

While Dena took the good china out of the hutch, Reggie collected the flatware. She found a half-finished cross-stitch project in with the serving pieces and laughed.

Dena grinned. "Mom, we found your counted cross-stitch. The one of the giraffe."

Their mother walked into the dining room. "Where was it? I've been looking for it forever."

"Hutch drawer."

Leigh took it and waved it. "I'm putting this in the basket by my recliner. If I forget, please remind me."

Belle wandered into the dining room, looking more worried than usual.

"What is it, little girl?" Reggie asked. "Do you want to go out?"

She led Belle to the back door and opened it. The dog stood there, sniffing the cold air, visibly shivering. Reggie closed the door, then grabbed one of Belle's jackets. Once she was bundled up, the dog reluctantly went into the backyard and finished her business before darting back inside.

"I know," Reggie told her, unfastening the coat. "It's much colder here than in Seattle. Sorry."

Before Belle could agree—nonverbally, of course—the doorbell rang.

"Reggie, be a dear and get that."

Reggie walked to the front of the house and pulled open the door, only to stare in disbelief. The "friends" her mother had mentioned were Toby, Harrison and Toby's grandmother, Judy. At least, that was what she assumed, seeing as they were standing on the front porch, looking expectant.

"Ah, hi," Reggie managed weakly, all the while wondering what on earth her mother had been thinking. "Happy Thanksgiving."

TOBY'S SEMI-SMUG FEELING that came from knowing Reggie had arranged the Thanksgiving invitation evaporated. Based on her shocked expression, she'd known nothing about them joining her family for dinner.

"Come in," she said, stepping back. "You must be freezing."

Everyone trooped inside. Dena appeared and helped with coats while Belle danced around Harrison, delighted he'd shown up in her house. Toby handed Reggie a covered dish.

"My grandmother made these."

"Lefse," Judy added. "They're a family tradition."

"It's a Norwegian flatbread," he added.

Reggie looked at him as if he was an idiot. "I've had it. At your house."

When they'd been dating, he thought, surprised she remembered.

She smiled at Judy. "Thank you for this. My family's in for a treat."

Reggie's parents appeared and ushered everyone into the family room. Vince turned off the game and put on music, and Harrison dropped to the floor to play with Belle. Toby saw Reggie duck into the kitchen with the *lefse* and followed her.

"You were surprised," he said, causing her to spin to face him.

"Yes. My mother said friends were coming over but didn't say who. I assumed it was one of her ladies-who-lunch group or somebody who works for Dad at the auto shop. I wasn't expecting you."

"So, not a good surprise."

"I didn't say that."

"You don't sound delighted."

"Delighted? Really? Like I should squeal?"

He leaned against the counter and raised an eyebrow. "You squeal when you're delighted? That's kind of unfortunate."

"Oh, please. I don't squeal." She took a step toward him. "At the risk of once again not sounding 'delighted.'" She made air quotes. "How did this happen?"

Her hair curved just beneath her jaw and emphasized her large brown eyes. She had on dark jeans and a sweater that was yellow, red and orange—all the colors of fall. She looked good. Different than she had in high school, but still good.

"The invitation?" he asked.

"Yes."

"Your mother came by the store and asked if we'd like to come over for dinner."

"My mother? That's confusing. I didn't know."

"I got that."

"Why did you say yes?"

An interesting question, he thought, not sure how to answer.

"It's been just the three of us. We agreed joining a family would be a fun change."

She didn't look convinced, but then shrugged as if accepting the explanation.

"It's always nice to have more people around the table," she said. "Thank you for coming."

He smiled. "Anytime."

Her lips twitched. "I can't imagine what you thought when my mother walked in and invited you to Thanksgiving dinner."

"Yes, you can."

She sighed. "Yes, I can. You thought it was me doing the asking."

"It wasn't."

"No."

"Awkward," he said in a high-pitched, sing-song voice.

She laughed. "Yes, but I'm okay with it if you are."

"I am, and we really are looking forward to dinner."

Their eyes locked, and he felt a flicker of attraction low in his gut.

"Want to talk about your dog?" he asked, more to distract himself than to learn about Belle.

Reggie smiled. "We already have. She's a rescue."

He nodded at the coatrack by the kitchen door. "I meant her wardrobe. I've seen her around town. She has quite the fashion collection. Where do you buy clothes for a dog her size?" He frowned. "Or any dog?"

"There are plenty of pet boutiques, including one across from your store in The Wreath. Dog clothes are a thing."

"I thought they sold dog food. I hope you're kidding me about the clothes."

"I'm not. But Belle's size makes her difficult to fit, so I make most of her clothes. She complains when I put them on, but I know she appreciates me keeping her warm."

"She complains? How?"

"It's mostly on the inside, but I'm good at reading her mind."

"You're good at assuming what she's thinking," he corrected her. "In truth, you have no idea."

She grinned. "You're wrong. I work with inventors, helping them get their products ready for market. Right now I'm dealing with an automatic vacuum that terrifies her. When she looks at it, I know exactly what she's thinking."

"She's a big girl. Why doesn't she just destroy it?"

"We've had that exact conversation, and Belle has no idea how powerful she is. I'm trying to self-actualize her, but it's slow going."

He smiled at her. "I would imagine."

Reggie looked at him. "You know I'm helping Dena with the charity project, right?"

"She mentioned you would be in charge."

"I'll try to be a benevolent dictator."

"Probably a good plan. Eight-year-olds are often ready for an uprising."

"We can't have that," she said lightly. "There's too much work to be done, and it's for a good cause. I've been practicing my loom knitting. I think the kids will enjoy it, and the loom will be easier for them than regular knitting."

"You knit?"

"Where do you think Belle gets her sweaters?"

"Impressive."

Reggie's mother breezed into the kitchen. "There you two are. Come join us. We're trying to remember when you two started dating. Your father says you weren't allowed to date when you were a sophomore, but I told him you were. Which is it, Reggie?"

"Mom, we're not going to talk about that."

Leigh smiled at them both. "Too late! Besides, isn't it better to get all this awkward talk out of the way so we can enjoy our dinner in peace?"

Toby glanced longingly toward the back door. Reggie intercepted the look and shook her head.

"No way. If I have to endure it, then you do, too. We'll come up with an alternative topic to distract them."

"Good luck with that," he said, his voice teasing.

"You need a more positive attitude."

"I'll leave that to you."

DENA PAUSED IN the courtyard by the carriage house. She was full and a little sleepy. The day had been a good one—she enjoyed her family's company, and having Toby, Harrison and Judy join them had made for an interesting meal.

It was barely seven but felt later, and the night air

was freezing. Still she hesitated, not sure if she should knock on Micah's door or not. The decision was taken out of her hands when the door in question swung open and Micah stepped out into the night.

"You lost?" he asked lightly.

She laughed and waved the bag in her hand. "I brought you leftovers. It seemed like a good idea at the time, but then I started second-guessing myself."

"Don't ever do that." He stepped back in obvious invitation.

She went inside. He took the bag and studied the contents.

"There's a lot of food here," he said.

"Turkey, both stuffing and dressing. My family has both for reasons we don't need to get into. Green beans and three slices of pie."

He looked at her. "I really did have dinner with Steve and his family."

"I believe you."

"Then why the food?"

"I'm a nurturer. I can't help myself."

He motioned to the sofa. "Have a seat."

She hung her coat, then settled in a corner of the couch. Part of her hoped he would sit right next to her, draping his arm across her shoulders before whispering that he couldn't stop thinking about her and then pressing his mouth to—

"Can I get you anything?" he asked.

"Huh? Oh, no. I'm good. So, did you have fun today?"

"I did. I like Marti, Steve's wife. A couple of the guys who work for him joined us. Dinner was at two, which is a strange time, but traditional."

"We ate at three."

His expression turned concerned. "How did you do?"

"You mean did I throw up at the table?"

He grinned. "I wouldn't have put it that way, but yes."

"I was fine. I got queasy a couple of times, but there was no actual regurgitation."

"Progress."

"I wish, but I think it's too early for my hormones to be calming down. Soon, though."

She looked at him, telling herself not to get lost in his blue eyes. He was a guest and possibly a friend—nothing more. Besides, he was still getting over the loss of his wife and their baby. He was looking to recover, not get involved with a very ordinary, pregnant woman.

"Was the day difficult?" she asked.

"Parts of it. Adriana wasn't one for traditions, so we usually traveled on the holidays."

"I've heard people do that. I can't imagine not being in Wishing Tree for Thanksgiving and Christmas. It's what I've done my whole life." She paused, thinking she could not sound more boring. "Except for when I went to college, I haven't lived anywhere else."

"You're a small-town girl."

Great. Because *that* was a thrilling description. "I am."

"Is that why there's no guy?"

"I don't know. Maybe. I had a serious boyfriend in high school and again in college, but neither was the one."

"You believe in the one?"

"I believe in falling in love. I want to give my heart

to someone and have him do the same with me. I want to know we're going to spend the rest of our lives together, no matter what."

"People get divorced."

"Sometimes people make a mistake, but sometimes they let go too quickly. I'd want to try harder."

"You're an idealist."

She wasn't sure if he thought that was good or bad. "My parents have been married nearly thirty-five years."

"I remember. They're renewing their vows."

"Exactly. They're still crazy in love. Just being around them makes me happy. I wanted that for my kids. But after college, I never found anyone. I dated a couple of guys, but the relationships never went anywhere."

His gaze was steady. "You mentioned that you were tired of waiting for the one."

"I still hope to meet him, but whether or not I do, I want children. So I decided to get pregnant."

"Using a turkey baster."

She laughed. "Yes."

"That's a bold move. It takes courage."

"People have said that to me, but I don't see it that way. I'm not being brave. I'm being practical. Women are biologically different."

The smile returned. "Yes, and most men enjoy those differences."

"I meant we have a limited time during which we can get pregnant. Men can father babies much longer. I didn't want to wake up the day I turned fifty only to realize I was never going to have a family. I have plenty of support, I can afford it, and I want to be a mother."

"Like I said, brave."

"You're giving me too much credit."

"I think it's just enough credit, but we can argue about that later."

She wanted him to kiss her. She wanted him to do a lot more. She wanted touching and all kinds of man-woman things that she hadn't experienced in far too long. The man was a musician. Didn't that mean he would be extra good with his hands? She wanted them naked and… Okay, while she was wishing for the moon, she wanted a Micah-induced orgasm. Which meant she really had to get out of here before she did something stupid, like tell him that.

"I should go," she said, coming to her feet.

He rose. "Thanks for stopping by."

"I promise not to make a habit of it."

"Don't say that. I like your company."

He did? Great. Only what did that mean, exactly? As a friend? As a friend he'd like to give an orgasm to?

"You're a guest," she said, hoping her tone was light rather than breathy with a big dose of desperation. "You need your privacy."

"You have too many rules."

"Plans," she corrected him. "I have plans."

"Same thing."

They looked at each other. For one brief second, she would have sworn his gaze dropped to her mouth. Anticipation swelled up inside of her and she—

"You have a good night," he said, walking toward the door.

She deflated like a popped balloon. Micah didn't want her. He considered her a friend, nothing more.

She really had to remember that, because if she didn't, she was going to do something they both would regret, and that was not how she wanted him to remember her.

Ten

"THIS IS GOOD," Reggie said, her words creating fog in the cold night air. "If we walk enough, dinner will settle, and then I can eat leftovers."

Beside her, Toby laughed. "You can't be hungry. We just ate the equivalent of six meals in a single sitting."

"Hey, no judging. I'm not hungry now. I'm less stuffed, which is progress."

He patted his stomach. "It was the second piece of pie that did me in."

"And you would be a man who appreciates pie in all its forms."

He chuckled, and she smiled in return.

This was nice, she thought. Comfortable and easy—kind of a trick, considering their past and all the talk about it at the dinner table. Still, she and Toby had worked as a team, deflecting and changing the subject.

"This was a good day," she said.

"Thanks for inviting us."

"Thanks for coming. I have no idea what my mother was thinking, asking you to join us, but I'm glad she did."

"Me, too."

She kept an eye on Harrison and Belle, who walked in front of them. The boy had a firm grip on the leash— not that Belle ever tried to get away. She didn't enjoy adventures. In her mind, danger always lurked. Still, it was sweet that he was protective, considering how big she was. Her head was about level with his chest.

"She really likes your son," Reggie said, watching the Great Dane step a little closer to Harrison.

"She's a surprisingly sweet girl. She was polite at the table, unlike Burt."

"He's a beggar, but he mostly stays by my dad, so it's less of a problem for the rest of us."

They arrived at the dog park. It was nearly eight and bitingly cold, so no one else was there. They all went inside the gate. Reggie unclipped Belle, who looked at her doubtfully, as if asking why she would do that.

"Come on, Belle," Harrison said, running across the park. Belle loped after him, her long strides allowing her to catch up easily.

"She'll keep an eye on him," Reggie said.

"Isn't it supposed to be the other way around?"

"Maybe."

Reggie wasn't sure what to make of their post-dinner walk. She had assumed that after cleanup, Toby would collect his family and leave. Instead, when she'd mentioned going to the dog park, he offered to go with her. Harrison had come along, while Judy was visiting with Reggie's mom.

Now, in the cold night, with the stars twinkling above them, she wondered why he'd wanted to prolong the evening. Not that it mattered—he was good company.

"How does it feel to be back in Wishing Tree?" she asked.

He looked at her. "It's been over a year, so it doesn't feel new anymore. This was home before and is home now." He flashed her a smile. "It is kind of nice to return as a success."

She laughed. "I'll bet. You used to be such a bad boy. There has to be a lot of satisfaction in showing people what you've accomplished, pretty much all on your own."

"I wasn't that bad."

"Maybe not for a big city, but for Wishing Tree?" She grinned. "My parents were very nervous."

"I won them over."

"You did, and they were grateful that you didn't start a trend. You were my one and only bad boy."

He leaned against the fence. "Why did you want to go out with me?"

"Is that a serious question?"

"Yes."

She thought about how he'd been back then. So good-looking, with an irresistible swagger. All the girls had wanted to go out with him, but he hadn't been the type to date much. Still, when she'd caught him watching her, she'd decided to pursue things.

"You were irresistible," she admitted. "You had to know that."

"I *was* pretty hot," he said with a grin.

He still was, not that she would be mentioning that.

"We were both young," she said instead. "Funny how things turn out. I never would have thought you'd come back."

"Judy's getting on in years. I couldn't ask her to move somewhere else. She's lived here her whole life."

Which spoke well of him, she thought.

He checked on Harrison and Belle, then turned back to her. "Jake? Really? My nemesis?"

"Oh, please. You were rivals on the football team. You both wanted to be captain. That hardly makes him your nemesis. So don't put that on me."

"Fair enough. So, Jake?"

She laughed. "You're not going to let it go, are you?"

"You never had a thing for him in high school. You were into bad boys."

"No, I was into you. And you're right. I barely noticed him back then." Once she'd given her heart to Toby, she hadn't been interested in anyone else. "Our relationship was unexpected. He'd moved here to be assistant manager up at the resort. I was home, visiting my folks. We ran into each other. Literally. I was coming out of Jingle Coffee and he was going in. My drink and Danish went flying, and we started talking, and then we went out."

"You were going to marry him."

She wasn't surprised he'd heard about that. It had happened about the time Toby had moved back, so there would have been chatter.

"He proposed on a Friday, we had a party to celebrate on Saturday and he dumped me on Sunday," she said, careful to keep her tone light. It had been nearly a year and— She paused. "Oh, wow. It was a year ago this weekend."

"He proposed the Friday after Thanksgiving?"

"He did. At the Lighting of the Trees."

"Way to make it memorable."

"I don't think the day really mattered after the other stuff."

He looked at her. "Are you over him?"

"Yes, and that happened more quickly than it should have. It makes me think I didn't love him as much as I thought I did. Sad, but true. I wish him well, wherever he is."

"I'm sorry."

"Don't be."

"It seems kind of crappy to propose and then break up all in the same weekend."

"Yes, it does. He never said why. He just showed up at my parents' house on Sunday and said he was sorry and he couldn't be with me anymore. I was hurt and confused, but there was no talking. There was nothing. He just left. I drove back to Seattle with my heart broken."

She glanced at Toby. "And that is the sad story of my Jake relationship."

"You should stick to bad boys."

She smiled. "You might be right about that."

TOBY WAVED TO Harrison, but his son was already busy showing his friends the fifty-cent piece he'd found on the sidewalk on their quick walk to the birthday party. For kids who had grown up in the digital world and saw their parents pay for most things with a credit card, an unusual coin was noteworthy.

The birthday party, complete with lunch and games, would go until three thirty. Brave parents, Toby thought. The most he'd been able to pull together was a party at the Wonderful Life Cinema, where they offered hot dogs and popcorn, along with priority seating on a Saturday afternoon movie.

Harrison had been happy hanging out with his friends, and the kids had all seemed to have a good time. Toby wondered if he should try to do more this year. The hard part was, he wasn't creative—not in that way. He was more business-oriented. He didn't decorate or do crafts or know what color went with what other color.

He walked the short distance back to his house. There were two large vans parked in front and a couple of guys up on ladders, stringing lights. Inside, several people were putting up large Christmas trees—one in the downstairs family room and one in the dining room. A woman stood on the stairs, looping garland around the banister. He stepped around open bins filled with lights and silver and red ornaments. He wove his way through the chaos and ducked into his grandmother's room.

Judy stood by her desk, going through the plastic tote he'd brought in for her. She smiled when she saw him.

"They're making a bit of a mess out there," she said.

"They'll clean up before they leave. Is there too much noise? Is this bothering you?"

She made a clucking sound with her tongue. "Toby, I'm old, but I'm not infirm. They're fine. I just wish you'd let me decorate the house."

"They're putting up a fifteen-foot tree in the family room. I don't think either of us could have handled that. In a week or so, Harrison and I will go get a real tree for the upstairs media room, and the three of us will decorate that one together."

She held up a string of old-fashioned bubble lights, filled with a fluid that bubbled when the lights heated up.

"You think those still work?" he asked.

"I hope so."

"If not, we'll get new ones."

"You don't have to keep doing that," she said, her tone a little rueful.

"What?"

"You're always buying me things. I have plenty. I don't need new lights."

He moved close and hugged her, trying not to notice how fragile she felt in his arms. He kissed the top of her head. "You're not the boss of me."

She laughed. "I used to be."

She stepped back and went to her closet, where she pulled a few boxes off a shelf.

"I want you to look at what I bought Harrison. If you think he'll like the gifts, I'll drop them off at Wrap Around the Clock later."

He glanced through the boxes. There was a baseball board game and a joke book. The last box contained a kit that would teach Harrison how to do simple magic tricks.

"All winners," he told her. "And these are plenty. You don't have to get him anything else."

She waved away his advice. "He's my great-grandson. I enjoy spoiling him."

"You're good to him."

"I love him."

A simple statement filled with meaning. Judy had

loved him, as well. Growing up, he'd known she was the only one. At least until Reggie, and that had been a very different kind of love.

"I know you do," he said. "Want me to drop the gifts off at Wrap Around the Clock for you?"

"I can do it. I want to check on Camryn and see how she's doing."

Camryn had been a couple of years behind him, so he'd known *of* her in high school, but hadn't hung out with her or her friends. She'd recently lost her mom and had moved back to Wishing Tree to take over the family business and take care of her much younger twin sisters.

"The holidays are going to be tough," he said. "On all of them."

Judy eyed him speculatively. "Maybe you should stop by yourself. Just to be friendly."

"Why would I do that? I barely know her."

"You could get to know her better."

As her true meaning sank in, he held in a groan. "Don't even think about it. I'm not interested in dating Camryn."

"You can't know that. You just said yourself you barely know her. She's very pretty."

"I'm sure she is, but no." The last thing he needed was his grandmother messing with his personal life. Not that he had one, but the principle was the same regardless.

"What about Reggie? You two got along well last night at dinner."

This was more dangerous territory, he thought. Last night had been fun, and he'd enjoyed hanging out with

Reggie and getting to know the person she'd become, but that was a far cry from wanting to go out with her.

"You know I don't date."

"You can't judge every woman by Lori. She was a horrible person. Reggie isn't like that."

"I'm not going to get involved with someone. Not while Harrison is still young. I have to protect him."

His grandmother sighed. "You shouldn't be alone. It's not right."

"I'm fine." He softened his words with a smile. "I was going to stop by the office. You feel up to being in charge of the decorating?"

"There's not much for me to do. They're taking care of it all."

"That's what I'm paying them for. I'm picking Harrison up at three thirty. We'll be home after that."

"All right. Don't work too hard."

He kissed her cheek, then made his way to his SUV. He knew Judy was only trying to help. Her comment about not being alone was one he thought about every now and then.

The truth was, he *did* want someone in his life. He wanted to give his heart to someone, to be cared about and to care back. He wanted all the little things that made up a relationship—just not now. He'd been wrong about two women in his life, and both of those decisions had rocked him to his core. One had given him his son, and the other had damaged Harrison in a way that would scar him for years.

Toby couldn't risk having that happen again, and the easiest way to make sure his son was safe was to never get involved. Not seriously. Not until Harrison could protect himself.

It was similar to the way he handled the reality of being the son of an alcoholic. He didn't know if whatever caused the disease had been passed on to him, but he wasn't taking any chances. He didn't drink much and when he did, it was a single beer or one glass of wine. He never got drunk—not even when he'd been younger. Maybe he would be fine, but he wasn't willing to take the chance.

MICAH WAS THINKING that instead of pursuing music, he should have learned a trade. People always needed their cars fixed—maybe he would have been good at that, because he sure couldn't write a song anymore. He tore off yet another piece of paper and balled it up before tossing it into the nearby recycling bin.

He'd wasted the entire morning making zero progress. He couldn't find a spark or theme or anything that would help him find his way into the song. At least if he'd learned a trade, he would be skilled at something useful. As it was, he had—

A loud crash caught his attention. The sound came from the other side of the wall. He knew there wasn't another suite there—the carriage house only had the two, and Dena was upstairs. He grabbed his coat and went outside, then around the building.

The big garage door stood open, and Dena was up on a ladder in front of rows of shelving, pulling down big plastic bins. One was on its side on the concrete floor.

"What are you doing?" he asked, moving to the bottom of the ladder. "Get off of there. You shouldn't be climbing up and down."

She laughed. "Don't say 'in my condition,' please.

Last I heard, being pregnant doesn't affect equilibrium, and I'm hardly off balance from the extra point-three pounds I'm carrying."

She looked adorable. Her nose was red from the cold, and she wore a thick red sweater and jeans.

He softened his tone. "Get down, please. You can tell me what you want and I'll get it down."

"You're being weird."

"I'm the guest, so you have to do what I say."

"Fine," she grumbled, making her way to solid ground. "I only need those last three bins. I've already taken in most of them."

He went up the ladder and carried the bins to the floor. They were bulky but lightweight and filled with holiday decorations.

"How many are there?" he asked.

"About sixty. The public spaces are pretty big, so we put up a half dozen trees. I had a couple of high school kids come in and help with that this morning, so they're up and decorated. Now I just have the rest of it."

"You're doing this yourself?"

"I told you. I had help this morning. It's fine."

"You're pregnant."

"Have I mentioned it's a lima bean, because it is."

"You said you had a support system."

She laughed. "Yes, for when I have the baby. Micah, you're sweet to worry, but I've been doing the decorating here at the B and B for years. Before I inherited it, I worked here part-time. Even after I was teaching, I took shifts in the summer."

It all sounded logical, but he couldn't get past the fact that she was doing all this alone.

"You've got me now. I'll run these inside. Then you

can get off your feet and point to what needs to be done."

"I don't think so. Remember the guest thing?" She looked at him. "Are you deliberately being difficult?"

"I'm a talented guy. Take advantage of that." At least, he used to be talented. On the bright side, helping her decorate meant that for an entire afternoon, he wouldn't have to deal with his inability to write. That was enough of a win for him.

"Thank you. You're sweet to offer."

"It's not an offer. It's an act." He picked up two bins and started for the main building. "Don't even think about picking one up," he said without turning around.

She laughed and followed him inside.

He saw right away she hadn't been kidding about the number of storage containers. They were stacked everywhere. A big decorated tree stood in front of the living room's main window, with two smaller ones flanking the fireplace. He could see others by the reception desk and in the dining room.

He set down the bins he held, collected three empty ones and went back to the garage. It only took a couple of trips to take the rest inside and bring out the empty ones. Once that was done, Dena showed him the decorating plan.

"The bins are color-coded," she said, pointing to several bins with big dots on the side. "Red for the living room, blue for the dining room, green for the reception area and so on."

She opened a red folder. The drawing of the fireplace in the living room was crude, but he could see exactly where the dancing bears were supposed to go, along with the decorative pine and the glass bulbs.

Other drawings showed different parts of the room and what went where. There was a folder for each space, along with a diagram of where all the wreaths would go.

"Did you do this?" he asked. "It's impressive. Easy to follow, and the instructions are clear. Nothing gets mixed up, and when you put it away in January, you simply keep the sections together in the bins."

She smiled. "Thank you. I worked on this for a couple of years to get it right. Decorating used to take weeks, but now I can do it over the long weekend. I get help on the trees, and I have professionals putting up the outdoor lights first thing in the morning."

"I'm glad you're not thinking of tackling those yourself."

She laughed. "I know my limitations."

"No, you don't. Where do you want me to start?"

"*We* are going to start in the living room."

He wanted to push back, saying he would take care of it, but he knew that was ridiculous. She was right about barely being pregnant. Except for her morning sickness, she was strong and healthy. There was no reason she couldn't handle a few Christmas decorations.

"The living room it is," he said, his gaze briefly dropping to her mouth before he turned away. Not only could he avoid his lack of talent, he would get to hang out with Dena for the rest of the day.

He liked her company, he admitted to himself. He liked *her*.

She had him hang wreaths, showing him how to loop the ribbon around the hooks. He hadn't realized how many windows there were in the big space, and each one had its own wreath. She took care of the fireplace, centering the dancing bears before filling in with the faux boughs and large glitter-covered glass bulbs.

Little rabbit figures were placed on the coffee table as part of a seasonal forest tableau. Tabletop trees had different themes. There was one decorated in all fish, including three happy and grinning goldfish, and one that was devoted to all things Cinderella. There was her coach, glass slippers and little porcelain Cinderella figurines.

"Tell me there's a boy tree somewhere," he said.

"There's a cowboy one in the dining room. Does that help?"

"Yes. Not that I don't love a woman in a blue dress." He frowned, touching one of the ornaments. "Why is her dress always blue?"

"I don't think it is. You should check it out."

He winced. "Yeah, I don't really want anything to do with Cinderella in my browsing history."

"Afraid people will think you have kinky porn needs?"

"I don't do porn of any kind. It's not interesting to me."

"I suppose in your position, you can get the real thing anytime you want."

"Speculating about my personal life?" he asked.

She grinned. "I am. Although no one has mentioned women coming and going from your suite." She tilted her head. "Do you have them drop by one at a time or in groups?"

"If there aren't at least three or four, where's the fun?"

"How would four even work?"

He laughed. "Okay, time to shut this conversation

down. We're going places that are weird, even for a former rock star. For the record, I was never into groups. I was into volume, but one at a time, and when I reached my late twenties, I got a whole lot more discerning."

"Thank you for clarifying," she teased, her brown eyes bright with humor. "My personal life has been far less exciting, but I'm okay with that. I wouldn't be a good groupie."

"That's not a bad thing."

"I suppose not."

They smiled at each other. He liked how comfortable he was with her. Dena was easy to talk to, and she had a positive outlook he enjoyed. Plus the nurturing. She was a natural-born caretaker.

"You must have loved growing up in Wishing Tree," he said.

"I did."

"It's just you and your sister?"

"Uh-huh." She paused to scan the living room folder. "I think we're good here."

He carried bins with blue dots into the dining room, and they got started there.

"How about you?" she asked, placing a display of ice-skating penguins into the hutch. "Brothers and sisters?"

"Just me. My mom died when I was young, and I don't remember her. My dad was the kind of man who could never settle anywhere. We traveled a lot. He encouraged me to learn to play guitar, telling me I could figure it out."

"He didn't play himself?"

"No, but he loved that I was enthused. About the time I turned twelve, I knew I wanted to be a musician when I grew up. I started writing songs and singing. When I was fifteen, we settled in a small town outside of LA. That's where I met Steve."

"I wondered about that."

"We connected instantly, mostly because we loved music. Steve is a great drummer. We started a band. When my dad wanted to move on, I told him I wanted to stay."

"He let you?"

"Yeah." Micah remembered the sadness in his father's eyes. "He knew he couldn't help me with my dreams, not with us always moving around. I never got the sacrifice he made for me until later."

When Adriana had been pregnant and he'd found out he was having a son. At that moment, he'd understood what his father had done for him.

"He passed away about ten years ago."

"Still moving from place to place?"

"Yeah, but he was doing it in style. When the band and I signed our first record deal, I used my share of the money to buy my dad an RV." He smiled at the memory. "He was one happy guy. With that, he would always have a home."

"So he got to see you famous and everything."

"He did. If he was near where we were performing, he would come to the concerts. He liked saying he was with the band."

"He sounds like a wonderful man."

"He was. Sometimes the hardest thing is to let someone go. I get that now."

"It's a good lesson to learn."

"So speaks the teacher."

He opened a tote and saw part of a Victorian village,

carefully wrapped in tissue paper. Dena pointed to the window seat.

"They go there. There's a plug under the seat. You'll see a little cutout where the cord goes. I think there are four bins just for the village."

He started unpacking the various buildings, trees and small streetlights.

"You said you inherited the B and B, right?" he asked.

"I did. My Grandmother Regina left it to me. She knew I loved it here. She left Reggie stocks and bonds worth about the same as the B and B, so it was fair."

He grinned. "Fairness matters."

"When you're talking about siblings, yes, it does." She looked around the room. "I love this place and I've enjoyed owning it, but honestly, I would give it back in a heartbeat to have Grandmother Regina with us."

He believed her.

"She would be very proud of you."

Dena looked at him. "I hope so. I think she would have been concerned about me having a baby on my own, but she would have loved a great-grandchild."

"So you never thought of selling?"

"The B and B?" Her voice was a yelp. "No! Why would I do that? What a terrible thing to say."

He held up both hands in a gesture of surrender. "Sorry. I was just asking."

"Don't. Not that question. Sell the B and B. As if."

He tried to hide his smile. "You have a lot of energy on a lot of topics."

She opened her mouth to reply, then went completely white. He set down the small toy store he'd been about to put in place and moved to her side. After grabbing her wrist, he pressed in several places, automatically matching his breathing to hers, as if that would help ease her discomfort.

She closed her eyes. He felt her try to relax as her color went from white to green and she pressed her free hand to her stomach.

"Inhale," he murmured, aware of how close they were standing and how he could breathe in the scent of her shampoo. It was a citrusy scent—clean and appealing. He studied the freckles on her nose and across her cheeks, and the shape of her mouth. Wanting stirred.

"Count to four," he said, even as he heard a faint melody in the back of his mind. The notes moved like leaves in the wind, back and forth.

Thought I was strong, but I was in pain.

Because healing mattered. The spirit of the holidays was about hope and forgiveness and—

"Better," Dena said.

He blinked, bringing himself back to her. Her color had returned to normal, and she'd opened her eyes.

"You are very skilled. You should do a video for YouTube or something."

He released her wrist. "I'm sure there are plenty of videos about pressure points online."

"But you'd be an added attraction. 'Learn How Not to Throw Up, with Micah Ruiz.'" She wrinkled her nose. "It would probably need a catchier title."

"I don't know. That one is direct."

They smiled at each other. They were still standing close together. He found himself wanting to take that last half step and—

And what? Hug her? Hold her? Kiss her?

All valid questions, for which he had no answer. But

he liked that he was asking. Since losing Adriana, he hadn't felt any kind of desire, no need and certainly nothing close to curiosity about a woman. While he'd been in physical rehab, he'd been required to work on healing his mind, as well. He knew that his emotions would heal more slowly than his bones, but they would still recover.

He accepted that one day he would be open to caring about someone else. Physical interest was a good first step, he told himself, although one he had no idea how to manage. He didn't have a clue about what to do next, or even if there should be a next step. Dena had deliberately gotten pregnant on her own—hardly the act of a woman looking for a man.

"There wasn't even one guy you would have considered having father your baby?" he asked, before he could stop himself.

She blinked, as if trying to keep up with the change in topic. "You've seen Wishing Tree. It's not a big town, and I can assure you, there aren't a lot of age-appropriate single guys hanging around, waiting to fall in love with me." She smiled. "Besides, I'm not like you. I don't have a million guys falling all over me every time I walk down the street."

"Is that what you think happens?"

"Sort of."

"But I'm not into guys."

She laughed—a bright, happy sound that made him join in. The need to touch her cranked up just a little. He decided he would simply enjoy the feeling for now. If it lingered, then maybe he would do something about it.

"I meant, I don't have your array to choose from," she said.

"I'm not that guy anymore. I'm much happier being a one-woman man."

Her expression softened. "That's nice. I'll bet you were a great husband."

"I tried to be."

"Adriana was lucky," she said, turning back to the bins. "You loved her a lot. I'm sorry you lost the great love of your life."

It took him a second to realize what she meant. Dena was assuming he was saying that because there had been Adriana, there couldn't be anyone else, which wasn't what he'd meant at all. But given that he was only in town for a few weeks, and he wasn't sure how much he'd healed from the loss of his wife and son, it was probably best not to correct her. For his sake as well as hers.

Eleven

REGGIE CIRCLED HER MOTHER, taking in the lace overlay and long sleeves of the traditional wedding gown. It wasn't too fancy, and the fit was good. Her mother's devotion to Zumba and long hikes had kept her in excellent shape, so the V-neck sheath style should have looked amazing.

"I don't love it," Reggie admitted, stopping behind her mom and looking at her reflection in the full-length mirror. "I should. It's pretty, you're pretty, but it's just not…something."

Her mother sighed. "That's what I said. I look okay, but not great, and I don't feel good in it." She pointed to the open boxes on the bed behind them. "The others are the same. They fit, they're what I expected, but they're not right somehow."

"Maybe with your hair up," Reggie said, knowing she sounded doubtful.

Leigh shook her head. "That's not going to help. I don't know what the problem is."

"Why a traditional wedding gown?"

"Because I didn't wear one when we eloped. I wore a white suit that I hated."

"Is the goal to wear a traditional gown or to look and feel fabulous?"

"The latter."

"Then let's try something else. Why don't you change back into your regular clothes, and I'll go online and see what I can find that's going to make you happy?"

"Like what?"

"I don't know. I'm going to look at party dresses on the Nordstrom website."

"Okay, but remember, I'm not twenty-five anymore."

Reggie feigned shock. "You're not?"

"Ha-ha. Fine. Go look. I'll meet you in the kitchen in ten minutes."

Reggie started out of the room. Belle got up off the bed and followed her. As they walked into the hallway, Burt appeared from nowhere and darted toward Belle. He must have gotten close enough to nip, because she yelped and immediately danced backwards, bumping into the wall, then spinning as if to see who else was attacking her.

"Burt!" Reggie said, getting between them. "Pick on someone your own size." She stomped her foot to get his attention, but Burt was unimpressed.

"Put her back in with me," Reggie's mom called.

Reggie guided Belle into the bedroom and shut the door behind her. She glared at Burt.

"You think you're so big and brave, don't you? Belle is emotionally delicate. Why can't you be friends?"

Burt shot her an incredulous look before sauntering back toward the stairs. Reggie went into her own room to collect her laptop and headed for the kitchen.

She went onto the Nordstrom website. A quick search showed her that maybe party dresses weren't what her mother was looking for. They were all cute, and there were several Reggie would have liked to put in her own closet, but nothing really appropriate for a woman approaching sixty.

She tried mother-of-the-bride dresses next.

"Bingo," she said, scrolling through the collection.

When her mother walked in, Belle at her heels, Reggie patted the seat next to her.

"I think I've found a few really great options, Mom. The wedding colors are basically red and green, to take advantage of the holiday decorations in place. You'll want your dress to stand out."

Her mother wrinkled her nose. "Not black. I thought about that, and while I love a black dress, not for the wedding."

"I agree. So what about gray?"

Her mother's expression turned doubtful. "Gray? Really?"

Reggie showed her the dress she'd found online. The bodice had a sweetheart neckline, and the knit fabric was ruched on the bias. It was fitted to the waist, then fell straight to the floor. The sleeves, shoulder and back were done in matching lace.

"It's beautiful," Leigh breathed. "And it looks comfortable."

"The style would be so flattering, Mom. You'd need a strapless bra, but otherwise nothing special underneath."

Reggie showed her a second dress in more of a ball gown style. It had capped sleeves and a plunging V-neck. The top was embroidered and beaded to the hips, while the skirt was layers of matching tulle.

"Oh, I like that one, too. In some ways, it's a bit more of a wedding gown style." Her mother clicked between the two dresses. "Let's order them both and I'll try them on." She laughed. "One of them has to work or I'll be walking down the aisle in my bathrobe."

"That would certainly be memorable."

Reggie logged into her Nordstrom account and ordered the dresses, requesting a rush delivery to give them a little extra time.

"They should be here early next week," she said, closing her laptop.

"Good. If I keep one of them, I'll write you a check for the cost."

Her mother rose and walked over to the coffeepot on the counter. She poured them each a mug.

"So," she said, her voice casual. "Have you seen Toby since Thanksgiving?"

"Mom, it's been three days. When would I have seen him?"

"I don't know. Out and about. You take Belle for walks. You might have swung by his store. I don't keep track of you that closely. You know I'm not one of those mothers who meddles."

"Really? I wouldn't have guessed that, what with you inviting Toby over for Thanksgiving and not bothering to tell me. What were you thinking?"

Her mother sat across from her and smiled. "That Judy isn't a young woman anymore, and cooking a big dinner might be too much for her."

Which sounded very lovely and kind, but Reggie knew there had to be more going on than the desire to help out.

"Aren't there other people in town who also would have enjoyed a family meal?"

"Maybe, but I don't know them as well. You know, Harrison is a very sweet boy. Have you ever thought about what it would be like to be a stepmother?"

Reggie stared at her. "That's not even subtle."

"I've never seen the point in being subtle. Why not just say what you're thinking? You and Toby got along really well at dinner. You used to be madly in love with him. I'm sure the sex was good, so why not see if you still have chemistry? He's very successful, and he's a good father, and everything I've heard about him is positive." She sipped her coffee. "I'm simply saying you could do worse."

Reggie opened her mouth, then closed it. "I don't even know where to start," she admitted.

Thankfully her phone rang just then. She grabbed it, not bothering to look at the screen. "I have to take this."

Her mother rose and started out of the room. "Fine. Be a coward."

"Hello?"

"Hey, you. What's going on?"

Reggie recognized her sister's voice. "Your mother is making me insane. She wants me to start dating Toby."

"First of all, she's your mother, too."

"Right now I prefer to think of her as just yours."

Dena laughed. "Second, dating Toby isn't the worst idea ever."

"It's going to make the top five. We don't know each other. It's been years. I live in Seattle."

"Details. You had a good time with him on Thursday."

Reggie smiled. "I did, but that doesn't mean we should get married."

"I thought Mom wanted you to date him."

"She asked if I'd ever thought about being a step-mother."

"That *is* a leap."

"Tell me about it."

"He's a great dad," Dena said, her voice filled with laughter. "In case you were wondering."

"Don't you start, too!"

"All right. I really called to talk about what we're doing for Mom and Dad for the wedding. I've spent the last two hours on Pinterest, getting ideas. There are a lot of different options, but I think the slideshow is the best one. We can set it up on a loop and have it play during the entire reception."

Reggie nodded. She and Dena had been talking about doing something special for their parents. Their brainstorming had produced a handful of ideas, but the one she kept coming back to was the slideshow.

"I agree," she said. "I'll go through the pictures I already have on my computer and then start upload-ing more today. The albums are still in the craft room, aren't they?"

"Last time I checked."

"Good. Mom will think I'm downstairs working, so it will be a surprise. I want pictures from when they were first dating through now."

"Can I help? I feel like this is all falling on you."

"Dena, you're teaching full-time, running the B and B, and you're pregnant."

"I know, but you're already dealing with the charity project and your own job. This is too much."

"How about if I send you the pictures as I add them, and you can write the captions? I don't think we have to caption them all, just maybe a handful. If we have the year, that would help with the timeline."

"I can do that. Send me the files as soon as you're ready."

"I will."

They talked for a few more minutes, then hung up. Reggie looked at Belle, who was curled up in her bed in the corner of the eat-in kitchen.

"You know, I have more to do here than at home."

Belle looked at her as if to ask whose fault that was.

"Yes, I know," Reggie told her. "I can't help it. I've never been able to say no to family. Or you, for that matter."

Belle's expression said never saying no to her was hardly a bad thing.

"You're right, baby girl. Because you're special."

Toby arrived at the community center a little after two thirty on Monday afternoon. The third-graders were due at three, and he knew there would be materials to set up. He'd practiced making hats over the long weekend and was comfortable that he could help the kids.

He told himself that any sense of anticipation was more about getting started than seeing Reggie. She was his son's teacher's sister, and that was all. Yes, they'd had a good time at dinner and on the walk afterwards, but they were simply old friends getting to know each other again. Nothing more.

Still, he found himself hurrying toward the largest of the spaces in the community center. The double doors stood open, and he could see dozens of boxes stacked on large folding tables. He found Reggie opening a box of the hooks the kids would use.

She glanced up and smiled at him. For a second, he was transported back to all those years ago, when she'd looked him in the eye and told him he should ask her out. Her smile had been just as disorienting.

"You're here," she said. "Thanks for coming early. I didn't totally grasp how much setup there would be until about an hour ago."

"You should have called me. I could have come then."

"I'm nearly done."

Belle ambled over to greet Toby.

"Very festive," he said, nodding at the red-and-green sweater.

"She loves the holidays." She snapped her fingers. "Belle? Go lie down."

The Great Dane sighed heavily before making her way back to a large bed in the corner.

"Want to get started opening those boxes of yarn? I figured the kids can pick colors." She paused. "Forty kids, plus the parents. How about unpacking about a hundred skeins of yarn, in different colors. We can store the rest in the locked storage room, so it's always close by."

She tossed him a pocketknife and went back to counting out hooks. He made quick work of opening the boxes, then set out skeins of yarn in a rainbow of colors. Once he had enough, he collected the keys for the storage room and put away the extra yarn. By the time that was done, Reggie had set up her computer and pulled down the big screen at the front of the room.

Right on time, about forty third-graders trooped in the door, followed by a half-dozen volunteer parents. Reggie greeted them and introduced Belle.

"She's very delicate emotionally," she said. "So you have to be careful or you'll scare her."

Several of the kids, not to mention parents, looked doubtful.

"I'm not kidding. Just because she's big doesn't mean she's brave. But she does love company. That's why I brought her. Okay, let's get started."

Reggie quickly separated them into smaller groups, each with a parent. Toby sat at Harrison's table. Materials were passed out and yarn chosen.

"I've prepared a video demonstration of what we're going to be doing. It's pretty easy and fun. We're going to be meeting today, tomorrow and Thursday." She smiled. "We're skipping Wednesday because it's December first and the start of the town Advent calendar."

"We have to be there for that!" one boy said.

"I know, right? So let's make some hats."

Reggie started the video on her computer and walked everyone through casting on. Once that was done, they went to work on the brim.

Reggie circled through the tables, answering questions and fixing mistakes. She was patient and friendly, putting the kids at ease. He liked how she didn't rush anyone. Every now and then, she glanced at him and smiled. Something he wouldn't have noticed if he hadn't been looking in the first place.

He told himself to pay attention to his knitting and managed to make good progress on his hat. As he worked, he saw Belle get up and drag her bed a few feet before lying down again. It took him a few minutes to realize her destination.

"You have a fan," he told his son, who glanced at Belle and grinned. Harrison patted his thigh, and Belle dragged her bed the rest of the way before settling close enough to be within petting distance.

Once the brim was finished, Reggie explained how to work on the body of the hat. Toby got up and checked in with the students at his table, to make sure everyone got how to make the transition. After a few minutes, Reggie put on Christmas music.

At the end of their hour-and-a-half session, Reggie handed out paper bags for the half-finished projects. The kids wrote their names on the bags so they could start back up tomorrow. By five, everyone had left.

Reggie shut down her laptop and turned off the portable speaker she'd brought.

"That was great. Nearly everyone got through at least half a hat, and with some parents doing extra, we're going to have a good number to take to the shelter."

"I'll make a few over the weekend," he offered.

She laughed. "I would pay money to see that."

"You've already seen me working on my hat."

"Yes, but it's different here than in your kitchen."

"I'll work in the media room with manly sports on the TV."

"Of course you will."

Harrison sat by Belle, petting her back. "Dad, can Reggie and Belle have pizza with us tonight?"

A great idea and one he should have thought of. He

looked at her. "Monday is pizza night. Not Judy's favorite, so she stays home."

Reggie glanced between him and Harrison. "I'm afraid Belle isn't allowed in restaurants."

"Oh." Harrison studied the dog, then looked at Toby. "We could get pizza to go."

"Are you sure?" He turned to Reggie. "The pizza place has pinball machines. Harrison's been getting good."

Harrison wrapped his arms around Belle's neck. "Yes. I don't want Belle to be alone."

"She'd be with my parents," Reggie told him.

"Yeah, but Burt's mean to her."

Reggie smiled. "Thank you, Harrison. That's a big sacrifice to make. Belle and I would be delighted to join you for dinner."

"Come over at six?" Toby asked.

"Sounds good. I'll take Belle home now and feed her. While she loves pizza, it doesn't love her back."

"Does she get sick?" Harrison asked, looking worried.

"Nope. She gets gas and it's bad."

Harrison started laughing. "Belle, do you fart?"

Belle licked his cheek.

Reggie picked up Belle's leash. "Come on, sweet girl. Let's get you fed. We're going out tonight."

REGGIE AND BELLE arrived right at six. Reggie told herself not to read too much into the invitation, as it had come from Harrison and not Toby. This was just an evening with friends, nothing more, despite her mother's speculative look. On the bright side, Leigh had offered a Bundt cake for dessert.

"Hi," Toby said, opening the door. "Right on time. The pizza should be here in a few minutes."

He stepped back to let her and Belle inside.

Belle moved cautiously, unsure. She'd just started to tremble when she spotted Harrison and nearly broke her leash trying to get to him.

"You're here!" Harrison rushed forward, grinning.

Reggie unclipped Belle's leash. "Maybe you could show her around so she gets comfortable. Oh, and watch her tail. When she wags it, she can clear off a coffee table in seconds."

The next few minutes were filled with unwrapping Reggie's layers and then helping Harrison find the right place for Belle's bed. Reggie chatted with Judy while Toby and Harrison set the table. Reggie admired the giant tree in the family room and the elegant garland on the stair banister.

"Professionally decorated," Judy said with a shake of her head. "Toby and his father used to walk out into the woods and chop down a tree."

"We'll have a real tree upstairs next week," Harrison said eagerly. "Then we all decorate it ourselves. I can't wait!"

The doorbell rang, and Toby went to get the pizza. Judy retreated to her room. Reggie, Toby and Harrison sat at the kitchen table, with Belle lying in the corner.

"Today was fun," Harrison said, taking a slice of pepperoni pizza. "We're going to make a lot of hats."

"We are," Reggie said, going for the mushroom pizza. "It's a good project. I'm glad you thought of it."

The pizza was delicious but couldn't distract from the surreal nature of the moment, she thought. Hard to believe that until a couple of weeks ago, she hadn't thought of Toby in years, and yet here she was, in his home, eating dinner with him and his son.

His home appeared new, with expensive touches. He'd come a long way from the teenager who'd lived in what was then the poorer part of town. Back then his number one goal was not to be a drunk like his dad, but beyond that, he hadn't had much direction. Obviously he'd found his way.

Twelve

ONCE THEY'D FINISHED dinner and had put away the left-overs, the four of them went upstairs. Harrison showed Reggie and Belle his room, then begged his father to let him watch a movie with Belle. The Great Dane was all in when it came to lying on the sofa with her favorite boy. Reggie and Toby left them and went to his spacious office at the end of the hall.

"How many rooms are there?" Reggie asked as he put down the wine bottle and glasses he'd carried upstairs.

"The usual amount."

She thought about what she'd seen downstairs. "Let me guess. Five bedrooms, a bonus room, a home office and possibly a basement."

His appealing smile turned sheepish.

"That's right. We have just over five thousand square feet."

"Nice."

This office had a big desk, built-in bookshelves and a comfortable-looking sofa against the far wall. Behind it were pictures—of Harrison from infant to now, and of Judy's Hand Pies food trucks and a storefront she didn't recognize.

He followed her gaze. "That was the first one," he said. "I opened it in Austin."

"You have an empire."

"Of sorts."

They took seats on the sofa, and he poured her a glass of wine. She took it and looked around.

"I'm shocked. You didn't have the decorators turn this room into a Christmas paradise. Why is that?"

"You know I don't care about that kind of stuff for myself. It's important to celebrate for Judy and Harrison."

"You like it, too."

"Not as much as they do."

"The tree downstairs is beautiful. Magazine-worthy. But I'm going to guess the one you do with Judy and your son is more meaningful."

"It is."

She eyed him over her glass of wine. He looked like what he was—a successful and content man. His gold-blond hair was a little darker than it had been back in high school, and the shape of his face was sharper. His eyes were the same color blue. Sort of medium with a hint of gray.

He'd been good with the students today, helping them with their hats. Not that she should be surprised. He was a great dad. So, why wasn't he married, and where was Harrison's mother?

Although she wasn't comfortable asking the question directly, she didn't mind hinting at it.

"You were young when you had Harrison," she said as casually as she could.

"Twenty-two." He set down his glass. "When I left here my senior year of high school, I just wanted to get away. I ended up in Texas. I figured it was big, and there were plenty of spaces to get lost."

"Your goal was to get lost?"

"I was all of eighteen. I might have been a bit dramatic in my thinking."

"How did you support yourself?"

"I worked construction. I would hang out at sites, and if someone didn't show up, I filled in." He smiled. "Not with the big equipment. They didn't let me do that, but there's always plenty of grunt work that doesn't require training. I became a regular, and the money was decent. I started in Lubbock, then went to Dallas. While I was there, I met a girl."

"Just one?" she asked, careful to keep her voice light and teasing. She wanted him to keep talking.

"Okay, more than one, but this particular one was more significant. Her name is Anne, and she was…" He paused, then studied her. "A lot like you."

"Everything you've ever wanted in a woman?" she joked.

The smile returned. "It was more a personality thing. Or maybe *attitude* is a better word. Anyway, we were a thing for six months, but then I wanted to move and she didn't. The parting was amicable enough and I headed to Austin."

He sipped his wine. "I liked it there. I got a steady job, still in construction, rented a decent apartment instead of some crappy room, and decided I would settle there."

Interesting, considering he was now back in Wishing Tree. "And?"

"About ten months later, I got a text from Anne. She wanted to see me." He shook his head. "I assumed she couldn't live without me and wanted to talk about moving to Austin so we could get back together." He glanced at Reggie. "I was wrong."

"She was pregnant? No, wait. Ten months later means she had to have already given birth."

"Yeah, that. We agreed to meet at a coffee place. I was excited to see her, making all kinds of plans in my head. But she didn't want to get back together. She walked in carrying Harrison and said he was my son."

He looked past her to something she couldn't see. "I didn't know what to think or say. One second I was a happy, single guy, and the next, I was a father of a three-month-old."

He returned his gaze to hers. "She said she couldn't do it—she couldn't be a mom. It was too hard, and Harrison needed too much. She was offering him to me. If I didn't want him, she was going to turn him over to the state."

"What?" Reggie nearly came out of her seat, unable to believe what she was hearing. Seriously? Anne had done that? What kind of human being was she? "She was going to give him up? Just like that? She is nothing like me. I would never do that."

He smiled. "I know, and you can relax. The story has a happy ending."

"Are you going to defend her and say it's not her

fault? She's the mother. She should have tried. And where was her family? Why weren't they helping?"

Amusement darkened his eyes. "You have some thoughts on the subject."

"Of course I do. Dena's going to be a single mom, and you know we're all going to be fighting over time with the baby. We'll be there for her. I'm already planning to move back home for the first few months after the baby's born so I can help."

"I'm not even surprised."

She picked up her wine and waved at him. "Okay, go on. I won't interrupt again."

"Yes, you will."

"Probably, but we can hope I don't."

He chuckled. "I told her I'd take him. She had all his stuff in her car. She'd written down a few instructions. Once she gave those to me, she told me to find a lawyer, and she would sign whatever she had to. She was done being a mother. And then she drove off."

"Leaving you standing by the side of the road, with a baby in your arms? That's insane. How would you know what to do? You'd never even changed a diaper."

"You're right. I didn't know anything. My first call was to Judy to ask her to come stay with me. My second was to a guy I worked with. He was married with a couple of little kids. They let me come over, and his wife showed me the basics. By the time I picked up Judy at the airport, I could fix a bottle and change a diaper. But I still didn't know how I was going to survive. Who was going to take care of Harrison while I worked?"

"The dilemma of single parents everywhere."

"It is. Judy was willing to stay for a few weeks, but then she had to get home to my dad."

She heard the edge in his voice and knew better than to ask about his father. She wanted to hear more about his early years with Harrison, and talking about Toby's father would send them spiraling to a place neither of them wanted to go.

She still couldn't believe how Anne had acted. If she hadn't wanted the kid, why have the child in the first place? Or if she wasn't willing to have an abortion, then arrange for an adoption from birth. There were thousands of wonderful couples eager to adopt a baby. But to keep him and then change her mind? That wasn't right.

"We brainstormed ways for me to make money from home," he said. "It's harder than you'd think. None of the ideas worked for me. I didn't have any work-from-home skills that I could use, and trying to work as a handyman didn't solve the day care situation. Then she suggested selling hand pies."

His mouth twisted. "There were plenty of times when I was a kid that the money from those was all we had. Remember how she would sell to friends and neighbors?"

"I do," Reggie said, her voice soft. "My mom always wanted to know when Judy was making them. We loved having them for dinner."

"I took a couple of days off work. We baked all weekend. Made as many as we could. Then Monday, I sold them at the construction site. They were gone in minutes. Tuesday, I brought in even more and took them to another construction site. The same thing happened. By the time she was ready to go back home, word had spread about the hand pies, and guys were showing up at the two construction sites, buying me out in less than an hour. I had my home business."

"How did you make it work with Harrison?" she asked, trying to absorb everything he told her.

"It was hard at first, going to construction sites with Harrison in his car seat. I started making pies as soon as I got back from selling them at lunch. I worked until about midnight, then grabbed a few hours of sleep before getting up and working more. That was all I did—I was either taking care of him or making pies. Once my bills were paid, I used the extra money to buy a couple more ovens and a second refrigerator." He smiled. "I'm sure I violated a lot of health codes, but I never got caught."

"Ah, the heart of a bad boy never changes."

"In some respects. It took me six months to save up enough to buy a food truck, and that helped a lot. I set up different locations where I would be every week and started developing a following."

"One truck became three and so on?" she asked.

"Pretty much. Within two years I had a fleet of food trucks in the Austin metro area. Five years later, I'd expanded to the big cities in Texas and was moving into California. I'd also opened a couple of stores, and they were successful. Today I have two hundred trucks and ten stores, and we're in fifteen cities."

Jeez, that was impressive. She'd known he was successful, but hearing it from him was different.

"Including Wishing Tree," she said with a smile.

"It's my favorite store. It means I get to be around whenever Harrison needs me."

She glanced at the wall of pictures. "You should

have its picture up there." She frowned, then leaned forward to study the photographs. "Is that bottom one of the old hardware store?"

"Yes."

She looked from it to him. "I'm surprised. You always had a complicated relationship with the store."

He'd been twelve when he'd first started working there, trying to help out when his dad was too drunk to care about things like opening or stocking inventory. As Toby had gotten older, he'd taken on more responsibility. Once they'd started dating, they'd spent hours together in the store. She'd learned all about tools and how to repair things like a faucet or a light fixture.

"It wasn't the store," he said. "It was my dad." He exhaled. "Judy had that picture framed for me when I was putting up photographs. I didn't want to tell her I'd rather not stare at it every time I came in here."

Involuntarily, she reached out and touched his arm. "I'm sorry. That's hard for you."

"It's a picture. I can handle it."

She dropped her hand back to her lap. "Your dad sold the store right about the time you left, didn't he?"

Toby looked at her. "He didn't sell it, Reggie. He lost it. He didn't pay the lease or for his inventory, and they took it from him. He got mad and blamed me for not doing enough." He looked away. "He came after me with a baseball bat the day he lost the store. I knew then if I stayed, he would kill me. So I took off."

"What?"

The word burst out before she could stop it. One corner of Toby's mouth turned up.

"You thought I left because of you?"

There was no way to change the truth, she thought,

fighting embarrassment. "It crossed my mind. We'd just broken up, and it was all your fault. I thought you were handling it badly."

"I did. I was crushed, but I didn't take off because of you."

"I'm chagrined."

"Don't be. It's a logical thing to assume. And speaking of mistakes, I didn't blab about that night."

She stared at her wine, not sure what to say.

The night of prom, after dating for more than a year and knowing she would love Toby forever, she'd finally been ready to give herself to him. They'd gotten close dozens of times, but she'd always held back on going all the way. But that night, knowing how much he meant to her, she'd given him her virginity. Tuesday morning at school, Paisley had warned her everyone was talking about the fact that Toby had told the football team she was the best sex of his life.

She'd been devastated by the betrayal and humiliated beyond words. She'd called her mom to ask if she could come home. When her dad found out, he'd threatened to take Toby out back. She'd told him she would take care of Toby herself and had broken up with him. Three days later, he'd been gone.

"It wasn't me," he repeated. "Reggie, you know me well enough to know I wouldn't do that."

She raised her gaze to his. "I didn't think you would, but then how did it happen?"

"I don't know. I only told Brian." He grimaced. "It was in the locker room, so someone must have overheard us. That's the only thing I can think of to explain what happened." He looked into her eyes. "I loved you, and I would never have knowingly hurt you."

Despite the years and the miles, hearing him say he'd loved her still gave her the same tingle it had back when she'd been all of seventeen.

"I know," she told him. "I didn't then, not at first, but I do now, and I believe you. It was just such a shock and so awful. Even after we broke up, I assumed we would figure it out, but then you were gone."

"I'm sorry."

"It's not your fault."

"I should have told you why I left."

She smiled. "I should have listened when you wanted to explain."

They looked at each other. Reggie felt some shift in the energy between them, but didn't know what that meant. Nor was she going to pursue the topic.

"You were a good boyfriend," she said with a smile. "I'm guessing that's still true, so why didn't you bring a wife back to Wishing Tree?"

She'd thought he would give her a funny response, but instead his face went blank and he turned away.

"I'm not getting married anytime soon."

There was something in his voice, a finality along with a hint at dark secrets she knew she couldn't ask about.

As quickly as his mood changed, it shifted back again to easygoing Toby.

"What about you? It's been over a year since you and Jake broke up. There must be a guy in your life."

"One would think," she said lightly. "But one would be wrong." She shrugged. "It took me a while to get over him, and since then, I've gone out some, but just casually. So far I haven't met anyone relationship-worthy."

A statement that seemed designed to make things

awkward, she thought, setting down her wineglass and coming to her feet.

"This has been fun," she said. "But I need to get Belle and head home. She gets really cranky if she doesn't get enough sleep."

For a second she thought Toby was going to call her on her bolt for freedom, but he only nodded and rose.

"A cranky Great Dane can't be fun. Come on, I'll walk you out."

Fifteen minutes later, as she drove home, Reggie told herself she'd made the smart decision. Lingering would only have led to—well, she wasn't sure what, but something complicated. She and Toby had a past, but that was no reason to assume they had a future. Better to keep things casual and friendly. Or maybe just safer.

MICAH FIGURED HE'D clocked about ten miles since he'd left the B and B. He was still frustrated by his inability to write, so he'd decided to walk until he had something close to a creative thought.

He'd walked through several residential sections of town before heading west to Gray Wolf Lake. Then he'd gone south, bundled up against the freezing temperatures.

All the houses he passed were decorated for the holidays. Santas and reindeer dotted lawns, and wreaths hung in windows. About an hour into his journey, he realized there weren't any snowmen anywhere. Obviously not real ones, what with there being no snow, but also no plastic or ceramic ones. Now that he thought about it, Dena hadn't used snowmen in her decorating at the B and B. Was it a town thing? Some tradition he didn't know about? He would have to ask her.

He paused to check for traffic before crossing the street. There weren't a lot of people walking and not that many cars. He knew if he headed for the center of town, he would run into more pedestrians. The area around The Wreath was always busy.

He wondered what Adriana would have thought of Wishing Tree. Would she have seen the charm of the place, as he did, or would she have thought it was too small? Neither of them had grown up with much in the way of a community. The longest he'd lived anywhere had been when he'd stayed with Steve in high school. He and Adriana had bought the house in Malibu—the one he rarely went back to. Not so much because of any memories, but more because he didn't see the point of returning. It had never been a home for either of them.

He supposed if she hadn't been killed, everything would have been different. That house would have been where they'd brought their baby. They would have made memories there. As it was, he knew he should sell the place, and he would. Just as soon as he figured out where he was going to settle.

He continued south on Celebration Pass, then turned left on Virginia Street. About a dozen kids came running toward him, passing him with an eagerness that told him it must be just after three and school had let out. His step quickened as he hurried up the front stairs and into the main building. This hadn't been his destination, but now that he was here, it seemed rude not to stop by and say hello.

He checked in at the front office and asked if he could go by Dena's classroom. The receptionist recognized him from his last visit and waved him down the hall.

"She's still here," the woman said with a smile.

Micah walked toward the classroom. A couple of older students were in the hallway, talking intently. He saw the door standing open and walked inside, only to find Dena speaking with what he would guess was one of the parents. Both women turned when he entered.

He came to a stop. "Sorry. I didn't mean to interrupt. I'll wait in the hall."

Dena smiled at him, but before she could speak, the other woman, a pretty redhead in her early thirties, gaped at him.

"OMG! You're Micah Ruiz. No, you can't be." She turned to Dena. "Is he? OMG! Is it really you?"

Dena laughed. "It's really him. Micah, this is Lindsey, one of my classroom moms."

Lindsey still looked wide-eyed. "I love you. I mean, I love your music. This is incredible. How are you here? What's going on?" She looked at Dena. "You *know* him?"

"We go way back," Micah teased. "As for how I got here, I flew. Not me personally, of course."

"I'm shaking," Lindsey admitted, holding up a trembling hand. "Can we take a picture? Please? This is incredible."

Micah moved close. "Sure. Let's take a couple."

He handed the phone to Dena, who looked slightly chagrined as she snapped several photos. Lindsey checked them out before nodding.

"These are great. Thank you so much. I'm having a day. I stopped by to tell Dena that I can't finish my class mom duties this month. My husband's in the army, and he's stationed in Germany. My parents surprised me with airline tickets for me and the kids to join him, and we're leaving in three days. Then I met you."

Tears filled her eyes. "It's just I miss him so much, and he's a big fan, too."

Micah sensed her emotions were spiraling out of control. "Your children are going to be excited to see their father," he said, trying to distract her from focusing on him. "They'll remember the trip a lot longer than any toy. Is it a direct flight?"

"What? Oh, we fly to Frankfurt, then go from there. They're so excited to see him. I am, too."

"Then you need to go home and start getting ready," Dena told her. "Lindsey, don't worry about anything here. I'll get someone to fill in for you. As for Martina's schoolwork, I'll have her assignments pulled together before you leave. She's such a bright girl and always motivated. Don't worry about her missing out. She'll catch up easily. Besides, this is a trip of a lifetime. She's going to get so much out of it."

"I know, right?" Lindsey collected her bag. "Thanks for understanding." She looked at Micah and waved her phone. "Thanks for the pictures."

"Anytime."

When she'd left, Dena sat on the corner of her desk. "To quote Lindsey, OMG. She went crazy."

"Naw, that was nothing. She was polite, she spoke in complete sentences and she didn't ask me to sign any part of her body or offer to have sex with me."

"That happens?"

"It does." He sighed regretfully. "You've never once fawned over me. I'll admit I'm disappointed."

Something flashed in her eyes, then was gone. "I've

never been the fawning type, but I can try to make the effort."

"No. If it's not genuine, it doesn't count." He slumped his shoulders. "I'll get over the pain."

She laughed. "I'm happy to hear that. I would hate to be responsible for breaking the spirit of a famous rock star."

He straightened. "Thanks for distracting her by gently asking her to leave."

"I didn't ask her to leave," Dena said. "I just pointed out she was busy. And now that I know how difficult things can get, I'm glad I did."

"What does a classroom mom do?"

"Sometimes it's a dad," she said. "He or she comes in for a couple of hours every week for the month, usually with a snack, and does something with the students. It can be a craft or activity. Sometimes the parents just read to them."

She moved behind her desk and sat down. "The purpose is to give the teacher a little time to get caught up on paperwork or whatever it is we're behind on that day."

"Could I do it?"

She stared at him. "Why would you want to?"

"You need help. I'm available. I like kids."

"Micah, that's sweet, but you don't want to take this on. The snack alone is complicated. It has to be kid-friendly, but no nuts and not all sugar-based. And it's two hours. That's a long time with fifteen eight-year-olds staring at you."

He shrugged. "It's just for December, right? And school gets out for the holidays, so it's what? Three times? I can handle it."

"But—"

"People are going to be busy," he added, determined to convince her. Being the classroom dad would give him something to look forward to and would be a distraction. Right now, given his complete lack of talent, he needed to be distracted. "You won't be able to find someone on short notice, so here I am, volunteering. You should say yes."

"You're trying to write a song."

"Yeah, well, that's not going well. Besides, I liked career day."

"I guess you could play music. They'd like that."

He wanted to ask if she would as well, but told himself going there could make things weird between them, and he liked how they were right now.

"Good. Give me the particulars and I'll get started on my lesson plan."

Her lips twitched as if she were trying not to smile. "It's two hours and a snack, Micah. You're not going to need a lesson plan."

"I like to be prepared."

Thirteen

REGGIE STOOD WITH her mom in the lobby of the resort. Although she hadn't been inside for over a year, she felt as if she knew every inch of the space. When she and Jake had been dating, she'd often met him here after he was done working. They would grab a drink or dinner, then head upstairs to the suite where he lived.

She took a breath and tried to figure out if she was feeling any lingering discomfort being back, but there didn't seem to be much beyond the sense that she wasn't really a big hotel wedding kind of person. If she were to get married—and her plan was that one day she would—she was thinking maybe a summer wedding in her parents' backyard. Or a beach destination wedding.

She heard a familiar voice calling her name and smiled when she saw Paisley approaching.

"Right on time," Paisley said, hugging them both, then smiling at Leigh.

"How's our lovely bride?"

"I'm excited. This is such a beautiful hotel, and I love all the holiday decorations."

"We do our best."

Paisley led them down the wide hallway toward the ballrooms. There were ten-foot Christmas trees lined up on both sides. When they reached the main ballroom, even larger trees flanked the double doors.

"This is it," Paisley said, opening one of the doors and motioning for them to go inside. "Now, don't be concerned about how big and open the ballroom is. We're going to be dividing it for you. One third will be seating for the ceremony, and the rest will be set up with tables and the dance floor."

The space was large, with high ceilings. There was a huge fireplace at each end, and beautiful chandeliers hung overhead. Reggie knew there was a great sound system for the DJ to tap into.

Paisley glanced at her notes. "You wanted round tables of eight. Is that correct?"

"Yes. Eight is more intimate than ten. I want people to be able to talk to each other."

Paisley showed them where the room would be split and then laid out a few floorplans for the tables. Leigh quickly picked the one she liked.

"I have linen samples to show you," Paisley said, then shook her head. "Which I left in my office. I'll be right back."

She excused herself and hurried out of the ballroom. Reggie's mother looked around.

"It will be so beautiful. They're going to have poinsettias on shelving in the shape of Christmas trees all along the walls, and the centerpieces are green and silver."

"Perfect for either of the dresses on order."

Her mother turned to her. "Is this too hard on you, darling?"

"What are you talking about?"

"Being here? I should have come on my own."

"Mom, I have no idea what you're talking about."

"Being here at the resort. Does it bring back memories of Jake? You two hung out here all the time. He used to be the assistant manager. I've been thoughtless. I'm so sorry."

Reggie shook her head. "Mom, no. Don't give it another thought. I'm fine. Jake and I are long over, and the hotel is perfect for you and Dad. I'm glad you chose it."

Her mother studied her. "Are you sure it's all right?"

"Totally and completely."

"All right. I'm choosing to believe you."

"Thank you."

Leigh sighed. "This town needs another hotel. This one is always full. Dena's B and B does great business. I think we could handle more tourists."

Reggie grinned. "You should bring that up with the city council."

"I just might."

Paisley returned with several cloth napkins and a huge three-ring binder.

"Let's sit over here," she said, leading them to a long folding table with several chairs. "We'll pick out linens, then talk about the menu."

She showed them the options for tablecloths and napkins.

"With the poinsettias and the centerpieces, we'll be heavy on red already," Paisley said. "So I would suggest we steer clear of those. We can go with classic white, or various shades of green." She pointed to a black napkin. "Black is elegant, but I'm not sure it's the tone you want to set so close to Christmas."

"Not black," Leigh said. "I like the white, but I'm afraid it will be too plain."

"Do you have table runners?" Reggie asked.

Paisley brightened. "We do. In all these colors."

Reggie folded the green napkin into thirds, then placed it over a white napkin. "What about this? You go with white and add a table runner. With silver chargers under the place settings, it will give a little color but not overwhelm the table."

"I love it," Leigh said. "Oh, Paisley, show Reggie the centerpieces."

Paisley pulled a picture from her folder. Reggie studied the arrangement with three thick red candles surrounded by greenery and decorated with small red ornaments.

"We offer a house centerpiece over the holidays," Paisley explained. "We buy these in bulk and then have them available for all the events scheduled."

"Your father and I only have to pay a small percentage of the cost," Leigh added. "I think they're lovely."

"They are." Reggie smiled at her friend. "That's a great idea."

"Thank you." Paisley grinned. "I thought of it myself and everything."

They finalized the linens and discussed how the table would be set, then moved on to menus.

Paisley opened the large binder. "Dinners for our

weddings are a pre-set menu, but you can choose from multiple options of three courses. The cost includes plated service and the tip, so what you see is your out-the-door price. We can also provide appetizers, either as stations set up around the room or served on trays."

She took out several pages and spread them on the table. "The different prices of the meals reflect the number of options and what the options are. A chicken breast is less than a steak. Three options for an entrée cost more than just two. Oh, and a vegetarian entrée is always included in the price, so even a two-option selection will give you a vegetarian entrée at no additional charge."

Reggie was glad she was sitting. The dinner prices started at eighty dollars a person. Eighty!

"What about the cake?" she asked, grateful she didn't sound too breathless as she spoke.

"I've already ordered that," Leigh said as she looked through the various menus. "I like this one."

Reggie glanced over her shoulder and nearly shrieked when she saw the hundred and forty dollar per person price.

"Mom?" she asked, her voice faint. "That's the one?"

"Yes." Leigh passed it over. "What do you think?"

The dinner started with a soup-salad combination that included butternut squash soup with truffle oil. The main course selections were filet mignon, lamb or wild salmon. The vegetarian entrée was a portobello mushroom stuffed with cornbread and wild mushrooms. Dessert was a trio of a mini chocolate pot de crème, a chocolate cheesecake lollipop and a shot of Baileys Irish Cream in a chocolate cup.

"I think I'd want seconds of everything," Reggie

murmured, terrified to do the math of a hundred twenty guests at that price per person.

"Me, too," Leigh said. "We'll do that, plus some appetizers. I think a couple of stations is easier for everyone than having servers walk around."

Paisley entered the information on her tablet, then discussed the wine selections. As Reggie didn't know much about wine, she stayed out of that discussion, and for her own peace of mind, she didn't look at the price of the various bottles.

An hour later, they were finished. Leigh handed over a check to cover the deposit on the food costs and thanked Paisley, and they were on their way. Once in the parking lot, Reggie turned to her mother.

"Are you sure about this?" she asked. "It's a lot of money. Shouldn't you and Dad be saving for your retirement or something?"

Her mother smiled at her. "Darling, we're going to come live with you. Didn't we tell you?" She laughed. "You're a love to worry, but we can afford this. The business does very well, and we've never been extravagant. This is something I've wanted to do for years. Now that it's happening, I'm going to make it as special as I can."

"If you say so. Don't get me wrong, everything is going to be incredible, but the prices."

"I looked them up online, so I had an idea what I was getting into," her mother admitted. "Otherwise, I would have fainted at the table."

"I nearly did."

Her mother laughed. "On the bright side, it's going to be a night to remember."

Reggie was sure she was right about that.

THE WAVE OF nausea came without warning. Dena struggled to press her fingers on her wrist and forearm, but it was too late. She barely made it to the B and B kitchen sink in time to throw up.

Ursula, her fortysomething chef, wrinkled her nose. "Really? You couldn't run to the bathroom?"

Dena was still busy trying to catch her breath and decide if this was a onetime thing or she was going to barf again. She stayed where she was, breathing and willing herself to be calm. The sensation passed, leaving her only a little shaky.

"Sorry," she said. "I didn't have any warning."

"This is why I never had children," Ursula grumbled. "First you throw up, then they throw up. It's too many fluids for me."

Dena laughed. "There's more to having a baby than fluids."

"Yeah, you can't drink and you get hemorrhoids. I remind my friends of that when they try to convince me God's a woman. There's no way God's a woman."

Dena quickly rinsed out the sink, then reached for the disinfecting cleanser. Ursula swooped in and grabbed it from her.

"You can't use that. What if you breathed in the fumes and gave birth to an ostrich? No way, missy. Wash your hands and take the food out to the dining room. I'll clean the sink."

"You're very sweet to me."

Her chef glared at her. "I'm not. Never say that. What are you thinking? I'm crabby and difficult. Now, wash your hands and get out of here."

Dena did as she was told. Once her hands were clean, she pulled two serving platters from the cupboard and set them on the counter. She removed large baking sheets from the two ovens, inhaling the scent of melting cheese, potato and bacon. Her stomach growled.

She moved the loaded potato skins to the platter and carried them into the dining room, where several guests were already gathering, most of them with wineglasses in their hands.

"Hello," she said cheerfully, surprised to see Micah among the crowd. "You're going to love these, I promise. Ursula has worked her usual magic. If anyone needs me to change a dinner reservation to later, just let me know."

"Because we're going to get full?" Mr. Bingly asked with a laugh.

"You're going to be very tempted," she said as she put down two platters. "Be sure to try all the sauces. Each one is delicious."

She pushed the stack of plates closer to the food, moving a snow globe with silver glitter and a cardinal to the side to make room, then stepped back.

"Enjoy, everyone."

Her guests all lined up to try the potato skins. Only Micah hung back, walking toward her rather than the food.

He looked amazing, she thought, ignoring the hitch in her breathing. Not just his face, but how he held himself, and when he smiled, she wasn't sure if she was going to melt from the inside out or go up in flames. Not exactly appealing visuals, but genuine nonetheless.

"Hi," he said, stopping in front of her. "How are you feeling?"

"I threw up in the prep sink," she admitted with a sigh. "Ursula was totally grossed out."

"Ursula needs to give you a break." He held out a small box. "I ordered these for you. I'm not sure if they're going to work, but you can try them."

She looked down at the small brown box. "You bought me a gift?"

The smile returned. "Don't get too excited. They're bracelets people wear to stop motion sickness. There are instructions inside, telling you where to place them. Based on the research I did over the weekend, they help about seventy percent of women with morning sickness."

"I don't understand," she whispered. "You did research, then ordered these for me?"

"Sure. You're not feeling well. What else would I do?"

Her pesky hormones went into overdrive, making her lower lip tremble and her eyes fill with tears. He was being nice. *So* nice, and he was so easy to look at, and she just wanted to throw herself at him and have him hold her and kiss her and—

Stop! She had to stop or she would humiliate herself!

She took a step back and tried to smile. "Thank you, Micah. You're very thoughtful. Now, you really need to try the potato skins. They're delicious and they go fast. Try the dill sauce. It's my favorite. I think you'll really like it. She uses fresh dill because, well, that's what you'd use, right?"

She knew she was babbling but didn't know how to stop, so she thanked him again, then turned and bolted. When she was safely upstairs in her apartment, she quickly texted her sister.

**I need to see you. Please tell me you can get away
and meet me somewhere.**

The reply came almost instantly.

**Sure. Mom and Dad are out with friends and I was
just about to rummage in the refrigerator for some
dinner. Want to meet at Joy's Diner?**

Perfect. See you there in ten minutes.

You okay?

Dena had no idea how to answer the question, so
she texted back a quick I'm fine before grabbing her
coat and gloves, then heading outside for the quick
walk to Joy's Diner.

She arrived first and was able to grab a booth in the
back. Reggie arrived about two minutes later, hurrying to join her.

"Hey, you," her sister said, hugging her before sliding into the booth. "What's going on? Are you okay?"

"I'm fine. The baby's fine. It's just…" Dena honestly didn't know how to explain her situation without
sounding ridiculous, but maybe that was the point. She
was ridiculous and should just accept it.

Their server appeared at the table to take their order.
They agreed to split a chocolate mint milkshake. Dena
chose the chicken salad croissant sandwich, substitut-
ing a salad for the fries, while Reggie asked for a Reu-
ben with extra fries.

"Because I know the salad is just for show," her

sister said when the server left. "You'll start sneaking fries off my plate and then I won't have any."

Dena tried to smile. "That is a real possibility."

Reggie leaned forward. "You sound okay and you look good, so that's encouraging, but panic is right here, under the surface. Please tell me what's going on."

Dena nodded. "Do you know who Micah Ruiz is?"

Reggie frowned. "Sure. He's the lead singer for Darryl John James. I like his music. How would you know about him? You only like country music."

"Yes, there is that, but this isn't about music so much as the man himself." She drew in a breath and reminded herself that her sister loved her and would never laugh in her face or otherwise hurt her feelings.

"I have a crush on him. A big one, and it's getting hard to control."

Reggie rolled her eyes. "We all do. Have you seen him? He's the definition of gorgeous. Those eyes."

"Not like that. I mean in real life."

Their server returned with their milkshake already split between two smaller glasses. He winked. "I gave each of you a little extra whipped cream."

"Thanks," Reggie said with a laugh. "A man who understands women. We appreciate it."

When they were alone, Dena leaned toward her again. "I know him. He's staying at the B and B. We've met. We've talked. He came to career day at my class. He's funny and sweet and when I get nauseous, he does this thing with my wrists that makes it all go away."

Reggie's eyes widened and her mouth fell open. "You know him? Are you telling me Micah Ruiz is in Wishing Tree right this second and you're just telling me now? How did I not know this? I'm so going to complain to Paisley. She's supposed to know everything happening in town. She tells us there's going to be a Snow King and Queen next year, but she doesn't think to mention Micah Ruiz has moved to town?"

Dena motioned for her sister to lower her voice. "You're missing the point."

"I don't think I am. He's really here?"

Dena groaned. "Yes. At the B and B, probably eating potato skins and worrying that I'm slipping into madness. I would have told you before, but he's a guest, and I try to respect their privacy, and it didn't seem important."

"We need to work on your definition of *important*."

"Again, hardly the point."

"Oh, I would say it's totally the point." Reggie stared at her. "Micah Ruiz? Start at the beginning."

Dena explained about the music and running into him and how they'd shared late-night mini pizzas and the pressure point technique and that he was the new classroom dad for the month of December.

"I felt something the first time we met," Dena added. "But that was just superficial chemistry. Now I know him, and I like him even more."

She had to stop talking while their food was served.

"He's nice. Really nice. And every time I look at him, my heart beats faster, and I want him to kiss me." She grabbed one of Reggie's fries and bit down hard. "I'm terrified I'm going to make a fool out of myself. I don't know what to do."

"Why do you have to do anything? Why can't you enjoy the moment? You like a guy. So what? It happens. He's probably used to women having a crush on him."

"I don't want to be a groupie. I want to be a real person."

"You are a real person. Right now you're a real person who's not making much sense. Dena, what's the actual problem?"

"I want him to like me!"

Reggie picked up her sandwich half and took a big bite. Dena had a feeling it was a lot more about buying time than because she was hungry.

Reggie swallowed. "You want a relationship."

"Yes. No. I mean, I do, but I can't."

"Why not?"

"For one thing, he's him and I'm me."

Reggie tapped Dena's plate. "Eat, please. You have to be healthy."

"Exactly. That's one reason. I'm pregnant. Who wants that? Plus he's so good-looking and he's nice and famous and talented. Oh, and he's a widower. He's still in love with his late wife, so that sucks."

She paused. "Not that I don't totally respect his feelings, but they make him even more unavailable. I'm just this ordinary, not pretty, pregnant schoolteacher. He'd never fall for me."

The tears returned, but as she was with her sister, she didn't bother fighting them very much. Reggie never judged.

"Stop saying you're not pretty," her sister told her firmly. "You are, and if he doesn't see that, he's a jerk. As for the rest of it, so what? Famous people want to fall in love. They want connection. The being in love with his late wife is a complication, possibly the biggest one. I don't know how to fix that."

"Me, either. Plus he's leaving. He's only in town for

the holidays." She didn't mention the trouble he was having writing a song. That seemed too personal to share.

"Do you want to sleep with him?"

Dena yelped, then spun to see if anyone was sitting close enough to overhear. "Don't ask that."

"Why not? It's the obvious question. Do you?"

Dena thought about how she felt when Micah took her hand in his, even just to do the pressure point thing. She thought about his smile, his laugh, and how squishy she got inside when she was near him.

"Yes," she whispered. "I know that's bad, but I do."

"So, find out if he's interested."

"Oh, please. How do I do that? Send him a survey? Besides, I already know the answer. He's helping me because he's lonely, and his wife was pregnant when she was killed in a car accident, and me being pregnant makes him feel closer to her."

"Really? She was pregnant?"

"Yes. Five months. They were having a boy."

"I really need to keep up with pop culture more." Reggie put down her sandwich and wiped her fingers. "Let's recap. You're interested in a famous rock star who is only in town for a short period of time. He's a recent widower whose wife was pregnant when she died. You like him, and while you accept it could never be anything more than a fling, you're interested in the fling, but worried that being normal and pregnant might be off-putting. Is that about right?"

Dena nodded.

Her sister picked up her milkshake. "I love you like a sister, kid, but I've got nothing. Seriously, I don't know how you got yourself in this mess, but you are completely and totally screwed."

"I was hoping for something more uplifting in the way of advice."

"Then you need a different problem, because when it comes to this one, I'm an empty vessel. But I still love you."

"Nice, yet not the least bit helpful."

Fourteen

TOBY LEANED BACK in his chair and picked up his mug of coffee. His computer screen was divided into a grid with six pictures—his weekly virtual meeting with the corporate leadership team.

When he'd considered moving back to Wishing Tree, he'd known he would have to relocate the headquarters. His goal had been to bring as many key employees as possible. There was no way to settle them all in Wishing Tree. While he loved the small-town life, he knew it wasn't for everybody.

Seattle had been the obvious solution. The proximity to the water and the mountains made it ideal for those who enjoyed the outdoors, and the urban areas could go toe-to-toe with any major US city. It was less convenient for him to have to go back and forth, but there was only one of him.

"You can see this from the data," said Finian York,

Toby's favorite number cruncher, drawing Toby's attention back to the meeting. "The testing shows there's no measurable degradation of appearance regardless of how the pies are prepared. Taste tests show a ninety-seven percent satisfaction rate when cooked from frozen and a ninety-five percent satisfaction rate when cooked from thawed."

"Wait," Talia Nagy said. The marketing director sounded confused. "You're saying the pies taste better when cooked from frozen?"

"No. That's what the data's saying."

Talia grinned. "You know what I meant."

"Yes, but that's not what you asked. I answered your question as spoken."

Talia laughed. "Toby, we so need to get Finian a pet. Something he can't predict or control. Something with a little attitude."

"I like control."

Toby held in a smile. The familiar banter told him all was well with the team.

"I'll review the data later," he said. "This is the three-month test?"

"Yes." Finian consulted his notes. "Three months and four days. The next taste test is at six months." He looked into his computer camera. "Boss, I think people are going to like the frozen pies."

Toby looked at his sales manager. "Nate, you've convinced Finian. I'm not sure I approve of that. You're starting to gang up on me."

Nate laughed. "We're just doing what's best for the company. The frozen food market is big and getting bigger."

Talia leaned forward. "I've been holding off on a marketing plan. Should I get started on that?"

Toby knew it would take her and her team time to develop a strategy. "Yes, go ahead. Kelly, get going on what it would take to get a supply chain up and running. I want real numbers."

Kelly shook her head. "When have I not given you real numbers?"

"You're right. I meant that comment for myself rather than you. I want to make this decision based on data."

Because he was the most reluctant member of the team. The idea of selling frozen pies still bothered him, and he was going to have to figure out why. So far all the information pointed to incredible profitability while maintaining the excellent quality of the product.

They went through the rest of the meeting agenda. When they were done, Toby thanked everyone for their work.

"If you think you can handle things there on your own, I'll hold off my next visit until right after the first of the year," he said.

"We'll be fine," Nate told him. "You enjoy whatever you do over there in Wishing Tree."

Nate's tone indicated he couldn't begin to understand why anyone would want to live in a place like that, but then, Nate was a city boy down to his bones. While most of the executive team had bought houses in the suburbs, Nate had a downtown condo with great views. Nate always said he liked nature…from a distance.

"You're all missing a great day here," Toby told them. "At four o'clock, people will gather in The

Wreath for the start of the Advent calendar. Then there's a big celebration. The first day is always a fun activity, but later days will be everything from a community-based giving project to caroling or sledding."

"What kind of community-based project?" Kelly asked.

"Last year one of the suggestions was a random act of kindness, paying someone's grocery or gas bill."

"That's nice." She smiled. "I like Wishing Tree." She paused. "Not that I don't love Seattle, because I do."

Toby grinned. "Don't worry. I'm not forcing anyone to move here. Everyone have a good week."

"You, too, Boss."

He disconnected from the video conference and closed the program. He probably should make his way to Seattle for a few days, but he didn't want to be gone during the holidays. Not with everything going on. Plus, now there was the Advent calendar.

He smiled, thinking he had a very good life. He and Harrison might have had a rough start together, but they were doing fine now.

He turned his chair so he could look out his office window. A huge Christmas tree and two smaller trees were already in place at the north end of The Wreath— the trees of Christmas past, present and future. The Advent calendar had been set up at the south end. The calendar was actually boxes stacked in the shape of a tree, each box about four feet square. Harrison had been surprised at how big it was and how everyone participated in at least one of the activities. He'd gotten very excited about collecting coats for a coat drive on the day that box had been opened last year.

Toby remembered when he'd been a teenager. He'd

considered himself too sophisticated to care about the Advent calendar, even though he'd secretly been interested to see what was going on. Once he'd started dating Reggie, refusing to participate hadn't been an option. She'd insisted they be there, right at four on the first day, to enjoy every second of the celebration.

That night they'd returned to The Wreath for an outdoor sing-along. Even though her voice was average at best, she'd been an enthusiastic participant. Reggie had never been afraid to simply jump in and get started on anything.

Thinking about her made him recall the second day of knitting at the community center. Each of the kids had finished their first hat and had eagerly started a second. Reggie had been right there, cheering them on, with Belle offering a headbutt of support.

That dog, he thought with a chuckle. She always had on a sweater or a warm shirt of some kind, and she adored Harrison.

He turned back to his computer, ready to get to work, only he found himself picking up his phone instead.

He scrolled through his contacts, then started texting.

Advent starts at 4. Want to join me and Harrison? Belle would be welcome—just make sure she dresses warmly.

He waited a few seconds, then saw three dots.

Sounds like a great time. I want to go and the company will be fun.

Excellent, he thought. Harrison and I will be by to pick you two up at three thirty.

We'll be ready.

He returned his phone to his desk, then glanced at the clock on the wall. It was only eleven in the morning. Three thirty felt like a long way away.

REGGIE TOLD HERSELF not to read too much into Toby's invitation. The first day of Advent was a huge deal in Wishing Tree, with the calendar taking center stage. Family and groups of friends often went together. Plus, his son and her dog were coming along—it was hardly a date.

Yet she found it difficult to concentrate on work after he'd texted, and then she felt the need to put on makeup. She tried to be casual when she mentioned the outing to her mom. Fortunately, Leigh simply nodded and told her to have a good time.

At exactly three thirty, the doorbell rang. Burt barked from the family room, while Belle stayed safely behind Reggie until she determined who was at the door. When the Great Dane saw Harrison, she pushed Reggie aside to go greet her boy. She danced around him, licked his cheek, then placed her big head on his shoulder.

"I think it's more than a summertime fling," Reggie said with a laugh, waving them both inside. "I just need a second to get her in a coat and boots." She grimaced. "Belle doesn't mind the clothes, but she really hates the boots. Still, when it's this cold, I worry about her standing in one place for too long. Her little toes could get frostbite."

She told herself to stop talking, but it was tough. The second she saw Toby, she felt an unexpected surge of nerves. Being nervous always made her babble. Him looking all tall and manly in his thick coat and leather gloves didn't help.

"She has dog boots?" Harrison asked, glancing down at her feet. "How do you keep them on?"

"They have a hook-and-loop closure system. You can help me with them, if you'd like."

She turned to collect Belle's warmest jacket, along with the booties. Burt came running into the room, his tail wagging. He sniffed Toby's boots, then turned toward Harrison. Reggie realized a second too late that the little dachshund had gone into nipping mode. She reached for him. She couldn't get there in time. But before he could sink his teeth into Harrison's pant leg, Belle spun and shoved herself between Harrison and Burt. She pushed Harrison back a couple of steps, braced herself, lowered her head and growled at Burt.

The low, menacing sound startled all of them. Burt yelped and ran down the hall. Reggie stared at her dog.

"I didn't know she could do that," she said. "That was an impressive sound. Belle, you defended Harrison. Good for you."

Belle straightened, looking a little sheepish, her tail wagging tentatively. Harrison flung his arms around her.

"You protected me!"

"You're a good girl," Toby said, petting the dog. "Thank you."

Belle accepted all the praise, then allowed Reggie

to strap on her coat. She submitted to the booties with slightly more grace than usual, then led the way outside.

"Can I take her leash?" Harrison asked.

Reggie handed it over. "Remember, she'll only let you go on the sidewalk, so don't try anything, Harrison. Belle's a rule follower."

Harrison laughed, then let Belle pull him toward the center of town and The Wreath.

"She was something," Toby said, falling into step next to her.

"I know. She's never acted like that before. Burt doesn't ever come after me, so I don't know what she would do if he tried, but obviously she's going to take care of Harrison." Reggie was oddly proud of her dog. "Normally she's so timid. I'm impressed."

"She was motivated," he said.

They were joined on the sidewalk by other families making their way to The Wreath.

"Big crowd this year," Toby said, waving at people he knew.

"It is. Probably because the weather is so nice."

The sun was already sinking in the west, but the sky was clear, and the night promised to be filled with stars.

Filled with stars? Reggie held in a groan. She wasn't sure what was wrong with her, but whatever it was, she needed to get over it and fast. While she wanted to believe her strangeness was due to her dog's unexpected bravery, she had a bad feeling that being around Toby was the real cause. Apparently Dena wasn't the only Somerville sister to have a reaction to a man this holiday season. And speaking of Dena...

She looked around, trying to spot her sister, wondering if Dena had managed to invite hunky Micah Ruiz to join her. But she couldn't see her anywhere.

"Who are you looking for?" Toby asked as they joined the crowd entering The Wreath.

"Dena. I thought she might come with a few of her guests."

She saw Paisley and Shaye buying hot chocolate at a cart by the huge stack of calendar boxes. Paisley saw her and started to wave her over. Then she spotted Toby, and her expression turned knowing. Reggie knew there would be lots of explaining when next they spoke.

Music played from speakers set up around the perimeter. Other vendors sold cookies and more adult beverages than hot chocolate. The old-fashioned streetlights were decorated with garland, and giant ornaments decorated the circle. Harrison and Belle huddled close as more and more people poured into the space and the big clock, also erected for the season, ticked closer to 4:00 p.m.

At three fifty-eight, "We Wish You a Merry Christmas" started playing.

"This is it," she told Harrison, trying not to shiver in the cold.

The minute hand moved to twelve, and everyone cheered. The first box was opened, and the screen at the east side of The Wreath lit up.

Moonlight Mini Golf in The Wreath. 7 p.m. tonight. Live music and fun for all.

Harrison spun to face his father. "Dad, Dad, can we?"

Toby grinned. "I wouldn't want to miss it." He looked at Reggie. "Want to join us?"

She told herself once more not to read too much into

the invitation. They were going to be out in public, hanging out with an eight-year-old. Again—not a date.

"Sounds like fun," she said. "I'll have to leave Belle at home, and I'll want to put on more layers."

"It is chilly," Toby said. "And it will get colder now that the sun's gone down. Say quarter to seven, by the clock?"

"I'll see you there."

Toby stood by the clock at six forty-five. As he'd predicted, the temperature had dropped, making him grateful for long underwear. He'd dressed Harrison in layers, piling them on until his son had complained he wouldn't be able to move. Toby had pointed out that mini golf didn't require a whole lot of mobility and had added a scarf. Everyone was just as warmly dressed—the smallest of the children so bundled they were nearly as round as they were tall.

He spotted Reggie walking around the edge of The Wreath. She, too, had on layers, including a bright red hat that had ear flaps decorated with fabric horseshoes. Her scarf was the same color, with horses on it.

"Very stylish," he teased as she stopped in front of him. "I like the hat and the scarf."

"That's not all," she said with a laugh as she pulled out a red wallet. "If I'd had a red phone case, I would have changed that out, too."

They smiled at each other, their gazes locked. The music and conversations around them seemed to fade away until all he could see and hear was her. He remembered this feeling of getting lost in her, of existing only with her, from when they'd been dating. He'd missed it with the other women he'd gotten involved with and had assumed it was just because he'd been a kid. Now, feeling the need to move closer, to touch her cheek and press his mouth to hers, he wondered if instead, it was a Reggie thing.

After a few seconds, she looked away. "Where's, ah, Harrison?"

"He went off with a few of his friends. I'm meeting him back here at eight thirty. I'm not gonna lie, it's tough being dumped."

"Knowing you're not as exciting as a bunch of eight-year-old boys?"

"Yeah. I used to be the fun dad."

"He's learning to be independent. Be happy that he's fitting in."

"I am, but hey, mini golf."

They both turned to look at the makeshift course. Most of the players were families with small children and groups of teenagers huddled together. A night this cold was a good excuse to put your arm around a girl, he thought, remembering when he'd been fifteen or sixteen and girls had been a total mystery. In some ways he supposed that hadn't changed.

Reggie studied the line to start the course. "We could absolutely play or we could go to Holiday Spirits and get a drink."

Toby laughed. "Sold."

They walked the short distance to the bar and discovered they weren't the only adults to have that idea. The place was busy. He looked around and spotted a small table in the back corner.

"Over there," he said, pointing.

As they walked, he began to peel off layers. Reggie did the same. When they arrived at the table, they hung jackets, scarves and sweaters over the rack by the wall. She pulled off her horseshoe hat and smoothed her hair.

"When did you cut it?" he asked.

"My senior year of college." Humor flashed in her eyes. "I couldn't go the rest of my life with a ponytail."

"I don't know. I always liked it."

Mostly he'd liked the way it moved. The bounce was sassy, like her.

Howard walked up to their table. "I know what you want, Toby. What about you, Reggie? The special tonight is a pomegranate martini. Basically it's a cosmo but with pomegranate juice instead of cranberry juice."

"That's for me," she said, smiling at Howard.

He nodded and left.

"What do you always get?" she asked.

"A beer."

"And he doesn't mind?"

Toby wasn't sure how to explain without causing her to lose her easy smile.

"He knew my dad, so the first time I came here and said I only drink beer, he didn't push me."

As he'd expected, her mouth straightened. "I'm sorry. I didn't mean to bring up a difficult topic."

"You didn't. My father was an alcoholic. Everyone knew it. I don't know how much of the disease is genetic and how much of it is just bad luck. Either way, I'm careful."

"No hard liquor?"

"Nope. One beer or one glass of wine and that's it for me." He consciously relaxed his posture. "It doesn't bother me to see other people drink, so don't worry about it. It's like oysters. I don't get it, but if you like them, go ahead."

"I heard your dad stopped drinking a few years before he died," she said. "I didn't really know him."

Something Toby was grateful for, he thought. He'd always kept Reggie away from the house if his father was around. No way he'd wanted her to experience what it was like to be near his old man.

"He stopped drinking, but he never stopped being mean."

"I'm sorry."

"Don't waste energy on it. He was who he was. Once I left, I rarely came back. Harrison and I visited once, right after he'd stopped drinking. It didn't go well."

"He wasn't a kid person?"

Toby thought about how Harrison, only four at the time, had been playing a toy drum. His grandfather had told him to stop making so much noise. Harrison had—for about two minutes. Then he'd started up again. Toby's father had backhanded the boy, sending him stumbling into a wall. Only Judy physically putting herself between Toby and his father had kept him from going after the old man. He'd packed up their suitcases and they'd left, never to return. Only Toby had come back for the funeral.

"Let's just say he never saw the point in children," he told her lightly, grateful when Howard arrived with their drinks.

"You said before you work with inventors," Toby said, as much to change the subject as because he was interested. "What does that mean?"

"I started out in applied design. Working with engineers to make sure the product was something that humans could interact with easily. I was a tiny cog in a very big company. When I was offered a buyout, I took it." She smiled. "By then I had a lot of contacts and wanted to try making it on my own. So I started a little business, and by little I mean it's just me."

"And you help inventors bring their products to market?"

"Not in a marketing sense. I help them make sure their product is easy to use. The start sequence for a high-tech blender has to pass the grandma test."

"Not fifteen buttons and a Bluetooth hookup?"

"Exactly. It's fun work. I set my own hours and I meet interesting people. Sometimes it's frustrating because success isn't automatic. Great products that will never get to market."

"But you still get paid?"

The smile returned. "Sometimes. A lot of my clients are rich with ideas but not so much with the actual cash. If I believe in what they bring me, I'll get a cut of the action. If they make money, I do, too. If they don't, then I chose badly."

Which sounded easy enough, he thought, but required an incredible business sense and a trust in her gut instincts.

"What's your success rate?" he asked.

"About sixty-forty. Sixty percent have done well. Some have done very well."

He leaned toward her. "You're rich." His tone was both humorous and accusing.

"I'm not." Her brown eyes sparkled with amusement. "I do okay."

"You own your own house?"

"I bought a place a year ago. It's a cute little bungalow just north of Seattle. I also have a retirement fund, so there."

"Congratulations."

"Thanks. Like I said, it's a small business, but I'm happy. I'm saving up to remodel the kitchen." She picked up her drink and took a sip. "Are you happy back in Wishing Tree?"

"I am. I like that I can keep an eye on Judy, and Harrison is thriving."

"He's a sweetie and Belle adores him."

"I'm still impressed how she protected him."

"Me, too. I've always thought that if someone broke in the house, she would wait in the closet until the situation resolved."

He chuckled. "I can see that."

Conversation shifted to mutual friends who'd stayed in town. Reggie was still easy to talk to. Toby kept getting distracted by her smile and the way she talked with her hands—all exactly as he remembered. Good memories, he thought.

When it was time to go get Harrison, Toby paid their bill and helped her into her coat.

"Braced for the cold?" he asked.

"Yes. We just have to keep moving so we don't freeze in place."

They were still laughing when Paisley and Shaye walked into Holiday Spirits and spotted them.

Shaye only looked mildly interested, but Paisley's eyebrows shot up, and her gaze took on a speculative look.

"Hey, you two," she said, eyeing Reggie. "You didn't want to play mini golf?"

Reggie grinned. "We're leaving that for the family crowd."

"Interesting." Paisley glanced at him, then returned

her attention to Reggie. "Rumor has it one of the Advent events is putting together toiletries kits for a women's shelter. I thought we could make it a girls' night out kind of thing. Assuming you can *get away*."

Reggie sighed. "Really? You had to go there?"

"I did." Paisley grinned. "You would have done the same."

"Maybe. Yes, to the girls' night out. I'm looking forward to it. You two have fun."

Reggie pulled Toby along by the arm.

"Sorry about that," she said when they were outside. "Paisley is a great friend, but she can be a little intrusive sometimes."

"It's a small town, Reggie. Someone was going to say something about us hanging out together."

She looked at him. "You okay with that?"

What he would be okay with was kissing her. Despite the cold and the potential for becoming inspiration for a lot of gossip, he wanted to pull her close and find out how grown-up Reggie was different from the teenage girl he'd known all those years ago.

"I'm fine with it," he said, taking her hand. While the kissing was tempting, he wasn't sure it was a good idea. "Now let's go get my son. He'll be freezing and hungry. We can swing by the store and eat a few hand pies."

"But the store is closed."

"It is, but I have a key."

"A man with power. How can I resist?"

Fifteen

REGGIE ARRIVED HOME frozen to the bone. She let herself in the front door and was immediately greeted by Belle, who demanded a full face rub and lots of reassurance.

"Hey, where's the wild dog who took on Burt?" she asked, unwinding her scarf.

"She seems to have forgotten her lone moment of bravery."

Reggie jumped and turned to see her mother walking in from the family room.

"You scared me," Reggie said, pressing a hand to her chest. "You waited up."

"It's nine thirty. I haven't gone to bed yet."

Reggie got her breathing under control and took off a couple more layers, then handed her mother a bag.

"Hand pies," she said. "We stopped by the store and had a snack. Toby sent these home with me for dessert, I'm still hungry, so I could go for one. Want to split them with me?"

Her mother smiled. "Trying to distract me from asking about your date?"

Reggie laughed. "Mom, it wasn't a date. I met Toby and Harrison for mini golf. That's hardly romantic." Which was the truth. The fact that instead Harrison had gone off with his friends while she and Toby had gotten a drink wasn't something she was going to discuss.

"I was hoping for more," her mother said, pouring them each a glass of milk and sitting at the kitchen table. Belle took her usual seat, beside Reggie's chair— just in case something fell.

Reggie pulled out the two pies she'd brought home and handed her mother one. She grabbed a couple of napkins from the dispenser.

"You're going to need this," she said. "They're extra crumbly tonight."

"I love the hand pies, but they can be messy. And when you get them at the store, all they give is one of those little bakery tissues and a napkin. You really should talk to one of your inventor friends about making some kind of sleeve."

"I'll get right on that, Mom."

"You're dismissing me, but it's a good idea. So, no kissing?"

The unexpected change in subject gave Reggie mental whiplash.

"No kissing." Toby had been friendly, nothing else. Alas.

"Too bad. I was hoping you two would discover there was still chemistry. Not to pressure you, but I really need one of my daughters to get married. You're nearly thirty, Reggie. It's time. I had high hopes for Dena, but she's chosen another path."

Reggie thought about her sister's mad crush on Micah Ruiz, but knew better than to mention it to her mother. Leigh would demand details and start planning an engagement party before the end of the week, and Dena had enough going on.

"I want to fall in love and get married, too," Reggie said instead. "But it's not happening."

"I don't know why. You're pretty. You're smart. You have a great career." She eyed Belle. "You don't think it's your dog, do you? Belle is intimidating."

"She's a marshmallow, and no, she isn't the reason I haven't found Mr. Right."

Her mother took a bite of her butterscotch pie. "Jake was a disappointment. I'm still angry at him for how he treated you."

"You have to let it go. He could have handled the breakup better than he did, but otherwise, he wasn't wrong, Mom. I got over him way too easily, which makes me wonder if the marriage would have lasted."

"I just want you to be happy."

"I am."

"I meant with a man."

Reggie grinned. "Oh, that." Her smile faded. "I want that, too. I just can't figure out how to make it happen."

MICAH DROVE THE short distance from the B and B to The Wreath and found parking. Under normal conditions, he would have walked the short distance, but given how much he had to carry, that wasn't practical. He went inside The Christmas Feast and saw Mrs.

Heins-Smith waiting on another customer. She spotted him and waved, indicating she would be right with him.

He walked around the store while she finished up. There were aisles of dried pasta from Italy, and bottles and cans of olive oil. The next row over had different kinds of hot sauce, including one with white truffle oil—a combination he didn't understand. A cold case offered cheeses from around the world, a bacon sampler and clotted cream, and the frozen food section was an array of ice cream, gelato and frozen desserts, including soufflés.

Mrs. Heins-Smith walked over. "We have your order ready to go," she told him. "They turned out very nicely." The sixtysomething woman winked at him. "We're borrowing the Santa idea for our weekend crowd. I think the parents will be very impressed."

"I saw the idea online. It wasn't me."

"Ah, a modest man. They're as rare as hen's teeth."

She pulled a bakery box from the cold case and opened the top. Inside were three dozen "Santas." An upside down whole strawberry had been cut in half, with a slice of banana placed in the middle. The banana slice was the face, complete with tiny chocolate chip eyes. Cottage cheese created the beard, just below the banana. The second treat was more traditional—Rice Krispies balls in holiday colors.

He'd confirmed the dietary restrictions with Dena, and had given the information, along with the suggestion for the Santas, to Mrs. Heins-Smith. Now all that was left was to hope the kids liked the snack.

He carried the treats to his car and drove the short distance to the school. It took a bit of juggling to carry in two guitars along with the bakery boxes, but he managed, then signed in at the front desk and made his way back to Dena's classroom.

He stood in the hallway, watching her through the window in the door.

She was completely absorbed in what she was doing. He could tell by the way she was standing and how she kept her gaze on her students. Her smile was easy, her command of the moment absolute.

He liked how she gave herself over to whatever she was doing, whether teaching or decorating the B and B. Her long brown hair hung in a ponytail down her back, moving with her. The color caught the sunlight.

She wasn't wearing much makeup, and her clothes were more practical than fashion-forward, but he liked that, too. There was something about her that appealed to him. Maybe how accepting she was, or maybe how much she cared about people, or maybe how she was about the bravest person he knew.

She looked up and spotted him. Their eyes locked, and he knew in that second that if there wasn't a door between them and a classroom of third-graders watching, he would close the space between them, pull her close and kiss her until they were both breathless.

The image was nearly as startling as the desire that accompanied it. He smiled. After all this time, he was ready to start living again. Had it really taken a schoolteacher from Wishing Tree to bring him back to life?

Dena hurried to open the door. "I'm not sure you could carry much more than you are," she said, taking the bakery boxes from him. "You could have asked someone from the office to help."

"I was fine."

She smiled at him. "Thanks for coming. The kids

are so excited. I made the mistake of telling them you'd be back, and they've been wild with anticipation ever since."

She led the way into the classroom. The students went quiet and all stared at him. He spotted Noah and winked at him.

"You all remember Micah Ruiz from career day," she said. "He's going to be our room parent for the month of December. Say hello."

"Hello, Mr. Ruiz," they chanted.

"Hello, everyone." He smiled. "It's going to take me a bit to learn your names, so please be patient." He looked at Dena. "How does this work?"

"I usually feed them first. Then we do whatever it is you want us to do."

"I'm going to teach everyone about guitars. I brought two with me—one's acoustic and one's electric. We'll talk about the differences. Then I'll play both of them." He grinned at her. "I should probably close the door."

While the kids lined up for their snacks, he moved an extra adult-size chair to the front of the room. He unpacked his equipment and plugged in the amplifier. By the time everyone had taken a paper plate and napkin back to their desk, he was ready to go.

He sat in the chair and drew in a breath. The odd sensation in his stomach surprised him, until he identified it as nerves. Funny how he could walk onto a stage in front of fifteen thousand people and not feel anything but anticipation, but in front of a room full of eight-year-olds, he was tense.

"As Ms. Somerville said, I'm Micah Ruiz. You can call me Micah. I was lead singer in a rock band called

Darryl John James. I've been playing guitar for a long time." He reached for both guitars.

"Who knows the difference between these two?"

Noah's hand shot up.

Micah smiled. "Anyone who isn't the son of a famous drummer?"

A dark-haired girl tentatively raised her hand. "One's acoustic and one's electric?"

"That's right." He strummed a chord on the acoustic guitar. "Acoustic guitars have a different sound. They're physically bigger overall, and the strings are heavier. Some people think they're harder to learn on, but I think they're worth the effort. In the band, we used electric guitars exclusively, but when I write songs, I use an acoustic guitar."

He put it down and picked up the electric guitar and strummed. There wasn't any sound. The students laughed.

"Who knows what's wrong?"

"You have to plug it in," one boy yelled.

"You're right, I do. And then turn it on." He touched the strings again and sound filled the room.

"Now, who knows what a chord is?"

He went through the basic parts of a guitar and demonstrated the major and minor chords, first on the acoustic guitar, then on the electric. He played "Twinkle, Twinkle, Little Star" on both before answering questions.

One little girl raised her hand.

"I told my mommy you were here for career day, and she said she would have died to see you and that you're going to be on TV soon. What's the show?"

"I'm going to be on a live variety show close to Christmas."

"From here?"

He smiled. "No. I'll fly to Los Angeles. The show is being broadcast from there."

"Do you get scared to be on TV?"

"I've done it lots of times, so it's not scary anymore. Being live is different. If I make a mistake, everyone will know."

The students laughed.

"To be honest," he told them, "I was a lot more scared to come here and play for you."

"For real?" a boy asked.

"Sure. I don't know how to be a teacher. But Ms. Somerville said I could do it, and I believed her."

Just then a bell rang. Dena had everyone file out for afternoon recess, then turned back to him.

"That was so great," she said. "Thank you. What a fantastic afternoon. You were a hit."

He found himself less interested in what the kids had thought of him than how Dena felt about the lesson.

"It was appropriate for them?"

"They were mesmerized. Everyone learned something, even me." She smiled. "I was supposed to be getting work done, but I couldn't stop listening to you." The smile widened. "It's the famous rock star thing, huh?"

"Possibly."

She held up the empty bakery boxes. "Even your food was a success. You did great."

He unplugged the guitar and coiled the cord. "Thanks. I meant what I said—I was nervous about this."

"You had no reason to be. So you're in a live show?"

"A few days before Christmas." He grimaced. "I agreed to it in a moment of weakness. I'll fly down to LA, do the show, then come back here." He looked at her. "I want to be in Wishing Tree for Christmas Day."

"It's a pretty fun day here. There's a reindeer 5K run—runners wear antlers—and caroling and lots of other things going on. Small-town stuff, though."

"I'm kind of enjoying small town stuff these days."

Without thinking, he moved toward her. The door to the classroom was open, not that closing it would matter—there was a window. Although he had no idea why he was thinking about closing doors—unless he really did want to kiss her, which he thought maybe he did. He had a feeling Dena was a great kisser and that her mouth would feel good on his.

From that thought, it was a quick and easy journey to wondering how she would feel in his arms. Did she hold back a little or did she melt?

I was afraid to risk my heart. Again. Swore I could exist apart. Again.

The melody and words descended from nowhere. Micah froze in place, not wanting to lose either. They played again and again in his head, taunting him with the idea they could be something.

"I should get going," he said, putting his guitars into their cases. "The kids will be in from recess soon, and I need to get back to my place and do some writing." He tried to sound friendly as he spoke, rather than dismissive.

Dena stepped back, her smile tight. "Of course. Thank you again."

He nodded and left, trying to hang on to the music

in his head. *I was fine. I was okay. I'd loved and lost—that's just life's way.*

He jogged to his car with the guitars and did his best not to speed on his way back to the B and B. Once inside, he pulled out his guitar, started the recorder on his phone and began to play.

REGGIE WALKED INTO Wrap Around the Clock, more for ideas than to buy something. She needed a heavier paper than regular wrapping paper, but it also had to be food-grade.

The store had a huge selection of wrapping paper—some precut and ready to take home, others in thick rolls, allowing the customer to buy as little as two feet or as much as a hundred feet. There were sections for birthdays, weddings and, of course, Christmas.

"Can I help you?" Camryn Neff was a couple of years younger than Reggie, so they hadn't run in the same social circles at school. The Camryn Reggie remembered was an attractive, outgoing redhead with an easy smile, but the woman in front of her was pale, with swollen eyes and a trembling mouth.

"Are you all right?" Reggie asked.

Camryn tried to smile. "Sorry. I'm having a bad day." She waved her hand, then wiped her tears. "We're getting close to Christmas, and my mom hasn't been gone that long. Sometimes it's hard."

Her voice cracked on the last word. Reggie instinctively moved close and hugged her.

"I'm sorry," she whispered. "This has to be such a huge shock. Dealing with the loss of your mom, raising your younger sisters. Of course you're overwhelmed."

Camryn nodded. "Thanks. Most days I'm fine, or

as close to fine as I can get." She drew in a breath and exhaled. "Okay, I'm going to get through the rest of our conversation without breaking down. Tell me what you need."

"How about the next time we invite you for a girls' night, you join us?"

"Paisley already talked to me about the service project in a couple of nights. I'll be there."

"Good. I look forward to us hanging out. Okay, I'm actually not sure what I'm looking for." Reggie lowered her voice. "You know the hand pies at Judy's?"

"Of course. They're our favorite dinner at least twice a week."

"They're delicious but messy. Even with bakery tissue and a napkin, the filling can get all over."

"I stained my favorite sweater with berry juice."

"I've been wondering if there was a way to create a simple pie holder. You know, like the little cardboard boxes French fries come in. Some of the fast food places use something similar for their desserts, but they wouldn't work for Judy's hand pies. The shape is all wrong. I want something inexpensive and food-safe. A heavy paper of some kind, folded. I don't know. At this point, I'm just playing."

"We have a lot of paper choices," Camryn told her. "I have no idea if they're food-safe. How would you even find out?"

"I'm working on that. In the meantime, I thought I would try different weights of paper and use Play-Doh to simulate the pies."

"Sounds like fun. Okay, these are the craft papers. Let me show you the heaviest weight we have, and we'll go from there."

Sixteen

REGGIE SWUNG BY the B and B to pick up Dena on her way to the community center. As Paisley had mentioned, the Advent activity for the day was to do something to help a homeless shelter. Paisley had texted that all the supplies had arrived, along with the time they were to meet.

Reggie had barely pulled into a parking space when she saw her sister walking out of the main building.

"I was watching for you," Dena admitted, climbing in the car.

"I am the fun sister, aren't I?"

Reggie meant the comment to be teasing and was surprised when Dena didn't laugh.

"What?" she asked. "You feeling all right?"

"I'm fine. I have pressure bracelets that seem to be helping with the morning sickness, although I'm still really tired."

Reggie started for the community center. Between the knitting project and tonight, she was spending a lot of time there.

"So, your lack of enthusiasm over my sparkling humor is because you're tired?"

Dena sighed. "No. I'm sorry. You were very funny."

"What's wrong?"

"Nothing. It's stupid. I'm fine." She offered a big smile. "See? I'm great. Happy."

"Uh-huh. You can't fake your mood with me. I know you. Come on. Tell me."

Dena groaned. "It's totally ridiculous and you'll laugh and I'll feel bad."

"No laughing. I swear." A thought occurred to her. "Is this about Micah?"

Dena covered her face. "Yes," she said, her voice muffled. "I'm such an idiot." She straightened. "He's the classroom parent for the month, and yesterday he brought snacks and guitars and sang and was just so amazing."

"He sounds irresistible."

"He is. It's a nightmare. Afterwards, we were talking, and I swear I thought he was going to kiss me."

She turned to Reggie, as if waiting for laughter.

Reggie pulled into a space in the parking lot before turning off her engine. "I'm listening."

"It was a moment. I swear it was. Then he got this weird look on his face and left. He barely said goodbye. I don't know what happened. What I'm most afraid of is I imagined the moment because, I don't know, I'm pregnant and single and he's Micah Ruiz. Maybe all this is happening in my head, and the reason he ducked out is he thinks I'm pathetic."

Reggie reached for her sister's hand. "I have no experience with this," she admitted. "I've never dated a celebrity of any kind, so I don't know how it usually goes. My first thought is if you thought he was going to kiss you, then he was probably going to kiss you. That's not the sort of thing you get wrong."

"And then?"

"I don't know. Maybe he had gas."

Dena stared at her for several seconds before laughing. "Gas?"

Reggie grinned. "It's the best I could come up with under the circumstances. I don't even know the guy— something you should change, by the way. Invite him over for dinner."

"At our parents' house? That is so not happening. No. Just no." She sighed. "Maybe I really did imagine it."

"Maybe he had gas."

"It wasn't gas. Stop it."

"He also poops."

Dena got out of the car. "What are you? Five?"

"I'm just saying everyone does it."

"I can't believe you're my sister."

Reggie grinned. "Because you know you're so lucky to have me in your life? I get that."

They were still laughing as they walked into the community center and found the room where they would do their project. Paisley was already there, placing shipping boxes onto the long tables set up in the middle of the room.

"Hey," she called, motioning to the coatrack in the corner. "Strip down, then help me. We have to open the boxes to see what's inside, then figure out how we're going to load the backpacks. Oh, and you each owe me two hundred dollars."

"I already have my check," Reggie said, pulling it out of her back jeans pocket and waving it. "Thanks for doing all the shopping."

"I have mine, too. And I'm with Reggie. You were great to coordinate this."

Paisley brushed aside the praise. "Once I knew what the project was, I made a few calls, placed a few orders." She paused. "Wow, I guess I am the superior friend, huh?"

They hugged each other.

Reggie and Dena helped put the rest of the boxes on the tables, then began to open them. There were three huge boxes filled with backpacks. The slightly less large boxes contained things like socks, hand towels, tampons and pads, toiletries, cosmetics and wallets. The last one was filled with snack-size bags of M&M'S.

"Once we get everything sorted by type, we can form an assembly line," Paisley said. "We'll get the backpacks filled, then load them in my SUV, and I'll take them back to the resort. There's a truck going to Seattle tomorrow and the backpacks will be on it, getting there well before Christmas."

Camryn and Shaye arrived just then. Shaye wheeled in several boxes on a hand truck, and Camryn held two covered trays that looked a lot like snacks.

"I apologize in advance," she said, setting down the trays. "The twins helped me, and they have strange ideas of what makes a good snack. These are for us to eat while we work, by the way."

Paisley eyed the plastic coverings. "Should we be afraid?"

"Do you like celery stuffed with cream cheese and walnuts?"

Paisley paused to consider the question. "I've never had it, but I think I might. I mean, come on, it's cheese. Where's the bad?"

They all laughed.

After Shaye and Camryn took off their coats, Shaye unpacked her boxes.

"Books and fun things," she said. "Yo-yos and puzzles. I thought they would be a surprise, along with the practical stuff."

"Nice," Paisley said. "All right, people. We are ready to get to work."

They rearranged the tables to create a U shape with the boxes filled with backpacks at one end. They put out the supplies in the order they would go into the backpack, with the bulkier items on the bottom and the M&M'S and games on top. Once that was done, they each took a backpack and started to go down the line, filling it with the various items.

"How's everyone doing?" Dena asked. "Are the holidays getting crazy?"

"Some of us have time to get a drink with a good-looking man," Paisley pointed out. "Some of us should talk about that."

It took Reggie a second to realize her friend was looking at her. "You mean me?"

"I wasn't the one getting drinks with Toby at Holiday Spirits."

Everyone turned to stare. Dena pouted. "You never said anything."

"There's nothing to say. It was one drink."

Camryn smiled. "That's how it always starts, with a casual drink. So, how did you end up at Holiday Spirits?"

Reggie should have realized the topic would come up and prepared her story. As it was, she was left with little more than the truth, which even in her head sounded a little…unexpected.

"He texted me and asked me to go to Advent with him," she began, only to be interrupted by Paisley.

"He asked you out?"

"No. It was just friendly. Belle and Harrison came. It wasn't a date."

"I don't know. You ended up in a bar. Sounds pretty date-like to me."

Dena grinned. "She's right. It's kind of Dating 101."

"No. I was joining him and Harrison for mini golf, but Harrison went off with his friends and it was cold, so we went to Holiday Spirits instead. It wasn't anything."

Shaye put a pink yo-yo in her backpack. "I can't decide if it was just one of those things, or Toby had a plan from the get-go. I can see either happening."

"There was no plan," Reggie grumbled, putting her first full backpack against the wall and collecting a second empty one.

"That you know of."

"Did you have fun?" Dena asked.

Reggie dropped in a large box of pads and one of tampons, then reached for socks. "Yes. He's always been easy to talk to. That hasn't changed. But it was just as friends, I swear."

Which was a hundred percent true and a tiny bit

disappointing. Not that she wanted anything to happen with Toby. It was just she hadn't been out with a guy in a while, and being with Toby was fun. Plus he was very easy to look at, and he made her laugh. He'd always been a good kisser—she wondered if that had changed.

"So boring," Paisley said with a sigh. "As my love life has become a desert wasteland, I expect my friends to provide me with vicarious entertainment." She looked at Shaye. "How sad is it you're the only one of us in a relationship?"

Shaye smiled. "With the best man who ever lived."

"Young love," Paisley grumbled. "Save me."

"You just said you wanted to live vicariously," Camryn pointed out. "You can't turn around and complain about young love after that."

"I am charming with the contradictions." She grinned. "What about you, Camryn? Any hunky guy visiting for the holidays?"

Instead of joking back, Camryn turned away. "No."

Paisley immediately blanched. "I'm sorry. Did I say something bad? I didn't mean to."

Camryn's smile was forced. "It's not anything you could have known." She paused. "I was seeing someone before my mom died. Actually, I was engaged. When I came back and found out how sick she was, I knew I'd have to relocate home so I could help my mom and take care of the business. The twins had already been through so much and were about to lose their mom, there was no way I could ask them to move to Chicago."

Reggie got a bad feeling in the pit of her stomach.

Camryn tucked in a bag of M&M'S and zipped her

backpack closed. "When I told my fiancé, he dumped me. He said he wasn't interested in moving to some town no one has heard of, and he wasn't willing to wait."

"What a jerk," Shaye blurted, then covered her mouth. "Sorry."

"Don't be sorry," Reggie said, moving to Camryn and wrapping her arms around her. "He is a jerk and worse. What happened to in sickness and health?"

Camryn gave her a grateful look. "I guess he didn't plan to mean that part."

Dena pressed her lips together. "Can we get someone to beat him up? I don't know anyone personally, but I could ask around."

Paisley looked impressed. "Girlfriend, you have depths."

"I hate it when men act like that. You needed him and he wasn't there. He should have taken care of you instead of abandoning you in your hour of need."

"I agree," Reggie said forcefully.

"This is why I don't date," Paisley announced. "Just when you think you've found your one true love, they crap all over you."

"I thought you weren't dating because no one had asked you out," Dena said.

Paisley grinned. "Yes, well, that, too."

DENA COUNTED THE number of construction paper bells, stars and Santas she'd cut out, then confirmed she had enough for the list. Her mother sat across from her at the B and B dining room table, carefully punching a hole in the top of each of what would be paper ornaments.

"I feel awful," her mother confessed. "I totally forgot about the giving tree we put up at work. I can't believe I let that slip through the cracks."

Leigh had called in a panic, asking for help to get the giving tree ornaments pulled together. With Reggie already involved with the wedding and handling the charity knitting project, Dena had been happy to help. She was on duty at the front desk at the B and B from after school until six, but with no one checking in or out, she wasn't expecting to be that busy. She'd put out a sign, asking anyone who came in to ring the bell to let her know they were there.

"Mom, it's fine. You help out with the business, and you're planning a wedding. It's not a surprise you momentarily forgot something. This is easy. We'll have all the ornaments done in a couple of hours."

The process was simple enough. The front of the paper ornament would have the child's first name, last initial and age. On the back was a list of three possible presents. Employees at the auto repair shop and the tire store could take as many ornaments as they wanted, then bring in the unwrapped gift and the ornament. A week before Christmas, everything would be taken over to Spokane and delivered to the children.

"I still feel like the worst human alive," her mother murmured. "I forgot the giving tree."

"For a second. It's getting done now." Dena smiled at her. "There's an open bottle of wine on the counter in the kitchen. Why don't you go pour yourself a glass?"

"You're suggesting I drown my shame in liquor?"

"That seems extreme, but if it helps, then yes."

Her mother rose and went in search of the promised wine. Dena measured out a length of yarn, then made sure it was long enough to allow the ornament to hang from a tree branch. Once she'd confirmed it was correct, she used it as a template to cut the other forty-nine pieces.

"Hello."

She jumped, then looked up and saw Micah standing by the table. As always, her first thought was the man was dreamy. Her second was that she hadn't seen him in a couple of days, and during that time, she'd missed him a ridiculous amount. Her third realization was that she was grinning like a fool. She forced her mouth into a more normal smile.

"Hi," she said, feeling shy and happy at the same time.

"I've been holed up in my room, trying to write."

"How's it going?"

He sat across from her and raised one shoulder. "I lack talent."

"I know that's not true."

He smiled. "If I was really gifted, Dolly Parton would have recorded one of my songs."

"Have you asked her to?"

He pressed a hand to his chest. "I couldn't. What if she said no? My heart would be broken forever."

"I can see that."

His gaze settled on her face. "I've missed hanging out with you."

What? She blinked, sure she'd misheard what he was saying or that her ears or brain or some other body part was playing a trick on her. No way Micah had said what she'd thought he said.

"I, ah… I—"

She was saved from more stuttering by the appearance of her mother. A circumstance that was both good and oh, so very bad.

"Hello," Leigh said, looking at Micah. "Who are you?"

He chuckled and rose to his feet, then offered his hand. "Micah Ruiz. I'm a guest here at the B and B."

"Leigh Somerville." She lowered her voice to a conspiratorial whisper. "I'm the mother."

"Congratulations. You have an amazing daughter."

Leigh's gaze turned speculative. "Do I?"

"You already know that, though, don't you?"

"Yes, but not everyone can see it."

They both sat down.

"Are you and your wife enjoying your time in Wishing Tree?" Leigh asked.

Dena suddenly wanted to sink under the table. "Mom!"

"What?" Her mother smiled at her. "It's a genuine question. All your guests should enjoy themselves."

"I am having a great time in town," Micah told her. "But there's no wife. I'm a widower."

"Oh, I'm so sorry. When did you lose her?"

"Okay, that's enough," Dena said firmly. "Micah, you should go now. Trust me on this. The Somerville women can be formidable. Seriously, go directly to your room and lock the door. But be back for Snacks and Wine. Ursula made steak tacos, and you don't want to miss them."

"I'm torn," Micah admitted with a lazy grin that had Dena's heart getting all fluttery.

"You probably *should* make your escape," Leigh

confided. "If you stay, I'll ask all kinds of inappropriate questions that will embarrass my daughter."

"I wouldn't want Dena to be uncomfortable," he said with a laugh.

"Isn't that nice to know?" Leigh leaned toward him. "Do you like children?"

"OMG!" Dena glared at her mother. "Stop right now. I won't help you with these ornaments if you don't."

"Yes, you will. Since when have you ever not helped a child?" Leigh turned back to Micah. "So, children?"

He rose. "Nice to meet you, Mrs. Somerville." He winked at Dena. "I'll see you for Snacks and Wine."

They both watched him walk away. Dena's mom reached for her glass of wine. "That is one good-looking man."

"Mom, you were terrible."

"Just getting the lay of the land. He likes you."

Words that made Dena happy—a foolish concept, but there was no escaping the truth.

"He's a handsome single man who was flirting with you. If you ask me, you should definitely go for it."

"Really, Mom? Like, throw myself at him?"

"There are worse things."

"He's Micah Ruiz."

"Yes, he told me."

Dena sighed. "He's a famous rock star."

Her mother pursed her lips. "Oh, that's why he looked familiar. Is there money, or did he blow it on drugs and women? I'm only asking because I want you to find someone who will take care of you."

Dena covered her face with her hands. "First, I can take care of myself. Second, I wouldn't be interested in someone who acted like that. Third, I'm pregnant, and fourth, Micah is a guest, and he's leaving. There will be no throwing or hinting or anything. He's a nice man, and we talk occasionally, and that's all."

Her mother's gaze turned speculative. "Your children could have real musical talent."

"Mom!"

"I'm just saying. It could happen."

Seventeen

"But we could sneak in Belle," Harrison said, his tone hopeful.

Toby touched his son's nose. "Belle's too big to sneak into the theater. Plus, how would she get comfortable in one of the seats? Half of her would be hanging out."

Harrison smiled at the image. "Okay, so not Belle, but you should call Reggie, Dad. I'm sure she'll want to see the movie with us."

"Maybe next time," he told his son.

Toby was less sure Reggie would be enthralled by the latest animated holiday feature, but that wasn't why he'd resisted issuing the invitation. His reasons were more complicated, and a little contradictory. He liked Reggie. He'd enjoyed their time at Holiday Spirits, and since that night, she'd been on his mind a lot, which was saying something because she'd been on his mind plenty before they'd gone for drinks.

He didn't know if it was the season, their past, or Reggie herself, but he kept thinking of things he wanted to talk to her about or reasons he could call or places they could go together. All of which spelled a level of trouble he didn't want to get into.

His not getting involved rule had always been easy to follow. It was rare for him to meet someone who made him want to rethink the whole "avoid women" plan. But Reggie was testing his limits, and he had no idea what to do about it.

He locked his SUV and took Harrison's hand as they walked toward the multiplex. The Wonderful Life Cinema had seven screens, one of which was always playing a Christmas classic, no matter the time of year. He remembered when he and Reggie had been dating. She'd insisted on seeing a Christmas movie on the first Friday of every month, no matter what great new movie might be dropping that weekend. She would go see the new one with him on Saturday, but the first Friday of the month was a holiday movie, no matter what.

He'd quickly discovered that they frequently had much of the movie theater to themselves, and if he positioned them in corner seats, he could get in a lot of kissing and a little over the shirt action. Suddenly *Miracle on 34th Street* had become a lot more interesting to his seventeen-year-old self.

He was still smiling when Harrison started waving and yelling.

"Reggie! Reggie!"

Toby turned to his left and saw the woman in question also heading for the movie theater. She saw them, too, and changed direction, walked toward them. Toby looked around for a male companion, but she seemed to be alone.

Harrison broke free, rushed toward her and hugged her. Reggie hugged him back, then grinned at Toby.

"Now, what could you two possibly be doing?" she asked.

"We're off to the movies," he said, trying not to acknowledge the jolt of pleasure her smile brought him.

"Me, too. I spent the afternoon transplanting Christmas cactus. They're going to be the favors for my parents' wedding, so I need to put sixty of them into little custom planters."

"You're a good daughter."

"That's what I'm telling myself." She looked at Harrison. "Let me guess. You're here to see *It's a Wonderful Life.*"

Harrison laughed. "Nope. The new cartoon. Come with us, Reggie. It'll be great."

"Harrison, Reggie has her own plans."

His son's expression fell as he nodded slowly.

"I just thought it would be fun if she sat with us." He paused, then brightened. "Reggie, would you like to pick the movie?"

"Good one," Reggie said with a laugh. "I would very much like to sit with you, and I pick the cartoon."

"Really?"

Toby looked at her. "You don't have to do that."

"I want to. I can see *It's a Wonderful Life* later. It's not as if I haven't seen it before."

Harrison jumped up and down. "Yay! Dad, can I buy the tickets?"

Toby handed over his credit card, and Harrison raced toward the ticket machines.

Toby returned his attention to Reggie. "Thank you for indulging him."

"I really don't mind. It'll be fun."

"I can tell you haven't been to a movie with a bunch of kids in a while. *Fun* isn't the right word. *Loud* works. Very loud."

"I will endure."

He found himself wanting to offer to take her to the Christmas movie of her choice later in the week. Something with just the two of them. Like a date.

Only he didn't date—not ever. He wouldn't chance getting involved. That would mean putting Harrison at risk, and he never went there, not anymore.

Harrison returned with the tickets. They went inside and found seats. They'd barely finished taking off their coats when Noah and two other boys raced over.

"Come sit with us, Harrison," Noah said eagerly. "We're all the way up front."

"Dad, can I?"

"What happened to watching the movie with Reggie?"

Harrison turned to her. "Please?"

"Cast aside for friends. I'm crushed." She softened the words with a smile. "I'm fine with it if your dad is."

Toby stood up so Harrison could slip past him and go with his friends. "Come find me as soon as the movie's over."

"I will. Thanks, Dad."

The boys hurried to the front of the theater. He looked at Reggie.

"*It's a Wonderful Life* might not have started yet."

"I'm committed now." Her smile faded. "Unless you'd rather not sit with me."

"I appreciate the company. If I'm by myself, then I'm that creepy old guy, alone in a kid's movie."

She laughed. "There is that. Does he abandon you a lot?"

"I'm getting used to it. I knew it would happen. I just thought it would be later."

They stood to let a family into their row. Seats were filling up.

She looked around the theater. "They've remodeled this place. The seats are new."

"Wait until you hear the sound system. It got an upgrade, as well."

"While I appreciate better sound, one of the things I like about Wishing Tree is how much stays the same. I like the traditions and that I can count on certain things whenever I come home."

"Do you come back often?" he asked.

She wrinkled her nose. "Yes, although you wouldn't know it by my recent behavior. Until this trip, I hadn't been back in over a year."

"Why?"

"The Jake thing."

Right. Because Jake had broken her heart.

"I thought there would be a lot of talk and I couldn't handle it," she admitted. "Ironically, no one has said a word. Not counting my mother, of course."

"Do you want me to talk about him, to make you feel better?"

She laughed. "That's very sweet, but no. I'm good. I just wish I'd come home sooner. I usually make the trip several times a year. I love seeing my folks and Dena. They came to visit me, but it wasn't the same."

"You've broken the ice, so to speak, so now you won't have an excuse not to come home."

"You're right. I've been hanging out with Shaye," she added. "I like her a lot."

"Me, too. She'd good in the store. She's waiting to establish her year of residency, and then she's going to college. If she does as well as I think she's going to, I'll be moving over some of the marketing work for her."

He paused, not sure why he'd told her that. He hadn't told anyone.

"She'll be thrilled." Reggie patted his arm. "Don't worry, I won't say anything."

He believed her. Reggie had always been good at keeping secrets. She'd seen plenty of bad stuff between him and his dad, and she'd never once mentioned it. The only time they'd talked about it had been when he'd brought it up.

"You were a good girlfriend."

Her eyebrows rose. "An unexpected leap, but thank you. You were a good boyfriend."

Until the end, he thought. Not that he'd betrayed her the way she'd thought, but she'd still ended up with a broken heart. And then she'd shattered his. How would their lives have been different if they'd been able to sit down and talk about what had happened? He would have told her why he had to get out of town. She was still in high school, so she wouldn't have come with him, but they might have stayed in touch. If he'd known Reggie was waiting for him, how would everything have been different?

The overhead lights lowered as the previews started. The theater had filled up, and the noise level around them barely dimmed as the first trailer played. Reggie shifted, moving the coats to the other side of her and sliding onto the seat next to him. Without considering what he was doing, he automatically pulled up the armrest. She moved closer still as he put his arm around her.

This, he thought, noting what was the same and what was different. This was how it had been all those years ago. Just him and Reggie. They'd had so many firsts together.

But it hadn't lasted forever, and now they were different people. But for this moment, it was nice to pretend that nothing had changed.

REGGIE STUDIED THE lines of the red dress. There were challenges when it came to designing for a Great Dane, or possibly any dog. Reggie's experience was limited to Belle. She'd decided against sleeves. She wanted something simple but dressy. Belle was going to be a flower girl at the wedding. Her mother was still on the fence about Burt, but had already bought a little tuxedo jacket for him to wear.

"I'm not sure about the lace," she murmured, holding it up against the neckline of the dress.

Belle sat patiently, waiting for Reggie to be done.

"You're a good girl," Reggie told her. "Thank you for enduring my indecision. It's just I can't concentrate this morning."

She also hadn't slept much the night before, and both problems were Toby's fault.

They'd had a good time together. Being with him in the theater, his arm around her, had reminded her of how things had been all those years ago. After the movie, the three of them had gone to dinner and had spent most of their time laughing. She enjoyed his company, and Harrison's, and she'd spent the rest of the night alternating between wishing he'd kissed her and playing a silly game of what-if.

Funny how she hadn't thought of him in years and now she couldn't stop thinking about him. She wanted to spend more time with the new grown-up Toby. Everything she'd seen so far—how he was with Harrison, how he interacted with everyone during their knitting sessions—told her he was still someone she could like a lot.

"Complications," she murmured, dropping the lace to the floor and pulling the dress off Belle.

"Thank you for helping," she told her dog. "I'll pick this up later when I'm able to make decisions."

Belle moved close, and Reggie wrapped her arms around her.

"You're a good girl," she whispered. "My best girl."

Burt watched from a safe distance away. Ever since Belle had growled at him, he'd been treating the Great Dane with more respect.

"See what happens when you stand up to a bully?" Reggie pointed out. "When someone does you wrong, you need to be brave."

She had more life lessons to share, but was interrupted by the sound of footsteps on the basement stairs.

"Reggie, darling, you have a visitor," her mother said, stopping halfway and motioning for whomever was following her to continue.

Reggie scrambled to her feet, surprised to see Toby. Her heart gave a little jump, and she suddenly didn't know what to do with her hands.

"I'll leave you two alone," her mother said pointedly as she started up the stairs.

"Thanks, Mom," Reggie called after her before turning to Toby. "She needs to get a life."

Only Toby didn't smile at her attempt at humor. It was then that she noticed his shoulders were stiff and he wasn't looking at her.

Belle gave him a quick sniff, then retreated to her bed.

"What's wrong?" Reggie asked when Toby continued not to speak. "Is Harrison all right?"

"He's fine. He's at school. Why would you ask?"

"You're upset about something."

He looked at her then, his gaze unreadable. "I'm not upset. Guys don't get upset."

"Well, you're something. Is it Judy?"

"Everyone's fine. That's not why I'm here."

There was an edge to his voice—something that warned her they were about to head into a place she wasn't going to like. She couldn't explain the feeling except that when they'd been dating, she'd known Toby as well as she'd known her own family members. She'd been able to read his mood even before he could articulate it himself, and right now, he was going to say something that would make her uncomfortable.

She pointed to the sofa. "Want to take a seat?"

"I'll stand." He looked at her. "I'm not getting married."

What?

"What?"

Not getting married. That was certainly an unexpected statement that made no sense. She wanted to respond with something equally weird like *There are fish in the cracker box*, only she didn't think this was the time for humor, and—

The reason behind his statement clicked into place.

Annoyance and some embarrassment settled in the center of her chest.

"And you obviously feel it's necessary to specifically warn me that you and I aren't getting married."

His gaze met hers, but he didn't speak.

The arrogance of the man, she thought, irritation growing. It had been a couple of hours at the movies, followed by dinner. Nothing had happened. The fact that she'd wanted him to kiss her wasn't the point. She'd never hinted at it, so he didn't know what she'd been thinking. Lucky for him, the whole kissing thing was a lot less appealing now than it had been.

"As I don't recall proposing," she told him, "I can only assume that you have such a high opinion of yourself that you believe a single evening in your presence is so overwhelming that women automatically want to marry you. That has to be tough to deal with. Fortunately, I seem to be immune."

"Reggie, I can't go there. Not while Harrison is young. I can't risk it."

"Fine. It's all clear now. I hate to have to return the ring. Oh, wait. We're not engaged." She slapped her hand against her forehead. "Silly me."

"Be serious."

"Why? This is a ridiculous topic. You're not getting married? Who says that? Who thinks it? Do you honestly believe I spend my life thinking about you? I don't. I haven't thought of you in years."

He watched her. "Last night was different."

"We went to the movies. Big whoop."

"It was more than that."

Was it? He'd felt it, too? Only she couldn't say that because he was currently being a butthead, or slipping into madness.

"We have chemistry," he continued. "That hasn't gone away. But you're not the casual sex type, and I don't do anything else."

She took a second to digest all of that. Yup, a butt-head.

"Wow," she said, letting herself build up steam. "Just to quickly recap, you've assumed I want to marry you, and you wanted to let me down on that one. Now you're telling me how I feel about sex. You don't actually need me for this conversation, do you? What's wrong with you? I mean that as a genuine question, because you've screwed this up from the second you opened your mouth. I suggest you take yourself home and figure out how to get your head out of your ass. I'm guessing when that happens, you're going to feel like a first-class jerk, which is good, because you are one."

She pointed to the stairs. "Get out."

"Reggie, we have to talk."

"No, we don't. Get out. I mean it. Go."

He nodded once and went up the stairs. She walked to the sofa and sat down. She had no idea what had just happened. Where had all that come from, and why had he felt the need to dump all over her?

She looked at Belle. "Never like a guy. I'm serious. They're nothing but trouble."

Anger churned inside her, along with just a hint of sadness. So much for him being like the guy she'd once known. If this was the real grown-up Toby, she wanted nothing to do with him.

"YOU'RE BEING DIFFICULT for no reason," Electra said, her full lips forming a pout.

Micah looked away from the computer screen, wishing he hadn't agreed to the online call. He'd known what she wanted to talk about and had mistakenly thought he could change her mind.

"I'm not interested in going away with you," he said flatly. "I'm not going to write with you, and I'm not coming back to LA."

She flipped her long red hair over her shoulder. "Why are you being like this? You know we write well together. Why are you resisting the inevitable?"

"There is no inevitable. Electra, look at me. No. I'm saying no."

Her green eyes narrowed slightly. "You need me, Micah. You're not writing on your own. If you were, I would have heard. I can be your inspiration."

"I doubt that."

"You're not even trying."

"I'm going now," he said, just as someone knocked on his door.

"Micah, wait. I have something to tell you."

"Come in," he called, not caring who was on the other side of the door. Any distraction was welcome.

He looked at the perfect face of his ex-wife. She was beautiful—he would give her that—but nothing about her appealed to him.

"Oh, I'm sorry. I didn't know you were busy."

The soft words had him spinning around to see Dena carefully backing out of his suite. He half rose, waving her forward.

"No. Don't go. I'm finished here."

"Don't you dare hang up on me," Electra insisted.

Micah smiled. "I have to go."

With that, he disconnected the call and looked at Dena.

"Sorry about that."

She looked startled. "Your, ah, girlfriend?"

"No. My ex-wife."

"Oh. She's stunning."

"Yes, but the inside doesn't match the outside."

Dena still looked as if she might bolt, and Micah didn't want her to leave. He closed the laptop, then moved toward her. "What's up?"

"I, ah… Oh, it's snowing. I don't know if it will last, but there's actual snow. I thought you'd want to see it…" Her voice trailed off. "It's a thing here. The first snowfall."

"I've heard."

"It has to snow for a full fifteen minutes. I'm afraid it might turn to rain." She looked at the floor, then back at him. "I shouldn't have bothered you."

"You're never a bother. Let me get my coat and we can go watch the snow together."

Dena looked at his computer. "You two stay in touch?"

"Not really. We used to write songs together, which was strange after the divorce. We got married because we were kids and we thought that's what adults did. But it was a mistake from the beginning. We weren't in love. Not really."

He fastened his coat, then pulled on gloves. "She wants us to write together again."

"What do you want?"

"Not to write with her. It was different all those years ago. These days I want something more substantial than she can offer."

She smiled. "I understand the words, but not what they mean. I'm nothing close to an artist."

"You're something even better," he said, opening his door. "You're a teacher."

"A lot of people are teachers."

"Only the best ones."

They stepped outside. Snow was falling, but it didn't feel that cold to him. Not that he knew anything about snow, beyond the fact that it formed up in clouds or the sky, so maybe that was the temperature that mattered.

"Does she still write?" Dena asked.

"No. Electra's not interested in songwriting as an art. She wants to get back into the music business. She wants to be relevant and she sees me as her way to make that happen. With Adriana gone, she's making a run at me."

"She didn't want to write with you when you were married?"

"She did, but Adriana was opposed to the idea. She didn't trust Electra."

Dena surprised him by smiling. "I think I would have liked Adriana very much."

He laughed. "She would have liked you, too."

He took her gloved hand and drew her out into the snow. The flakes were light and small. He looked up at the sky.

"Are we supposed to do something? Turn in a circle three times or hum?"

"We wait."

"I'm not especially good at waiting," he admitted.

"Breathe in the moment. Snow can be magical."

She raised her head and closed her eyes. Tiny snowflakes landed on her face and melted away. He studied her, thinking there was something about her. Something unexpected and appealing and—

Impulsively he leaned forward and lightly brushed her mouth with his. Her eyes popped open and she stared at him.

"You kissed me."

"I did."

He closed the scant distance between them and kissed her again, this time lingering. Her mouth was soft against his. Wanting stirred, but more important to him was the sense that he liked her. She was a good person who made him laugh, and when he was with her, he felt at peace with the world.

He pulled off his gloves and stuffed them in his pockets, then cupped her face in his hands and kissed her again. Her lips parted in an age-old invitation. He deepened the kiss, tasting her and—

Cold rain pelted them. Dena shrieked and pulled him back toward the carriage house. He followed, ducking under the overhang of the upstairs landing.

When they were both under cover, they stared at each other. He had no idea what she was thinking, but as far as he was concerned, the day had taken a very nice turn for the better.

He debated what to do next. Inviting her inside so they could pick up where they'd left off seemed the most obvious option. Not that he would push her toward his bed. It was too soon, and she wouldn't be comfortable with that. But he liked that he wanted to go there with her. Specifically with her.

Her big brown eyes searched his face, as if she were trying to read his thoughts. He smiled at her.

"You all right?" he asked.

She nodded. "You and Electra really aren't, um, you know?"

"We're not. You have my word."

"Okay. Then I should probably let you get back to work." She gave him a quick smile before hurrying away.

Micah watched her go, thinking she really was amazing. Then he stepped inside. Once he'd taken off his coat and hung it on the rack, he reached for his guitar.

Even before he sat on the sofa, he heard the words in his head. *But then the snow fell. There you were, with snowflakes in your hair. There you were, teaching me to care. As the snow fell, I fell.*

He stopped playing long enough to turn on the recorder on his phone. Then he started from the beginning.

Eighteen

IT TOOK TOBY far less than the twenty-four hours Reggie had predicted for him to, as she had put it, get his head out of his ass. Around two in the morning, after hours of tossing and turning, he began to understand that he'd handled everything badly. He'd been an idiot, and he'd made a fool of himself. Worse, he'd hurt Reggie.

That last realization was the one that bothered him the most, because he'd never wanted to do anything to upset her. Not when they'd first started dating, not when he'd fallen in love with her—which had probably been on their second date—and not now.

He liked her. He'd always liked her. He enjoyed looking at her. He found her sexy. He liked how her mind worked and how she was a genuinely nice person. He admired her smarts and her emotional courage and how she took care of her ridiculous dog.

And that was the problem. The liking. Yes, it had

just been one evening, but he'd found himself way too comfortable with her. Being with Reggie had always been easy, and that hadn't changed. The feel of her next to him, the warmth of her body, the way she'd laughed at the movie, had made him think about possibilities. He'd imagined taking things further—asking her out on a date, just the two of them. He'd pictured them getting to know each other again, finding out if the sparks were still there, and once they'd gotten started on sparks, maybe they could start exploring hearts.

Only he couldn't. No, he *wouldn't*. He'd screwed up once, and Harrison would be dealing with those emotional scars for the rest of his life. That was on him. Keeping his son safe at any price was his responsibility—he wasn't going to fail him again.

But he could try to repair things with Reggie. He could explain, at least part of it, and apologize. Because he'd been wrong and he hated the idea of her being mad at him.

To that end, he arrived at the community center a half hour before the knitting session was to start, hoping to find her setting up. Luck was with him. She was just pulling the large totes of supplies out of a locked closet.

As she turned to put them on a cart to wheel them to their room, he took the tote from her.

"I need a minute of your time," he said.

Her brown eyes flashed with a combination of anger and hurt, but she squared her shoulders and raised her chin. Because the Reggie he knew was always ready to take on the fight. She wouldn't start it, but she would stand up for herself, and she would see it through to the end.

"I'm sorry," he began. "I was wrong yesterday."

"Just yesterday?"

Despite everything, he felt his lips twitch. "Let's deal with one transgression at a time."

She didn't speak.

He put the tote on the cart. "I screwed up and sent things in a direction they didn't need to go. I warned you off, but the person I was talking to was myself."

Some of the mad faded. "I don't understand."

"Sometimes I don't, either. Being around you is complicated. There have been other women in my life, but I've only ever loved you. So seeing you now, grown-up, beautiful, successful, it's intriguing. I like spending time with you. The other night, at the movies…" He paused, not sure how to explain.

"Let's just say past and present got a little blurry, and I reacted to that." He drew in a breath. "But I meant what I said, Reggie. I can't get involved. I won't. There's too much risk."

She tilted her head slightly, her shiny hair swinging with the movement.

"Yesterday you said it was about Harrison. He was the reason you weren't getting married."

"Yes."

"So something happened with him and a woman you were dating."

"Yes."

"But you're not going to tell me what."

"It's not my story to tell."

He could see the questions forming, but she didn't ask any of them, for which he was grateful.

She pressed her lips together. "It makes me sad that you would think I would hurt him."

"I don't. This isn't about you. When it happened, I promised him I would never put him in that position again. I promised there would just be the two of us until he was old enough to take care of himself. He believed me."

"That was the wrong promise to make. It puts too much pressure on him." She shook her head. "But not the point, right?"

"I'm sorry," he repeated.

"Do you understand you behaved ridiculously and that the memory of it will haunt you forever?"

He held in a grin. "Yes, I do."

"Okay, then I forgive you. I'm sorry about Harrison, and I really want to find whoever that woman is and go after her in a way that leaves scars."

"You wouldn't enjoy prison."

"No, but I would feel better about the world, so there's that. People shouldn't hurt children, ever. There's no excuse."

He appreciated her energy on the topic. It was how he'd felt, as well. Being able to share the conflicting emotions only added to her appeal.

"Have dinner with me."

The words came without warning. Toby watched Reggie stare at him, her brows drawn together in obvious confusion.

"You're sending some seriously mixed messages," she told him.

"I am."

"Why?"

He wasn't sure if she was asking why he was sending mixed messages or why he wanted to have dinner with her, but it didn't matter.

"I like you and I want to spend time with you."

"But we're not having sex and we're not getting married." She smiled. "Just to clarify your position."

"I'm open to sex."

"Most men are."

"I think my interest in you is a lot more about who you are than anything else."

"You're weird. I don't remember you being weird. Back in high school, you were the superhot bad-boy-slash-football-captain."

"And now?"

"You're still hot, but I don't believe you're bad anymore. Now that I think about it, I'm not sure you were ever bad. I think it was just an act. Maybe a way to survive. If you were tough, people would leave you alone. Of course, then you were lonely, but you were willing to pay the price to feel safe."

Her eyes widened. "Oh, that's what this whole Harrison thing is about. It's not what you promised him. It's that you need to keep him safe, at any price. But safe is always a moving target—in some ways it's intangible. So the whole marriage thing is your way of controlling an uncontrollable situation. Huh. Interesting."

Her insights slapped him upside the head like a blow from a two-by-four. Mentally he staggered and wondered if he was going down. She was right, of course, but that she'd figured it out so easily stunned him.

He was still trying to recover when she turned and grabbed another tote from the closet.

"Yes, Toby, I'll have dinner with you," she said, handing him the container. "I think at the end of the evening, kissing is a possibility, but no on the sex."

She flashed him a smile that was nearly as lethal as the two-by-four. "At least for now."

DENA TRIED TO lose herself in the chapter on the third month of her pregnancy, but the words simply weren't gripping. Actually, that wasn't fair—the words were fine. The problem was her. Specifically, that she couldn't stop thinking about the fact that Micah had kissed her.

She didn't know what to make of what had happened. No matter how many times she turned the concept over, held it up to the light, replayed it in her mind, it didn't make sense.

He'd kissed her. More than once, on the mouth, and at the end, with tongue. Like a real kiss. A boy-girl kiss. Only they weren't in a boy-girl thing. So why had he done it, and what was she supposed to do now?

She set down the book and reached for her phone.

Are you done with knitting for the night?

Reggie's reply came immediately. Just wrapping up.

Can you swing by the B and B? I need to talk and I'll ply you with yummy snacks and delicious wine.

What's the snack?

Despite her confusion about what was happening with her life, or specifically Micah, Dena laughed. You're saying I have to lure you with food?

You promised me yummy snacks. I'm just confirming that's true.

Micah kissed me.

There were several seconds before the three dots appeared. **I'm on my way.**

Dena grinned.

Five minutes later, she was waiting in the living room of the B and B. She saw Reggie's SUV pull into a parking space. Then her sister got out and ran toward the front door. Reggie hugged her before glancing around to make sure they were relatively alone.

"He kissed you? For real? I couldn't believe it when Mom said she met him the other day. She said he was gorgeous and totally into you. I haven't met him and I'm supposed to be your favorite sister. OMG! Tell me everything. Then feed me. I'm starving."

"Let's go in the kitchen. Word got out that tonight's snack is Ursula's famous coconut shrimp, so we'll have a crowd. Thank goodness she always makes extra."

Dena set out place settings at the island in the kitchen. The part-time helper was already taking out large plates of coconut shrimp and bowls of the dipping sauce. The wine for the evening was a crisp Painted Moon chardonnay, already open and sitting in ice buckets.

Dena took one of the smaller plates of shrimp and put it on the island, along with some dipping sauce. She poured wine for Reggie and sparkling water for herself, then checked the refrigerator. Sure enough, Ursula had left her a fruit and cheese plate—with only safe, hard cheeses—along with hummus. In the pantry was a second plate with crackers and a sliced baguette. She carried both to the island, then sat next to her sister and motioned to the food.

"Good enough?"

"It's amazing, but honestly I would have settled for a saltine." She glanced around again and lowered her voice. "He kissed you? Talk!"

Dena explained about the snow earlier that afternoon and how she'd gone to tell Micah.

"I'd just gotten home from school, and I was waiting to see if it was going to last."

"I know what you mean. We were knitting away, and one of the kids noticed the snow. We all held our breath, but then it turned to rain. We really need snow. The poor ski resorts must be suffering."

Dena held in a smile and waited. Any second now, Reggie would remember what they'd been talking about.

Her sister picked up a piece of shrimp. "How did I get distracted? More on the kiss, please."

"We were out in the snow and I closed my eyes to let it fall on my face and he kissed me. On the lips."

A fact that still hadn't sunk in.

"That's so romantic."

"It was unexpected."

"You've got it bad."

Dena thought of the tingles and jolts she felt around him, but knew her sister was more interested in what mattered. "I do. He's very kind and funny and he's amazing with the kids."

Reggie's gaze turned speculative. "That's right. He's your classroom mom."

"Classroom dad."

"Whatever. Interesting. And he knows about the baby,

so obviously that's not a concern." Reggie grinned. "I can't believe you gave up on love only to find Mr. Right."

"No." Dena shook her head. "He's not that. He's a crush. That's all he can be. He's a famous rock star, and he's only in town temporarily. I'm a small-town teacher who is pregnant. We have nothing in common."

"Except the kissing."

"Which didn't mean anything."

"It meant something to you."

Dena knew her sister was right. It had meant something. The problem was, it shouldn't, because if she let herself dream too much, she was in serious danger of getting her heart broken.

"Time to change the subject," she said firmly. "Distract me, please."

"Toby asked me out."

"What?" Dena's voice was a shriek. She consciously spoke more softly. "When? Are you going? Why didn't you say something sooner?"

"Oh, big sister of mine, a kiss trumps a dinner date every time. And he asked yesterday, and I said yes."

"To quote you, he asked you out? Talk!"

Reggie laughed and told her about the "I'm not getting married" conversation, followed by the very sweet apology.

"Did he say why he's not getting married?" Dena asked.

Reggie hesitated. "He did, but I'm not comfortable sharing that part. I'm sorry."

Dena wanted to know, but she wasn't going to ask. She knew her sister would tell her when she could, and she trusted Reggie completely. When they'd been kids, they'd shared everything, but as they'd gotten older, they'd realized there were pieces of their lives they would always keep private.

"But you believe him?" she asked instead.

"Yeah, I do."

"So you're going out?"

"Tomorrow. I'm nervous." Reggie spread hummus on a slice of baguette. "It's silly, really, but there's something about him."

"You have a past and it was a good one. Until the end. Even if he didn't mean for word to get out about you sleeping with him, you were still hurt, and I blame him."

Reggie grinned. "You're a very good sister."

"Yes, I am."

They were both laughing when Reggie suddenly drew in a breath.

"So, Micah. Tall, gorgeous, with dark hair and blue eyes?"

Dena's throat went dry. "That's him."

"He's about to walk into the kitchen. Lucky me. I get to meet him."

Dena barely had time to process that nugget when the back door opened. She turned to see Micah shrugging out of his thick jacket and hanging it on the coatrack by the door. Then their eyes met and the rest of the world fell away.

He looked good—which wasn't news. What was different was the way his gaze locked with hers. Like they had a connection. He smiled, and her insides melted.

"Hey," he said, crossing to her. "It's a lot colder than it was before. If it started snowing now, it wouldn't stop."

She genuinely found herself unable to speak. There were words in her brain, but they couldn't seem to make it to her mouth. Fortunately, he didn't seem to expect an answer. He turned and smiled at her sister.

"Brown hair, beautiful eyes, and I recognize that smile. You must be Reggie."

"And you're Micah. Nice to meet you."

"Likewise."

Dena tried to control her nerves. "Reggie's working with all the third-graders for the holiday charity project. They're using a circular loom to knit hats for homeless kids."

"Sounds like a worthwhile project. Is it hard to learn how to use the loom?"

Reggie smiled. "It's pretty easy, and while we could always use an extra pair of hands, I think the loom would be a waste of your talent. If you want to help, why don't you bring your guitar and entertain us instead?"

"Reggie!" Dena glared at her, then turned to Micah. "She's kidding."

"I could do that," he said slowly, as if considering the possibility.

"No," Dena told him. "Just forget she said anything."

Reggie gave her an arch smile, then looked at Micah. "How are you enjoying Wishing Tree?"

"It's a great town. The traditions are fun. I like the holiday enthusiasm." He shoved his hands in his jeans front pockets. "Last year I was in a bad car accident. My wife was killed and I ended up in the hospital for several weeks, followed by a lot of rehab. I kind of missed the whole holiday season. Being here this year is a great way to get back into the spirit."

He smiled at them both. "I'll leave you two to your conversation." He lightly touched Dena's arm before heading out to the main dining room.

"He likes you," Reggie said when he was out of ear-shot. "He likes you a lot."

While Dena wanted to believe her, she knew her luck wasn't that good—not when it came to the guy department.

"We're friends."

"Who kiss."

"It's not like that. I think he's still in love with his late wife. You heard him. He loved and lost her, and she was the one."

"He never said she was the one."

"He wouldn't have married her if she wasn't. He lost his one true love." She wondered why she hadn't seen that before. Of course he had. He couldn't write, and he was emotionally lost. He was looking to heal, not to re-place her. She would be foolish if she hoped otherwise.

"I don't believe in your theory of one true love," Reggie said flatly. "I was in love with Jake, and now I'm not. People change. Hearts heal. His heart has def-initely healed."

"You don't know that. I think he'll mourn Adriana forever."

"I'm not saying he won't still love her. It's not as if their love died with her. I'm just pointing out that he's moved on, and he's ready for a relationship."

While Dena wanted that to be true, she knew her sister was wrong. She needed to be careful and protect her heart or she was going to find it broken in a way that might not ever be repaired.

Nineteen

REGGIE TOLD HERSELF not to get too excited about her dinner out with Toby—a somewhat difficult task considering she'd been thinking about him all day. Worse, they'd spent most of their afternoon knitting session looking at each other and smiling. It was like being back in high school all over again.

Which was part of the problem, she thought, crossing the street on her way to Buon Natale, the incredible Italian restaurant in town. High school. There were too many good memories, too many habits and patterns to fall back on. She had to keep reminding herself that adult Toby was different. Oh, his character was similar, and she was definitely attracted to him, but she had to be smart and remember that he'd been very clear about not wanting to have a serious relationship with anyone. This was just dinner with a friend, and if she made it more than it was, then shame on her.

"I can do dinner," she murmured as she opened the door to the restaurant. "I eat several times a day. I'm good at it."

Her musings were cut short by the scent of garlic and basil and other delicious ingredients. Immediately her mouth began to water and her stomach grumbled, reminding her that not only had lunch been light, it had been hours ago.

The décor was simple, with dark walls and white linens. Classical music played on the sound system, and the atmosphere was both welcoming and elegant. Buon Natale was the kind of place you went when you wanted to celebrate an anniversary or job promotion. They served things like risotto with lobster and truffles or Mediterranean sea bass with carrot puree.

But all thoughts of food fled when she spotted Toby in the waiting area. Gone were the jeans and flannel shirt—he had on black pants and a deep blue shirt under a well-fitting leather jacket. He looked good enough to be the main course with just a hint of bad boy adding spice.

She had a brief moment of gratitude that she'd taken extra time with her appearance, wearing her sexy boots and applying more makeup than usual. His smile told her she'd done well.

"So we're dining fancy tonight," she said as she approached.

"Fancy is required when a person messes up like I did," he told her, lightly kissing her cheek. "You look beautiful."

"Thank you. You clean up nicely, as well."

The hostess showed them to a table by the window. When they were seated, he leaned toward her.

"I could have picked you up," he told her. "It's freezing out there."

"I'll let you drive me home. Besides, the walk took less than ten minutes. My parents' house has a great location."

He smiled. "Still doing okay, living with them for so long?"

"It's fine. I know my little house back in Seattle is lonely, but it will recover. Belle appreciates all the attention, and ever since she went after Burt, they've developed something of a friendship." She paused. "Okay, *friendship* is strong, but there's definitely a truce. I'm hoping she can get a little more confident in the rest of her life."

"Belle will always have a place in my heart."

Because she'd protected Harrison, Reggie thought.

Their server appeared and took their drink order. Toby mentioned he would have a glass of wine with dinner, so he ordered a soft drink. Reggie hesitated, not sure if she should get a cocktail.

"Order what you want," he told her. "Get something girly."

She laughed and asked for a cosmo.

"How was your day?" she asked when they were alone again.

"I had to deal with crabby tourists," he said. "I went downstairs to get lunch and found Shaye being yelled at by this young couple who'd come up yesterday morning because snow was predicted. They complained that the town should have held the celebration because it had snowed."

"But not long enough, and why were they yelling at Shaye? She works in a hand pie shop."

"I know That's what I said." He smiled. "That annoyed them even more, so they stalked out swearing they were never coming to Wishing Tree again."

"It's going to snow when it snows," she said, thinking Dena was probably waiting for that to happen, hoping Micah would kiss her again. Despite her sister's insistence that he was still in love with his late wife, Reggie hoped that Micah was getting serious about Dena.

"What are you smiling about?" Toby asked, his voice teasing. "If it's another guy, then you and I need to talk about that."

She laughed. "I suppose technically it *is* another guy. Micah Ruiz."

He frowned. "The singer? Why were you thinking about him?"

"He's in town. Didn't you know? He's staying at the B and B and flirting with my sister. I'm hoping it's more than just a passing thing."

"Dena and the rock star. I like it."

"Me, too," she admitted. "I'm glad Dena's having a baby. That's going to be so great for all of us, but I wish she hadn't given up on love so soon. She's a wonderful person, and she deserves love in her life."

"You're a good sister."

"I try to be." She looked at him. "Okay, enough about that. What are you getting Harrison for Christmas?"

They talked while she sipped her cocktail, then ordered dinner. Conversation flowed easily. Toby was as interesting as he'd ever been, and they still shared a sense of humor. He had her laughing at descriptions of failed hand pie flavors when she sensed someone approaching. She turned and felt her laughter fade when she saw Jake Crane standing by their table.

"Hello, Reggie."

TOBY'S FIRST REACTION was annoyance, followed by a somewhat violent urge to punch Jake in the face. He and the other man had been rivals in high school, which didn't matter much, but they'd also both loved Reggie, which suddenly mattered a lot.

He glanced at her, trying to gauge what she was thinking. Her wide-eyed expression made it clear she'd had no idea Jake was back in Wishing Tree, let alone in the same restaurant.

"Jake," she said, her voice surprised. "Hi."

Jake smiled at her. "I was walking by and saw you. I thought I'd come say hello. It's been a while."

"It has."

"I'm in town to spend the holidays with my mom. This time of year is hard for her, what with her missing my dad and all." He turned to Toby. "Newkirk."

"Crane."

Reggie glanced between them. "You two do know you each have a first name, right?"

Toby kept his gaze on Jake. "It's a guy thing."

Jake looked back at Reggie. "I'll let you get on with your dinner. I just… It's good to see you."

Good to see her? What the F did that mean? Only Toby could guess, and he didn't like it one bit. Jake had proposed to Reggie and then dumped her, all within forty-eight hours. Guys who did that weren't supposed to say it was good to see her. They were supposed to crawl into a cave somewhere and never come out. Or at the very least, they were supposed to stay away from Wishing Tree and not interrupt dinners.

Jake nodded at both of them before walking away. Reggie watched him go, then turned her attention to Toby.

"That was strange. No one told me he was back. I'm going to have to talk to Paisley and find out if she's failing at being my best source for gossip or if she was scared to tell me."

Her tone was more quizzical than concerned, and if he had to guess, he would say that she was surprised to see Jake but not emotionally overwhelmed. Still, she had agreed to marry him and spend the rest of her life with him, so she had to be feeling something.

"You okay?" he asked, still irritated but determined not to show it.

"I'm fine." She smiled at him. "I'm also ready to change the subject."

"You have to feel something, seeing him after a year."

Her expression turned questioning. "I guess. It was odd and unexpected."

"You were going to marry him."

"I was, and then we broke up." She studied him. "Toby, what are you getting at? I'm sorry he interrupted our dinner, but other than that, why would Jake coming back mean anything to you? While I'm having a good time, you've made it incredibly clear that you're not interested in having any kind of a relationship with me. So whatever I think or don't think of my ex-fiancé shouldn't affect you."

Her point was an excellent one, he told himself. He shouldn't care at all. But he did, and he didn't like what had just happened.

"You're right," he told her. "We should change the subject."

They looked at each other. He tried to consciously relax.

"I think the Seahawks have a good chance at making it to the playoffs," he said.

She grinned. "When in doubt, talk about sports?"

"It's always a good fallback position."

"You're such a guy."

"I am."

The rest of dinner went more smoothly. Normal conversation resumed, and Toby was almost able to forget that Jake had ever shown up. After he paid the bill, he walked her to his SUV, then drove her home. He circled around to open her door for her before he took her hand and walked her to the front door.

"Thanks for dinner," she said, shivering slightly in the cold. "I had a good time."

"Me, too."

They looked at each other for a second. He leaned in, intending to offer a perfunctory kiss, but the second his mouth brushed against her, everything changed.

Wanting exploded, sending heat pouring through him. He pulled her close, needing to feel Reggie against him. Her arms came around him, as if she'd been swept away, too. The kiss turned hungry, then deepened, his tongue sweeping inside to tangle with hers.

Past and present blurred as he remembered that kissing her had always been the best part of his day. He wanted to touch her and be touched, each of them slowly exploring, driving the other mad with desire.

The wanting increased until it became a driving

force, unlike anything he could remember. Only steel-laced self-control kept him from fumbling with the buttons on her coat and exploring her curves, right there on her parents' front porch.

Desperate for control, he pulled back, his breathing labored, his dick hard and aching. She looked as stunned as he felt. Her face was flushed, her eyes wide with surprise. She drew in a breath.

"So," she murmured. "The chemistry is still there."

"Yeah, it is."

"An unexpected turn of events."

"Tell me about it."

She smiled. "Okay, then. Um, thanks for a really nice evening."

He nodded and watched her duck into the house. When the front door closed behind her, he breathed in the cold air, waiting for his body to calm down. Five minutes later, it was just as aroused as it had been. He sighed heavily as he walked to his SUV, knowing it was going to be a very long night.

DENA KNEW THAT being a planner was one of her best qualities. It kept her life organized and allowed her to get through her day. She was almost always prepared, and she liked that. When there was a problem in her life, she thought it through and came up with a plan, which explained why she was standing outside Micah's suite, ready to tell him she'd come up with a solution.

Not that the kiss had been a problem, exactly. It was more of an issue. Or a complication. One she was going to deal with directly, because that was what she did. Mostly.

With that in mind, she knocked firmly, then stepped

back and waited. The door opened seconds later. Micah smiled when he saw her.

"Dena, hi."

The combination of the extra-sexy smile and seeing him was a little more of a turn-on than she'd expected. Her toes immediately curled in her boots, and she felt herself smiling in return.

He stepped back to let her in.

"I was thinking about you," he said, taking her coat and hanging it on the rack. "You just back from school?"

"I am."

He took her hand and led her to the sofa. His fingers were warm, and he looked good when he drew her down next to him. She just wanted to shift closer and have him wrap his arms around her and—

Ack! She scooted back a couple of feet. No! She was on a mission. She had a plan.

"We need to talk about the kiss," she told him.

The smile returned, only even sexier this time, which she wouldn't have thought was possible.

"I'd like to talk about the kiss," he said as he took her fingers in his and rubbed his thumb along the back of her hand. Tingles immediately moved up her arm and settled in her girl parts.

Surrender seemed the easiest option, she thought, swaying slightly. Resisting him was futile. The man was—

The plan, she reminded herself firmly. This was about the plan.

"We can't," she said, as much to herself as him. She pulled her hand free of his mesmerizing touch. "Kiss. We can't kiss again."

His smile faded. "Why not?"

"You're not ready. In some ways you're still recovering from your accident. Even more significant, you're dealing with the loss of Adriana. She was your one true love, and that changes things. You have to honor the pain you're feeling. I think that's why you can't write, and you need to be writing, Micah. I know you miss it. I just want to help."

He frowned. "You're assuming a lot."

"I know, but I'm not wrong. This isn't a good time for kissing."

"It seems like a fine time to me."

She ignored him. "We're friends. Let's keep that going. We get along, and we have fun together. It's important to have people in your life, especially at the holidays. I want that."

His gaze was steady. "To be my friend?"

"Yes. It's the most sensible plan."

He rose and pulled her to her feet. "You know what? You should be going, because I just got an idea for a song I want to write."

She brightened. "You did?"

"Yes, and you're the inspiration."

She pressed her hands together, trying not to let her excitement show. "I can't believe that. I inspired you?"

He held out her coat. "You did. I'm going to call it 'Crazy Women I Have Known.'"

Her happiness balloon burst. "You're making fun of me."

"I am, and you deserve it." He put his hands on her upper arms, leaned down and brushed his mouth against hers. "You're not the one who gets to decide when I'm ready to kiss someone, Dena. Just so we're clear on that."

Before she could wrap her mind around what he was saying, she was suddenly outside in the cold, and his suite door was closing in her face. She stood there, not exactly clear on what had just happened. The only thing she knew for sure was the fact that she was going to need a different plan.

"I'M INCREDIBLY DISAPPOINTED in you," Reggie said with a laugh as she sat in her SUV outside the community center. She shifted her cell phone to her other ear.

"I know. I'm so ashamed I didn't know Jake was back in town." Paisley's voice was thick with humor. "I'm usually so in the know about local gossip. My network has failed me, and I promise everyone in it will receive a stern talking-to." She paused. "Seriously, though, are you okay?"

Reggie considered the question. "Seeing him again was strange and out of the blue. Plus the whole 'having dinner with Toby' thing added a layer that made it harder for me to process what was happening. I don't feel any regrets, if that's what you're asking. I've moved on."

Even if she hadn't, the passion she'd felt in the brief kiss she and Toby had shared would have pushed her over into the "totally done with Jake" column.

"I suppose he really could be in town for his mom," Paisley mused. "They were always a tight family, and with the loss of his dad… But it seems early to be back for the holidays. I wonder if there's something going on at the resort. I'll ask around."

"Not on my account. I don't need to know anything about Jake."

"I'll be asking for myself. Job security and all that. So, how was the date?"

Reggie smiled. "It wasn't a date. We just went to dinner."

"Did he kiss you?"

The smile broadened as her body remembered the very amazing kiss they'd shared.

"Maybe."

Paisley laughed. "Then it was a definitely a date, and I'm going to want details. Just not right now because I gotta run. I have a meeting in like two minutes. See you soon."

"Bye."

Reggie dropped her phone into her bag, then started for the community center. While she wanted to claim that last night had been no big deal, Paisley was right—the kiss changed everything.

She was still smiling as she took a cart to the storage closet and loaded all the totes with their supplies. The stack of boxes containing completed hats was growing by the day. She would have a full carload when she delivered them in a couple of weeks.

She returned to the room they used and found a couple of parents had already arrived to help set up, which wasn't unusual. The surprising part was that Micah was there as well, holding a guitar case and looking wildly out of place. When he saw her, he crossed to her.

"I'm here to provide entertainment," he said, his smile almost dazzling enough to make her stumble. How on earth did Dena not fall over in a faint every time she saw him?

"Ah, hi." She looked at the guitar case, then at him. "You're really going to play for us?"

He raised and lowered the case. "It's not empty."

"But I was kind of kidding when I suggested you do that. I mean, you're you."

"I've heard that. I am me and you're you and they are they." He frowned. "That doesn't sound right."

She laughed. "And yet I know what you mean. If you're serious, everyone will be delighted to listen, but I'm giving you the chance to run while you still can."

"I don't scare off so easily."

"Good to know." She waved to the room. "We work at the tables. Feel free to set up wherever you'd like."

He nodded and took a chair to a corner of the room. The parents who had been hovering walked closer.

"Is that… I mean, it can't be, but he looks just like…" Brittany, mom of one of Harrison's classmates, verbally stuttered to a stop. "Is that Micah Ruiz?"

"It is. He's friends with my sister and offered to help with the project. I was joking when I pointed out having him entertain us would be a lot more fun than having him knit a hat. So here he is."

Brittany, a pretty thirtysomething with three kids, looked at him. "He's so sexy, I can't stand it."

The two dads standing nearby grimaced, but Reggie didn't care. *Sexy* was a good word when it came to Micah.

She introduced the adults to him, then got back to unloading supplies. She'd just started on the last tote when she heard a familiar voice.

"You should have waited for me," Toby said, coming up beside her. "I would have helped."

And just like that, Micah's bright, shining star

dimmed to nothing special. She turned and saw Toby smiling at her. Her lips curved up, and the rest of the world faded away until it was just them and what had happened the previous night.

"It's not hard work," she said, resisting the need to step into his embrace and have him kiss her again. Something that wasn't going to happen—at least not during their craft session.

As if to prove her point, a dozen kids streamed into the room. She greeted them by name and helped them get settled. When next she could spare Toby a glance, he was sitting by Harrison, chatting with the boys at his table and knitting away.

Micah was a big hit. He played and sang, taking a few requests and making the time speed by. Reggie knew she wasn't the only one trying to integrate the fact that Micah Ruiz was giving them a private concert. When the session was finished, a few of the parents crowded around him, asking questions and wanting selfies. Reggie made her way over, wondering if she should intervene, but when Micah caught her attention, he smiled and shook his head.

"I've got this."

"You probably have experience."

"A little."

Toby retrieved the open box of completed hats from the storage closet, and together they added the finished ones.

"I'm keeping a count," she told him, liking how aware she was of him. The hum of sexual interest was kind of nice. Kissing would be better, but in a crowd, she would take what she could get.

By the time she'd completed her inventory, Micah

had dealt with all his fans. He walked over and introduced himself to Toby.

"I heard you were staying at the B and B," Toby told him. "Dena does a good job there. My son and I stayed there when we first moved to Wishing Tree."

"You're a new resident?" Micah asked, putting away his guitar.

Toby grinned. "Yes and no. I grew up here but took off when I was eighteen. Harrison and I relocated here last year."

"Couldn't stay away?" Micah asked.

"Something like that."

"I get the appeal." Micah chuckled. "It's quirky." He turned to Reggie. "Thanks for letting me hang out."

"Are you kidding? We had a private concert. It was fantastic."

"Anytime."

He waved and left. Reggie watched him go, wishing she could have figured out a way to ask him about Dena. She had a good idea of her sister's feelings, but was less certain if Micah's heart was headed in the same direction. He seemed perfectly normal—if she didn't know about his late wife, she would have no idea he was still in mourning. So was he mostly healed and ready to give love another try, or was he, as Dena believed, happy having experienced his one true love and not interested in anyone else?

"Not going to get an answer to that question anytime soon," she murmured.

Toby looked at her, but before he could ask what she was talking about, Harrison held up a bag of yarn.

"We didn't put this away," he said. "I'll go put it in the right tote."

"Thanks, Harrison," Reggie said, walking around the room to check for any other supplies left behind.

Toby began pushing in chairs. When Harrison was out of earshot, he looked at her, his gaze heated. "So, about last night."

She smiled. "Yes. Last night. It was very—"

A desperate scream came from the back of the building. Before Reggie could figure out what was happening, Toby was running in that direction. The screams continued, getting more frantic with every second. Reggie raced after him, quickly realizing the horrific sound was coming from the storage closet.

"He's trapped inside," she said, aware Toby had already figured that out.

He pulled on the door, jerking it several times until it finally burst open. Harrison ran out, flinging himself at his father. He was pale, and tears poured down his cheeks. Even from several feet away, Reggie could see he was shaking.

"I've got you," Toby told him, cradling him close. "I've got you, Harrison. I'm right here. I'm here. Breathe, son. Just breathe. I'm right here."

She hovered, not sure what to do. Toby turned his head.

"Would you get our jackets?"

She nodded and hurried down the hallway. After collecting coats, scarves and gloves, she returned to the hallway. Harrison was still crying, but with less intensity. He reluctantly released his father long enough to put on his coat. Toby helped him with his gloves, then shrugged into his own gear before picking up his son and carrying him out of the building.

Reggie stood alone in the hallway, not sure what

had just happened, but knowing in her gut that Harrison's reaction to being stuck in the closet hadn't been the ordinary concern the average eight-year-old might feel. He'd been terrified in a way that left her worried and chilled all the way down to her soul.

Twenty

DENA SAT IN her doctor's waiting room, more excited than nervous about her appointment. The routine exams would be part of her life now, becoming more frequent as the baby grew inside her. She was feeling good, sleeping well, eating right, getting in plenty of walking. All the things she was supposed to be doing.

An older woman came in and gave her name to the receptionist, then took a seat close to Dena. She smiled.

"Less of a crowd today," the woman said conversationally. "Mornings are the worst."

"Are they? Good to know." Until getting pregnant, Dena only saw her ob-gyn for an annual checkup. The medical practice was a busy one, with three doctors and a couple of nurse practitioners.

"Usually I'm surrounded by very pregnant women," the other patient said with a laugh. "Just watching them trying to stand when their name is called makes me wince. I'm so glad those days are behind me. My kids are grown, with kids of their own." Her gaze settled on Dena's wrist. "But I see you're just starting your journey. How far along are you?"

"What? How did you…" Dena glanced at the motion sickness bracelets she wore. "Oh, these." She smiled. "Eleven weeks. I'm finally starting to feel better, but now that I've found these, I'm afraid to take them off."

"A couple more weeks and you won't need them." She glanced at the door. "Is your husband parking the car?"

Dena held in a groan. People assuming she was married was something she was going to have to get used to. She reminded herself to keep her smile in place as she drew in a breath.

"I'm not married. I had artificial insemination. I'm having the baby on my own."

"Oh, that's very modern." The other woman's expression turned pitying. "I imagine you think you're very brave, but don't you worry about giving up on ever having a man in your life?"

"Why would you say that? Having a baby doesn't mean I can't find someone to be with."

Although her reasons for getting pregnant in the first place had been guided by that assumption. Not that it would never happen, but that she was tired of waiting for a man to come along. She wanted children, and she'd been in a position to make that happen.

"Women with children get married all the time," she added.

"Yes, they do, but they were married before. Your decision says you don't need a man, and they don't like not to be needed. No one does. You should accept the fact that you're going to be alone forever."

The side door opened and a nurse stepped out. "Hi, Dena. We're ready for you."

Dena picked up her bag and coat and followed the nurse to the examination room. She told herself that the words of some stranger shouldn't matter at all. That she had a great life, with plenty of love and support, and the woman didn't know her. She wasn't giving up on love—she was being proactive. She was strong and determined, and if some guy was put off by that, then he was a fool, and she didn't need him in her life.

Which sounded really brave, but left her feeling sad and more than a little scared about her future.

REGGIE WATCHED THE "smarter" vacuum finish up in the kitchen, making notes about the weird chirping sound that it had recently started making. She'd texted Gizmo about it, but he hadn't had many ideas, nor had he seemed all that interested in the video she'd sent. Apparently his epic holiday light show was consuming his time these days.

"I can only do what I can do," she reminded herself as she watched the vacuum return to its home base. It chirped a couple more times, then went silent as it began recharging.

More interesting than the test or the noise was the fact that Belle had spent the last hour comfortably dozing on the sofa, barely raising her head to take note of her former enemy. Apparently her lone act of bravery in protecting Harrison had lasting and very positive repercussions.

"Who knows what you'll be doing in a few weeks?" she told Belle.

Her dog stretched and closed her eyes, as if saying she wasn't ready to discuss that just now. Reggie smiled, then went into the kitchen to empty the dishwasher. Her parents were both at work today—her mom subbing for the office manager who was home with a bad cold.

She put away dishes and what felt like every bowl in the kitchen. They'd made pancakes that morning, and for reasons she couldn't explain, that process involved more bowls than seemed natural. She hesitated before putting away the old-fashioned egg beater, not sure where it belonged. It was probably the last working one in the country, but her mother insisted that it was required to beat the eggs before they were added. Fluffy eggs meant fluffy pancakes.

She finished with the dishwasher, then stood in the center of the room, not sure what to do with herself. Another inventor was sending her an invention to review, but it wouldn't arrive until tomorrow. Belle's dress for the wedding was finished, and she'd transplanted all the Christmas cactus. She still had to tie ribbons on them, but wasn't ready to start that project. She supposed she could work on the slideshow that would be playing during the reception, but wasn't sure she could sit still for that long. She felt restless and unsettled, and she knew the reason: Harrison.

She'd been unable to stop thinking about what had happened to him and how he'd reacted. She had questions, of course, but wasn't sure she should ask them. Even more troubling, she hadn't heard from Toby since the incident. She'd texted a few hours later to ask if

Harrison was feeling better. Toby's brief He's fine hadn't seemed very friendly. She didn't think he was blaming her for what had happened, so she wasn't sure why he'd been so terse.

The doorbell rang, causing both dogs to come to their feet. Burt went running toward the front of the house, barking all the way. Belle stretched before following. Reggie crossed her fingers, hoping that Toby had decided to stop by to explain things, but when she opened the front door, there was a different man on the porch.

"Jake!" She stared at him. "You're a surprise."

"A good one or a bad one?"

"A good one."

She waved him inside, then stepped aside so Burt and Belle could greet him. Her Great Dane had always liked Jake—not with any kind of Harrison enthusiasm—and she wanted her head scratched before she was willing to get out of the way.

"I hope this is an okay time," he said, looking at her. "I thought we could catch up."

Weird, but sure, she thought, taking his coat. "I just finished up a report for work, so I'm available." She led him into the family room. "Can I get you coffee or something?"

"No, thanks."

They sat on opposite ends of the sectional, facing each other. Having him here was unexpected, but not as uncomfortable as she would have thought. Jake looked good. Lean and fit, with curly dark hair and hazel eyes that changed color depending on what shirt he had on. Today they were green, reflecting the sweater he wore.

"How's your mom doing?" she asked.

One shoulder rose and lowered. "She has good days and bad days. This is her first Christmas without him, so it's going to be hard on her."

"And on you," Reggie added. "You and your dad were always tight."

"Mostly." His mouth straightened. "I can't believe he's not here anymore. It was so sudden."

Reggie nodded, not sure what to say. Jake's father had gone to his office one morning, and after sitting down at his desk, he'd suffered a fatal heart attack. The sudden passing had rocked the town. Reggie remembered her mother calling, wanting Reggie to know what had happened. Reggie had sent a note to Jake's mom and had made a donation to the suggested charity, but hadn't gotten in touch with Jake. They'd split up five months earlier, and reaching out to him had felt strange.

"I wasn't sure what to do when he died," she admitted. "I was thinking about you…" Her voice trailed off.

He looked at her. "I get it. After what had happened, you wouldn't be sure what to say. I know you wrote my mom, and she appreciated that."

"I always liked her."

"She liked you. She was disappointed when we broke up."

"Is that what she thinks happened?" she asked before she could stop herself. "That we mutually decided to end things?"

His gaze was steady. "No. She knows it wasn't like that. She knows I…" He seemed to search for the words.

"Proposed on a Friday, went to an engagement party with me on Saturday, then dumped me on Sunday?" she offered.

One corner of his mouth turned up. "That's a very clear way of talking about it"

"It's what happened."

"I know. I'm sorry about that. It's why I'm here. To explain what happened." He held up a hand. "I realize you may not want to hear anything from me, and if that's the case, I'll go quietly. But I thought you might like a little closure. I've found it helps to know the truth when it comes to moving on."

Wow—she hadn't seen that coming. Reggie briefly considered telling him she couldn't be less interested in his excuses, only she found she *did* want to know. Everything had happened so fast. She'd still been in the staring-at-her-ring stage of their engagement, and then it was over. They hadn't fought or even disagreed. They'd had a great couple of days, and then poof, that was it.

"I would like to hear what happened," she admitted. "*Closure* is probably a little strong, but finishing the story would be helpful." She thought about adding that she was completely over him, then decided against it. She knew she'd moved on, and what he thought of her was a whole lot less important than it had been a year ago.

"Thank you," he said, his gaze locking with hers. "I want to tell you. I wish I'd told you then." He surprised her by smiling. "I'm going to start by saying I was an idiot."

She raised her eyebrows. "I'm not going to disagree. Go on."

"I was in love with you. I want to be clear about that. I meant every word I said when I proposed. But before you, there was someone else."

"I didn't think you came to me an emotional virgin."

"A few years before, I'd met and fallen for a woman named Iona. It was one of those things. A lightning strike. Love at first sight. Whatever you want to call it. I saw her and I knew she was the one and I would be spending the rest of my life with her."

Hmm, not the direction Reggie had wanted the story to go. She told herself to just listen and not judge—that whatever had happened before she and Jake got together wasn't her business.

"I didn't tell her any of that," he continued. "Not for a while. She was like a drug. I couldn't get enough of her."

Reggie resisted the urge to tell him to get to the idiot part because she had a feeling she would like that bit of the story a whole lot more.

"I was just about to propose when she dumped me. She'd fallen out of love with me and wanted to move on with her life. I was devastated and crushed and every other breakup feeling. I couldn't believe it. Living without her was like going from a world filled with color to one that was black and white." His expression turned sheepish. "Or so I thought at the time."

"It's a little dramatic."

"Yeah, that's how it felt. It took me a long time to get over her. I was starting to question whether I would ever be interested in another woman when I ran into you."

"Literally."

"Yes. You smiled at me and I felt something I hadn't in a while. I realized I was over her and ready to give my heart again."

That made Reggie feel marginally better. At least she could know his feelings for her had been real.

"One thing led to another," he said. "We fell in love and I could see myself spending the rest of my life with you. We got engaged. Then, Sunday morning, Iona showed up."

Reggie nearly sprang to her feet. "Here? In town?"

"On my doorstep. She told me she'd made a horrible mistake and that she still loved me. She begged for another chance."

"Which you gave her."

"No." He looked at her. "I told her we were done and she left. But after she was gone, I couldn't stop thinking about her, which made me question a lot of things about myself. Not knowing what to do, I broke up with you, then went away to clear my head. It was a rookie move, and I apologize for that. And for not explaining what had happened. I see now if I had, we might have worked it out. We should have at least talked."

Reggie didn't know what to do with all the information. She was confused and unsettled. The timing of Iona deciding she wasn't as over Jake as she'd claimed didn't help. What if it had been a month later, eight weeks sooner? What would have been different? If he'd just, as he'd said, come to talk to her? How would everything have changed?

"I don't know what to say," she admitted. "After you'd had time to think, why didn't you talk to me?"

"Iona followed me. I don't know how she found me, but she did. She begged for a second chance, and eventually I gave it to her."

Reggie looked at him. "I believe what you're saying

is, she begged, you slept with her, and *then* you gave her another chance."

"Yeah, that's probably closer to the order of events."

"Once you'd slept with her, you couldn't come back to me. It would have been as if you'd cheated, so why not see if things would work out with her?"

He winced. "I'd forgotten how well you knew me and how easily you could get to the heart of the matter."

"It's a gift," she said with a lightness she didn't feel. While she wasn't looking to return to the past, hearing all this wasn't as easy as she would have thought. "I take it the relationship didn't last."

"No. About four months in, I knew I'd made a mistake." He drew in a breath. "And that's my story. There are no excuses for what happened, and I'm sorry I hurt you. I acted badly. I regret that."

He hesitated as if there was more, then surprised her by standing. "I won't keep you any longer. Thanks for hearing me out."

She walked him to the door.

"I feel as if I should say something," she told him as he put on his coat. "Maybe profound or bitchy or funny."

He chuckled. "You have my number. Text me when you decide what it is. I'll be around through Christmas." He bent down and kissed her cheek. "I am sorry, Reggie. More than you know."

He opened the front door and stepped outside. After he was gone, she stood in the entryway, her mind swirling. What on earth was she supposed to think of everything he'd told her? There had been too much information and no time to process it. She needed a way to clear her head.

Taking Belle for a walk was the obvious solution,

but she decided to wait at least ten minutes. She didn't want to leave only to run into Jake somewhere.

She walked back to the family room, thinking she would flip channels until she felt it was safe to go outside. She needed something to distract her and—

Her phone buzzed with an incoming text. She pulled it out of her pocket and saw it was from Toby.

Immediately guilt bubbled up inside, which was ridiculous. They weren't involved. Yes, there had been that great dinner and the kiss that had followed, but he'd made it clear he wasn't interested in an actual relationship. Besides, she and Jake had only been talking. No guilt was required.

That established, she read the text.

Harrison has something he wants to talk to you about. Can you come by tonight around seven?

The only possible topic that came to mind was Harrison getting stuck in the closet. Was he afraid she was going to tell people that he'd screamed and cried? She wouldn't, but better to tell him that.

I'll be there.

Thanks. See you then.

EVERY PART OF Toby wanted to tell his son he was making a mistake. Protecting his son was his primary job, and watching him walk into a dangerous situation had him on edge. But Harrison was insistent and Toby had been unable to change his mind.

"It's okay, Dad," Harrison told him. "I want Reggie to know what happened."

The obvious question was why, but Toby had already tried that. His son trusted Reggie, and that was the end of the discussion.

So here they sat, waiting for Reggie's arrival at the house. Toby couldn't help wishing for a call from her, saying she couldn't make it. But right on time, the doorbell rang.

"Don't worry," Harrison told him, sounding far older than eight. "She's not like Lori."

Something Toby could only hope was true.

They let her in. Usually the sight of Reggie's easy smile kicked him in the gut, but not tonight. Instead there was only unease. He knew he should trust her, but he was a father first.

They exchanged the usual greetings as Reggie took off her coat and hung it, along with her scarf, then they went into the family room. Reggie hid her curiosity well, only smiling when Harrison told her where to sit. Toby took a chair across from her so he could watch her and jump in if he needed to. Harrison remained on his feet.

"I wanted to tell you what happened in the closet," Harrison said. "At the community center."

"You don't have to tell me anything," Reggie said, her voice gentle. "I mean that, Harrison."

He nodded, his expression serious. "I know, but I want you to know." He looked at Toby, then back at her. "When I was six, Dad had a girlfriend. Lori. She and Dad were going to get married."

Reggie's eyebrows rose slightly, but otherwise she didn't say anything.

"Lori told Dad that she liked me a lot, and when it

was the three of us, she was really nice, but when it was just her and me, she was different."

Toby was watching closely, so he noticed the subtle stiffening of Reggie's shoulders and the tightness around her mouth.

"Sometimes she was mean," he continued, his voice matter-of-fact. "There were a lot of rules, and when I didn't follow them, she punished me."

"Did she hit you?" Reggie asked quietly.

"She locked me in a closet under the stairs. There wasn't a light or anything. She would put me in there and not let me out for a long time."

Reggie flinched, and tears filled her eyes. She quickly blinked them away.

"That would have scared me a lot," she whispered. "Were you scared?"

Harrison nodded, then sat on the sofa. "I didn't know what to do. Lori said if I told Dad, the police would take me away from him. I didn't know what that meant, but I knew I had to be quiet."

Reggie looked at Toby, her gaze questioning.

"I had no idea," he said. "Harrison grew less enthused about Lori, but other than that, I had no reason to think anything was wrong. When I tried to ask him what was going on, he said everything was fine."

"Dad went away for a few days," Harrison continued. "He left me with Lori."

"You must have been so scared."

He nodded slowly. "I tried to be good. I tried not to break any rules, but I did, and she put me in the closet. Only this time it was a really long time, and she didn't let me out." He looked down. "I started screaming and screaming, and she said the more I screamed, the longer I would have to stay there."

More tears filled Reggie's eyes, and a few trickled down her cheeks. "I'm sorry, Harrison." She pressed her lips together. "May I hug you?"

He nodded and flung himself at her. She held him tight, then kissed the top of his head. Toby felt his tension ease.

"I came home early," he said, picking up the story. "I didn't tell her because I wanted it to be a surprise. I walked into the house and Harrison was screaming. I couldn't believe it."

He still remembered the horror of that moment. How it had taken him a second to figure out what the sound was and where it had been coming from. He'd freed his son and had held him, knowing whatever Lori had done was his fault. He'd been the one to bring her into their lives. He'd been the one to trust her with his son.

He remembered the body-shaking sobs and how Harrison was crying so hard, he couldn't catch his breath. He remembered Lori's defiance. "What's the big deal? It's how my mom punished me. It's not like I beat him or anything."

Harrison straightened and smiled at Reggie. "I'm okay now. Dad found a doctor for me. I talked to Dr. Nina, and she helped me understand I hadn't done anything wrong. I'm better, except I don't like being in the dark."

"That makes sense," Reggie told him. "You're so brave. I'm glad you had someone help you heal. I've already talked to the manager of the community center, and I told her about the sticky door. It won't happen again, Harrison. Not there."

"Thanks, Reggie. I knew you'd understand." He looked at his father. "I'm going upstairs now, Dad."

"Okay. I'll be along in a bit."

He watched Harrison climb the steps to the family room. When they were alone, he looked at Reggie.

"He wanted to tell you."

"I think I'm going to be sick," she admitted. "Toby, how did you stand it? You must have wanted to hurt her."

"I did. Once I got him home and settled, I wanted to go back and exact my revenge."

Her mouth twisted. "I know you didn't, even if she deserved it. What did you do?"

"Called a lawyer. I was ready to sign a complaint to press charges, but Harrison didn't want me to. So I got him in to see a child psychologist."

"Dr. Nina?"

He nodded. "She was incredible. When he first started seeing her, he couldn't sleep with the lights out, and he had nightmares every night. Within a couple of sessions, he was doing better. Now he's rarely bothered, but the closet at the community center threw him."

She pressed a hand to her chest. "I can't begin to imagine. Oh, Toby, I'm so sorry. You must have felt awful. Poor Harrison. What was that woman thinking?"

"You mean what was *I* thinking."

"How could you have known? No one would ever believe another human was capable of that."

"I didn't know."

She stared at him as if he were crazy. "You would never leave Harrison in a dangerous situation. No rational person would consider it. He's your son, and you would die for him. None of this is your fault. She's a sick, sick woman, and I'm sorry you didn't press charges."

"Me, too. But he didn't want to go through it."

"I understand that, but it leaves me with a lot of rage and nowhere to put it." She gave him a faint smile. "Sorry. Not your problem. I'm sure you felt the same, but ten times worse."

"It was a tough time."

"I hate her."

He smiled. "That's my Reggie."

"I mean it."

"I know you do."

She looked fierce and determined, but also frustrated. None of that surprised him. He should have known she would react like this. His worry had been silly and a waste of time.

"She's the reason you don't want to get involved," she said slowly. "You fell in love with Lori, and she turned out to be a monster, so now you can't trust yourself."

"I didn't love her," he admitted. "I thought Harrison needed a mother, and she was a likely candidate." He'd enjoyed her company and had cared about her, but his feelings hadn't been deeper than that.

"Dumb reason to get married," she told him. "Harrison is thriving. You don't need to create a family for him. He has one already. Not just with you and Judy but in the town. This isn't a community that turns its back on people." She paused. "Okay, you weren't living here then, but I'm sure you had a circle of friends who were like family to Harrison."

Which was exactly what Dr. Nina had told him.

"I know that now," he said.

"But you're still not willing to trust." She held up a hand. "I get it. I really do. I don't know that I'd trust anyone after that. Does Dena know?"

He nodded. "I told her at the beginning of the school year, in case something happened."

"She hasn't said anything to me, and I won't say anything to anyone, either." She drew in a breath. "I just want to go hug him and never let go, and I want to find Lori and bitch-slap her." She smiled apologetically. "I'm sorry I can't do more than that. I'm not good at violence." She brightened. "If Belle continues to grow a little attitude, I could train her to growl on command. That would be scary."

Deep in his chest, a little of the guilt and fury broke free and evaporated in the warmth of her caring. Reggie had her flaws, but lack of loyalty and heart wasn't on the list. He remembered how she'd stood by him when her parents and her friends had questioned her willingness to go out with a guy like him. She'd agreed to follow the rules her parents had set in place, but had refused to not see him based on rumors and a family history.

"You're a good friend," he told her.

"You're a good dad. I know you doubt yourself because of what happened, but we're not responsible for other people's sicknesses. That's on them."

"I lie awake at night and wonder if I missed a sign somewhere."

"Unless she had one on the wall that said 'hey, I lock kids in the closet,' then you didn't. Harrison has healed. He's brave and strong. Trust that and trust yourself."

Without thinking, he stood and pulled her to her feet, then wrapped his arms around her. She hung on to him, burying her face in his shoulder.

They stayed that way a long time, with him breathing in the scent that was Reggie and feeling his anger fade as wanting took its place. How would grown-up

Reggie be different from the teenager he'd known? What would be new and what would be the same?

Not that he was going to find out. While he was glad she knew what had happened, her knowing didn't change his fundamental belief that he shouldn't get involved with anyone.

He stepped back. "Thanks for listening," he said. "I'm sorry all this got dumped on you with no warning."

"Don't be. I'm honored Harrison trusts me with something that important." She stared into his eyes. "It's okay to forgive yourself, Toby. You don't have to forget, but you need to accept that you've learned from your mistakes and you'll do better next time."

"Always seeing the good in people?" he asked, his voice teasing. Keeping things light was a whole lot easier than dealing with the dark stuff.

"No. I see the good in good people, and that's you."

She moved close, put her hand on his arm, then raised herself on tiptoe and lightly brushed his mouth with hers. "Good night."

"Night."

He helped her with her coat, then stayed by the door until she'd driven away. When she was gone, he headed for the stairs, knowing that whatever he wanted from Reggie, he was going to have to learn to do without. He liked her and he trusted her, but Harrison had to be his priority right now. No matter how Reggie tempted him, he was simply going to have to keep letting her walk away.

Twenty-One

MICAH COULDN'T REMEMBER the last time he'd felt this good. It had been over a year—that he knew for sure. Losing Adriana and the baby had nearly destroyed him, but he was coming back to life. In some ways he felt stronger than he had before the accident. He believed even the darkest of times eventually eased. Scars weren't anything to hide in shame—instead, they told a story and made him who he was.

He'd finished the song. Dena informing him that he was still in love with Adriana and that there would be no more kissing had somehow pushed him over the creative edge, so to speak. He'd worked into the night, until the song was done.

"Because the Snow Fell" was good. Really good. It would be a hit and a comeback for him, but more importantly, it affirmed that he could still write. Ever since finishing the song, he'd been flooded with ideas and was spending hours every day writing as fast as he could.

Except for today, he thought, whistling softly as he walked the short distance to Dena's classroom. He shifted the boxes from The Christmas Feast so he could pull open the door. Instantly all the students called out to him, waving and grinning.

Dena stood at the front of the room, shaking her head in mock dismay. "I have lost control."

Her students laughed. She smiled back, then looked at Micah.

"You come bearing gifts."

Her tone was light enough, but the second their eyes met, he knew something was wrong. He could see it in the half-hearted curve of her lips and the sadness in her gaze.

Aware of the students watching him, he put down the boxes of snacks and pulled Dena into the hallway. "What happened?" His gaze dropped to her stomach. "Is everything okay with the baby?"

"We're both fine," she said, offering him another smile that didn't convince him of anything.

But this wasn't the time or place to have the conversation. He would talk to her after class.

"Okay," he said, holding open the door. "I have a surprise for the class."

They walked inside and found everyone looking at them with a combination of curiosity and concern.

"You have a surprise?" she asked loudly, instantly shifting the mood of the room.

"I do."

One he'd been excited about until just this second.

Unexpected doubt swamped him. Maybe he'd gone too far. Maybe he should have—

Only there was no time to change his mind because just then, the school janitor showed up with a large pallet stacked high with boxes.

Dena stared at the writing on the side, eyes wide with disbelief. "You bought guitars for the class?"

All the kids started talking at once. A couple jumped out of their seats as if they couldn't contain themselves.

"I thought it would be fun," he said, trying not to sound defensive. "I thought I'd teach them a few chords, then let them take them home. I tuned them this morning."

She blinked at him. "You bought everyone a guitar?"

"Is that against the rules?"

"I don't think so."

The students raced to the front of the room.

Micah had everyone form a rough circle on the floor.

He demonstrated "The First Noel" because it could be played with only three chords. The kids strummed along as best they could.

After he demonstrated the song, he drew the three chords on the board.

"We'll use D, G and A7," he said. "First I'll teach you the three chords. Then we'll talk through the song while using the chords."

The bell rang for recess. Dena smiled at her class. "If you want to go out and play, you're excused. If you want to stay and practice, that's fine, too."

A couple of students exchanged looks, but no one got up.

An hour later, the entire class could play the song. He went around the circle again, helping where he was needed. A couple of the kids were naturals. A girl in glasses was already experimenting with different finger placements. He stopped by her chair.

"Everyone's getting a songbook," he told her.

Her smile lit up her face. "I can't wait to play them."

"You have talent."

Dena had everyone pause for their snack and to pass out the books. Micah demonstrated several more chords, then answered questions about how to play until it was time for the kids to head home. They trooped out, proudly holding their guitars.

"I hijacked your afternoon," he told her. "Sorry. I should have realized the lesson would take longer than my time."

"Are you kidding? They enjoyed it. If you're willing, I'd love to do it again next week. We don't have a music teacher in school anymore."

"So you're not mad?"

"No. I'm going to have to explain the influx of guitars to my principal, but I doubt she'll mind."

They moved the desks and chairs back into place. Micah took out the trash, then returned to Dena.

"What's wrong?" he asked her. "Please, I want to help."

She sank onto her chair and let her tote bag drop to the floor. "Is it that obvious? I was in the waiting room at my doctor's office and this woman said…" She shook her head. "I don't know why I let a stranger get to me."

"Someone was mean to you?" He was careful to keep the outrage from his voice.

"No, not mean exactly." Dena bit her lower lip.

"When I told her I'm not married and am having a baby on my own, she said…she implied…" She sucked in a breath. "She said that no man would want to marry me because I'd already proven I didn't need one, and men like to be needed."

She looked away, as if gathering her self-control. "I don't know. When I say it like that, it's really not anything, only somehow it made me feel awful." She turned back to him. "I want to fall in love and get married, and I don't know why that hasn't happened. What if there's something wrong with me?"

"There's nothing wrong with you. You're strong and smart and brave and beautiful."

She managed a faint smile. "That's kind, but you don't know me that well, Micah. I've had serious boyfriends, but no one has ever wanted to spend his life with me. What if that's my fault? What if I'm too bossy or demanding or I'm terrible in bed?"

He didn't like her questioning herself. Dena was determined and hardworking. She got in the middle of things and accomplished her goals. She wasn't afraid, and that was a good thing.

"I'm taking you to dinner," he said, a plan forming. He glanced at his watch. "Be ready in an hour. Dress casual."

She shook her head. "You don't have to take me to dinner or do anything else. Seriously, Micah, I'll be fine."

"An hour," he said firmly. "Don't think you can get out of this. I know where you live."

She laughed. "All right. Thank you. I'll agree, but only on one condition."

Sex? Could it be that they made love? Because for that, he was all in.

"Anything."

"We're not going to talk about this again," she told him. "It makes me feel pathetic, and I don't like that."

"I won't bring it up. You have my word."

They both rose. He started for the door, then turned back.

"She's wrong, you know," he said. "That woman? She's wrong about a man not wanting you because you had a baby on your own. Being that kind of person makes a guy wonder how far you'd go for the man you loved. It makes him think it would be to the ends of the earth."

MICAH'S KIND WORDS stayed with Dena for the next hour. She had a quick talk with her principal about the guitars, then hurried home to change for her dinner with Micah. She had no idea where he was taking her. They were meeting at four thirty, which seemed a little early for the evening meal, but as she would be spending time with him, she wasn't going to complain.

As friends, she reminded herself. Only friends. Nothing more.

Dressed in jeans and a pretty holiday sweater, she was pulling on her scarf as Micah walked into the lobby of the B and B.

He looked good, which wasn't a surprise. She doubted he ever looked bad. There was something about his deep blue eyes, or maybe it was his smile. Or his easy stride or the way he walked directly to her, as if there was no one else in the room.

"That man," Winona murmured under her breath from behind the front desk. "He does give a woman pause."

Amen to that, Dena thought.

"Right on time," he said with a wink. "See, you're full of good qualities."

"Yes, punctuality is one of my strong suits."

"We'd better get going. We have big plans for tonight."

He hustled her out to his car and drove through town, by-passing The Wreath. She tried to think of any restaurants on the other side of town, but none came to mind.

"Where are we going?" she asked, curious rather than concerned.

He pointed to a sign as they turned onto Red Cedar Highway. "There."

She stared at the arrow pointing toward the private airport just east of town.

"There's nowhere to eat at the airport."

He flashed her a smile that had her hormones whimpering in delight. "I know."

So why would they be going to the— "We're getting on a plane?" she asked, her voice a little shrieky.

"We are. Now sit back and enjoy the drive."

Given the time of year and how far north they were, the sun had already set. They drove through the darkness, arriving at the brightly lit airport ten minutes later. Dena stared at a small, sleek jet waiting on the tarmac. As Micah parked, the door on the plane opened and stairs were lowered, as if they were being invited inside.

"We're getting on that?" she asked, unable to grasp the concept.

"We are. We're flying to Seattle. It should take about thirty minutes to get there."

"On a private jet?"

"I chartered it."

They got out of the car and started toward the plane.

"How does that work?" she asked. "You pick up the phone and ask for a private jet to be delivered."

"I have an account with the company, so yes. I was lucky one was available." The smile returned. "I didn't give them much notice."

She would guess not, what with him asking her to dinner less than two hours earlier.

One of the two pilots came down to meet them. He introduced himself as Ron Sullivan and escorted them inside. Dena tried not to gape at the well-appointed interior, including comfy-looking plush leather seats.

Ron explained the safety features, showed her how to work the toilet in the bathroom, and put out a very nice cheese plate, along with an assortment of liquor, wine, and plain and sparkling water. She and Micah sat across from each other, and minutes later, the jet rolled down the runway and up into the sky.

"Things like this don't happen to me," she said. "I mean ever."

He looked at her, his expression anxious. "You've flown before, haven't you?"

"Oh, please. Of course I've flown."

Twice, she added silently to herself. Both times she'd driven to Seattle and had caught her plane there. No one had ever sent a private jet for her. She didn't even know anyone who'd flown on a private jet.

"It must be really nice to be a rock star," she said.

He got up and collected a couple of cans of club soda and the cheese plate. "It is. Now only the hard cheese, right?"

"Yes, and I'm too excited to eat anything."

"Have a little cheese and a couple of crackers. We

have a stop to make before we go to dinner, and I don't want you getting too hungry."

She smiled at him. "You have a nurturing side, don't you? That's unexpected."

"I take care of the people I care about," he said, holding out the cheese tray.

Dena hoped she was able to keep her expression normal. At least her mouth didn't drop open. Care about? As in *care about*? What did that mean? Was he saying he was—

Friends, she told herself firmly. He liked her as a friend. They got along and had fun together and nothing more. She had to keep telling herself that. Besides, he was still mourning Adriana—he was incapable of anything other than simply hanging out. Whatever ridiculous fantasies she had, she needed to keep them to herself.

She nibbled on a couple of pieces of cheese and drank sparkling water. In what felt like five minutes, they were descending for their landing.

Once they were on the ground, Micah whisked her to a large black SUV, where a driver greeted them before heading into Seattle.

Dena was somewhat familiar with the city. She could get to 5th Avenue Theatre or the downtown Nordstrom or the university, but anywhere else was kind of vague for her, so she wasn't sure exactly where the driver was taking them. Not that it mattered. She was determined to enjoy every second of her time with Micah.

Their vehicle pulled into a large parking lot in front of a—

She turned to him, instantly fighting tears. "You didn't!"

He smiled at her. "I refuse to let some woman you don't know ruin the amazing thing you're doing. We're here to get your mind back on what's important."

She got out of the SUV and stared at the large, brightly lit baby store. The huge windows were painted for the season with a big happy Santa and all eight reindeer. The mood was upbeat and welcoming, and Dena couldn't wait to go inside.

She grabbed Micah's hand. "You're a good, good man, and I will remember this moment forever."

"I'm glad. Now let's go explore."

Inside, Dena was immediately overwhelmed by the size of the place, along with all they carried. Furniture, clothes, toys, and the diaper area had boxes piled nearly to the ceiling. A display of large stuffed animals, all sporting Santa or elf costumes, stood by the entrance.

This, she thought, suddenly fighting tears. *This* represented the happy part of her decision. The reality that she was going to have a baby and that she and her child would be a family, no matter what.

Micah touched his finger to her chin, raising her face so their eyes met. "Better?"

"Yes. I'm having a baby, and that is nothing but a blessing. I'm going to remember that. I'm in a good place in my life, surrounded by people who love me. The decision was right when I made it, and it's even more right now."

"Good. Let's go shop."

She laughed. "I'm not buying anything. Not yet. But I do want to look around and get some ideas. Later, I can come back with my mom and Reggie and do the serious shopping."

He pointed to the left. "So, furniture?"

"Yes, please."

He took her hand and drew her in that direction. She tried to pay attention to the faux rooms that had been set up, complete with pictures on the wall and adorable bedding, but it was difficult to think of anything but how his touch felt. Having Micah beside her, pointing out several options, made her heart happy. Having him this close made her girl parts want to scream like fans at a concert, but she was going to ignore them.

They walked through several rooms, discussing what they liked. Micah paused by a display with classic baby furniture done in a pale gray. His body tensed, and his smile faded.

"Adriana and I were going to buy this one. We were about to place the order when she and the baby were killed."

Dena stared at him, horrified to realize how difficult walking through the store must be for him.

"Micah, you shouldn't have brought me here," she said frantically. "I'm so sorry. I never thought. We're going right now."

Even though she tugged on his hand, he didn't move. Instead he pulled her in front of him and cupped her face in his hand.

"Being here brings back memories, and they make me sad, but aren't they supposed to? I'll always love her. I'll always regret we never picked a name for our son. It was a senseless loss, but that doesn't mean I'm incapable of moving forward with my life. I wanted to bring you here, Dena. Nothing about that has changed."

"I don't understand."

"Can't I be sad and happy at the same time?"

"I want to say yes, of course, but I'm not sure I believe myself."

His smile returned. "You're always honest."

"It's easier. There's less to remember."

He chuckled. "That's true. Now, come on. Let's go find a princess bed. If you're having a girl, I think it's a requirement."

"What if she's not the princess bed type?"

"Then you can blame it on me." He looked around the store, then pointed. "I see one over there."

As they walked to the very impressive princess collection, Dena wrestled with the realization that, if she did have a girl, by the time her daughter was old enough to complain about the furniture, Micah would be years gone. He was only in Wishing Tree for the holidays. Once they were over, he would be returning to wherever it was he lived, to pick up the pieces of his life.

She'd been so busy telling herself that he wasn't ever going to notice her as more than a friend for an assortment of reasons, including the fact that he was still in love with his late wife, that she'd forgotten an equally important fact. He wasn't staying. He never had been. So even if there wasn't an Adriana holding his heart, geography was going to do them in.

She would be a fool to allow herself to fall for him, and while she'd made mistakes before, she liked to think she'd never been foolish. Wouldn't it be a shame for her to start now?

Twenty-Two

REGGIE SORTED THE pictures her sister had emailed into chronological order. She wanted the slideshow to be about fifteen minutes long, which meant they would need close to two hundred pictures. She currently had about a hundred forty. Dena had a couple of albums for them to go through together.

Once she'd rearranged everything, she started the slideshow on her computer and sat back to watch. She'd barely gotten through the courtship part of their relationship when she heard Dena calling her name.

Belle rose from her bed and walked to the base of the stairs. As Dena walked down, Belle's long tail began to wag, going faster and faster as her favorite aunt got closer.

"Look at you, beautiful girl," Dena said, shifting two huge photo albums to her other arm and reaching for

Belle. "Are you enjoying being spoiled by your grand-parents? Are you a happy girl?"

Belle stepped close for plenty of pats, leaning on Dena and nearly causing her to stumble. Dena grinned.

"I always forget how powerful she is."

"Physically as well as spiritually," Reggie teased, getting up to collect the photo albums from her sister. "Now that she's gone toe-to-toe with Burt, she's kind of full of herself."

Dena dropped her coat and gloves on the sofa, along with her handbag, then took a seat at the big craft table where Reggie had been working.

"How are you feeling?" Reggie asked. "Your color is good. You were looking wan for a while."

"I'm doing great. The morning sickness is now pretty much only in the morning." She held up both arms. "I'm still wearing my motion sickness bracelets, and they're helping a lot."

"I'm glad. Those few weeks were really hard on you."

"They were. I'm glad they're over."

Reggie reached for one of the photo albums. "If we could find thirty great pictures, I'd be really happy."

Dena motioned to the computer. "Put on the slide-show so we can check these pictures against the ones you already have. Both should be in chronological order, right?"

"My part is, and you know Mom. She wouldn't allow anything else."

Dena leaned over the album while Reggie advanced to the next photograph. They found several pictures from when her parents were still dating, along with a few candid wedding shots that made them both laugh.

"Her suit was so poufy," Dena said. "Those sleeves!"

"It was the style."

"Yes. Look at how pretty she is. And so in love with Dad."

Reggie agreed. Her mother's expression clearly showed her feelings for the man she was marrying.

"I know we're grown-up and it shouldn't matter," Reggie said. "But I'm glad they're still together and happy."

"Me, too. I don't think it's ever easy if parents don't get along. Obviously better if the kids are adults, but it's always going to be difficult. I dread hearing that parents of one of my students are going through a divorce. It's heart-wrenching to watch."

Dena tucked the pictures back into place, then turned the page in the album. "Most of the time both parents are interested in the welfare of the child, but not always. A few years back I had a student who was really suffering, but all mom and dad cared about was hurting each other."

Reggie looked at her. "You're the keeper of a lot of secrets, aren't you?"

"What do you mean?"

"Harrison told me about his fear of confined, dark spaces and being trapped."

Dena's eyes widened. "He did?"

Reggie explained what had happened at the community center and how Harrison had invited her over to tell her about his past.

Dena leaned toward her. "I couldn't tell you. I hope you understand."

"Of course. You're the teacher. What happens between you and your students is confidential. Like I said, you're the keeper of secrets."

Dena's expression turned sympathetic. "I know it was a hard story to hear. I wanted to go find that Lori bitch and do something bad to her."

"I'm still trying to figure out where to put all my emotions." She looked at her sister. "Toby and I have been hanging out some."

Dena grinned. "Yes, I've noticed. Mom has, too, in case she hasn't mentioned it. That's kind of interesting. So, there are still sparks? He's a really great father, and back in the day, he was your world. Does knowing about Harrison bother you?"

"What? No. I'm angry, but not at him. I think he's adorable and brave and sweet."

"The thought of being a stepmother is interesting?"

"That is so far from where we are, I haven't even considered it." Reggie paused, not sure how to explain the problem. She supposed repeating some version of what Toby had told her made the most sense.

"He said he's not going to risk Harrison again. He's not willing to trust anyone enough to give his heart. Basically, he warned me off any kind of relationship with him."

Dena surprised her by waving her hand, as if brushing away the information. "That's not the reason. I'll admit that he's concerned about making another mistake. No one could go through what he did without having scars, but it's not why he won't allow himself to fall in love."

Reggie smiled. "And you know the real reason?"

"Of course. Look at his past. His father was a mean drunk who enjoyed beating the crap out of him. Judy, his grandmother, wasn't much help there. She protected Toby when he was little, but she never took her grandson and walked away. I don't get that. Protect the kid. That's what you're supposed to do. Instead she coddled her son until the day he died."

Dena shook her head. "Sorry. That's a personal button for me. Anyway, he falls for you and then screws up and loses you, so he takes off. Over the next couple of years, he's a drifter of sorts until some chickie he was dating shows up with Harrison."

"Chickie?" Reggie asked with a laugh. "You used the word?"

"You know what I mean. Here's my actual point. No one has ever loved him unconditionally. Not in a way that made him feel cared for and safe. Obviously Harrison loves him, but in that relationship, Toby's the protector. He's never been able to hand over his heart and know that it will be cared for and cherished. Every human longs for that, and when it doesn't happen, people shut down. Harrison's trauma is an excuse. Toby blames himself for what Lori did, and while that is a subject for discussion, it's also a convenient reason. He's hiding because he's afraid to trust."

Reggie wasn't sure how she felt about her sister's analysis, but she was impressed by the depth of the argument. "Wow. You've given this a lot of thought."

Dena shifted uncomfortably. "Yes, well, that's true." Guilt laced her tone. "Okay, you can't tell anyone I said this. Promise."

"Sure. I won't say anything."

Her sister looked at her. "When Harrison and Toby moved back to Wishing Tree last year, Harrison was put in my class. I had a long meeting with Toby. He told me about Harrison and Lori, and I'll admit, part of me wondered if it was true. I knew about his past with his father. Frequently when a kid is abused, he grows up to be an abuser."

Reggie stared at her sister. "You weren't sure there even had been a Lori. You were concerned he was the one who had locked Harrison in the closet."

"It was a reasonable concern," Dena said defensively. "So I spent a little extra time with Harrison, and I scheduled extra sessions with Toby." She sighed. "I quickly discovered that he was a warm, loving father who would do anything for his kid. Harrison got more outgoing and happier by the day. Now he's a well-adjusted kid with lots of friends and a great sense of self."

"He is," Reggie said. "And you're an amazing teacher."

Dena grinned. "On my good days. During one of the sessions, Toby admitted he felt guilty about Lori. Not only for the abuse but because it had been so unnecessary. He wasn't in love with Lori—he was going to marry her to give Harrison a mother. Not the actions of a man who believes it's safe to give his heart. That's why he told you he wasn't going to get serious with you."

"You are wise beyond your years, Obi-Wan."

"I wish that were true. The question for you is, how do you feel? Are you willing to get involved, knowing he might never trust you enough to fall in love, or do you walk away?"

"Are those my only two choices?"

Dena smiled. "You're kind of the only one who can answer that."

"I know. I like him, but I'm not in love with him."

How could she be? They weren't hanging out all that much. Sure, she saw him several days a week at the knitting afternoons and they'd had dinner, but it wasn't like they were dating.

"Don't you think the fact that he warned you off is significant? If he wasn't interested, he wouldn't have bothered." Dena leaned toward her. "I think he was talking to himself as much as to you."

"I need to think about this. You've sent me in an unexpected direction." She held up the album. "We have to get through this."

"We do."

They chose a dozen more pictures, including several with their mom seriously pregnant.

"Adorable," Reggie said, positioning the photograph in the scanner.

Dena flipped to the next page and stared. "Was this my crib?"

Reggie glanced over her shoulder. "It has to be. That's you as a baby." She smiled at the stenciled castle painted on the head-and footboard and the draped fabric hanging overhead. "It's like a princess crib. Mom went with a teddy bear theme with me. Probably because I'm the second kid, and doing the princess thing again was too much work." She chuckled. "Imagine if we'd had a third sibling. That one would have probably slept in a tent."

She glanced at Dena, waiting for a quick retort, but her sister was staring at the picture as if she'd never seen it before.

"What?" Reggie demanded.

"I'd forgotten about the princess bed," she whispered. "But if I have a little girl…"

Reggie stared at her. "Are you crying? What's wrong? Do you know you're having a girl? Isn't it too early to know? Did you have to do blood work? Are you all right?"

Dena waved her hands in front of her face in a futile attempt to hold back the tears.

"I'm fine," she said, her voice thick. "Totally fine. It's not a health thing. It's just I didn't remember what my baby room looked like. I've seen the pictures, of course, but when we were in the store, looking at baby furniture, I didn't recall the similarities."

Reggie angled toward her. "Hey, what are you talking about? When did you go to look at baby furniture? There's no store here."

Dena shrank back, obviously fighting guilt. "Yes, well, um, I was in Seattle a couple of nights ago."

"What? How? There's no way you could have taught school and driven over in time to get to a store, and then get home in time to teach. That's crazy. Do not tell me you drove the pass at night, by yourself."

"I flew."

"Okay, this is just crazy talk. You flew? Dena, you're not making any sense."

Her sister surprised her by smiling. "Micah chartered a private jet and flew me to Seattle. We went to a baby furniture store and then out to dinner."

While Dena explained about their evening together, Reggie found she was having a little trouble staying upright in her chair. Falling over in a dead faint seemed the most obvious reaction to what she was being told.

"Wait," she said, forming a T with her hands. "Rock star Micah flew you in a private jet all the way to Seattle so you could look at baby furniture?"

"And then we went to dinner. Yes. I'd had a bad day. He wanted me to feel better."

"Holy crap. He's falling for you!"

Dena blushed and looked away. "He's not. He's very sweet, but it doesn't mean anything." She touched Reggie's arm. "At the store, he mostly talked about missing his wife, Reggie. This isn't about me. It's about the fact that I'm pregnant. He's reliving his relationship with her, in a way. I think it's about the baby and the season."

She sighed. "Believe me, I wish it was something else. I wish it was chemistry and having fun together, but it's not."

Reggie's head was spinning. She wasn't sure how many more revelations she could handle in one sitting.

"I don't believe it's all about his late wife," she said. "I think there's a very good chance he's interested in you."

Dena shook her head. "He's a very sweet man. Believe me, if I thought for a second there was a chance with him, I would be all in. But there isn't. He's not over Adriana. I'm not sure he's ever going to be. And after Christmas, he's leaving, and I'll never see him again."

"That makes me sad."

"Me, too," Dena admitted. "I'm trying to be smart and not get too involved, but it's difficult. He's just so amazing."

"And sexy."

Dena grinned. "Yes, there is the sexy part." She looked at Reggie. "Men are just so difficult."

"Tell me about it."

IT WAS TIME to face the Christmas cactus again, Reggie thought, holding a watering can and a spool of ribbon.

All sixty plants needed to be watered, and then she was going to tie bows on every container. Why couldn't her mom have chosen custom cookies, delivered in a lovely little box? With them, all she would have to do was put on a sticker. She was good at stickers. But alas, no.

She watered the plants, careful not to overfill the—

Her cell phone rang. She reached for it, hoping for pretty much any distraction.

"Hello?"

"Hi, Reggie. It's Jake."

Unexpected, she thought. "Hi. Ah, how's it going?"

He chuckled. "About how you'd imagine. My mom has me decorating the house. I never noticed how many Christmas trees she likes to have up. Did you know she has one decorated in little china teacups? They're all painted with a Christmas theme and they hang by ribbons. Oh, and some are from different countries, so they have little flags on them."

Reggie tried not to laugh. "I didn't know that. You're a good man for helping her."

"The holidays are still tough for both of us. I'm glad I can be a distraction. I just wish there weren't, you know, teacups."

"I would love for you to text me a picture."

"So you can mock me? I don't think so."

She gave in to laughter. "Oh, Jake. Trapped with a wild woman who loves teacups. The things our parents make us do. My mom has decided every couple who comes to her wedding is taking home a Christmas cactus. I had to repot them all, and now I'm about to tie on a little ribbon."

"Still not worse than teacups."

She giggled. "You might be right."

"So, I was wondering if you'd like to have dinner together tonight."

The change in topic caught her off guard. Dinner with Jake?

Her mouth dropped open. "Are you asking me out?"

"Yes."

"As friends or as a date?"

"I was thinking more date."

She pulled the phone away from her ear and stared at it. Was he serious? She was about to ask when she heard a thud followed by a high-pitched yelping. Belle immediately jumped to her feet and raced up the stairs. The yelping became more like a horrible scream.

"Something happened," Reggie said, following Belle up the stairs to the main floor. "I have to call you back."

She found her mother on her knees by Burt, who was lying on the floor, screaming in pain.

"I don't know what happened," her mother said, wringing her hands. "I think he fell off the sofa. I've told your father and told him that we have to be careful with Burt's back."

"We need to take him to the vet."

Leigh pulled her phone out of her pocket. "They're on my contact list. Call them and let them know we're coming." She reached for Burt to pick him up. He screamed when she touched him.

"I can't do this," her mother said. "I can't move him. What do we do?"

Reggie grabbed an old blanket from the back of the sofa. Belle hovered, whining softly. Burt continued to yelp.

Once the blanket was next to the poor dog, Leigh was able to shift him onto it. He screamed several times, but never tried to bite her. Reggie's stomach was a mess as she called the vet and said they were on their way. They got coats and gloves. Belle began to bark, as if protesting she couldn't possibly be left behind.

"You have to be brave," Reggie told her as she hurried back to Burt. "Please, Belle."

Her dog sat down but continued to whine steadily.

Reggie and her mom each took an end of the blanket.

"On three," Leigh said, then counted. They lifted him together. He yelped loudly, then settled down to moans and heavy panting. After carefully setting him in the back seat of Reggie's SUV, they got in the vehicle. Leigh sat next to him, patting his face.

"It's okay, little guy. You're going to be fine." She wiped away tears. "I have to tell your dad what happened."

"Let's wait until we're at the vet," Reggie said, driving across town and pulling into the parking lot. "You can call while he's being examined."

They got him inside on the blanket. A tech was waiting to show them into one of the examination rooms.

Two hours later, they carried a very drugged Burt back to the car. According to his vet, his fall hadn't broken anything, and none of his disks had ruptured. Burt had soft tissue damage and would need time to recover.

"She told us no jumping," Leigh said from her place next to Burt in the back seat. "Has she met a dog before?" Her mom pressed her lips together. "We have ramps for him, but he resists using them. We're going to have to be more firm. I'm just glad he's all right."

"Me, too," Reggie said, more than a little shaken. "That was awful. Poor little guy."

They drove home to find Reggie's father waiting. He and Belle were pacing in the living room, and they both rushed to help Reggie and Leigh with Burt.

"Is he all right?" Vince asked anxiously. "I know you said he was, but is he?"

Leigh passed over the dog so Vince could hold him.

"He's been given an anti-inflammatory and a pain medication. At eight tonight, we can give him a pain pill to help him sleep. He has to stay quiet for the next couple of weeks, so we're going to have to be extra careful with him."

Vince gently placed Burt in his bed. The dog tried to raise his head, then sighed and closed his eyes.

"They really drugged him," Reggie offered as she hugged Belle, hoping to reassure her. "His doctor said he would be out of it for the rest of the day."

"Best thing for him," her father murmured. He looked at Leigh. "We have to put up the ramps and make him use them. No more jumping."

Her mother gave him a soft smile. "That's a good idea. You're right."

"I'll go get them from the basement."

He went downstairs. Leigh looked at her dog, then shook her head. "I just aged ten years."

"You still look good."

"Thanks. It's like having a kid all over again."

"Only Burt won't ever want to borrow the car."

"There is that. I'm going to make some coffee. Or possibly a cocktail. Want one?"

It was only two in the afternoon, but Reggie found herself nodding. "That would be great. Thanks, Mom."

Leigh retreated to the kitchen. Reggie watched Belle anxiously circle around Burt before settling down next to him, her big head on his bed, their noses almost touching. Burt stretched out just enough to lick her face, then closed his eyes and sighed again.

Reggie got out her phone, scrolled through her contacts until she found Jake's number, then texted him an update on what had happened.

I feel like I should stay close tonight. We're all kind of traumatized.

Three dots appeared. Seconds later, he answered.

No problem. I get it. Poor guy. I hope he's feeling better. As for dinner, should I ask again or leave you alone?

An interesting question, she thought. Having Jake back in her life was nothing if not unexpected. But seeing him again? Going out with him? Fool me once and all that.

Only she didn't think he'd fooled her. He'd been caught up in events and his past. He'd been wrong not to tell her what was going on, but other than that, he hadn't been deliberately terrible. A year ago, she'd planned to spend the rest of her life with him.

She stared at her phone, then typed.

Ask again.

Twenty-Three

TOBY'S PLAN TO let Reggie walk away had seemed right at the time, but as days passed, he found himself missing her.

Maybe if he could spend some time away from her, he could get her off his mind, but four days a week he dutifully showed up at the community center to knit hats with his son's third-grade class. He did his work, all the while listening to her talk with the kids, or make jokes with Micah, who now regularly showed up to entertain them as they knit.

At first he'd wondered if something was going on with the former rock star and Reggie, but he hadn't seen any hint of attraction between them. She was friendly but not flirty, and Micah seemed to treat her like a sister. Which was good. Toby didn't want to have to take him out back and beat him with a stick.

No, he told himself as soon as the thought formed.

Reggie was just a friend. He'd been the one to tell her he wasn't doing relationships anymore. He couldn't take the chance. Based on that logic, he should be disappointed that Reggie and Micah weren't together, only he wasn't. He couldn't be.

Even as his fingers worked the yarn, going carefully around the loom, his mind was a dark, swirling mess of wants, needs and shoulds. He needed to keep his son safe. He should focus on Harrison rather than himself. But he wanted to spend time with Reggie. He wanted to make her laugh and listen to her talk and just enjoy the contented feeling that came over him whenever he was around her.

When the day's session ended, Reggie collected the completed hats. Harrison smiled at his dad.

"You remember I'm going over to Noah's for dinner tonight."

He grinned. "You've told me forty-seven times, kid."

Harrison laughed. "Na-uh. I've told you forty-six times."

Harrison left with Noah and Noah's mom. The other parents left with their kids, leaving Toby and Reggie to handle the cleanup.

"This has been a great project," she said, adding a few more hats to an already overflowing box. "Harrison should be proud of himself. He came up with a terrific idea."

"He's pretty happy." Toby collected unused skeins of yarn and put them into an empty shopping bag, which he then dropped into an open tote. "I haven't seen you in a couple of days. How's it going?"

"All right," she said, giving him a quick smile, then turning away. "Oh, Burt had a terrible fall and hurt his back. He's recovering, but he's in a lot of pain, so he spends his days drugged. Poor guy. Belle has appointed herself his nurse. She rarely leaves his side. They're becoming quite the couple."

Toby couldn't help thinking that there was something going on with Reggie. She was keeping her distance physically, and she wouldn't look at him—not the way she usually did.

He cleared his throat. "Nate, my sales manager, wants us to expand into the frozen food market. It's tough to break into, but if you can make it there…"

She smiled. "You get a film deal in Hollywood?"

He chuckled. "Something like that. He's trying to convince me it's the right direction for the company. I remain difficult to convince."

She tilted her head. "I'm not sure how I feel about Judy's Hand Pies in the grocery store frozen case. I think the store experience is worth having. But that's a limiter."

"That was my exact conversation with Nate. But he's not someone who gives up easily. We have frozen pies and are taste-testing them. As we speak, I have pies in my freezer that are three months old. Want to come over and have some previously frozen hand pies? I could make a salad, as well."

Was it just him, or did he sound pathetic? And why was he suddenly nervous?

Reggie looked at the floor, then back at him. "Thank you for the invitation, but I need to get home. My folks have plans for tonight, and I have to babysit Burt."

She picked up the last of the totes and started out of the room. "But you have fun. I'll want to hear all about the experience."

She walked away without looking back, leaving him with the distinct feeling that he'd been dismissed. The obvious solution to the Burt problem was for her to invite him back to her place. He could heat the pies there and they could spend the evening together. Only she hadn't suggested that at all. If anything, she seemed eager to not be with him.

He grabbed his coat and gloves and headed for his SUV. As he slid onto the cold seat, he told himself he should be happy. Reggie had gotten the message, and now he didn't have to worry about misleading her. Nothing was going to happen between them. Not now and not anytime soon. He should be celebrating. But instead of feeling happy, he was filled with a sense of dread that came from knowing he'd just lost something important—something he hadn't realized he would miss until it was gone.

> *As the snow fell,*
> *I fell*
> *And you fell.*
> *The past was gone,*
> *Only love remained.*
> *Reaching us and teaching us and making us into*
> *one.*
> *Now I'm going to spend Christmas*
> *With you*
> *And all my next Christmases,*
> *Too.*
> *Because the snow fell.*

Micah relaxed back on the sofa in his friend's house and waited for Steve's response. It was late. Steve's wife and kid were in bed, and it was just the two of them in the quiet.

His friend picked up his beer and took a sip. "It's good."

"Yeah?"

"You know it's a hit. Does Claiborne know?"

Claiborne was Micah's agent and the one who would negotiate any sale of the song.

"No. I told him I needed time to think and that I would see him when I go to LA for the Christmas special. He's been respecting my space."

"You should give him a heads-up about the song. He's going to want you to record it right away. They can get the single out in time to get a few sales before Christmas." Steve waved his beer. "You should sing it at the special. The network would do a backflip."

Micah strummed a few chords. "I'm not sure about singing it at the special," he said. That felt too public, somehow. "I was thinking of going old school."

"Acoustic?" Steve shook his head. "You need an orchestra, man. That's the way to debut the song. Then go into the studio and cut the acoustic version. Release the live and the studio recordings. The fans will go wild."

Micah couldn't write a score for an orchestra, but he had a friend who could. Someone he trusted.

"Electra's expecting me to sing 'Moonlight for Christmas.' She's counting on the royalties."

"Dude, the song is what, fifteen years old? The people want something new." Steve tapped the sheet music on the kitchen table. "Forget Electra."

"I don't care about her. I just feel responsible for her."

"I know you do. You always have. But you don't owe her anything."

Micah knew that was true. Maybe he could offer to release a new version next year. A duet or something, so he could sing "Because the Snow Fell" this year.

"If I go the orchestra route, I'll need to let Claiborne know. They'll have to be hired. That's not cheap."

Steve chuckled. "You know you're Micah Ruiz, right? If you needed the moon for your performance, the network would get it."

"The moon's kind of big," Micah joked. "Where would we put it?"

"Play the song again."

Micah did as his friend requested. After struggling for so long, he felt good knowing he'd finally found the words and melody. He let the song sink in and become a part of him.

When he'd finished, Steve toasted him with his beer.

"You did it. That's going to be a classic for sure. Just one question. Is it a song or a message?"

"Why would you ask that? It's a song."

Steve didn't look convinced. "Don't get me wrong. I'm all in favor of you healing and moving forward with your life. Adriana was an incredible woman, but you've got a lot of years in front of you. I'd like you to spend them with someone."

"I have no idea what you're talking about."

But even as he made the statement, Micah knew he was lying. Steve was asking the obvious question. Who had inspired the song, and did that inspiration mean anything?

Steve had known him long enough to understand when he should keep his mouth shut. After over a minute of silence, Micah sighed.

"It's not what you think."

Steve only looked at him.

"Fine. I like her and I admire her. She's pregnant and alone and—"

"Dena? Okay. Noah's crazy about her. She's well-liked in town. Family's respected."

Micah swore softly. "You think I could get her for three horses and a couple of cows? What's wrong with you?"

Steve grinned. "I'm just telling you what I know." His smile faded. "You're not as tough as people think. If this is going somewhere, you need to be careful. Not just with her heart, but with yours."

Micah strummed his guitar. "You're going down a road I don't even see on the map."

"You're saying there's nothing going on?"

Micah thought about their recent trip to Seattle. He'd been willing to do anything to erase the sadness from her eyes, and he'd been successful. She'd been happy the whole evening. After leaving the baby store, they'd gone to dinner, where they'd stayed until closing. On the quick flight back to Wishing Tree, she'd fallen asleep in his arms—a memory he would keep close always.

Dena was... He mentally paused as he realized he had no idea what she was to him. Someone important. Someone he cared about. For now he was content to let it just be that and figure out the rest of it later.

"We're just friends," he lied.

Steve snorted. "Yeah, right. Sell it somewhere else. You're gone on her and you're just not willing to admit it." He tapped the sheet music again. "Not just a song, my friend. It's a message and one you should pay attention to."

REGGIE CARRIED THE last bag to her SUV. Belle was already in the back seat, wearing her newest holiday sweater: an elf design, complete with an elf ears headband.

Normally a trip to The Wreath could be accomplished on foot, but Reggie was heading to a gift-wrapping party.

She'd just settled in her seat and was about to start the car when her phone buzzed with a text. From Jake.

Dinner tomorrow?

Short and to the point, she thought as she studied the words. Not sure how to answer, she dropped her phone in her purse and fastened her seat belt.

She made the short drive to Wrap Around the Clock and found a spot in the rear parking lot. Belle helpfully carried in one of the shopping bags, her teeth firmly clamped around the handle. Reggie grabbed the rest and managed to make her way inside with only one trip. Camryn was at the checkout desk with a line of customers. When she spotted Reggie and Belle, she laughed.

"I love your dog," she said. "You're in room six."

"Thanks. She loves to be loved."

Wrap Around the Clock had several private party rooms. There were big tables, plenty of chairs and all the supplies one would need to wrap presents. The host simply requested a certain type of wrapping paper, and a dozen or so selections were provided. Meals could be catered by a variety of local restaurants and drinks provided by Holiday Spirits.

Reggie walked into room six and found Dena, Paisley and Shaye were already there, sorting through the holiday wrapping paper Camryn had provided.

"You're here," Paisley said, rushing toward her and hugging her, then dropping to her knees to embrace Belle. "You're such a good girl. Look how cute you are! And carrying a bag for your mom."

"I went simple," Paisley said, waving toward trays of food. "Bacon chicken salad sandwiches, a veggie plate, chips and dip, with brownies for dessert." She pointed to the large and small pitchers. "A non-alcoholic holiday-themed drink for you, Dena, compliments of Howard. And for the rest of us, cranberry coolers."

Reggie hung up her coat. They all handed over their share of the cost of the meal, then pulled up chairs at the table, distributed plates and napkins, and filled their plates with food. Belle looked briefly hopeful until Reggie told her to go lie down.

"I've never been to a wrapping party before," Shaye admitted as she took her seat.

"It's fun," Paisley told her. "You get it all done at once. The nice part, for those of us who don't have giant houses, is we don't have to keep all the supplies around. When we're finished, Camryn tallies up the supplies we used. She'll even ship packages, if you want. I love being able to choose from all those cute decorations without having to go buy them myself."

"Plus the tutorials," Dena said, pointing to the posters on the wall. "See how there's a picture of the wrapped package and then a list of the supplies needed, along with the cost?"

"Easy for those of us lacking craft skills," Shaye said, her tone admiring. "This is my first Christmas in town, and I'm enjoying every second."

Reggie picked up her sandwich. "Yes, but how much of that is Wishing Tree and how much of it is being in love with Lawson?"

Shaye grinned. "It's about fifty-fifty."

"Young love," Paisley said with a sigh. "I want me some of that." She raised her glass. "To a rich, handsome man checking into the resort and sweeping me off my feet."

"Oh, not that," Dena said quickly. "If he checked into the resort, then he wouldn't be local, so if he swept you off your feet, you'd be leaving."

Paisley patted Dena's hand. "But I would never not be your friend."

"I like having you here. I'm already dealing with the fact that Reggie doesn't live here anymore." Dena looked at her sister. "You could move back, you know. You can do your job from anywhere."

"I have a life in Seattle," Reggie said, but her protest was mild. Truth was, she was enjoying her time back home. She'd missed the town and had stayed away too long.

Her own fault, she reminded herself. No one had been keeping her from returning. Jake hadn't even been here anymore.

"Just think about it," Dena said.

"So, what's new with everyone?" Paisley asked. "My life is boring. I'm working impossible hours with holiday events up at the resort."

Reggie surprised herself by blurting, "Jake asked me out."

The small room went silent. Three heads turned in her direction. Paisley and Dena looked two parts surprised and one part annoyed, while Shaye was only curious.

"Jake the ex?"

"That's the one," Reggie said lightly.

"He asked you out?" Dena demanded. "You said no, right? You had to say no."

Her fiercely protective tone had Reggie smiling. "You don't have to worry about me."

"I do. The man was a total jerk. There's no excuse for what he did."

Reggie ate a couple of chips. "There kind of is."

She explained about Iona and how she'd unexpectedly appeared in Jake's life the morning after their engagement party.

"He was an idiot," she said. "He should have told me, and we should have talked. But he wasn't deliberately cruel."

"That's a subtlety I can't get behind," Dena said flatly. "He had you, he claimed to love you and then he dumped you. There are no second chances after that."

"Oh, I don't know," Paisley said, picking up another sandwich half. "Jake's not a bad guy. Until the dumping, I liked him. He was easy to work for. He was smart and very fair with the staff."

Dena didn't look convinced.

"Do you still love him?" Shaye asked quietly.

"No. I'm over him."

"But you were going to marry him. Is that love gone? Or do you want to give him another chance?"

"Saying I want to give him another chance is kind of more than I'm comfortable with," she admitted. "But I'm not angry or hurt anymore."

"I think Shaye's asking the right questions," Paisley

said firmly, waving her drink. "Dena, I know you're going to play protective mama bear on this, but it's not like he cheated or anything. He freaked out, then broke up with her. At least he didn't go out behind her back. Taking responsibility for making a mistake is huge."

"Maybe, but it's not good enough," Dena insisted.

Paisley raised her eyebrows. "Interesting. What if Toby wants to date her? He broke her heart. Does he get a second chance?"

"That's totally different. He was a kid, and what happened in high school isn't his fault."

"So Toby gets a do-over, but not Jake?"

Shaye leaned toward Reggie. "Are you okay with them evaluating your life this way?"

Reggie smiled. "I'm feeling the love."

She didn't mind the discussion. It allowed her to look at her life from a relatively disinterested perspective. She understood Dena's reluctance to trust Jake and her willingness to give Toby a second chance. In truth, Reggie would rather be dating Toby, but he wasn't asking. As for Jake, she honestly had no idea how she felt about him.

"Look at it this way," Paisley said. "You were in love with him, and you wanted to marry him. Isn't that worth something? At least go on a date with him and find out if any of the old feelings are there. If not, you thank him for a nice evening and you're done. If they're still there, then have a go at it. But if you don't at least try, you may always wonder."

Dena stared at Paisley. "I hate it when you make sense."

"I know. Isn't it great?"

The two women laughed. Reggie glanced at Shaye, who shook her head.

"Uh. I don't have an opinion on this one. I'm just the new girl. It's your life, Reggie. What do you want?"

Someone to love, she thought. She wanted to fall in love and get married and have a family. She wanted silly traditions and laughter and Belle watching over their first child as protectively as she watched over Burt.

"I want us to change the subject," she said lightly. "This is supposed to be a party. So, what are we wrapping tonight?"

Her friends accepted the shift in conversation. Later, when they were done eating and starting to set up to wrap the presents, Reggie excused herself and stepped out into the hall. Paisley had made a lot of good points. What would it hurt to find out if she was really over Jake or if there was still something there?

She pulled her phone out of her pocket and texted back her response.

Dinner would be great. When and where?

Twenty-Four

DENA HAD NO idea why she was torturing herself. She knew it was a bad idea, yet here she was, typing in Micah's name in the search bar, along with Electra and Adriana. The list of links all took her to dark and dangerous places with pictures. So many pictures.

None of them were bad or gross or naked. Instead, what upset her was how incredibly beautiful both women were. Electra was a striking redhead who dressed in a lot of leather and platform heels. Adriana was an ethereal beauty with pale blond hair and blue-gray eyes. She looked more like a fairy than a human. A fairy supermodel.

Their styles and looks couldn't have been more different, except for the fact that they were as gorgeous as Micah was handsome. The photographs were physical proof that she was an ordinary mortal, and she'd read enough Greek mythology to know what happened to mortals who tried to involve themselves with the world of the gods. The mortals always ended up little more than a bag of dusty bones.

"That's cheerful," she murmured, sipping her herbal tea before glancing longingly at her coffee maker. "I still miss you, by the way. My love is true."

The coffee maker chose not to reply, so she turned her attention back to her screen and watched a couple of music videos before clicking on more links.

There were hundreds of pictures of Micah, with and without his wives. She spent a full minute staring into his soulful blue eyes before closing the browsers and turning away from her computer.

She had to accept the truth. She could daydream and wish as much as she wanted, but the truth could not be denied. She and Micah were friends. He was a good man who was very sweet to her, but that did not a true love make.

She wasn't his type. She wasn't beautiful or special or talented. She was an ordinary woman, living an ordinary life. A man like him would never want that. The Micahs of the world gravitated to the very special, and while she thought she was a good person with a lot to offer, *special* was probably stretching it.

Obviously she had to figure out a way to get over him. Because as much as she wanted to tell herself her attraction was all about the pretty outside of the man, she knew it was way more than his smile or his shoulders. It was him. The inside him—his generosity, his kindness, his sense of humor, his talent. The man had flown her to Seattle because she was feeling down. He'd bought guitars for her kids. He showed up at nearly every knitting afternoon and entertained everyone. How was she supposed to resist that?

Only she had to. Because if she didn't watch herself, she was going to get her heart broken when he left, and leave he would. He'd told her and she believed him.

"I need a distraction," she said out loud, closing her laptop and coming to her feet. As there was always something she could be doing at the B and B, she grabbed her coat and headed for the stairs. She could go over the monthly billing and check out linen inventory. That would take her mind off the man she couldn't have.

She hurried the short distance from the carriage house to the main building. The temperature was close to zero, but there was still no snow in the forecast. What was up with that?

She went inside and hurried to the fireplace to warm herself. Once she could feel her fingers again, she walked over to the reception desk and smiled at Winona.

"How's it going?"

The B and B manager gave her an odd look. "So, this thing happened."

"What does that mean?"

Winona gave her a pained smile. "A guest came down and said the bathroom sink was leaking. Micah was standing right here. Before I could pick up the phone to call the plumber, he said he would take care of it. I must have lost my head, because I showed him where we kept the tools, and he's up there right now."

Dena had trouble taking in the words. "You let a guest repair the plumbing of another guest?"

"I know. When you say it like that, I'm mortified.

It's just, I guess I don't think of him as a guest so much as your friend and, well, I screwed up. I'm sorry."

"What room?"

"Eight."

Dena took the stairs to the second floor and made her way to the far end of the hall. The door was partially open, so she let herself in, calling out as she entered.

"Knock, knock. It's Dena."

"In the bathroom."

She followed the sound of Micah's voice and found him kneeling on the tile floor, reaching into the cabinet. Seconds later, he straightened and smiled at her.

"Here to check on my work?"

That smile. Why did it get even more dazzling with time? Shouldn't she be a little more immune?

"You can't be doing this," she said, ignoring the smile problem. "You're a guest here. No one expects you to take care of maintenance items."

"It was a leaky faucet, Dena. I replaced a washer. It took ten minutes." He rose to his feet and turned on the tap, then turned it off again. There weren't any drips. "See? All done."

"But you're a guest."

His smile gentled. "You're welcome."

She flushed. "Thank you for helping out, but it's not expected."

"I like helping you. This was fun. I enjoy puttering, and I haven't been able to do it for a long time."

She didn't understand. She supposed that was the real problem. "Why would you bother?"

He chuckled. "You're not listening. I heard about the problem and I wanted to take care of it if I could."

He used a rag to wipe down the sink, then collected his tools and walked toward her. She instinctively backed up, so he led the way to the door.

She stared up at him, thinking he was too good to be true. Even more unsettling was how much she wanted to step into his embrace and kiss him. Really kiss him. And then have sex. Hot, wild, all-day sex. The kind where the rest of the world disappeared and it was only the two of them. And she wanted it to be more than a onetime thing. She wanted it to be real—all of it. She wanted Micah to fall in love with her.

The truth slammed into her with so much force, she nearly staggered. No. No, no, no. She was not going to give her heart to him. She couldn't. It wasn't just a recipe for disaster, it was the recipe and the ingredients and so much more.

"This was fun," he said, staring into her eyes.

"You're a crazy man."

The smile returned. "Maybe. I finished the song."

"You did? That's great. Do you like it? Are you happy with how it turned out?"

"Yes. I am. You inspired me."

"I… What?"

He touched her cheek. "You inspired me. You're the reason I can write again."

"I don't know what to say to that."

"You don't have to say anything. I just wanted you to know."

Her heart pounded in her chest, and she worried that at any minute, the hallway was going to start spinning. Did his words mean anything significant?

"When can I hear it?" she asked.

"I'll be singing it live on the Christmas variety show."

When he would be leaving to go to LA and possibly never coming back? So much for any daydreams about him caring for her. Listening to the song with fifty million other people, while Micah was performing live on television, wasn't exactly romantic.

"That will be exciting," she said brightly, hoping her disappointment didn't show. After all, she had no right to expect a private performance. Micah didn't owe her anything.

She took the toolbox from him. "Thank you for fixing the faucet. That was very nice of you. But from now on, try to remember you're our guest."

"I'll do my best."

She wanted to say more. She wanted to ask about the sex thing, only she knew she wouldn't. His recoil and rejection would be more than she could stand. So instead of risking humiliation, she smiled, waved and purposefully started for the stairs.

REGGIE FELT A strong sense of déjà vu as she handed her car keys to the valet and walked into the resort to meet Jake for dinner. When they'd been together, she'd come up here on a regular basis. To be doing that again, after all this time, felt strange.

She told herself to just let her emotions be what they were going to be. She would analyze them later. For tonight, she was having dinner with an old friend—in part to catch up and in part to find out if there was anything left between them. At least, that was her agenda. She had no idea what he expected.

She walked through the lobby and took the elevator to the third floor, where the fine dining restaurant was located. As soon as the doors opened, she saw Jake waiting. He smiled when he saw her.

"Right on time," he said, walking to her and lightly kissing her cheek.

"Traffic was light," she joked.

"There was traffic? We have, what? Less than a dozen stoplights."

"There might be a new one out by the highway," she said with a laugh.

He put his hand on the small of her back and guided her into the restaurant. "I've already picked out our table."

"Of course you have."

"One of the perks of knowing the owner."

"Or being her son."

Jake stopped by a table in the corner and held out a chair. "That, too."

He hung her coat on a nearby coatrack and then took a seat across from her. There were already menus on the table, but Reggie ignored them.

"How does it feel to be back?" she asked.

"Good. A little strange, but good."

"Where did you go when you left here?"

"Colorado."

"How *is* Aspen?"

He grinned. "Fun. Those people are serious about their skiing."

"I've heard."

"It was good to get away."

"Iona went with you?"

He grimaced. "Yes, she did. For a while. And then she left." He leaned toward her. "Reggie, I'm so sorry about what happened and how I acted. I deeply regret how I treated you and how I hurt you with my behavior."

She reached across the table and touched his hand. "You don't have to say that. You already apologized and I've let it go. I was just asking, not hinting or prying."

"I know, but I still feel like a jerk. We had something great."

She looked into his eyes and smiled. "Yes, we did."

"Speaking of great, you look amazing."

"Thank you. You're kind of pretty yourself."

He laughed, that deep, genuine laugh she'd always liked. The one that told her he wasn't pretending to find her funny.

She studied him, thinking she'd been telling the truth. He did look good. He was more classically handsome than Toby. More polished. Jake had been raised with the kind of expectations that molded a man. In his case, the outcome was impressive.

Their server appeared and told them about the specials, then took their drink orders. When she'd left, Reggie looked at Jake.

"Do you think you make them nervous when they have to serve you? I mean, you're going to be the general manager here one day, so technically you're their boss. Or boss-to-be."

"They can handle the pressure."

"I wonder if they flip a coin or something to see who has to take the table."

"Do I get the winner or the loser?"

She laughed. "I have no idea. Which do you want?"

"I'll take either. We have good people working here. They're all up to dealing with me."

"And when is that going to be a permanent thing?" she asked. "Any idea when you'll be taking over the crown jewel of the Crane family empire?"

"The empire is smaller these days."

"Do tell."

"We sold our properties in Savannah and Boston."

"Why?"

"We want to focus on our West Coast hotels. Those two were outliers."

No doubt they'd gotten millions and millions from the sales, she thought.

Their server appeared with their drinks. Jake nodded at the pink liquid in her glass.

"You're such a girl."

"It's seasonal," she protested, holding up her Candy Cane Cooler. "It's peppermint-infused vodka, brandy, half-and-half and some other yummy things." She reached for the candy cane carefully placed across the glass. "Plus a treat. What's not to like? Better than your stuffy Manhattan."

He laughed again. "I see you haven't changed." He raised his glass. "To the girl who got away."

She smiled. "To the boy who let her go."

They touched glasses. She took a sip of her drink and sighed.

"As delicious as I remember. So, how's your mom?"

His humor faded. "She's doing all right. She still misses my dad."

"Of course she does. They were together nearly forty years."

He nodded. "She's taking more of an interest in the

business, which is good. She's also taking more of an interest in me, which is less good."

"I can imagine." Jake's mother was sweet and funny, but she could be determined and intense.

"How's work?" he asked.

"Excellent. I have a few new clients who are keeping me busy."

They talked about several inventions she'd helped bring to market and which ones had failed. After placing their order, they chatted about their friends and what was going on in town.

"The snow is late," Jake said. "This is going to be a tough ski season."

"I know. Usually the first snowfall is in late October. We're well into December. This has never happened before. Everyone is freaking out."

"Are you going to The Wreath for the first snowfall?" he asked.

"Absolutely. I'm usually not home for it anymore, so if it happens while I'm here, I'm celebrating until I freeze."

His expression turned quizzical. "You said *home*. I would have thought Seattle was home now."

"Slip of the tongue. Part of it is I've been back since before Thanksgiving, so I'm returning to my native daughter status." She grinned. "Oh, I have to tell you about Belle. You'll never guess what happened."

"She carries a handbag now?"

"Better. She stood up to Burt."

"You're kidding. She's terrified of him."

"Not anymore. She growled at him and it totally changed their relationship."

"Tell her I'm proud of her."

"I will."

The rest of the evening passed quickly. Reggie was pleased she and Jake never ran out of things to talk about, although she wasn't sure there was any lingering attraction. He was nice and all, but she didn't feel any flutters or daydream about him touching her.

When they'd finished their meal, they talked over coffee before leaving the restaurant. Once they were on the main floor of the hotel, Jake walked with her toward the lobby. Partway there, he pulled her off to the side, into a secluded alcove. He drew her close and kissed her.

Reggie closed her eyes, wanting to fully focus on the kiss. She felt the warm, gentle pressure of his mouth. His touch was familiar and nice. Happy memories made her lean in. She'd enjoyed her evening with Jake and kissing him was…was…

She held in a sigh. It was nothing. Pleasant, but there was no sense of anticipation. She wasn't tingling or excited about taking things to the next level. He didn't make her breathless or happy or overwhelmed by passion. Not anymore. What they'd been to each other, when they'd been in love and engaged, had been lost.

He broke the kiss and stared at her, his expression tight with regret.

"It's gone," he said quietly. "Whatever we had. It's over."

The sadness in his voice affected her way more than the kiss. She fought against unexpected tears. "Yes."

"I'd hoped for more," he admitted.

"Me, too."

"I guess we had our chance and I blew it."

"No." She took his hands in hers and squeezed. "No,

that's not on you. If we'd really been each other's one and only, the feelings would still be there. Hiding, maybe, but they would have come back to life. It's only been a year, Jake. But they didn't, which makes me think they weren't that strong to begin with."

"Hell of a thing."

"I agree." She smiled. "I'm glad we did this. I'm glad we know."

"Me, too."

He walked her to the valet and waited until her car came, then helped her inside. As she drove off, she told herself that knowing how it ended was important and that she was stronger with the knowledge. She would never again wonder what would have happened if he hadn't broken up with her.

Funny how not that much time had passed and yet they'd gotten over each other completely. It wasn't like that with Toby. Despite the years, he still made her quiver in all the right places. He was—

She stared into the darkness, going slowly around the corners. When she reached the outskirts of town, she pulled into the first gas station she saw and parked over to the side. After taking her phone out of her bag, she sent a quick text, then settled down to wait for a reply.

JUST AFTER NINE THIRTY, Toby's phone buzzed. He glanced at the screen, then frowned. It was late for Reggie to be texting him.

I know it's late, but I was hoping we could talk for a second. Can I stop by?

The unusual request surprised him, and his first thought was that something was wrong. His second, far more powerful and intriguing, was that she wanted to come over to do anything *but* talk. His brain immediately supplied dozens of images of him making love with Reggie, fast the first time, both of them driven by passion, then slow the second time, each of them discovering the other until they had no choice but to surrender to the inevitable.

He shook off the fantasies, ignored his instant erection and quickly responded.

Sure.

Be right there.

He put down his book and walked downstairs. Judy had gone to her room about an hour ago, and Harrison was already in bed. The house was quiet.

He clicked on a few lights and waited by the front door. A couple of minutes later, headlights swept across the front of the house. He opened the door and watched as she got out of her car and hurried toward him.

When she stepped inside, he tried to gauge what she was thinking. There were no signs of panic or concern, so he could let his worry go. But she also wasn't throwing herself at him, so the whole fantasy evening thing was probably a no.

"What's up?" he asked, taking her coat, then leading her into the formal living room. It was away from Judy's room, so their talking wouldn't disturb her. Only after he sat across from her on the sofa did he register what she was wearing.

The fitted black dress clung to every curve, emphasizing the best parts of her body, and she had on makeup. This was not daytime Reggie who was always beautiful, but casually dressed. She'd been out somewhere. Possibly to a party, or maybe on a date.

The idea of the latter made him want to interrogate her, but he knew he had no right. He'd made it clear he wasn't interested in any kind of relationship with her or anyone, so he couldn't complain if she went out with someone else. But telling himself that didn't ease the sudden tightness in his chest or the need to demand answers.

She sat on the edge of the cushion.

"I had dinner with Jake," she said bluntly, her gaze meeting his. "Up at the resort."

The tightness became a band that made it impossible to breathe. Jealousy and anger battled for dominance, although he knew neither was appropriate.

"I wanted to tell you myself because I knew you'd probably hear about it from someone else." Her mouth curved in a half smile. "I'm not saying that I'm so interesting that everyone is dying to talk about my life, but Jake is certainly news, and we were engaged."

She raised one shoulder. "I went out with him because I was curious. Were any of the old feelings still alive?"

"Are they?"

He told himself the answer didn't matter, that Reggie wasn't for him because being with her would require a level of trust he no longer possessed, but he still didn't breathe until she responded.

"No." She shook her head. "They're not, which makes me sad. I was going to marry him. Shouldn't there still be something? Which isn't what I came to talk about."

Too bad, because he could talk about how much she wasn't interested in Jake all day.

"My point is," she continued, "I wanted you to hear it from me. I know we're not dating, but there's still something going on, and I didn't want you thinking I was sneaking around behind your back."

She paused, her gaze locking with his. "You're wrong to ignore what's happening between us. You say you won't get involved because you have to protect Harrison, but I think that's just an excuse. You've been burned enough times that you're not willing to risk your heart, but to admit that makes you uncomfortable. You've come up with a convenient excuse so that you never have to put anything on the line."

She shifted on her seat. "While that's fine in the short term, eventually you're going to look around and see what you've given up. Chances are it's going to be too late to try again. Your no-dating rule is ridiculous. You know it, and I know it, and you really should think about being more honest with yourself. After that, you should ask me out, because if you don't, you're going to regret it forever."

She stood. "I know the way out. Have a good night."

And then she was gone.

Toby sat on the sofa, stunned by her words and in awe of her courage. Reggie had always been honest and brave, but tonight she'd been exceptional. Wrong about him, but incredible in every way possible.

He knew he had to protect his son. That mattered more than anything. But she was right about him regretting losing her. He knew that was something he was going to be dealing with for a very long time.

Twenty-Five

MICAH CAREFULLY RAN the credit card charge, then handed the receipt to the woman trying to keep control of her two small children. The youngest, a little girl of maybe four or five, darted across the Christmas tree lot, toward the exit. Micah sprinted after her, catching her before she got out onto the sidewalk.

"Thank you so much," her mother said, hurrying up with her older child in tow. "She's a runner, that's for sure."

Micah handed over the little girl and smiled at the mom. "You and your family have a good holiday season."

"We will."

She paused as if she were going to say more. Micah turned away, walking over to where her husband was tying the large Christmas tree on top of their car.

"You have enough rope?" he asked.

The man made a final knot, then patted the tree. "I do. We're not going far and I'll drive slow."

"Enjoy the tree."

Micah returned to the lot. Despite the fact that it was the middle of a weekday, business had been steady, with several trees sold every hour.

Steve had called that morning, asking if Micah could help him out. His regular person had caught a stomach bug and couldn't make it in at the last minute. Micah had agreed. Not only would he do anything for his friend, but he thought the experience would be good for him. He'd been spending too much time in his room, writing. So far he had two more songs that were nearly completed and ideas for about eight others.

His stomach growled, reminding him he'd missed breakfast. Micah glanced at his watch. It was nearly one. His replacement would show up at three, so only a couple of hours to go.

He assisted a few more families with trees, and carefully put a small flocked tree in the trunk for an older woman.

"You need me to swing by when I get off work and carry this inside for you?" he asked.

The white-haired woman smiled at him. "That's very sweet, but my neighbor will do that for me when he gets home from work. He's good that way. I've already made a batch of frosted sugar cookies to thank him."

"Sounds like you have a good thing going on." Micah double-checked the ropes, then patted the raised trunk. "You drive slowly. You wouldn't want to hot-rod around a corner and have your tree go flying."

The woman laughed. "No, I wouldn't." She got in her car and slowly drove away.

Micah returned to the lot and was surprised to see Reggie waiting by the checkout desk. For a second, he hoped Dena was with her, but he knew she would still be in class.

He crossed to Dena's sister. "Afternoon. Looking for a tree?"

"No, my mom's already taken care of that. You have a second?"

"Sure." He smiled. "I'd invite you into my office so we could sit down, but I'm afraid this is as good as it gets."

"I'm fine." She looked at him, her gaze steady. There was an air of determination about her. "I don't know how else to ask the question, so I'm just going to blurt it out. When it comes to my sister, what are your intentions?"

His first instinct was to laugh. No one had ever asked him that before. He wasn't sure anyone in this century had used that phrase. But on the heels of that came the warmth of knowing that whatever happened in her life, Dena was never going to be alone. She had people who loved her and would always be there for her. He wanted that for her. He wanted her taken care of and looked after, even if she would resist, saying she was fine.

"You're worried I'm going to hurt her."

"Yes. Don't take this wrong, but you're Micah Ruiz. On the surface, that's hard to resist. You're good-looking and charming, plus the whole singing thing. You're a big-time guy, temporarily living in the regular world. I'm not sure why you're here, but I do know you're leaving, and that worries me." She wrinkled her nose. "Actually, I'd be worried even if you were staying. I love my sister and I know she's amazing, but I'm not sure you see it."

"I do."

"I don't believe you. I mean, I want to, but I don't. She's not like the other women you've been with."

"What do you know about them?"

Her smile was self-deprecating. "Nothing specific, but I can imagine. Dena's not that." The smile faded. "You're the kind of guy who's easy to fall for. Dena doesn't have experience in your world, and that scares me. She's tough and she always has a plan, but I don't think she can prepare for the likes of you."

He supposed he could have been insulted by her assumptions, but he was too happy to witness how close the sisters were.

"I would never hurt her," he said.

"You might not want to, but to me, it feels inevitable. Are you staying in Wishing Tree?"

A question he'd never considered. Stay here? He liked the town and he certainly needed to settle somewhere. He was tired of avoiding the house in Malibu. It was time to do something about that.

"I don't know."

"See, that's the thing. You need to know. I wasn't kidding about having a plan. Dena likes them. They make her feel safe. She's always had a plan—even about getting pregnant. Don't play her."

"I wouldn't do that. I care about her."

Reggie looked doubtful. "Sure. For now, but then what? I'm afraid you'll get bored and walk away. I'm afraid she'll be crushed."

He didn't want that, either. How could he get bored with Dena? She was always so easy to be with. Energetic and fun and sweet and funny and sexy. But that wasn't Reggie's point. She was telling him that he needed to get his act together and figure out what he wanted. That hearts could be on the line.

"You're right about all of it. Thank you for talking to me. You've given me a lot to think about."

Reggie stared at him. "What does that mean? Are you being sarcastic?"

"No. Not at all. You're right. I can't just let things happen. I need a plan."

"So you like her?"

"Very much."

She shook her head. "This did not go the way I thought it would. I appreciate you not getting mad."

"You're looking out for Dena. Why would that make me mad?"

Reggie pressed her lips together. "Don't take this wrong, but you're way weirder than I'd expected."

"Don't take this wrong, either." He leaned over and lightly kissed her cheek. "No matter what, never stop protecting her."

Her eyes widened in surprise. "I won't."

REGGIE FINISHED TYING the last of the bows around the ceramic pots. She'd worked her way through her entire to-do list. The video slideshow was finished, she'd emailed her report on the vacuum to Gizmo, she'd confronted Micah about her sister, she'd completed all her wedding planning items and her mother had found the perfect dress to wear to her wedding. Life was good. Great, even. Well, except for the giant knot in her stomach.

Why had she told Toby he would regret letting her go? At the time, it had seemed so logical and obvious, but with the passage of time, she was starting to find the moment cringe-worthy. Wasn't she assuming a lot? Maybe Toby had figured out she was interested in him, and his whole song and dance about protecting Harrison was just an easy way to let her down. Maybe her trip down memory lane wasn't happening for both of them, and now she was stuck with feelings that weren't reciprocated.

She'd always been willing to say what she felt. Even in high school, she'd walked right up to him and told him he should ask her out. Something she hadn't thought about in forever, but she'd done it. She'd been brave. Of course, back then, she'd known how he felt about her. She'd caught him watching her, seen him hanging out where she hung out. Back then she'd known he wanted to date her. But today she was a lot less sure.

Yes, they had a good time together and yes, their kisses had been even hotter than they had been before, but that didn't mean he was secretly wishing he could take her out. Maybe she should—

"Stop," she said out loud, startling Belle, who was sleeping comfortably next to Burt. Her dog raised her head and gave her a hurt look, as if to ask what she could have possibly done wrong.

Reggie petted her. "I'm sorry, baby girl. I wasn't talking to you."

Belle's whip of a tail wagged a couple of times, a sign of forgiveness. Then Belle put her head down next to Burt and closed her eyes, Reggie slumped back on the family room sofa.

She was done questioning herself. She couldn't stand it anymore. She couldn't take back what had happened, and deep down, she wasn't sure she would if she could. She did think Toby was an idiot to avoid what was happening between them. Whatever they'd had before was still alive, and as far as she was concerned, that was pretty special. But maybe he didn't see it that way.

She picked up the folded paper hand pie holder she'd designed. It was compact yet sturdy, with a simple, economical design for pushing broken pieces of pie toward the top. She'd found three manufacturers who could make them, and she'd gotten bids from each of them. Dropping the holder and the bids in the mail was certainly one way to get Toby the information, but that felt too cowardly. Running and hiding had never been in her nature. She was the kind of person who put it all out there and let the consequences be damned. Sort of.

She went upstairs and put on makeup, then replaced her University of Washington sweatshirt with a cute sweater. On her way out, she grabbed the hand pie holders she'd been playing with, along with the folder containing the bids, and stepped into the cold.

But as she approached Judy's Hand Pies, her courage faded until she started doubting herself. She nearly turned back twice, but told herself she had to be brave. Later, when she looked back on this moment, she would be glad of that.

She found Shaye behind the counter, helping a couple of customers. While they tried to decide between beef with mushrooms and beef burgundy pies, Reggie waved at her.

"I need to talk to Toby. All right if I go up to his office?"

Shaye smiled at her. "Absolutely. The stairs are through the back."

Reggie nodded and walked behind the counter, then into the prep area, where a huge oven baked the pies. She opened the door at the end and found herself at the foot of a staircase.

"Courage," she whispered before squaring her shoulders.

She took the stairs two at a time, then walked down the short hallway. Only one door stood open, so she moved toward it and found Toby at his desk, his attention on his computer.

He looked good, she thought, admiring his broad shoulders and the way his intense expression made him even sexier. In that second before he spotted her, she imagined him smiling— a welcoming smile with a hint of wicked. Then he would stand and cross to her before pulling her close and—

"Reggie?"

His tone of confusion and faint wariness was not what she'd been wishing for, she thought, holding in a sigh. She faked a bright smile.

"Hi. Yes, it's me. I'll only keep you a second."

She took a seat in one of the visitors' chairs.

"Fear not. I come in peace and to talk business."

His expression warmed. "We weren't fighting. There's no need to come in peace."

"Fine. Then I promise not to tell you all the things wrong with your life."

"You always did have firm opinions."

"I still do."

"So I heard. How are you?"

The question surprised her. He wanted to do the friendly chitchat thing? "I'm fine. It's supposed to snow tomorrow. We'll see if that happens. At this point, I'm more anxious than hopeful."

"Everyone is tense about the snow. Or lack of snow."

"We are a desperate people." She opened her bag and withdrew the holders, but kept them in her hand. "Your pies are messy."

His eyebrows rose. "Okay. Thanks for sharing."

She groaned, knowing she was going about this all wrong. "Don't get mad. I'm not being critical. I'm stating a fact. Sometimes the pies are messy. They're always delicious, but if the crust cracks, then the whole thing falls apart in your hand. The bakery tissues don't help, and if you forgot napkins, you're stuck with pie filling all over your fingers. The pie holders a lot of fast food places use are the wrong shape for your product."

He studied her as if not sure of her point. "And?"

"And I was thinking about it. Part of my job is to help my inventors with their designs. I offer suggestions on how to make whatever it is easier for the end user. It's my thing." She handed over one of the holders. "So I made this."

He took it from her and turned it over in his hands. "To hold the pies."

"Yes. It's still paper, but it's thicker, and the folds make it much sturdier. Even if the pie cracks, it's not going anywhere. The paper is scored so the user can fold it in a fan shape to push the broken pieces toward the top. The paper is food-grade, and if you order enough of it, you can have a logo on it. I know the cost is multiples of bakery tissue, but the ultimate pie-eating experience is so much better with it."

She told herself to stop talking and let him be. The fact that she had no idea what he was thinking was her problem. She knew the design was good and the concept sound. Yes, there was a cost differential, so he could easily dismiss what she'd done, but that didn't change the quality of the product.

He looked at her. "When did you do this?"

"I've been working on it for a while." She pushed the folder toward him. "I found three manufacturers and asked for bids. Just to give you some idea of costs."

He swore under his breath. "Two nights ago you told me I was an idiot for not wanting to date you."

"I don't think those were my exact words."

"Close enough. And while that was happening, you were doing this?"

"I don't see what one has to do with the other."

"Why didn't you just toss this in the trash?"

She drew back in her chair. "Because it's a good idea. I worked hard on this. If you don't want to consider it, that's fine, but there's no reason to tell me my idea is garbage."

"No," he said, leaning toward her. "Reggie, that isn't what I meant. I was asking why you would still want to help me?"

"Oh. Because we're friends."

His gaze locked with hers. She had the sense that he was looking for something, but she had no idea what it was. Finally he smiled at her and waved the holder.

"This is great. Let's go try it with a few pies."

"You want to?"

"Yes. Very much."

"It's simple yet strong. I like that in a design."

He stood. "It's amazing, and I'm embarrassed I didn't think of it myself."

"You're not a design kind of person. It's okay. We all have flaws."

He surprised her by laughing. The happy sound made her concerns fade. Even if she and Toby never found their way to being a couple again, she was glad they could get back to being friends.

"There were customers in the store," she said. "We could ask them what they think. Oh, and Harrison. He eats the pies all the time. He would be a great tester. If a kid can keep from spilling, then we know it's going to work."

"I already know it's going to work, but we're going to try it out anyway."

"Sound good. I'm in the mood for pie."

He motioned for her to precede him down the stairs. "Me, too."

TWO HOURS LATER, Toby knew he was going to be making a change in all the stores. Reggie's holders had worked perfectly. They'd taken a dozen pies to the back and had cracked some, eaten some from the middle to the ends and had cut some in two before putting them in the holders. The folded paper had kept in the filling and had withstood the pressure of dripping sauce. The design was simple and intuitive.

"Did you bring a contract?" he asked when she'd declared she was too full to eat another pie.

"What are you talking about?"

"I want to buy your design."

She rolled her eyes. "There's no buy. I did it because I wanted to. It's yours. Enjoy."

"Reggie, this is going to change the industry. You need to get it patented and license it to me. You should be paid for this."

She smiled. "Change the industry? We're talking about the hand pie world?"

"It's bigger than you think, and the holder will have other applications. This is good work, and it's what you do. I assume you have a patent attorney."

"Yes, and let me tell you, he's not as funny as you'd think."

"You're not taking me seriously."

Her brown eyes crinkled with amusement. "Not in the least."

"This could be worth a fortune."

"Hardly. Now, if I'd invented sticky notes —that would be a fortune." She patted his arm. "You're sweet to worry about me, but I meant what I said. I did this for you because I like to solve problems. It's your design to use. Consider it a gift." She glanced at her watch. "I need to get home to walk Belle. Let me know when you run the numbers on the holders. I want to know if you're going to do them or not."

With that, she shrugged into her coat, put on her gloves and scarf, then headed out of the store. He was left alone in the back room of his pie shop, holding the design she'd just given him, as if it was no big deal.

As he took the last of the holders up to his office, he admitted to himself that he didn't get it. Not her, not what had happened, not any of it.

When he reached his desk, he sat down and stared at

the holder. He wanted to tell himself it was just folded paper, but he knew it was more than that. Reggie had seen a problem and then had decided to figure out a solution. She'd put time and effort into the project. He would guess there were multiple attempts to get it right, and the whole time she'd been working, she'd never even hinted at what she was doing.

Even more astonishing was the fact that a couple of nights ago, she'd pretty much told him she wanted them to start dating. Meaning she was interested in him romantically—something he was still trying to ignore. Instead of accepting her enticing offer, he'd told her he couldn't take the chance and had let her walk away. A reality that had kept him up for the past two nights.

But even after all that, she'd still shown up here and had *given* him the pie holder design. For nothing. Who did that? No one he knew. Why wasn't she mad at him? Why did she ever want to see him again?

He crossed to the window, hoping to catch sight of her, but she'd already left The Wreath. He stared out at the other stores, at the bright blue sky, as if the answers to his questions were hiding somewhere.

He knew Reggie well enough to believe she wasn't trying to trick him. Instead she was just being herself. Giving, generous, honest. If he were to ever trust another woman, she would be on the short list. But to take the chance was to risk too much.

Or was it?

Was she correct to tell him he wasn't protecting Harrison as much as he was protecting himself? He'd never considered the possibility. What Lori had done had scarred them both. But if there was even a whisper of truth in her theory, shouldn't he consider her words?

He had no answers, no clear idea of what to do next. The only thing he knew for sure was that she was right about one thing. If he let her go without trying, he would regret it for the rest of his life.

Twenty-Six

"YOU'RE NOT EATING," Dena pointed out, grateful she'd put on yoga pants after she'd gotten home from work. Ursula had outdone herself with the food. "Did you not see that there are bacon jalapeño poppers *and* mini black bean and cheese tostadas? Plus chips and guacamole. You're from LA. This should be your thing."

She was sitting with Micah in the dining room. They'd agreed to meet for Snacks and Wine, something she'd been looking forward to all day.

Micah, as gorgeous as ever, in jeans and a sweater just a few shades darker than his eyes, smiled at her. "Sorry, I've been thinking."

"You can't think and eat?"

He chuckled. "I can and I will." He rose with lazy grace. "Be right back."

She knew it was wrong, but she turned to watch him walk away. The man had an amazing butt. And long legs. He was so incredibly perfect that she couldn't help wishing they were more than friends. Seeing him naked would be a memory she would treasure the rest of her life. She wasn't crazy enough to wish for sex, but just a casual glance at his awesomeness would be pretty incredible.

Ah, dreams, she thought, then did her best not to laugh.

He returned with two plates. One had several appetizers on it, and the other had a scoop of guacamole and a handful of chips. He pushed that one toward her.

"Because of the reverence in your voice when you said *guacamole*," he teased.

"I can't help it. Washington State grows lots of fruits and vegetables, along with amazing grapes for wine. We even produce most of the country's hops, which beer drinkers everywhere should celebrate. But we don't have a climate for avocados. Sad but true."

She grabbed a chip and scooped up guacamole. "It's the small things that make life so nice." And the company, but she was careful not to say that.

It was near the end of the Snacks and Wine hour, with only a few guests lingering before heading back to their rooms or out for dinner.

"I should have had a salad," she said, picking up another bacon jalapeño popper. "Although technically this is a vegetable, right? Hmm, I have beans for protein, cheese, vegetables."

"You're saying you're having a healthy dinner?"

She laughed. "Maybe. Kind of. It's not awful."

He ate a tostada. "People keep talking about it snowing tomorrow."

"We're all hoping. It's so late this year. The town

makes a big deal of the first snowfall, so tourists always want to be here when it happens, but there's no way to be sure of the date."

His gaze lingered on her face. "I'm sorry I'm going to miss it."

"You are? But you can't. Where are you—" She held in a sigh. "Is it already time for you to go to Los Angeles for the variety show?"

"Yes. I fly out early in the morning."

Ugh. He was leaving. Worse, they were already well into the second half of the month. Her parents' wedding was next week. Then it was Christmas, and then Micah would be gone.

He surprised her by taking her hand in his and lacing their fingers together. "I'll be gone three days, and then I'll be back."

She tried to smile. "Oh, I don't know. You might land in LA and realize what you've been missing all this time."

"I know what I'll be missing, and it's not anything in Southern California."

Ah, what? Did he mean he would miss her? Was there a way to ask without risking having him laugh in her face?

"They grow avocados in Southern California, so at least you'll have that," she said instead.

He laughed, then leaned in and lightly kissed her. "Yes, they do. I'll bring you some."

"That would be very sweet."

"Anything else you want from the city?"

"Just you."

The words fell out before she could stop them, and

then they just hung there, big and alive and un-call-back-able.

Oh, no, oh, no, oh, no. How was she supposed to explain that?

"I, ah, um, meant to say," she began, only to have him shake his head.

"Don't take it back. Please."

His blue gaze was steady, his expression intense. Her heart fluttered a few times as she tried to keep up with the conversation.

"Your parents are renewing their vows next week," he said.

The change in topic was both a relief and a little disappointing. "They are."

"Are you taking anyone to the wedding?"

"You mean like a date? No."

"Would you like to take me?"

She would have squealed, but as he asked the question, he began brushing his thumb across the back of her hand. It was nothing, really, or it should have been nothing. He probably wasn't even aware of the movement. It wasn't his fault that her entire body went on alert.

"If you'd like to go," she said, grateful she didn't stutter.

"I would."

"It's up at the resort. I'll have to get there early, so I'll text you the time." OMG! She was going on a date with Micah! "Oh, unless you get busy in LA."

"I'll be back for the wedding. I promise. Are you going to watch the show?"

She laughed. "Is that a serious question? Of course

I am. I've never seen you perform, and I want to hear the song. You said I inspired it."

"You did." One corner of his mouth turned up. "Now, you have to be gentle. I'm no Dolly Parton."

"I think we've already established that."

But instead of laughing, he got serious. "I'm going to miss you."

Okay, this whole Snacks and Wine evening had been filled with unexpected twists and turns.

"I'll miss you, too."

"Oh, Dena, we're having the best time."

Sadly, Dena was forced back into the real world. She released Micah's hand and smiled at Mr. and Mrs. Cuyler, a lovely older couple from Fort Worth who visited at least twice a year.

"I'm glad," she said, standing to speak with them. "The forecast says we're getting our first snow tomorrow."

Mrs. Cuyler pressed a hand to her chest. "We've heard, and we're so excited. We've never been here for the first snowfall."

"Remember, we need fifteen full minutes of snow to make it official. When you hear the horns, bundle up and go to The Wreath. You'll have such a good time."

"We're looking forward to it," Mr. Cuyler told her before the two of them started for the stairs.

She sat back down and tried not to sigh. She adored the Cuylers, but she really wished they hadn't walked up right then. Talking to them had broken whatever strange spell she and Micah had been in.

She reached for another tostada, telling herself at least she had carbs to comfort her.

"They seem nice," he said.

"They are. Some guests are easy and some aren't. They're always lovely."

"Dena, would you spend the night with me?"

Thank goodness she'd already swallowed, because otherwise she would have choked for sure. She swung her head to stare at him, not sure she'd heard what she thought she'd heard.

"Did you just ask me —"

His gaze was steady. "Spend the night with me. Nothing's going to happen. You have my word. But I would very much like to hold you in my arms."

And just like that, the bubble burst.

"Why don't you want to have sex with me?" she asked, only to gasp in horror as she realized what she'd said. She glanced around frantically, grateful that they were the last people in the dining room. At least no one else would witness her humiliation.

Micah's lips twitched, but he was gallant enough not to smile.

"Have I mentioned how I adore your directness? I'm thinking it's a family trait. For the record, I want to make love with you. It's hard to think about anything else. But it's too soon, and I'm leaving in the morning. I don't want to put you in that position. It's not fair."

Nothing about this conversation was normal, but then nothing about Micah was normal, either. He was larger than life and existed in a world she knew nothing about. Her body told her to say yes, that just spending the night being held by him would be magical. Her head warned her that he was dangerous and that even without "anything happening," she could be at serious risk of losing her heart to him. And if that happened, how would she ever get it back?

I can't. She thought the words, knew they were right and really, totally planned to say them. But when she opened her mouth, what came out was, "I would like that."

His smile dazzled her. "Thank you. Let's take care of the dishes, and then you can tell me what time to be at your place. If that's all right."

Her heart was beating so fast, she thought it might take flight. "That would be fine."

Fine. What a silly word for such a consequential moment. Yes, the man was going to break her heart, but she refused to regret the night. Not even for a second.

AFTER THE KITCHEN was clean, Dena hurried back to her apartment, then stood in the middle of the living room, not sure what to do. Clean sheets weren't a problem—she'd changed them yesterday. As for the rest of it, well, she had absolutely no frame of reference to help her make her decision. Assuming he was right and this was just a sleepover, a sexy nightie would be too much. Not that she had a wide selection of sexy lingerie from which she could choose.

If she was going to be by herself, she would put on her regular winter pj's and call it a night. Literally. But she wasn't going to be by herself, so cats in Santa hats might not be appropriate. And while she was on the topic of what was or wasn't going to happen, should she shower? Shave her legs? Wish she'd gotten a bikini wax, although she never had and she wasn't sure she should start while she was pregnant. She kept things tidy, but it wasn't as if he was going to see anything, so...

"Take the man at his word," she told herself. Nothing was going to happen. As much as she hated to admit it, he was right. She loved the fantasy of sex with Micah, but the reality was a little more intimidating. For one thing, she'd never been with a man she didn't have fairly significant feelings for. She just didn't see the point of sex for sex's sake. For another, he was leaving in the morning, and while he swore he was coming back in a few days, maybe he would get to LA and realize everything he'd been missing. Plus, she was a mother-to-be. Didn't that call for a little more decorum?

She walked into the bedroom and pulled back the covers, then put a night-light in the attached bathroom. She surveyed her pj wardrobe and decided she had nothing Micah-worthy, so she went with the Santa cats. After washing her face and brushing her teeth, she texted him that she was ready.

As soon as she hit Send, her stomach dropped to her toes. What if he'd changed his mind? What if this was just a very bad joke? What if—

She heard a knock on her door. OMG! He was here.

She let him in, then watched while he hung his coat and stepped out of his boots. Without them, he was barefoot, wearing sweats and a T-shirt. She raised her gaze to his face.

"I'm incredibly nervous," she blurted before she could stop herself.

"Me, too."

"Really? But you're so urban. I wouldn't have thought you were capable of being nervous."

He gave her a lopsided smile that had her toes curling. "It's my first time, too."

Before she could fully absorb the tender wonderfulness of his words, he was pulling her into his arms and holding her tight. He didn't try to kiss her. Instead, he rested his cheek against her hair and sighed.

"This is nice," he murmured.

"It is."

"I like the cats."

"They're new this season."

She felt him chuckle. "Do you get new holiday pajamas every year?"

"Sure. I start wearing them Thanksgiving night. Then I switch back to regular pj's on New Year's Day."

"I know I said this before, but I'm going to miss you. I wish you could come with me."

She stepped back. "To Los Angeles? I've never been. My parents took us to San Francisco when I was sixteen, and I flew over it when Reggie and I spent a week in Mexico." She wrinkled her nose. "My parents were more into vacations like driving to Mount Rushmore than taking us to a big city. Although I would like to see Disneyland one day."

He cupped her face and stared into her eyes. "I'll take you there."

She smiled, hoping he was telling the truth. She would like to go to Disneyland with Micah. Or anywhere. A couple of weeks in an uncrowded tropical resort was her favorite fantasy. Just them in a big hotel room with lots of walks on the beach and time in bed. Yeah, that would be fantastic.

"Shall we?" Micah asked, dropping his arm so he could take her hand. "It's late, and you have work tomorrow."

It wasn't really late, but she didn't protest. No way they were going to curl up on the couch and stream something. Not when he was here to specifically get into her bed. Not for, you know, but still, they were going to be lying down together. And, she assumed, cuddling. That should give her enough happy memories to last her well into her eighties.

She led the way into her bedroom. She'd turned off the overhead light and had left the nightstand lamps on. Micah was tall—thank goodness she had a king-size mattress.

"Which side?" he asked.

She felt herself blush. "Either works fine."

He looked at her. "Dena, it's your bed. Which side?"

"The right."

He went around to the left and got in bed. She slid onto her side, not sure what to make of the moment. A month ago, if someone had told her she was going to be spending the night with Micah Ruiz, she wouldn't have believed them. In part, she supposed, because she hadn't known who Micah was, but that wasn't the point. This was really happening!

He slid toward the center of the bed and relaxed on his back, with his arm out. The invitation was obvious. She was to get close to him, maybe put her head on his shoulder, maybe rest her hand on his chest. And while she had imagined doing that in her mind, she was less sure about making it happen in person.

"What are you thinking?" he asked.

"I don't know what to do with my hands."

He laughed. "What do you want to do with them?"

The blush returned. "I meant that if I put my head on your shoulder, my right arm and hand need to go somewhere. I'm not sure I can rest them on my side, and I don't know you well enough to, um, put them on you."

"You're a thinker."

"I am. And bossy. It's probably why I'm single."

"You're single because all the men you've met until now have been blind. And maybe because I'm a lucky SOB. Lie down."

She did as he requested, moving close enough to put her head on his shoulder. He immediately took her hand and put it on his chest. As if they did this sort of thing all the time. As if they belonged together.

He was warm everywhere they touched. His shoulder was muscled, as was his side. Slowly, cautiously, she shifted her right leg so it rested across his thigh.

"You can touch me anywhere," he told her. "What's mine is yours."

"I wish I was brave."

He smiled. "What would you do if you were?"

Wanting flared. "I think we both know the answer to that."

He tangled his fingers in her hair. "Yes, we do, and best not to go there. I have a limited amount of control, and I meant what I said. This isn't the right time."

Did he want to mention when the right time might be? Just so she could clear her calendar and maybe get a pedicure at the nail salon?

"How's your morning sickness?" he asked.

Now there was a change in subject. "Much better. It's very much only in the morning and less and less each day. I'm still wearing my bracelets, but at some point, I'll risk going without them."

"You'll be entering your second trimester soon."

"I know. It's exciting and scary at the same time. Mostly exciting. So far my stretchy clothes are all fitting, but that will change in the next couple of months.

It's so odd to think about. I know I'm pregnant, but sometimes I don't feel it."

"You'll get there. You're going to be a great mom."

"Thank you."

"Now close your eyes."

She tilted her head to look at him. "What? I'm not tired."

"You are. Your blinks are getting slower and slower."

She wanted to protest that wasn't true, but before she could say anything, he shifted so he could kiss her. For a second, he loomed over her, and she wished with all her heart that they were going to make love tonight. Just this one time.

But after brushing his lips against hers and staring deeply into her eyes, he reached over her and turned off the lamp, then did the same with the one on his side. He rolled onto his back again and pulled her close.

"Go to sleep, Dena. I'll be right here."

He felt so good, she thought, snuggling close and resting her hand on his chest. Warm and safe and everything she'd ever wanted. Not that she was going to sleep. She planned to stay awake so she could remember every moment. She would need the details for when she was eighty and reliving the past.

Only the next time she opened her eyes, the bed was empty and Micah's side was cold. She turned to look at her clock and saw it was nearly five thirty. She had no idea what time he'd left or if he'd slept at all. All she knew for sure was that he was gone, and now she had to wait to see if he would come back.

Twenty-Seven

TOBY STARED OUT the window, looking at the sky. The clouds had come in overnight—thick and heavy and gray. Had it been any other year, he would have been sure of snow, but this year had been disappointing for everyone. Still, he was hopeful. It was cold enough, and the local weather forecaster had promised. By two o'clock, it was supposed to be snowing across northern Washington State, with the snow lasting at least two days.

He had plenty of work he could be doing, but waiting for snow seemed more interesting. That and thinking about Reggie. He hadn't been able to get her off his mind, not since her recent visit, when she'd given him the pie holders. He'd contacted the manufacturers and had confirmed the bids, then had held a Zoom call with his team. Everyone had been blown away by her design. He'd overnighted samples to the Seattle office, and they were already sourcing food-grade paper and looking for ways to get a logo on it.

What he hadn't shared was how generous she'd been, simply giving him the design. He still didn't understand why she'd done it. Yes, she'd said she was helping a friend, but he couldn't wrap his mind around that. The best explanation he'd come up with was that he was so used to holding back from people, he'd forgotten they could act the way Reggie had.

Fluffy white flakes started to fall. He checked his watch to mark the time, then willed them to keep falling. Ridiculously, anticipation filled him. At the five-minute mark, the snow was even more steady and starting to cover the ground. At seven minutes, he shut down his computer and picked up the backpack he'd prepared yesterday morning. It already contained plastic glasses, napkins and cookies, along with chocolate-covered strawberries he'd ordered on impulse. He grabbed his outdoor gear and went downstairs.

Shaye stood at the open door, watching the snow. She smiled when she saw him.

"It's so still, like the whole town is waiting."

"It is. When you hear the horns, you can close the store and head to The Wreath. Text Lawson to meet you there."

Her smile widened. "Really? You sure?"

"Yes. It's the first snow of the season and your first snow in Wishing Tree. Enjoy it."

"Thanks, boss." She was already pulling her phone out of her back pocket.

Toby waited a few more minutes, then reached for his own phone.

We're going to have a white Christmas. Join me at The Wreath?

Reggie's reply was instant. Love to.

I'm going by the school to pick up Harrison. I'll meet you there.

He went into the back and opened the big industrial refrigerator. Inside were a bottle of sparkling cider and another of champagne that he'd brought in that morning. He put both into the backpack, shrugged into his coat and pulled on his gloves, then walked the short distance to the elementary school.

Kids were already pouring out of the building, being met by equally excited parents. Toby spotted Harrison and called to him. His son ran over and hugged him just as horns and sirens went off all over the city.

"It's official," Toby said, tugging his son's hat down on his head. "Let's get to The Wreath."

They hurried north, waving at friends, joining the thickening crowd. When they arrived, the round space was filling rapidly. Music played over speakers, and carts selling everything from bird feeders to hot chocolate had appeared as if by magic.

"Reggie's joining us," he told Harrison. "Do you see her?"

They both searched the crowd.

"There!" Harrison called, pointing. He ran over and grabbed her hand, then pulled her back to where Toby was waiting.

She was laughing as she came to a stop in front of him.

"It's snowing!" She spun in a circle. "I'm so happy. I

love Wishing Tree when it snows." She smiled at him. "How are you?"

He impulsively leaned forward and kissed her on the mouth. Her lips were soft and warm, and the second he touched them, he wanted to do so much more. Wanting filled him, nearly painful in its intensity. Wanting for her, but also wanting for *them*. For what they could be.

But this wasn't the time or place to explore that, so he drew back and smiled at her.

"I'm good. I brought champagne."

She laughed. "You are a very smart man. I like that."

He opened the backpack and poured Harrison some sparkling cider, then passed out the cookies. He opened the champagne and poured them each a glass. The three of them toasted the snow. Harrison drained his glass, then asked to go play with his friends.

"Stay in The Wreath," Toby told him.

Harrison grinned. "Dad, I'm not going anywhere. You don't have to worry about me."

Toby knew in some ways that was true, but in others, he was a dad. He would always worry.

"There will be snowmen," Reggie said, leaning against him.

"For sale?"

She smiled. "In town. Remember? There aren't any snowman decorations until the first snowfall. Right this second, people are putting them out everywhere. Isn't it wonderful? I love this town."

She was smiling as she spoke, her eyes bright with happiness, her mouth curving. He wanted to kiss her again, lingering this time, teasing her, tasting her, arousing her until—

"Let's go shopping," she said, capping the cider bottle and tucking it into the backpack. She held the open bottle of champagne. "I guess we'll have to carry this."

"Or drink it."

She laughed. "Yes, we could do that. I want to buy a bird feeder, and they always have the best ones for sale on the first snowfall."

He secured the backpack and put his arms through the straps to get it out of the way. He took the bottle from Reggie.

"So you have a free hand to shop."

"You're so sweet. Thank you."

The music continued to play. Several couples were dancing in the middle of The Wreath. The younger children were making snow angels where they found untrampled snow. Harrison and several boys his age were throwing snowballs at each other.

Reggie led the way to the carts and booths, admiring the crafts and carefully studying the bird feeders. She purchased two, then bought some fudge from another vendor. Then they found a free bench and sat down to enjoy their champagne.

"My team is very impressed with your design," he told her, pouring more of the sparkling liquid into her glass.

"I'm glad. I hope the numbers work."

"I think they will."

He set the champagne down and angled toward her. She had on a thick coat, gloves and a hat, and he wasn't sure he'd ever seen her look more beautiful. This was Reggie—he knew her. He'd known her much of his life.

"I've been thinking about what you said," he told her. "Working things through."

Her gaze met his. "I'm glad."

"You're right about some of it."

One corner of her mouth turned up. "Only some?"

"I still worry about Harrison."

The smile faded. "I know you do, and with good reason. If I were you, I'd never let him out of the house."

"I'm not sure keeping him locked up helps with the healing."

"But it was your first instinct?"

"Yes."

She took his free hand in hers. "I get that, Toby. I really do. You're a good father, and he's such a great kid. But as to the rest of it, you know there's something between us. Something I think is worth considering. It's not just nostalgia, believe me. I went out with Jake, and the fact that there was nothing still there was painfully obvious. We're not like that."

She looked down at her champagne, then back at him. "I still wonder about what would have happened if you hadn't had to leave town. If instead you'd stayed and we'd talked and I'd listened."

He already knew the answer to that. "I would have convinced you to give me a second chance."

"You didn't need one. You hadn't done anything wrong."

"You know what I mean."

She nodded.

What would have happened? But even as he asked the question, he already knew the answer. If they'd gotten back together, they would have stayed together. He never would have left town, never would have started over. He would have made it work here, so they could be together always. He would have married her.

"We could have had three kids by now," he said absently.

"Three? That's a lot."

"Two, then?"

"Yeah, two kids." Her smile turned regretful. "But there's no going back. Only forward."

She leaned toward him. He met her halfway and kissed her. The wanting was just as strong, but this time it was accompanied by something else. A sense of rightness. He didn't know what it meant, but he was going to let it sit for a while and figure it out later. In the meantime, he was going to pretend he was still eighteen again and kissing his girl.

REGGIE WALKED HOME enjoying the steady snow and her general sense of happiness. As per tradition, snowmen had appeared everywhere. They were on porches and front steps and in yard displays, and the city workers were hanging snowmen banners on light poles. The snow had arrived, and now all was well in the Wishing Tree world.

On a more personal note, her parents' wedding was less than a week away, and she felt good about being ready. The Christmas cactus were beribboned, her mother's dress was back from the alterations lady, and according to her last call with Paisley, all was well with the resort. Which meant she was perfectly free to think about Toby's kisses.

They'd been pretty good—in some ways better than she remembered. Or maybe it was that all the other kisses in her life were a poor second.

He'd seemed different today. More relaxed and open. She knew better than to get her hopes up—he had a lot to work through before he would be willing to risk a relationship—but maybe a little progress had been made.

That was what she wanted. She wanted Toby and Harrison in her life. She wasn't sure when she'd decided it, but today, celebrating the first snowfall together, she'd known. He'd been a great guy when she'd known him in high school, and he was a better man now. He was a terrific father, an intelligent businessman, and a kind soul who loved his grandmother, and he kissed like a dream.

She felt things with Toby she'd never felt with anyone else. Talking about how different their lives would have been if he hadn't left town had helped her see what was important. Toby was the one. Maybe he'd always been the one. A thought that made her dizzy with happiness. Unless, of course, he was going to be difficult. He'd always been stubborn, and once he got something in his head, it was tough to change his mind.

"Not a problem for today," she said, walking up the path of her parents' house.

A large inflatable snowman sat in the middle of the yard. There was a family of snowmen by the front door, making her smile as she let herself in.

"You've been busy, Mom," she called, starting the unraveling process.

She hung up her coat and scarf, put her hat on the little shelf and unlaced her snow boots before stepping out of them. Hmm, there hadn't been a response from her mom, and Belle and Burt hadn't come running.

"Mom?"

"Is that you, Reggie? We're in the basement."

Reggie headed for the stairs. When she was halfway down, her mother moved to the bottom of the stairs.

"Don't be mad," she said, her expression two parts guilt and one part amusement.

"Unless you decided on a different favor for your wedding, I couldn't possibly be mad. What's going on?"

Leigh pointed to the far end of the basement, where Belle was stretched out on the carpet, Burt resting beside her. At first Reggie couldn't figure out what her dog was doing, but then she saw the scattered pieces of what had been Gizmo's vacuum. Belle was chewing on a piece of the casing.

"It's my fault," her mother said quickly. "I was running late, so I thought I'd let your little invention take care of the upstairs. When I got home from running errands, I didn't think anything of it, except Belle didn't come to greet me, so I went looking for her. This is what I found. She must have carried it down here to kill it."

"Oh, Belle," Reggie said, trying to sound stern. "Gizmo is not going to be happy."

Belle wagged her tail.

Reggie wasn't overly concerned about her client. Gizmo had at least a half dozen of the machines at his workshop. It wasn't as if Belle had destroyed the only one, but still, this was so unlike her.

"You've become a sassy girl," Reggie said, pulling out her phone and taking a picture of the damage. "You might need a little extra training when we get home."

She texted the photo to Gizmo, along with an explanation.

Bill me the cost of the vacuum. And maybe look at making it a little more dog-proof. Belle won't be the only one going after it.

Three dots appeared.

Belle is awesome. And you're right. The casing isn't tough enough. After the first of the year, I'll work on modifications.

Reggie tucked her phone into her jeans, then looked at her mom. "I'll get this cleaned up."

Her mother's mouth twitched. "Too bad we don't have a fancy electronic vacuum to take care of it."

Reggie started to laugh.

MICAH STOOD ON the deck of his Malibu home, staring at the impossible blue of the California sky and the Pacific Ocean. Despite the fact that Christmas was less than ten days away, the temperature was a balmy seventy-two degrees. He could smell the salt air, admire the beauty of the view, and he wanted nothing more than to be back in Wishing Tree, waking up next to Dena.

Rehearsals had gone smoothly. The producers had been wild about the new song and had brought in an orchestra to play with him. There was one more run-through this morning, then the live show tonight.

He took his coffee back inside. The cleaning service had done a good job of stocking the refrigerator for him. There were clean linens on the master bed and fresh towels in the bathroom. He couldn't complain about the service or the view or the house itself. The only thing that didn't belong was him.

He and Adriana had bought this place while they'd still been engaged. They'd planned on making it their forever home, but somehow that had never happened. They'd traveled together, enjoying seeing the world. He and the band had still been performing from time to time, so that had kept him busy, along with writing. It was only the last few months, when Adriana had been pregnant, that the two of them had spent any serious time in the house.

Despite that, despite the pictures of her on the walls and her clothes in the closet, she wasn't here. Micah had gone looking for traces of her in the house, trying to recapture her, to feel what he had when she'd been alive, but she was gone. He loved her, he would always love her, but she wasn't a part of him anymore. He had moved on.

He returned to his office, where several boxes were stacked together. He hadn't been able to sleep, so he'd spent much of the night collecting personal items and moving them in here. A few mementos from his marriage, photographs, some artwork he'd bought over the years. Before he went back to Wishing Tree, he would get someone in to go over what he was keeping. All this, his clothes, and everything in the music studio downstairs. Not only the guitars and his piano, but the cabinet filled with half-written songs and ideas, and the notes on everything he and the band had performed. That he would take with him. The rest would stay with the house. He'd sell it furnished. Some up-and-coming rock star or movie executive would appreciate not having to furnish the place.

He showered and dressed, then walked back out to the deck and took a picture to text to Dena.

You'd look good here.

By now she would be in class, so he wouldn't hear from her for a while, but he was okay with that.

The missing felt good. Wanting her, wishing she was with him, made him feel alive. After so many months of not feeling much of anything, he'd reached the other side and was finally going to start living his life again. There were details to be worked out and decisions to be made—some about his career and the logistics of making his home in Wishing Tree.

His phone buzzed. He glanced at the screen, hoping to see a text from Dena, but instead it was the limo driver saying that he was in the driveway, ready to take Micah to the studio. Micah replied that he would be right out.

Traffic was oddly light, and they arrived in less than forty minutes. Micah carried his guitar inside and was immediately met by one of the assistants who would shepherd him through his rehearsal. Before he could introduce himself, Electra burst out of nowhere and threw herself at him.

"Finally!" she said, her voice thick with drama. "Dammit, Micah, why didn't you call me? I can't believe you've been in town for two days and didn't get in touch."

She wrapped her long, thin arms around his neck and ground her body into his. She smelled of expensive perfume, and her jewelry clinked as she moved. She was all angles and edges, and when she tried to kiss him, he quickly sidestepped and drew away.

Her big green eyes widened with surprise. "What's up with you?"

"It's good to see you," he lied.

"Not good enough." Her mouth formed a pout. "Micah, what's going on? You *always* let me know when you're in town."

That wasn't true. Once he and Adriana got involved, he hadn't seen Electra at all. They'd talked on the phone maybe twice a year, but that was it. After he'd lost Adriana, seeing Electra had been the last thing on his mind.

"I thought we could have dinner," she said, lightly touching his arm. "I've missed you so much."

"I have plans tonight."

The light touch became a slap. "No, you don't." She glared at him. "I want to talk about us working together. Come on. I know you're not writing, and we used to be a great team. We could be again."

She wasn't going away. He should have remembered that she could be persistent. He shifted his guitar case to his other hand and gave her his full attention.

"I'm writing just fine," he told her. "I appreciate the offer, but I'm not interested in going backwards. You have a lot of talent. You'll find someone else to write with."

"No one's as good as you."

He faked a smile. "I appreciate the compliment, but it's not going to happen. I'm sorry."

She would think the apology was about the songwriting. Later tonight she would find out that he wasn't going to be singing "Moonlight for Christmas," and then it would all hit the fan. But by then, he would be surrounded by his manager and agent and counting down the hours until he returned to Wishing Tree.

As if she could read his mind, she said, "Something happened in that stupid little town, didn't it? It's where you started writing again."

"I have no idea what you're talking about."

"We both know that's not true." Her sharp gaze searched his face. "You've really changed."

He thought about teaching Dena's class how to play guitar, and the B and B, and Reggie telling him to be careful with Dena's heart.

"I have."

"I don't like it."

She turned and stalked away, her high-heeled boots clicking on the concrete floor. He watched her go, thinking he'd made a lucky escape.

When he was back home, he would tell Dena about the encounter. Then he would pull her into his arms and kiss her. He would tell her how he felt, and they would talk about the future. Maybe they would go back to her place and make love for the first time. He wasn't sure of the details or how it would all play out, but he knew for sure that he'd found something solid and precious, and he was never going to let it go.

Twenty-Eight

PERHAPS A LITTLE late in life, Dena realized she didn't have it in her to play it cool. She was a bundle of nerves, and she couldn't seem to fake casual interest or lack of worry. She'd felt sick to her stomach since waking up that morning. By quarter to eight in the evening, she was a mess.

"Maybe you should pace," Reggie offered helpfully as she stirred the brown sugar, corn syrup and butter that would become the coating for the homemade caramel corn they would be sharing during the live holiday special that was about to start. "Burn off some energy."

"I'm nervous," she admitted.

"The man's been texting you multiple times a day. He misses you."

"I hope so."

In her head she knew Reggie was right. Micah had been staying in touch regularly. But her heart was more concerned about his absence. He was down in LA, where life was different. His old life was there—what if he decided he liked that better than the slow, easy pace of things in Wishing Tree? What if he met a cute, not-pregnant woman?

As if that wasn't enough, she was also wondering about the song. He'd said she'd inspired him, but she didn't know what that meant. Would it be meaningful? Or was it a silly holiday song about talking rabbits and she was reading way too much into his comments?

Why hadn't they talked about their feelings before he left? What if he never came back? What if she'd snored and he was disgusted and never wanted to see her again?

Their mom walked into the kitchen. "All right, girls. It's time."

They brought the caramel popcorn into the family room. A commercial ended, and then they were staring at a beautiful stage decorated for the holidays. The announcer spoke.

"Live from Los Angeles, California, a celebration of the season with our guests." He started listing the artists, giving a special shout-out to Micah Ruiz. Dena's stomach flipped. The show was two hours and Micah was toward the end. She didn't know how she was going to hold it together that long.

Finally, after dozens of performances, the camera panned across a large orchestra before stopping on Micah, seated on a stool. The audience went still, waiting.

The first notes of the beautiful melody had her catching her breath. Then he began to sing.

I thought I'd be alone this Christmas.
Again.
Wouldn't have a home this Christmas.
Again.
And I was fine.
I was okay.
I'd loved and lost—
That's just life's way.

But then the snow fell.
The snow fell.
The snow fell.
The past was gone,
Only memories remained.

Dena stared at him, not sure what to think, what to feel. Was the song about her? About their first kiss?

There you were, with snowflakes sparkling in
your hair.
There you were, teaching me to care.
Again...
Inviting me into your heart.

As the snow fell,
I fell
And you fell.
The past was gone,
Only love remained.
Reaching us and healing us and making us into one.

Now I'm going to spend Christmas
With you

And all my next Christmases,
Too.
Because the snow fell.

The last note lingered, the violinists stretching it out until the audience began clapping and cheering. Dena stayed in her seat, frantically telling herself it was just a song. They were words he'd strung together, and whatever inspiration she'd been didn't mean what it sounded like he meant.

"That was so pretty," her mother said, her voice incredibly calm. "Had you heard it before, Dena?"

"No, he didn't play it for me."

"The man is very talented. I liked that a lot. I wonder what Taylor is going to sing. I do love her."

Vince smiled. "Maybe she'll do a Christmas version of 'Shake It Off.'"

Leigh laughed. "That would be fun, wouldn't it?"

"You okay?" Reggie asked, eyeing her.

"Sure. Of course. Why do you ask?"

"The song. Did you know what he was writing?"

Dena brushed off the question with what she hoped was a convincing laugh. "Oh, they're just words that rhyme."

Reggie's gaze seemed to probe a little. "You sure?"

Just then her phone rang. "I'll go in the kitchen." She raced there and hit the Talk button. "Hello?"

"Hey."

The sound of Micah's voice made her knees go weak. "Hi. The song was great. So beautiful."

He said something, but she couldn't hear him over all the background noise. She heard people calling his name and congratulating him. Someone nearby was saying something about getting into the studio that night.

"Micah? I can't understand what you're saying."

"I have to record a single. I'm not coming back to-morrow."

"Oh."

He said something else she couldn't hear, then what sounded like, "I'll call later," and then he was gone.

She stood alone in the kitchen, not sure what to think. He'd phoned her—that had to mean something. And the song…well, she had no idea what it had meant. Could she believe he might care about her? Was it safe to let her heart open to him? Or was it too late to be asking the question? Because there was a very good possibility she'd already fallen for him. And if the lyrics were just that, she was heading for a very painful heartbreak.

MICAH ENDURED THE praise and congratulations. He would catch Dena later, when it was quiet and they could talk. He didn't like not being able to connect with her. Next time, he promised himself. Next time he would bring her. Or do his part remotely, so he didn't have to leave Wishing Tree. With technology the way it was, he could easily perform from a studio there.

"You didn't sing our song!"

The sharp accusation had him turning to face Elec-tra. She glared at him.

"You said you were singing 'Moonlight for Christ-mas.' I was counting on that. You lied to me."

"I didn't lie. There was a change in plans."

"You didn't warn me, Micah. You didn't mention it."

"Why would I?" He grabbed her arm and pulled her

away from the growing crowd into the relative quiet of the hallway. "Electra, we haven't worked together in years. I don't owe you anything. I'm sorry you're disappointed, but it's time to move on. Find someone else to write with. We're not going back to what we were."

Electra's green eyes unexpectedly filled with tears. "But she's gone. She can't keep us apart anymore. Why don't you want me, Micah?"

He stepped back. "It wasn't like that. She wasn't the reason I didn't want to write with you. That was on me."

Being with Adriana had allowed him to see Electra for who she was. Adriana had shown him what it meant to be a good person—someone who cared. Dena was like that, perhaps more so. She had an honest and open heart.

He shook his head. "Move on, Electra. There are plenty of songwriters who would kill to work with you. Hold auditions. Find a couple of good ones and move on."

"Go to hell."

He walked back to his dressing room, where his manager was waiting. He would record Dena's song and then he would go home. Christmas was coming, and he had a wedding to attend. But most of all, he had to see Dena. Without her, nothing was right.

"BELLE, HONEY, THERE'S just no room," Reggie said, staring into the soulful eyes of her dog.

Belle nudged her hand with her nose, then whined.

"Yes, I know Harrison is coming, but it's his project. He gets to help deliver the hats."

Belle looked at her and whined again. Reggie felt her resolve crumbling.

"Why am I such a soft touch when it comes to you?"

Reggie turned back to her SUV and began pulling boxes from the back seat to put them up front with her. If she could squeeze one into the footwell and stack two more on the seat, she could make room for Belle.

She shoved and pushed, then used the seat belt to hold the stacked boxes in place.

"Happy?" she asked the dog.

Belle wagged her tail.

They went inside and she got Belle into a warmer sweater, then called out to her mom that she was leaving.

"I should be back a little after five," she said. It was about an hour each way to the drop-off point. The charity in Seattle had arranged for her to meet a driver heading to Seattle at a truck stop on Highway 2. That saved her from having to make the five-hour drive to the city.

Once Belle was secure in the back seat, Reggie swung by the elementary school, where classes were just letting out. She spotted Harrison and honked. He came running toward her car.

"I can't believe we're finished with the project," he said, hugging her before climbing into the back seat. "Belle! You came."

"She insisted," Reggie told him, making sure his seat belt was secure. "Once I told her you were coming, she wouldn't stay home."

She got behind the wheel and started her SUV. "Ready?"

"Uh-huh." He looked around. "This is a lot of boxes."

"It is. You did a good thing, Harrison. A lot of kids

are going to have hats for Christmas. They'll be warm and it's because of you."

He grinned at her. She smiled back, then checked for traffic before pulling out onto the street.

It only took a few minutes to head west on Pacific Silver Highway that would take them south to where they would meet up with Highway 2 and find the truck stop. Reggie had already texted with the driver she was meeting. Apparently the man traveled with a Chihuahua named Rex. He'd seemed very proud of his companion, and Reggie had refrained from texting back a picture of Belle. She didn't want to give Rex a complex.

The snow had stopped the day before. Although it was due to start back up in the morning, for now the roads were relatively clear. She merged onto the highway and was careful to watch for icy patches. The temperature was plenty cold, and she wanted to stay safe.

She and Harrison talked about his day at school and how excited he was about Christmas. He told her he was too big to believe in Santa but they still put out their stockings every Christmas Eve.

"Dena and I do, as well," Reggie told him with a laugh. "My mom insists, and honestly, I'd be disappointed if I didn't wake up to a full stocking on Christmas morning."

A truck sped past going about twenty miles an hour over the speed limit. Reggie watched the vehicle zip by. Whoever was driving was an idiot, she thought. It was going to get dark in an hour, and they'd just had their first snow of the season. Better to be cautious.

She checked her mirrors and saw another pickup coming up behind her. It was also going way too fast, and she felt a flicker of tension in her midsection.

"Get over, you fool," she whispered, glancing in her rearview mirror.

The driver didn't seem to be watching, because the pickup got closer and closer. She sped up, but it kept coming, then suddenly jerked to the left, as if to go around her. But the driver miscalculated and clipped her left rear corner.

Her SUV instantly began to spin. Reggie consciously relaxed her grip on the steering wheel, waiting for her SUV to pick a direction. She steered into the spin, easing off the gas, slowly bringing the vehicle under control.

"It's okay, Harrison," she called. "Hang on to Belle."

She knew their seat belts would keep them safe. Thank God she'd insisted Belle be strapped in.

She'd nearly gotten control of her car when she saw the truck that had hit her was still spinning on the highway. It swerved wildly, as if the driver didn't know what he was doing, then suddenly headed for her. She tried to drive out of the way, but it slammed into her, pushing her SUV off the road.

The world spun as her vehicle rolled. Harrison screamed, Belle yelped and Reggie felt something heavy slam into her head.

REGGIE CAME TO SLOWLY. Her first thought was to get to Harrison. Her second was that she was going to throw up. It was only then the pain exploded in her head and her side.

She knew exactly what had happened. She'd been hit twice, and the SUV had flipped. It was back on its wheels now, the windshield cracked, the engine off. It was only then she noticed the quiet.

"Harrison?" she managed. "Harrison?"

"I'm okay."

His voice came from behind her.

She turned and saw him in the back, Belle next to him. They both looked shaken.

"Are you hurt?" she asked as Belle whimpered.

"Reggie, you're bleeding!"

"I'm okay."

The words were automatic. She unfastened her seat belt and assessed the damage. She was pretty sure she could walk. She brushed her face and realized that she'd hit her head on something. The blood was warm and sticky.

"Move your fingers and toes," she said, trying to find her handbag. "Can you?"

"Yeah. My chest hurts a little from the seat belt, but I'm okay."

She opened the car door. She had to find her purse and call for help. Out on the highway, she saw several cars stopping and knew they would call 911, but she had to let Toby know what had happened.

"I need my phone."

"I'll get it."

Harrison released himself and Belle, then got out of the SUV. Belle followed. She shook herself off and trotted around to sniff Reggie, as if making sure she was all right. Harrison opened the passenger door.

"Got it."

He ran around and handed her the bag. She dug out her cell and scrolled through for Toby's number, only she couldn't find it. Then she realized she couldn't focus. Her vision was blurry and the nausea had returned.

"Call your dad," she said, feeling herself start to fade. "Listen to me, Harrison. Call your dad and tell him what happened. Then get in the back with Belle. Use her to stay warm. She'll protect you."

She motioned to the people racing toward them. "Ask them for a blanket. Make sure someone called 911. Okay?"

He moved toward her. "Are you all right?" Tears spilled down his cheeks. "Reggie, don't die."

She managed a smile. "I won't die. I hit my head. Just stay warm and look after Belle."

"I will."

He pushed the button to connect him with his dad. Two men reached the SUV. One of them looked at her and swore.

"Help is on the way," he said, and that was the last thing she heard.

DENA APPRECIATED THE fact that her day had been busy—it gave her less time to think. She taught her students, then hurried home to man the reception desk at the B and B. Winona needed to duck out for a couple of hours, and Dena was filling in. Midweek, there weren't a lot of guests checking in or out. Most would stay through the holidays. She was still getting regular emails from the Pinkertons, who were hoping for a last-minute cancellation, but so far there hadn't been any.

All of which was a nice distraction from the fact that she hadn't heard from Micah all day. Last night had been a whirlwind of emotions, from waiting for Micah to play to hearing the song to wondering what it meant. Not that she had been able to ask. When he'd called back sometime after midnight, he hadn't wanted to keep her on the phone long. Before she could say she was fine with talking, he'd hung up. Which left her feeling unsettled and confused.

"He'll be back soon," she told herself. He'd promised, and she trusted him to keep his word.

She went into the kitchen and started getting ready for Snacks and Wine. Ursula had outdone herself with shrimp-scampi-filled and wild-mushroom-filled puff pastry. Dena was going to try to limit herself to only a couple of each. She really had to get in her vegetables, and if she stuffed herself with flaky goodness, that was not happening.

She'd just finished setting out the wine when she heard the sound of the bell over the front door. Instantly her entire body went on alert. Had Micah surprised her by coming back early? Was he here?

She ran into the main room, hoping to find him standing by the reception desk, but the person there wasn't Micah. Instead it was a woman—a thin, beautiful redhead, with angry eyes and a petulant expression.

"I'm looking for this room," Electra said, slapping Micah's key on the counter. "Micah Ruiz sent me to check him out of this place and get his things packed up." She looked around. "What a nightmare. Whoever did the decorating never heard the phrase 'less is more.'" She turned back to Dena. "His room? Where is it?"

Dena struggled to understand what was happening. Electra was here for Micah's things? But he was coming back. He'd promised.

"Mr. Ruiz didn't leave any instructions to let someone else into his room." She forced herself to offer a pleasant smile.

Electra waved the key. "I don't need permission,

do I? I have the key. He's busy recording and can't be bothered to come here to take care of the details."

Dena didn't know what to think. Micah couldn't have gotten back together with Electra. Not so quickly. He'd sworn he didn't even like her that much. But Electra had his key. How would she have gotten it if he hadn't given it to her?

"I'll show you the room," she said stiffly, walking toward the main entrance. "It's in the carriage house."

"It's so cold here. And the snow. What's up with that? When he's done recording, we're going somewhere tropical. Just the two of us. I can't wait. Sun, sand and sex for three weeks. Then we'll come home and start writing. It's going to be wonderful."

Dena came to a stop in front of Micah's door. Electra used the key to let herself inside. She looked around and wrinkled her nose.

"What a dump. How did he stand it here for so long?"

She walked through the living room, into the bedroom, then returned. "I'll take his guitars with me. Send the rest of it to his manager. Here's the address."

She handed Dena a business card.

"Bill him for the shipping."

In less than five minutes, Electra was gone. She carried out two guitars, leaving everything else, including a stunned Dena, who stood in the center of Micah's living room and tried to remember how to breathe.

He was gone. Just like that. He hadn't told her, hadn't hinted. He'd just sent that horrible woman to get his guitars. And now she was supposed to pack up his things and send them to him? Like his time here hadn't meant anything at all? Like *she* hadn't mattered?

What about the song? What about the night they'd

shared? What about the kisses and all the things he'd said? She'd hoped that they were—

She collapsed on the sofa and covered her face with her hands. This couldn't be happening. It couldn't. She'd given him her heart, and he was going to get back together with Electra?

Her cell phone rang. She pulled it from her pocket, hoping against hope that it was Micah. Instead the caller was her mother.

"Hi, Mom," she said, trying not to sound like she was crying.

"Dena, Reggie's been in an accident. Her SUV flipped over and she's unconscious."

Twenty-Nine

TOBY DROVE AS fast as he could, given the road conditions. It was dark and he was on a mountain highway. Even though it hadn't snowed that day, there was still plenty on the side of the road, and he knew there would be ice.

He'd struggled with debilitating terror ever since Harrison had called to tell him about the accident. The only sound in his head was his son crying that Reggie wouldn't wake up and there was blood everywhere.

From what he'd managed to get from Harrison, some asshole driver had clipped Reggie, sending her into a spin. The jerk's truck had slammed back into them, sending them tumbling off the highway. At that point, Harrison had given the phone to a man who had stopped. The stranger had assured Toby that they'd already called 911 and that Harrison and Belle appeared unhurt. But Reggie was bleeding and unconscious.

Thankfully, the accident had occurred only a few miles outside of town. He was there in less than thirty minutes and had found two highway patrol cars and an ambulance already on scene. A couple of tow trucks pulled up behind him on the side of the road. He stopped a few yards back and jumped out of his SUV, then raced toward the group of people, calling for Harrison.

"Dad! Here!"

He found his son wrapped in a blanket and an EMT standing a respectful distance away from Belle, also in a blanket, who glared menacingly from Harrison's side.

"This your son?" the man asked.

"Yes." Toby scooped up Harrison and held him tight. His boy hung on like he was never going to let go.

"I wanted to check him out, but she won't let me near him."

Toby freed one arm and wrapped it around the Great Dane.

"You're a good girl, Belle. A good girl." He swallowed against the tightness in his throat. "Harrison, how do you feel?"

"I'm okay, Dad. We flipped over and it was scary, but I didn't hit my head or anything."

Toby handed him to the EMT and took hold of Belle's collar. "I'll keep her back. Where's Reggie?"

The man pointed toward the ambulance. "They're taking her to the hospital in Wishing Tree. She hit her head on something."

Toby looked at his son. "I'm going to see Reggie for a second."

"I'll stay here, Dad," Harrison told him.

He jogged over to the ambulance, taking Belle with him, then nearly stumbled when he saw Reggie. Blood soaked one side of her face and stained her sweater. She had a black eye and cuts on her cheek. Her eyes were closed, and other than the blood, she was paper-white.

He must have made a sound because she opened her eyes, then moaned.

"Reggie." He rushed over and grabbed her hand.

"My head."

Belle struggled to get close and frantically sniffed, then licked Reggie's unmarred cheek.

"Hey, girl," Reggie managed, her voice groggy. "Harrison. You stay with Harrison."

"She did. He's fine. I called your folks. They're meeting you at the hospital."

"The hats."

"Shaye and Paisley are on their way. They'll take them to the truck stop."

"That guy." She tried to open her eyes again. "You're spinning."

"Don't try to talk."

"He hit me, then spun back into me. I was so scared."

"I know, but you did good."

Another EMT walked over. "Your son seems fine. You might want to take him to his pediatrician tomorrow, but except for a little bruising from the seat belt, he came through unscathed. We need to get going. The other driver is already on his way to the hospital. He's pretty banged up."

Harrison ran over to join Toby. He hugged Reggie.

"You have to get better."

Reggie gave him a wan smile. "I will."

They put her in the ambulance and drove away. Toby checked in with the police officer and explained who he was and what Reggie had been doing.

"From what the witnesses told me," the officer said, "she had steered out of the skid and was doing fine. Then the truck slid back into her. No recovering from that." She grimaced. "People need to learn how to drive in snow and respect what cold does to a road. Your boy okay?"

Toby put his arm around Harrison. "Yes."

She pointed at Belle. "That is some dog. She wasn't going to let anyone near him. Must make you feel real safe."

Harrison rested his head on Belle's. "She's a good girl."

Belle's tail wagged.

Toby moved the boxes out of Reggie's car and took her purse, along with the contents of the glove box and the console between the seats. The banged-up truck was already gone. The tow driver made quick work of pulling her SUV onto his flatbed, then took off. Toby stayed at the side of the road, his flashers on, until Shaye and Paisley arrived.

Harrison sat in the back seat, his arm around Belle. He chatted about the accident and what they might have for dinner and asked if they could go see Reggie at the hospital. Toby did his best to act normal, even as his body began to react to the shock of what he'd been through.

He could have lost them both. If Reggie hadn't controlled the spin, if the other driver had hit her harder, if the accident had happened by a deep gully, they could both be gone. Just like that. With no warning, no way to change things. But Reggie had kept her head. She'd taken care of Harrison. She'd protected his son.

As had Belle. He glanced in his rearview mirror and saw the Great Dane leaning against Harrison, her expression still fierce, as if she would never back down. Harrison was her boy and she would never, ever let anyone forget that.

REGGIE HAD NEVER done the drug thing. Her idea of wild was a second ibuprofen if she pulled a muscle. But she had to say, whatever the hospital was giving her took the edge off her pain and gave her a nice internal buzz.

The wooziness had passed, and her vision was focused again. She still felt a little spacey, but that was probably because she had a concussion. Plus, you know, the drugs. Her parents and sister hovered around her bed.

"They've towed your car to the shop," her dad said, watching her anxiously. "We'll wait for the adjuster to give the okay to go ahead and start repairs. If it's totaled, then I'll come over to Seattle with you to help you buy something."

Reggie thought about pointing out she was perfectly capable of buying a car on her own, but knew her father wouldn't want to hear that. Not tonight. He was showing her, in his way, that he cared and was worried.

"Thanks, Dad."

Her mother fussed over her, wincing when she saw the stitches and tutting at the bruises.

"You could have been killed," Leigh grumbled. "The other driver should have his license revoked. Going too fast when we just had our first snowfall! Who does that?"

Reggie reached out and squeezed her hand. "Mom,

I'm fine. Go home. Have a glass of wine. Come back in the morning and bail me out."

Her mother's expression softened. "I should stay. They'll give me a cot."

Reggie shook her head, then wished she hadn't. "Don't even think about it. You go home and get some rest. Your wedding is in two days, and we still have to figure out what we're going to do about my shaved head."

Her mother's gaze immediately went to the stitches on the side of Reggie's scalp.

"I think the hair on top will cover it."

Her father winked. "Or we'll just tell the rest of the family you're having a punk rock stage."

"I'm kind of old for that," Reggie said. "Mom, I'm fine."

"You have a concussion."

"A mild one, and the nurses here will check on me every thirty minutes. You've seen them do it. I love you. Go home."

"All right." Leigh's voice was reluctant. She rose, then squeezed Reggie's hand. "I'll be back first thing in the morning. I want to be here when the doctor comes by."

She and Vince hugged Reggie, then Dena, before walking out of the room. Dena smiled at her.

"You need anything?"

"I'm good."

"You didn't eat."

Reggie grimaced at the thought of food. "Yeah, not tonight." She closed her eyes. "My head hurts."

"Wait until you look in the mirror. You're going to shriek."

"That bad?"

Dena took her hand. "You have a black eye and scratches. The wedding pictures are going to be epic."

"I don't know if I can cover a black eye with makeup."

"I already have a call in to Paisley to help with that. She knows more about makeup than any of us. And while we're discussing logistics, I should inform you that Paisley and Shaye made the delivery and are back home. So you can let that go."

"The hats. I totally forgot about the hats."

"You had a few things on your mind. Oh, and Belle is spending the night with Harrison. They both were pretty determined."

Reggie smiled. "Do not tell me I'm losing my dog."

"Never. It's a summer fling."

Dena's tone was light enough, but there was something in her eyes, Reggie thought. Unless that was the concussion talking.

"You okay?" she asked. "Did something happen?"

Dena stared at her. "Aside from my baby sister getting run off the road and flipping her car? No."

Reggie wasn't sure she believed her. "You're not lying?"

Before Dena could answer, Toby walked into the room. Despite the throbbing and the drugs, Reggie perked up at the sight of him. Probably because he looked good. Tall and strong and very serious.

"My cue to leave," Dena said, kissing her cheek. "I love you. I'm sleeping with my cell phone right next to me tonight, so if you need anything, text or call. Otherwise, I'll see you tomorrow."

She left.

Toby took her seat and reached for Reggie's hand.

"How are you feeling?"

"Not awful. Dena said I have a black eye."

He smiled. "You do. It's impressive."

"Great. And the wedding's in a couple of days. I'll look like a freak." She saw his gaze shift to the side of her head. "Yes, I know they shaved my hair. I just don't know how bad it looks."

"You look amazing." He raised her hand and kissed the back of her knuckles. "Thank you for saving my son today."

"I'm just glad he's all right. And Belle. I understand they're having a sleepover."

"I hope you're okay with that. Harrison is acting like he's fine, but I know he's a little shaken. With you in the hospital, I thought it would be nice if he and Belle could hang out. I promise to bring her back home first thing."

Reggie closed her eyes. "I'm glad they'll be together. He really did good today. He held it all together and was so brave. Belle, too."

"What you didn't see was, she stood guard. She wouldn't let the EMT near Harrison until I got there."

She opened her eyes. Wow, he was good-looking. Had she always known that?

"Really? Good for her. Although if he'd been injured, it would have been a problem. Dena said the hats got delivered."

"Everything's taken care of," he told her. "You worry about getting better."

She could feel the drugs taking over. She just wanted to sleep. And maybe have Toby join her. If Belle was having a sleepover, why couldn't she? And while she was on the topic…

"Why aren't we sleeping together?"

His eyes widened. "What?"

"You heard me. Don't pretend you didn't. We should be having sex. Lots of it. And since I've already gone there, you're stupid."

He stared at her. "Excuse me?"

"Stupid. You. I'm the best thing to ever happen to you. That was true all those years ago, and it's still true. I'm smart and capable and creative and we're good together. Oh, and Harrison likes me, and I have a great dog. You're in love with me. You never stopped loving me, but you're too proud or stubborn to admit it."

She felt her eyes closing and couldn't seem to open them. "Stop being dumb and just admit you care. You'll feel better."

Reggie never heard his answer. There was some mumbling about visiting hours being over, and then the nice nurse on duty took her vitals.

"I'll be back in an hour to give you more pain medicine."

"Goody," Reggie managed, and then there was only blissful sleep.

MICAH DIDN'T KNOW why Dena wasn't taking his calls or answering his texts, but whatever the reason, he knew it couldn't be good. After a day in the recording studio and another in meetings, he'd finally had enough. He chartered a plane back to Wishing Tree and walked into the lobby of the B and B a little after eleven in the morning. He would rather have driven directly to the school to talk to Dena, but knew she wouldn't appreciate the interruption while she was in class.

Winona was at the reception desk, looking anything but friendly.

"Why are you here?" she asked, her tone cold.

"I live here."

"Not anymore."

Dena not taking his calls was one thing, but what was up with the attitude?

"I have a room until after the first."

Winona glared at him. "*Had.* You turned in your key, and we've rented out the room to the Pinkertons. They come every year." She narrowed her eyes. "We like them."

Micah shifted the bag of avocados he'd brought with him to his other hand. "Wait a minute. I've been in Los Angeles. I never turned in my key."

"You sent a friend. A woman. She did it for you. Your stuff is all packed and waiting to be shipped back to your manager. I'll take care of that just as soon as it snows again." She smiled. "I'm going to accidently leave the boxes outside so they get nice and wet. Then I'll send them."

A woman had come to Wishing Tree? What—

He swore under his breath. "Electra. That's why I couldn't find my room key." He thought about the morning he'd started recording. She'd shown up to talk to him, but he'd refused to see her. He'd left his backpack on the table when he'd gone in to record. She could have easily gone through it. Taking his key and coming to Wishing Tree was just like her.

"You shouldn't be wasting your time here," Winona told him, obviously still pissed. "You should be heading for your tropical vacation. Let me see. What was it? Three weeks of sand, sun and sex. Yes, that's what she said. Dena told me. Through her tears."

Her words were a two-by-four to his gut. He nearly doubled over as the realization of what had happened swept through him.

"No," he said, sickened by what he'd put Dena through. He never should have stayed in Los Angeles. He should have convinced her to go with him, or he should have insisted he record in Seattle rather than LA.

"Electra talked to Dena?" he asked, already knowing the truth.

"You mean the skanky redhead? She did." Winona's lip curled in disgust. "And to think I used to like you."

"It's not what you think."

She held up her arm. "Tell it to the hand."

He looked at his watch. "She's in class, right? When is lunch? Eleven thirty? Twelve?" He set the bag of avocados on the desk. "Can you hold these for me? I'll give them to her later."

Winona's expression turned suspicious. "What did you bring her?"

"Avocados. She likes them, and this time of year they're hard to get in Wishing Tree."

Winona looked from the bag to him. "That's not much of an 'I'm sorry' gift."

"I didn't know what had happened." He looked at her. "Electra is my ex-wife. We've been over for years. She has no interest in me personally, but she does want us to write songs together. From what I can guess, she flew up here to make trouble. Now, you can believe me or not, but that doesn't matter. The important person in all this is Dena. I have to tell her the truth. She's suffering and hurt and believes she made a fool out of herself, and it's all my fault."

Winona looked in the bag. "They're nice-looking avocados." She returned her attention to him. "She's not at school. She's at her mama's house. Reggie was in a car accident yesterday, and Dena took the day to be with her."

She quickly filled him in on what had happened. Micah forced himself to stay and listen when all he wanted to do was run to Dena's parents' house. The only thing that kept him in place was the fact that he didn't know exactly where that was.

"But Reggie's all right," he said when Winona had finished.

"A little banged up, but otherwise, she's fine." She gave him the address and told him how to get there.

He started for the door, then turned back. "You really packed up my room and rented it to someone else?"

"We did."

"I'll be back for my stuff. Don't give it away."

Winona smiled. "I'll wait and do whatever Dena tells me to do."

"Fair enough."

Thirty

"YOU DON'T HAVE to stay with me," Reggie said for the fourth time that morning. "I'm fine."

"I'm keeping you company," Dena told her. "We're hanging out. It's fun."

"You're monitoring me."

Dena smiled. "If I'd been in a car accident, you'd be doing exactly the same thing, so get over it."

She was proud of herself for acting normal. So far, no one had guessed her heart was shattered into a thousand pieces that would never be made whole. She was devastated and emotionally battered, not to mention exhausted from not sleeping, but she knew that one day, years from now, she would feel better. That was what happened. People healed and moved on. She would do the same. It was just the time between then and now that was going to be awful.

If she thought about Electra showing up, she felt sick

to her stomach. She'd spent the night in tears, unable to believe Micah had betrayed her like that, and so ashamed that she'd believed in him. She'd been a dumb little country mouse, willing to hang on his every word. All that crap about wanting to spend the night with her. How he must be laughing at her now. Even more painful— a wonderful, tender moment she'd planned to treasure forever had been destroyed. She felt small and alone and embarrassed. But most of all, she felt sad. Sad that she'd given her heart and devastated that it had been rejected.

Reggie touched the injured side of her face. "Do you think we'll be able to cover any of this with makeup?"

"Paisley's going to come over later and assess the damage. If anyone can do it, she can. She was saying something about makeup that covers tattoos. Apparently that's a thing. She said she could order it shipped overnight so it will be here in time for the wedding."

Reggie winced. "I hope it works. I don't care about being a freak so much as I care about distracting from Mom and Dad's big day. Plus the pictures."

Dena squeezed her hand. "You'll be beautiful regardless."

"Beautiful? Really? I'll accept *pretty* or *attractive*, but not *beautiful*."

"Don't believe me? Ask Mom."

Reggie chuckled. "She's going to lie, same as you."

They smiled at each other.

"I'm glad you're feeling better," Dena told her, reaching across the bed to stroke Belle's face. The Great Dane wagged her tail but didn't open her eyes.

"I'm fine. Sore and shaken, but much better. I'm only seeing one of you. There was no reason to take the day off school."

"Are you kidding? You're my baby sister. I had to be here."

Reggie squeezed her hand. "You're good to me."

"I love you."

"I love you, too."

Reggie shifted, making more room on the bed. "All right, get comfy and let's binge-watch something. I'm thinking funny with an edge."

"Sounds like a plan."

But before Dena could sit on the bed, their mother walked into the room, her expression confused.

"Dena, you said Micah was still in Los Angeles."

Just the sound of his name was like a knife to her chest. Her breath caught, and she felt the blood rush out of her head.

"He is."

"I don't think so. The man is downstairs, and he says he wants to talk to you."

Dena's sudden need to throw up had nothing to do with morning sickness.

"He's here?"

Her mother and her sister stared at her.

"What's going on?" Reggie demanded. "Did you two have a fight?"

"No." Dena stood, then had to steady herself on the nightstand. "No," she repeated more loudly, telling herself to stop shaking. "We haven't spoken in a couple of days. I'm just surprised."

They both eyed her suspiciously.

"Do you want me to tell him to leave?" her mother asked.

"No. I'll talk to him." She faked a smile. "He's back. That's good, right?"

She darted out of the room before either of them could answer. At the top of the stairs, she paused, knowing she had to give herself a second to catch her breath and figure out what was happening.

Micah was here? But why? He didn't have to come back. They'd packed up his stuff, and Dena was going to run it over to the shipping store later that afternoon. After Electra's visit, there was nothing to say.

She drew in a breath. Maybe he wanted to apologize for what had happened. Maybe he wanted to ease his conscience or somehow try to make her think he wasn't the bad guy. She didn't think he'd come all this way to break her heart in person. She refused to believe Micah was that horrible. Of course, she'd been wrong about him in so many ways. Maybe she was wrong about that, too.

"The sooner I deal with this, the sooner I can get over him," she murmured quietly before starting down the stairs.

She found him standing in the middle of the family room. The second she saw him, the waves of pain became a tsunami. She wanted to rush into his arms and have him tell her everything would be fine. She wanted to see him smile and hear his laugh and know that it was all just a big misunderstanding. But that wasn't going to happen because everything he'd said or done was a lie. He'd been using her—maybe for entertainment, maybe for sport. She wasn't sure the reason mattered. All she knew for sure was, next time she would be a little more cynical, a little less willing to trust. A painful legacy from the man she'd fallen in love with.

"Dena!" He started toward her, then stopped and swore. "I'm sorry. She hurt you. No, I hurt you. I can see it in your eyes. Why didn't you call me and—" He shook his head. "Dumb question. You wouldn't do that. Please tell me what she said."

He wasn't making any sense. "You don't need me to tell you. You're living it."

His gaze was steady. Concerned. "I'm here with you, not wherever with her. Please tell me so I know what happened."

Either things weren't exactly as she'd thought or he was the best actor on the planet. Still not willing to trust him, she kept her distance as she said, "Electra showed up yesterday afternoon. She had your key and said she was here to get your stuff. You weren't coming back to Wishing Tree. Instead, you and she were going somewhere tropical for the holidays. Three weeks of sun, sand and sex."

He flinched. "I'm sorry," he repeated. "It's not true. Not any of it. There is nothing between Electra and me. That was over more than a decade ago. That was all her. She took my key from my backpack while I was in the studio, recording the song. She must be desperate to do what she did, and I wish she hadn't. I wish you'd called and talked to me."

He took a step toward her, and she took a step back.

"Stay away," she told him. The words all sounded so nice and plausible, but there was no reason to believe him. The hurt was just too big for her to want to trust him. "Just stay away."

Pain sharpened his expression. "Dena, no."

"Yes. I can't do this. I don't even know what *this* is. You're some famous rock singer. You don't belong here. You were just playing. I won't be entertainment when you're bored. This was a mistake."

"But I love you. Didn't you know? It was in the song."

Her whole body stilled, and she tried to make sense of what he'd said. He loved her? He what?

She opened her mouth but was unable to speak. She also wasn't breathing, but that seemed less important than trying to understand what he was—

He crossed to her, standing close but not touching her. "I meant every word in the song. You've changed me, Dena. You've opened my heart in ways I never expected. You're good and kind and funny and smart and so beautiful. I love you. I thought you knew."

"It was just a song," she blurted. "You never said anything, and then you were gone and singing on TV, and we didn't get to talk, and that woman showed up." Tears spilled down her cheeks. "It was so awful. I thought it had just been a game to you. I thought you were laughing at me."

He pulled her close and held her so tightly, she knew in that second he would never let her go.

"I'm sorry. It's all my fault. I handled this badly from the beginning." He drew back enough to stare into her eyes. "Please forgive me for not getting it right. I should have told you how I felt before I left. When I was in LA, I should have made it clear I was coming back, because I need you and want to be with you always. Only you, Dena. Always you."

She was still gasping like a fish when he leaned in and kissed her. At the first brush of his mouth on hers, she flung her arms around him and hung on. He loved her! Her!

He kissed her with enough love and passion to heal her shattered heart. Warmth spread through her. Not just because he was a hunky guy who had quite the erection, but because of what he'd said.

He raised his head. "I am so sorry I hurt you. Please believe me."

"I do," she whispered. "It's okay. It was awful, but I understand what happened." She brushed her cheeks before smiling at him. "We need to work on our communication skills."

He grinned. "Yes, we do. How about this? I'm not going back to LA without you. In fact, I'm not going anywhere without you. I'll work around your school schedule. You're the only woman in my life, and that's how it's going to stay."

Wow. Just wow. "So you're staying in Wishing Tree?"

"I'm staying wherever you are, if that's all right." He took both her hands in his. "I love you, Dena Somerville. Now and for the rest of my life."

"I love you, too."

He went still. "You do?"

She nodded. "I couldn't seem to stop myself from loving you."

He kissed her again. "Did you really give away my room?"

Oh, no! "I did. I didn't think you were coming back, and the Pinkertons have been phoning every week to ask if there was a cancellation."

He surprised her by smiling. "I deserved that. I'll call Steve and see if I can bunk with him."

She reminded herself he'd said he loved her and she believed him. "Did you want to stay with me?"

His eyes darkened. "Are you ready for that? I'll wait if you're not. No matter how long it takes."

"You can stay with me." She felt herself flush. "I'd like that a lot."

He stroked her cheek. "We'll have to remember to be quiet, what with the Pinkertons downstairs."

"That's never been a problem for me before. This should be interesting."

His smile faded. "I meant what I said, Dena. I love you and I want us to be together. I know it's too soon to talk about getting married, but I want you to know I'm excited about the baby. I look forward to it being the three of us, then the four of us. I'm in this for the rest of our lives."

Happiness filled all the empty spaces. "I am, too."

He kissed her. "I was thinking I'd go say hi to Reggie, and then you and I could go back to your place. Unless you think she'll need you."

She wanted to point out it was barely noon, but then decided she wasn't willing to wait, either.

"She doesn't need me."

"Good. Later I'm going to call a local real estate agent and see if any of the Victorian houses will be coming on the market. You'd be close to the B and B, and we'd have a great house for our family."

"You're a man of action."

"I'm motivated." He grinned. "I'm the guy who got the girl."

He put his arm around her and led her to the stairs. "You think Dolly Parton would consider doing a duet with me?"

"You should call her and ask."

"I just might do that."

THE MORNING OF her parents' wedding, Reggie stared at her reflection and knew that the green-yellow of her black eye was actually the least of her problems. The makeup Paisley had brought over the previous day covered pretty much everything. She would be passable in person and look fine in the pictures. Her headache was gone. The stiffness and aches from the accident were less than they had been. So her only real problem was Toby. Or the lack of Toby in her life.

She hadn't heard from him. Oh, there'd been a text checking on her, but aside from that, there'd been nothing but crickets. She'd practically thrown herself at the man, and he had yet to respond. Which, she supposed, was an answer all in itself.

He didn't want her.

The truth wasn't fun, but that didn't change the reality of the situation. She'd thought they had something. She'd thought they had, in fact, never gotten over each other. She'd thought they'd been given a second chance, but based on the silence from Toby's end, he didn't agree. And it was hard to be in love just by herself.

Disappointment settled on her, heavy and consuming. She reminded herself she only had to get through the wedding today, and then she could have a good sulk for the couple of days her parents were up at Whistler for their second honeymoon. They would be home Christmas Eve morning, and then the whole family would be together. A slightly bigger family, now that Dena and Micah were a thing.

So just today, and then her tasteful breakdown. After Christmas, she would head back to Seattle and pick up the pieces of her broken and discouraged heart. At least she had a good life there. Friends, a routine, her work. Plus she wasn't used to seeing Toby all the time there, so maybe she would miss him less.

Her mother breezed into her bedroom. "I've changed my mind."

Reggie looked at her. "About marrying Dad? I think it's kind of late for that. You two seem like a couple to me."

Her mother laughed. "No, about you and Dena being bridesmaids. I want you in the ceremony."

Reggie groaned. "Mom, it's too late. The wedding is tonight. We don't have dresses and—"

Her mother shook her head. "I've already talked to Dena. She has a beautiful dark blue dress that would be perfect, and you have one that's practically the same color."

Reggie was about to say she didn't have anything like that in her closet, only she remembered that she did. Not at home, but here.

"No," she breathed. "No, Mom. No. You can't make me wear that."

"Why not? I'm sure it still fits, and it's a very classic style."

"But it's my prom dress."

"What does that matter? Reggie, no one's seen it since you were in high school."

"I'm not worried that they've seen it. I'm worried it's out of style and not appropriate for a grown woman. I was seventeen when I wore that."

Her mother patted her arm. "Try it on. I'm sure it's going to look beautiful on you."

No. She couldn't. It was just too… She held in a groan as she realized Toby was coming to the wedding, and he would see the dress. What if he assumed she was wearing it to get him to think about the past and how they'd been together? Because telling him he was in love with her wasn't enough? It was all so humiliating.

"Mom, please. I beg you. Don't make me wear my prom dress."

"It's going to be perfect. You'll see."

TOBY WOULD HAVE said Reggie couldn't surprise him anymore, but he would have been wrong. In the thirty-six hours since she'd called him stupid and told him he was still in love with her, he'd been dealing with the ramifications of her verbal landslide, alternating between knowing her head injury was worse than the doctors thought and wondering if maybe she was right about him *and* them.

After dinner, Harrison went into the media room for his twice-a-week two hours of online games with his friends. Toby looked in on him to make sure he was playing the allowed game, then retreated to his office, where he told himself he was going to pay a few bills but knew instead he would be staring unseeingly at his computer screen while thinking about Reggie.

Had she nailed the problem? Was she the reason he'd never fallen in love with anyone else?

He thought about how he'd felt after leaving Wishing Tree and Washington State behind. He'd moved to Texas because it seemed like the kind of place where an eighteen-year-old running from his life could get lost. He'd made friends, he'd hooked up and he'd dated, but he'd never fallen in love. His relationship with Harrison's mother had lasted nearly four months, and then he'd moved on without looking back.

He didn't think there was anything wrong with him, nor did he not believe in love. He'd expected to find someone and settle down, but that hadn't happened.

He'd picked what he'd assumed was a safe choice instead. Lori.

Once he'd realized what she'd done, he'd vowed to never get involved until Harrison was old enough to take care of himself. A decision that had seemed sensible at the time but now felt more like...what? Giving up? Hiding? He didn't have an answer. Worse, he didn't like the question. He would rather think about Reggie. About her smile and her laugh. How even as she'd been fighting a head injury, she'd taken care of Harrison and Belle. He knew her. He'd always known her.

"Toby?"

He looked up and saw his grandmother in the doorway to his office. He was immediately on his feet.

"Judy, you don't have to climb the stairs to talk to me. Just use the intercom. I'll come right down."

She smiled. "I try to take the stairs at least once a day. It's good for me."

He ushered her to the sofa and sat at the other end, angled toward her. As always, he could see that she was getting older. There were more wrinkles, and her hair was pure white. There was something about her walk these days. It was slower, and she was a little more bent.

"I've been going through old pictures," she said, smiling at him. "Sorting them and labeling them."

"Don't tell me you're getting your things in order. I don't want to hear that."

The smile widened. "Oh, I'm getting on in years, but I plan to be around for a good long while."

"I hope so. Harrison and I need you in our lives."

"I'm sure that's true, but I think you might need a little more than just me."

Uh-oh. The conversation had taken a turn he was going to find awkward. He could feel it.

"I have a lot of pictures of your father," she said. "Less of your mother. I wish there were more."

Okay, not the direction he'd thought they were headed. He relaxed. "I have some of her. A handful. I'll give them to you to put in one of the albums."

"You were a handsome little boy. Very affectionate and helpful."

"Is that how you remember me?"

"It's how you were."

"I think I got in plenty of trouble, made messes and talked back."

The smile returned. "Some, but that's what children do." Her expression turned serious. "I have so many regrets with you, Toby. After your mother died and I came to live here, I didn't protect you enough."

He looked away. "That was a long time ago."

"Was it? Sometimes it feels like yesterday. Sometimes I wish I could go back in time and talk some sense into my younger self." She glanced down, then back at him. "I only had the one child. I wanted more, but I kept miscarrying. Maybe if I'd had my two or three, I would have been better at seeing your father for what he was rather than what I wanted him to be. I should have stood between the two of you more than I did."

He hated seeing her like this. Although he agreed with the sentiment—she should have taken care of him better—he didn't want to blame her or even talk about it.

"I did just fine."

Her gaze locked with his. "He beat you. He went after you time after time, and I did very little. As you got older, it got worse, and by the time you were a teenager, I was too afraid to get between you."

"I would never have hurt you."

"You weren't the one I was afraid of."

He moved toward her and took her hand. "Judy, I love you. I will always love you. That's all that matters."

"I love you, too. It's funny. They say that when people get old, they get clarity about what's important and what isn't. I suppose that's true. I don't miss that I never went to Europe or owned nice jewelry or had a fancy car. But I regret not being a better grandmother to you. I should have stayed with you when you had Harrison. I should have moved to Texas to help you."

"While I would have liked to have you around, I think it was better that you didn't. I learned how to be a dad because there wasn't anyone else. If you'd been with me, I would have depended on you too much. The situation might have been easier, but I don't think it would have been better for me and Harrison."

"You're being kind. You've always been a good man. You protect those you love. I know what happened with Lori was hard, but I think you're learning the wrong lesson."

"I picked her and she abused my son."

"I agree, but then you decided you would never trust again. That wasn't what you were supposed to take away from what happened. Be careful, but don't shut yourself off. It's not good for you, and it's not teaching Harrison what a healthy relationship looks like. How is he supposed to know how to be a husband if he's never seen one close-up? How is he supposed to choose the right woman when you're showing him that after one mistake, you give up?"

For a woman well into her seventies, she still knew how to throw a punch.

"That's not what I'm doing," he said automatically, even as he wondered if it was. "It's not what I meant to do."

"You deserve to be happy. You deserve to be with someone who will love you and Harrison and always have your back. I wish you'd take one more chance to find that."

"You're talking about Reggie."

Judy shrugged. "Am I? It's interesting she's who you thought of."

"She's the only person I've been seeing."

"You loved her once."

According to Reggie, he still loved her. A concept he couldn't get his mind around.

"If you don't do something, you'll lose her again. When the holidays are over, she'll go back to Seattle, and then what? What if she meets someone there? This is your chance, Toby. I don't like to see you throw it away."

With that, she rose. He stood as well, then hugged her.

"You're a powerful woman."

She patted his arm. "I have life experience. Learn from my mistakes. Don't have regrets. They're a painful thing, and they never go away."

He walked her to the top of the stairs, then waited to make sure she got down all right. She'd given him a lot to think about. Yes, Reggie was special, but how did he feel about her? What did he want, and how did he let go of his past mistakes enough to keep them from influencing his present?

Questions that had no answers, he thought, walking into the media room. Harrison was finishing up his video game. He turned off the player and grinned.

"I won, Dad! By a lot. Noah came in second. We're going to team up to play against some guys from school, and we are going to keep winning."

"Good for you." Toby sat on the sofa. "I want to ask you something."

"Sure, Dad."

"I was wondering how you would feel if I started dating Reggie. I didn't know if you were okay with that, because of what happened with Lori."

His son stared at him. "She's not like Lori, Dad. She's totally different. I like her a lot. She's nice and she's funny. Plus, there's Belle."

"You mean you like her because she has a dog?"

"Not just that." He frowned, as if trying to put his thoughts into words. "Some people think dogs don't matter, but they do. Reggie is good to Belle, so I know she'll be good to me. And at the accident, she was really worried about me, even though she was hurt and there was blood everywhere. She took care of me. I think we should love her."

Toby swore silently. Everyone was taking swings at him tonight.

"You should marry her, Dad. Then she could be my mom, and we could be a real family."

"We're a real family now."

Harrison rolled his eyes. "We're a family, but it's not the same without a mom. They're important. They do stuff like make cookies and worry about you, but they also hug you and want to know you're okay. It's nice when moms do that. I see it with my friends and their moms. I think Reggie could love us, Dad. I think she'd be good for us." He thought for a second. "That means we have to be good for her, too. We're going to have to figure that out."

Toby's throat got a little tight. He pulled Harrison onto his lap and held him. "Don't I give you enough hugs?"

"You give me plenty, but they're not mom hugs. It's just different."

"I kind of know what you mean."

His son looked at him. "So you'll ask her out."

"I will."

"Yay!"

Thirty-One

"I'M WEARING MY prom dress," Reggie said glumly. "Why does she hate me? I'm the baby of the family. I'm supposed to be special."

Dena's lips twitched, as if she was trying not to smile. "If it helps, the dress looks good on you. It's a little 2000s, but otherwise, very pretty."

"I feel like an idiot."

They were in the bride's room at the resort. Their mom was out getting her picture taken in her beautiful gown. Dena looked fabulous in a simple sleeveless V-neck, A-line gown, although part of her glow could be her newfound happiness with Micah. Dena had announced they were seriously involved, and unbeknownst to Dena, Micah had asked their father for his permission to marry his daughter.

Reggie, on the other hand, was missing a man who wasn't communicating with her. Nearly as uncomfortable, she was wearing a strapless dress trimmed in—wait for it—faux feathers, and except for the lining, made entirely of tulle.

"What was I thinking when I wore this?"

"You begged Mom to get you the dress. You said if she did, you would never ask for anything again."

Reggie grimaced. "I was so wrong."

"At least it fits."

"It has feathers! If I'd known I was going to have to wear it, I could have taken them off, but there wasn't time. I'm humiliated. The dogs look better than me."

Reggie pointed at Belle and Burt. Belle had on the pretty dress Reggie had made, while Burt was in a doggy T-shirt printed to look like a tuxedo. His back was better, and the two of them had kept their odd connection.

"There are going to be pictures," Reggie whined. "I'll have to look at myself in this dress forever."

"I'm trying to be sympathetic," Dena said, patting her bare shoulder. "It's a wedding. People dress weird."

"They don't usually dress in old prom dresses." Reggie sighed. "All right. I'm done complaining. After the ceremony, I'm taking the dogs home. Mom said I could change into the cocktail dress I'd been planning to wear. So it's only for, what? Another hour? I can survive that."

Compared to missing Toby and worrying that it was over for them, once again, the dress was kind of no big deal. Why hadn't the man called? Or texted? Or come by? They lived in a very small town—he could walk to her house from his office.

The complete absence of any communication had her worried that the silence was the answer. Maybe he'd heard everything she'd said and come to the decision that he wasn't interested in her that way. Maybe he never had to even wonder about it—maybe everything that had happened had been in her head. Now, there was a depressing thought that really put her feathers into perspective.

Paisley walked into the bride's room. "We're about ready to start." She paused and stared at Reggie. "Oh, my. You weren't kidding. That's your old prom dress. I remember because I was so jealous that you got to wear it. You were so beautiful and cool."

Dena grinned. "Mention the feathers. She likes that."

"Don't, I beg you."

Leigh hurried into the room, looking happy and beautiful. "This is so much fun. Your father is so handsome in his tux. I'm enjoying every second of the day."

She reached for her daughters. "My wonderful girls. Thank you for indulging me and being my bridesmaids."

"We love you, Mom," Reggie said. "We want to be here for you."

"Dressed however you want," Dena added with a laugh.

"You both look lovely. Reggie, I don't know why you were worried about the dress. It's very pretty."

"Thank you," Reggie said, doing her best to act like she meant the words.

Paisley got them lined up. They'd agreed Dena and Reggie would each walk a dog down the aisle. Then Leigh would follow. Paisley cued the music, and the procession started.

Dena went first, with Burt. His handsome self

caused the guests to laugh and point, but that reaction was nothing compared to the one when Belle made her wedding debut. She walked perfectly, the basket of flowers in her mouth, her whip-like tail wagging in time with the music.

Reggie kept her attention on her dog, trying not to look at the guests. She wasn't even sure if Toby was going to show up. Maybe he'd decided not to bother.

At the end of the aisle, she got Belle in position, then went to stand next to Dena. Involuntarily, she looked at the guests and immediately saw Toby. He was seated next to his grandmother, looking incredible in a dark suit. Their gazes locked, and she tried desperately to figure out what he was thinking. He'd shown up, so that had to mean something. At least, she hoped it did.

THE CEREMONY WAS beautiful and exactly right. Reggie cried more than she'd planned to, her parents were obviously still madly in love, and the dogs behaved. When everyone had headed for the reception, Reggie took the dogs back to the bride's room, where she quickly changed into jeans and a sweatshirt before grabbing her coat on her way to her car.

The trip back to the house only took a few minutes. Once she'd relieved the dogs of their finery, she ran up to her room and put on a slightly more contemporary cocktail dress. She was halfway down the stairs when the doorbell rang.

"Who on earth?"

She pulled open the front door and saw Toby standing on the porch.

"What are you doing here?" she asked, stepping back to let him in. "Aren't you staying for the reception? The food is going to be amazing. I should know. I saw the menu."

It was also going to be pricey for her parents, but why mention that? In fact, she should probably stop talking altogether. She tended to babble when she was nervous, and this situation was certainly nervous-worthy. After all, the last time she'd seen Toby, she'd told him he was still in love with her. Not exactly a memory she could relive without wincing.

"You changed your dress."

"I had to. The other one had feathers."

"I have very fond memories of that dress. Of you in it, and of taking it off."

She willed herself not to flush. "Yes, well, having sex after prom is kind of a tradition."

"That was a good night."

"It was."

He moved a little closer. "I've been thinking about what you said."

Oh? "That it's a great menu?"

"No. What you said about me being in love with you."

Ack! Okay, she would survive this. She was strong, and even if she didn't feel that way at the moment, she could fake strong. She didn't regret what she'd told him. She might have worded it differently, but she'd told the truth. If he was too stupid to see that, he was—

"You're right."

The soft words nearly didn't penetrate. Then they did, and all the air rushed from her body.

"I… What?"

"I'm in love with you. I probably never stopped loving you, which would explain why I haven't fallen for anyone else since we broke up."

"You haven't?"

"Not a one." He smiled at her. "You're so damned brave. Where does that come from? How do you have the courage to simply put it all out there? You always impress me, Reggie. I worry I can't keep up, but I'm hoping you'll help me be more like you."

Her head was spinning. He was saying the most wonderful things. He was talking like they were going to be together.

"So, you want to start dating?"

"No. I don't want to date you. I want to marry you."

The room went totally still. The only sound was the ticking of the old grandfather clock in the dining room. Reggie felt a prickling all over her body. Not goose bumps, exactly, but definitely a reaction from her sympathetic nervous system or some other system. It was the shock of the moment, or maybe her head injury was acting up.

"I love you," he repeated, although he could say it a million more times and she'd be fine with that. "I love you and want us to be together." He paused. "I'm assuming you're okay with that. Oh, and I'm a package deal."

"Harrison and Judy. Yes, I know."

The half smile returned. "Do you have any thoughts?"

"Yes."

She threw herself at him, wrapping her arms around his neck and kissing him. Happiness, pleasure and so much love filled her that she knew her heart couldn't hold any more joy.

"I love you," she murmured against his warm, sexy mouth. "A lot. And I have Belle. And I can move my business here, but I'll have to go to Seattle every few weeks."

"That works, because I do, too. We can carpool."

She laughed, still hanging on to him. "That's very environmentally conscious."

"It is. Plus, I have extra space in my building if you want to set up your business there. Oh, and think about keeping your house in Seattle. You can rent it out. It would be a good investment for you. And we all love Belle."

"She'll be thrilled. She's finally getting her boy. Oh." She took a step back. "What about Harrison? Is he going to be okay with us getting involved?"

"Married," he said firmly. "Not involved."

Married! She had a little trouble thinking the word. Not because she didn't want to, but because she hadn't dared to dream that could ever happen with Toby. She'd thought she'd lost her chance with him, but she hadn't.

"He's on board. We had a man-to-man talk last night, and he thinks you'll be a great mom and be good for us."

For the second time that day, she was fighting tears. "That's so sweet."

"It is." He pulled her into his arms again. "Now, what I really want to do is take you upstairs and make love to you for the next six hours, but we should go back to your parents' reception instead."

She sighed. "I really like that you respect my family. Thank you for that. But later tonight, my folks are driving to Whistler for a couple of days, so if you want to spend the night, you can."

His slow, sexy smile had her thighs quivering. "I'd like that a lot."

"Me, too."

He put his arm around her. "Tell me about this fancy dinner."

"Well, you have a choice of filet, lamb or salmon." She grinned. "Unless you want the vegetarian option."

"No, thank you. What else?"

"Dessert is a trio of a mini chocolate pot de crème, a chocolate cheesecake lollipop and a shot of Baileys Irish Cream in a chocolate cup. The kids get some chocolate drink in their cup."

He led her to the door, where they both put on their coats.

"Sounds delicious."

"It will be," she said.

"But I'd rather be with you."

She laughed. "I should hope so. I hate to think food is more important than sex."

He drew her against him. "Reggie, you're more important than anything. I will love you faithfully for as long as I draw breath."

"You're going to make me swoon."

"For the rest of your life."

Lucky for her, that turned out to be a promise he would keep.

* * * * *

Can't get enough of
The Christmas Wedding Guest?

Don't miss Home Sweet Christmas,
the next unforgettable book in
the witty and heartfelt Wishing Tree series from
#1 New York Times *bestselling author Susan Mallery.*